THREE
MÄRCHEN OF
E.T.A.
HOFFMANN

THREE
MÄRCHEN OF
E.T.A.
HOFFMANN

Translated and with an Introduction by
CHARLES E. PASSAGE

UNIVERSITY OF SOUTH CAROLINA PRESS
Columbia, South Carolina

833

CONTENTS

INTRODUCTION

Among literary traditions of the world, the literature composed in the English language has the greatest diversity of riches. But it has no Hoffmann. Nor any writer like him. The alleged parallels with Poe and Hawthorne are tenuous and his spirit is alien to them. Even within the realm of German letters he is unique.

For a century his works knew immense, though not quite universal, fame. In his native land he never lacked for admirers. Also, within a decade of his death the French had made a twenty-volume translation of his stories, to which Sir Walter Scott contributed the preface, and hardly a French Romantic but underwent his influence. In Russia it was the rage to read him in Russian translation, in French, or in the original German, especially in the years 1829–1835. Gogol produced some fine tales in the Hoffmannian manner before he grew petulant at the elusiveness of his model. Pushkin created *The Queen of Spades* on a Hoffmannian pattern, even though he claimed to disapprove of the pattern. Lermontov's fine but unfinished tale *Shtoss* is an ingenious reworking of a Hoffmannian theme. At least half a dozen lesser writers sought to synthesize the difficult Hoffmannian formula. Above all, Dostoevski, particularly in his early career, created new works by reducing Hoffmann's plots and characters to bare skeletons and then fleshing them up again with his own substance.

Musicians found the Tales evocative. Schumann sought to transfer Hoffmann's spirit into tone in two sets of piano pieces which reduplicate Hoffmannian titles, the *Kreisleriana* and the *Fantasiestücke*—the program notes to which are usually crammed with misinformation about the literary man. Wagner's *Tannhäuser* text reworks a Hoffmann story and *Die Meistersinger* represents an amalgam of Hoffmann's Nürnberg tales. Chaikovski's *Nutcracker* ballet enacts a Hoffmann Christmas story for children. Offenbach's opera, *Contes d'Hoffmann*, on the other hand, in spite of its charm, distorts three of the Tales to make its own three Acts, while its Prologue and Epilogue libelously misrepresent the author himself as an inept skirt-chaser, a cavorter with raucous students, and a sot.

In the twentieth century, Oswald Spengler cited Johannes Kreisler (the hero of the *Kreisleriana* and of *Kater Murr* and Hoffmann's alter ego), together with Faust and Don Juan as type figures for Western European civilization. Under Lenin's eyes in revolutionary Russia, one of the first Communist literary groups termed itself "The Serapion Brethren" in homage to the literary club to which Hoffmann belonged and which he portrayed in his most extensive collection of Tales.

By contrast, the Anglo-Saxon world remained unreceptive to Hoffmann's genius. Scott tended to admire him, but, perhaps on a cue from Goethe, cautioned against the Romantic unwholesomeness and wildness of the Tales. To Carlyle, Hoffmann was only one of several exponents of the interesting new German literature, and not the greatest of these. Both the two-volume translation of *The Devil's Elixirs* and the taste of the English reading public may be gauged by the comment of a *Blackwood's Magazine* reviewer in July of 1824, who claimed that Robert Pearce Gillies had "contrived to prune off all the indelicacy of his German original, without doing the smallest injury to the author's genius." Only minor works of English fiction owe any debt of influence to Hoffmann, save for Emily Brontë's *Wuthering Heights*, where the inspiration is perceptible but so diffused as to be undemonstrable. In America the case is hardly otherwise. Minor resemblances in Washington Irving are most likely coincidences. Hoffmannian echoes in Hawthorne's *Feathertop* and *Monsieur du Miroir* are faint, in *Rappaccini's Daughter* somewhat stronger. A Hoffmann-Poe connection has been debated in more than a hundred scholarly studies without arriving at a consensus, but the two authors are utterly dissimilar in spirit, as Dostoevski pointed out as long ago as 1861.

German enthusiasms in England and America during the latter nineteenth century were gentlemanly and philosophical and merely tolerated Hoffmann at the tail end of their canon. The infallibility of Goethe was an article of faith, and Goethe had complained of Hoffmann's corrupting the taste of a whole generation. In Germany itself Hoffmann came to be considered neither profound enough nor national enough after 1870 and the Tales were relegated to the status of mere entertainments of a bygone era. To that notion, English-speaking scholars tended to subscribe. A small work like *Master Martin the Cooper* might be edited for schools, anthologies of shorter pieces might appear and reappear in English, but the major items were consistently neglected. No comprehensive translation of Hoffmann was made before World War I, when most German literature moved into the penumbra of Anglo-Saxon distrust. No comprehensive translation has been attempted since then. And the genius of Hoffmann, like the genius of Balzac, seems slender and insubstantial until one reads in depth and the realization dawns that both are giants.

The decades since 1914 have not favored Romantic works, especially German Romantic works, and in those decades our author's name has declined to a legend of dim memory. Ignorance reports that he wrote ghost stories. In graduate study he is mentioned in passing. "Tales of Hoffmann" lingers as a catch phrase in the English language, but there are educated people who are not quite certain whether "Hoffmann" was an actual man or the hero of a forgotten continental romance.

The real man lived—from January 24, 1776, to June 25, 1822, and he was named Ernst Theodor Wilhelm Hoffmann. At some point after 1808 he suppressed the Wilhelm in favor of Amadeus, out of veneration for Mozart. Intimates commonly called him Theodor, posterity cites him as "E. T. A. Hoffmann." His life was full, even hectic, but neither heroic nor particularly stageworthy. In order to perceive the actual man and artist, layer upon layer of erroneous legend needs first to be stripped away, and no worse beginning can be made than to assume the historicity of Offenbach's preposterous opera hero.

He was born in the provincial city of Königsberg, a Baltic port of the once glorious Hanseatic League, in the northeast of German language territory. He always claimed to remember his gifted, if eccentric, father, who, when the boy was four years old, abandoned his wife of thirteen years, took his older son Karl with him, and migrated to another East Prussian town. Thus it was in his maternal grandmother's house in the Junkerstrasse, and not in the house of his birth, that the lad grew up. Life was cheerless at Grandmother Doerffer's, not from poverty, but from boredom, from stuffiness, and above all from the oddity of the household. The matriarch never left her room, where she brooded over her daughter's divorce and the decline of family prestige. The mother, who had never wanted to marry her first cousin in the first place, aspired to no second marriage and lived, sickly and frail, unto herself alone, even to taking her meals in the privacy of her room. Uncle Otto Wilhelm Doerffer was past forty, a bachelor, and a pompous bore, who often emerged sullen and humiliated from dressings-down by the matriarch. The latter assigned him and the boy to a single room and treated them both as small children. "O.W."—pronounced in German "O Weh!" (O woe!)—was also the boy's first teacher. Two maternal aunts offered all the affection, warmth, and mirth in the family. Guests never came. Upstairs lived Frau Werner, a raving lunatic who believed she was the Virgin Mary and her son the Messiah. The latter, five years older than young Hoffmann, was Zacharias Werner, the future writer of Romantic melodramas.

As a child, our author was already cast in the mold of looks and personality that were to be his through life. He was small, ill-favored, with thin lips pressed tight and with an alarmingly scant margin of forehead. Vivid in speech and sharp of wit, he was precocious at schoolwork, music, and drawing, and utterly devoted to a very few chosen friends. Of these, the most important was Theodor Hippel, a lad of the same age, who had been selected by the family to be young Hoffmann's playmate and studying companion on Wednesday afternoons, subsequently on Wednesday and Sunday afternoons. "O.W." went for a long walk on those days to leave the boys the privacy of the room.

At age sixteen Hoffmann was a good organist and pianist and

would gladly have begun a musical career, had not the family council determined on law. From 1792 to 1795, he dutifully studied law at the University of Königsberg, and did well at it. In his spare time he enjoyed Hippel's company, wrote three novels (all happily lost), gave music lessons, composed, wallowed in a hopeless love affair with a married lady who was one of his music pupils, read widely, and submitted to the home regime. He never attended a single lecture by the university's most renowned professor, Immanuel Kant.

By decree of the family council he was exported in the summer of 1796 to Glogau, seventy-eight miles away, to live with cousins and to seek a government post. The Doerffers of Glogau undertook to offset his infatuation with the married lady by engaging him to their daughter Minna. Dutifully, Hoffmann submitted. But a trip to Berlin with his uncle resulted in a government appointment in Posen, in Prussian Poland, and the engagement to Minna was eventually broken off. In Posen he dutifully performed his legal tasks, but he was restless. He struck a cynical pose, indulged in pranks and Don Juan escapades. At carnival time in 1802, he became involved in a petty social cabale, his contribution to the mischief being a set of caricatures of General von Zastrow. Complaints were made, even to the royal throne in Berlin, and two months later the prankster was banished to a dismal hinterland post at Plock. Among two thousand Polish Catholics and one thousand Polish Jews, with a thankless job, a surly chief, and mail twice a week, the young lawyer existed on letters from friends, on his composing, and on the string quartet he had organized. Almost as a counsel of despair, he accepted the advice of a well-wishing lady and married a local girl. His bride, "Misha," was Polish, Catholic, nineteen years old, utterly uninterested in the arts, and completely devoted to her husband. Her love was necessarily strong in order to survive his long years of indifference toward her.

Through the help of Hippel and other friends, a transfer was effected to a post in Warsaw. In 1805, a daughter was born. Briefly there was the prospect of conventional domesticity, coupled with association with musicians and literati. But on November 28, 1806, Napoleon arrived in Warsaw. The Prussian government was dissolved, his job and income vanished, his wife and daughter had to be sent to relatives in Posen, and the thirty-one-year-old official had to cast about for a livelihood. Even the Warsaw Music Academy, which he had helped to found, was dissolved. He went to Berlin, but Berlin was swarming with men in precisely his circumstances. For a time he worked at odd commissions for book illustrations. From Posen came word that his little daughter had died and that Misha was seriously ill.

Desperation in the summer of 1807 caused him to insert the following advertisement in the *Allgemeiner Reichsanzeiger*:

> A person who is fully experienced in the theoretical and practical aspects of music, who has himself turned out significant compositions that have met with success, and who has until now been Director of an important musical institution, desires, since he has lost his position through the war, employment as director in some theater or private orchestra. He is familiar with the management of scene painting and costuming, knows the entire range of theater activity, speaks French and Italian in addition to German, and is not only culturally but also literarily trained. He would also be able to take charge successfully of theater production. Further contact with him will easily lead to proof of the talents claimed, and in order to establish such, please communicate by postage-free letter with Referendary Hoffmann in Berlin, Friedrichsstrasse No. 179.

The talents were justly claimed, though the experience was slightly exaggerated. Hoffmann's musical publications up to 1807 included two symphonies, three overtures, two quintets, six sonatas, two Masses, several motets, and a quantity of smaller vocal works.

Of the three replies to his advertisement he chose the post in the south-German city of Bamberg. When he arrived there, with Misha, on September 7, 1808, he was five months short of age thirty-three and his essential life had not yet begun. Just before that date or soon after it, however, and amid unknown circumstances, he wrote his first story, *The Chevalier Gluck*, and despite its ready acceptance by the publisher Rochlitz, he seems to have entertained no thought of a serious literary career. Musical compositions in all forms, including operas, poured from his pen during the five Bamberg years, 1808–1813, while the first few "Tales of Hoffmann" materialized very slowly. Meanwhile he worked hard at the theater, directing plays, painting scenery, providing incidental music, conducting the orchestra, and to eke out his wretched salary he gave music lessons on the side. The gathering momentum for story writing was to come from personal experiences, particularly from his involvement with his voice pupil, Julia Marc.

At the center of the tragicomedy cast was Julia herself, thirteen years old at the beginning, sixteen at her marriage, and seventeen when Hoffmann last saw her. She was lovely, precocious, gifted with an ethereal soprano voice, and susceptible to the exaltation of music. The impecunious musician worshiped first the voice, then its owner. Her father was nowhere in evidence, but her redoubtable mother was single-mindedly concerned with making a wealthy match for her daughter. Friends of Hoffmann and figures from the tiny Bamberg court were the other participators in the tragicomedy. Faithful, jealous, neglected Misha stayed chiefly at home. When she pried into his diary and exploded over the phrase "spiritual adultery," the spiritual adulterer made crucial entries in German but used the Greek alphabet or else attributed his thoughts and feelings to a fictional personage named Johannes Kreisler. In this manner were gradually created the fifteen short sketches known as the *Kreisleriana*. Eventually there arrived on the scene young Mr. Gröpel of Hamburg, a wealthy merchant, a boor, and the winner of Julia's hand. On September 6, 1812, the brutal denouement came. Friends accompanied the engaged couple to a rural inn for celebration. The fiancé became tipsy and lascivious—the Leech Prince was pawing the Princess Gamaheh—and Hoffmann's tormented fury broke like a storm. A table was overturned and over the slobbering but still conscious Mr. Gröpel, Hoffmann vented the full hatred of his soul upon the conniving mother. The party had to be called off. Dead misery followed. Next morning an apology was sent to Frau Konsulin Marc, to which came the reply, "Something has come over Julia that makes it impossible for her to continue her lessons." Julia married Gröpel in December, and before Hoffmann left Bamberg in April of 1813, he learned that she was to be a mother.

Departure from Bamberg was ostensibly taken for the sake of

a new position as conductor-director of Joseph Seconda's opera company and orchestra, which performed in both Dresden and Leipzig. Actually it was a flight from unbearable circumstances. Before leaving, however, Hoffmann signed a contract with his friend Kunz, who was also his creditor and confidant, whereby Kunz would arrange for publication of Hoffmann's future literary works. Individually published pieces had so far met with success, Kunz's faith was limitless, and Hoffmann himself had ideas for tales which were yet to be written but which he felt sure were valid, both financially and artistically. Thus at age thirty-seven, his true career was about to begin.

Neither Mr. Joseph Seconda nor his opera company was in Dresden when the Hoffmanns arrived there, but Napoleon was, and the unemployed musician witnessed a battle before moving on to Leipzig. Hardly were rehearsals under way than the tides of war brought Napoleonic armies near Leipzig and forced the Hoffmanns to return to Dresden. No sooner in Dresden than the Russians surrounded that city, while the Emperor of the French steadily retreated westward. Through months of siege, short rations, and public clamor, the unemployed musician worked away at his new opera *Undine* and at stories for a future collection of tales to be published by Kunz. Though a Prussian by nationality, Hoffmann felt himself a wholly disinterested spectator of European events. Financially he survived first on a loan from Hippel, whom he had by fantastic chance encountered in the beleaguered city, and then, just at starvation's edge, on money accruing from the estate of the deceased relatives in Königsberg.

Through the adventures and misadventures of 1814, Hoffmann continued writing. Two thin volumes of the *Fantasy Pieces in the Style of Callot* appeared in print for Easter; a third volume, containing only the long *Märchen* entitled *The Golden Pot*, followed in the fall; the fourth and last volume of the set appeared in the spring of 1815. On the very day when the last item was completed, the full-length novel, *The Devil's Elixirs*, was begun. Financial existence meanwhile was managed by odd jobs, musical articles for newspapers, political cartoons commissioned by a publishing house, a hastily composed symphony published anonymously because of its shabbiness. In July,

Hippel visited Hoffmann, who was then back in Leipzig. The Prussian government was now reestablished, Hippel had obtained a post in it, and he urged his friend to follow suit. Together they concocted the application, and on September 26, 1814, Hoffmann entered upon his new duties in Berlin.

The seven Berlin years, 1814–1822, the seven last years of his life, saw the emergence of the Hoffmann known to posterity, the "essential Hoffmann." Characteristically, that figure had two sharply contrasting aspects. By day, Counselor Hoffmann, dressed in the uniform of the Prussian civil service, worked in the criminal prosecutions section of the Ministry of Justice. Evenings might find him at the theater, in the concert hall, in a café with a group of intimates who called themselves "the Serapion Brethren," or, especially in the final years, at Lutter & Wegner's tavern in the company of the Shakespearean actor Ludwig Devrient and other cronies. He also found time to visit and play with two small children, a boy and a girl, in the household of his friend Eduard Hitzig, and to construct elaborate toys for them. They are the real-life children, and he is the Godfather Drosselmeier, of his *Nutcracker* Christmas story. And by night he composed the greater part of the sixty-odd stories and two novels on which his reputation is based.

Legend claims that Hoffmann lived those seven years in a continuous state of alcoholic frenzy bordering on delirium. Mere common sense refutes the legend. He wrote by night, at home, while Misha sat silently at her knitting, interrupting her task at intervals to brew either tea or punch for her husband. The punch was no doubt strong, and it built on a foundation of punch and wine from the earlier tavern hours. With alcoholic fuel his creative powers blazed; without it, they smoked and smoldered. Once, in the wee hours of a morning in November of 1815, when he was writing *The Sandman*, he became so terrified at his own eerie creation that he woke Misha just to have the reassurance of human company. But other writers have found themselves carried away by their own literary inventions. Quantity and quality of the Tales, to say nothing of his regular office routine, deny the possibility that he was perpetually drunk or perpetually in a state of morbid hallucination.

The stories were written rapidly but not carelessly. There

was conscientious "labor of the file." Hoffmann wrote for popular magazines and his public was as insatiable as that of Sherlock Holmes. When a certain number of works had accumulated in scattered publications, the author would gather them up in book form, adding one or more new items to sweeten the purchase of the more expensive volumes. Thus emerged his second collection, *Night Pieces*, and his third collection, *The Serapion Brethren*, the frame-tale of which portrays the actual persons of "The Serapion Brethren" club to which the author belonged. The fourth collection was made by friends after his death. The previously mentioned novel, *The Devil's Elixirs*, appeared in 1816, but his second novel and universally acknowledged masterpiece, *Kater Murr*, was left unfinished, to the grief of all Hoffmann enthusiasts. Finally, there were the three sophisticated fairy tales which formed part of no collection: *Little Zaches*, published as an independent book in January, 1819; *Princess Brambilla,* written and published in 1820; and *Master Flea*, begun in the summer of 1821, completed by dictation from the author's deathbed, and published in April of 1822, less than two months before he died. Letters, diaries, and miscellaneous pieces fill at least one large volume, musical criticism another volume, and the musical compositions equal the bulk of the literary creations.

Little Zaches

Little Zaches is pure entertainment, and of a high order. Like Shakespeare's *Twelfth Night*, to which it is akin in spirit though utterly dissimilar in content, it serves no purpose other than to be joyous and to make joyous. It is serious in the sense that it is high comedy and not farce, satire, or a sermon in disguise. In the little foreword to *Princess Brambilla*, the author forthrightly says all that need be said about the allegorizers of *Zaches*, about the "philosophy"-distillers of *Zaches*, and about the source-seekers of *Zaches*. Truly, there is nothing to be done with this story except to enjoy it, and having enjoyed it, to put it by for a time and then enjoy it anew.

Technically, it is "loose and coarse-woven," as Hoffmann says. It starts slowly; its course meanders slightly, but in no intricate pattern; its characters are devoid of complexity. The student Balthasar is a conventional *jeune premier* engagingly portrayed, with little touches of absurdity to make him both lovable and credible. His few individualizing traits were derived from Hoffmann's fellow Romanticist, Adalbert von Chamisso, that fascinating French émigré turned Prussian aristocrat and Berliner, that world traveler, botanist, poet, and kindly personality. The heroine is "the lovely Candida," and no more than that; she exists only on the story's margin. Fabian and Pulcher are pleasing accessory figures. Even Zaches, for all that he is vividly pictured in his vanity, stupidity, and malice, is no more than the story's bone of contention. The real concern is with the two mature adults, Prosper Alpanus and the Fay Rosabelverde, and in their conflict lies the power and poignancy of the tale. When the fay's golden comb falls and shatters on Prosper's splendid pavement floor, the tiny crash is a small sound, but unforgettable. The interview surrounding the breaking of the comb is mixed of hilarity and pathos in accordance with a formula unique with Hoffmann. Unforgettable, too, is that first appearance of Prosper Alpanus in the forest. In fact, the scene is so fine and so expertly placed in the narrative that the author was unable to match it in the scene of Prosper's departure. The anticlimax of the latter episode is one of the blemishes in the jewel. The Ninth Chapter is a little miracle of the narrative art. The valet's stagy comedy at the outset soon gives way to the grim realism of the storming of Zaches's palace by the mob. In 1819, readers might well feel the chill of 1789 upon them as they read that scene. Zaches's appearance on the balcony combines puppetlike farce with grisly humor; it also persuades the reader that the nasty little bug deserves to be crushed. Yet, if his death is directly forthcoming, it evokes feelings of the preposterous, the slightly disgusting, and the pathetic. It would have been easy for the author to close his narrative with an innocent appeal to the reader's self-righteousness, but had he done so, the story itself would have turned malicious. Genuine pathos attends Rosabelverde's visit to the deathbed, and illusion triumphs after all over the truth of his nature. Again the author declines to allow pathos to be the final impression, lest his story turn overly sentimental. Burlesque follows, as the prince and his seven gentlemen take out their pocket handkerchiefs and weep in unison over the corpse. Be it noted, however, that for all the burlesque, the prince's grief— or at least his vexation—is real. The last touch of all is the pathetic absurdity of old Liese's obtaining the onion-selling concession for the royal luncheons. On that reedy note is concluded this chapter of many tonalities. The author admits that the Final Chapter is mere epilogue and born of the wish to make a happy ending, because happy endings are so much nicer than sad ones.

Princess Brambilla

By contrast, *Princess Brambilla* is a complex and controversial work. It has never lacked for admirers. It was welcome to the reading public of 1820; Heine remarked that anyone who did not lose his head over it, had no head to lose; Baudelaire praised it highly. On the other hand, the author's own "Serapion Brethren" read the work with dismay, and more than one reader since 1820 has begun it with all good will and put it impatiently by. Strangeness surely marks it, a strangeness which is both initial handicap and ultimate glory. Its concept is unique, its execution constitutes a dazzling tour de force, yet there is abundant human warmth in it, and abundant humor, a thoroughly engaging hero, and even an urgent message. This last need not disquiet the sophisticated reader. It is a message of concern mainly for theater people, quite free of any abstruse philosophy, and in a fresh statement might not be bad advice for the contemporary stage.

The genesis of the story in the author's mind was odd. On his forty-fourth birthday, January 24, 1820, one of the Serapion faithful, Dr. J. F. Koreff, presented Hoffmann with reproductions of a set of engravings by Jacques Callot (1592–1635). Under the title of *Balli di Sfessania*, the twenty-four engravings depicted scenes and characters from the old Italian *Commedia dell'Arte*. Both artist and subject were dear to Hoffmann's heart. His own first collection of stories consisted of *Fantasy Pieces* (i.e., "paintings") *in the Style of Callot*, and he profoundly admired the plays of Carlo Gozzi, which may be described as specimens of the old impromptu *Commedia*, artistically heightened by a fixed text in verse and by superb poetic invention. The birthday gift begot the idea of "deducing" a story from the pictures, eight of which would then be reproduced as an integral part of the text.

Precisely what "dances" (*balli*) Callot specified is not clear, since the word "Sfessania" is unexplained. Professor Joseph F. De Simone of Brooklyn College conjectures a coined noun from Italian *fesso*—"cracked, split, cloven" with intensifying s-prefix. From the twenty-four original engravings, each the size of a small postcard, Hoffmann selected his eight arbitrarily and in "deducing his story" rearranged their order, so that we have, in *Princess Brambilla*, numbers 12, 3, 8, 23, 17, 24, 9, and 21 of the Callot set. Nor are the eight reproduced just as Callot drew them. Eliminated are the tiny street scenes which, in a perspective different from that of the *Commedia* figures in the foreground, place those figures in a realistic daytime setting. The new background is a uniform brown, romantically mysterious, committed neither to day or night, but evocative of the nocturnal. Eliminated too are Callot's neat captions— "Scapino & Cap. Zerbino," "Riciulina & Metzetin," etc., and in their stead is a suggestion of turf for the *Commedia* figures to stand on. In this way Hoffmann was able to treat Callot's different personages as the same personages in successive stages of the story. And finally, each *Brambilla* picture is reproduced in mirror-image of the original, so that right-hand figures in Callot become left-hand figures in Hoffmann, and vice versa. The result is a set of radically new art works "by Hoffmann-Callot," and it is necessary to "read" them closely as part of the story entitled *Princess Brambilla*.

Further, the subtitle, "A *Capriccio* in the Style of Jacques Callot," warns the reader to expect a tale suggestive of the new Romantic *musical* form called a "*capriccio*," that swiftly and unpredictably changeful form which, in 1820, had not yet received full definition from composers like Mendelssohn, Schumann, and Brahms. Near its close the story lapses briefly into verse—competent verse but admittedly not high poetry, and in a striking passage at the opening of the Sixth Chapter there is a dialogized section which attempts, as far as words are able to do so, to simulate the sensations of strenuous dancing. And the total story deals with drama and the acting profession. Here, a generation before Wagner, is an attempted synthesis of all the arts, a *Gesamtkunstwerk*.

The youthful hero of the story is Giglio Fava—"Lily Bean!" —a vain matinee idol so corrupted by his success in bad neo-classical tragedies that he poses, struts, rants, and orates off-stage as on-stage, until he is a caricature of his princely roles, which are in turn caricatures of real art and real life. But within him and unbeknown to him is contained a future master of comic acting whose name will be the Assyrian Prince Cornelio Chiapperi. The heroine is a stage seamstress, Giacinta Soardi, who for all her peppery temper sincerely loves Giglio, as he sincerely loves her. Within her and unbeknown to her is contained a future mistress of comic acting whose name will be the Princess Brambilla. The narrative deals with the birth, growth, and development of these future selves. In a passage of more than usual grotesquerie we witness the birth of Prince Cornelio, who is so tiny that he can fit in a candy box, while a matching passage portrays the birth of Princess Brambilla as she rises from the neck of a wine bottle and stretches her tiny arms out toward Giglio. We are in Rome at carnival time, when the entire city becomes, as it were, a troupe of maskers in a swift, lusty, Devil-take-the-hindmost farce of the old *Commedia*. But before the carnival starts, the populace beholds the arrival of a masked procession more bizarre and opulent than anything in Roman memory. In realistic terms, a *Commedia* troupe is coming to take up quarters in the palace of their benefactor, Prince Bastianello di Pistoja. Thus, so to speak, the *Commedia* comes to the *Commedia*. Everything in the story will also come in pairs, in image and counter-image. Much of the time Prince Bastianello di Pistoja appears as the "mountebank" Celionati ("heaven-born"), and in this latter guise conducts discussions on the theory of humor and irony with the German students in the Caffè Greco. He is also the benevolent mage who steers the hero through the troublesome course of transmutation of personalities.

No sooner is Giglio's new Self born so small as to fit in a candy box than a struggle begins between the old Self of the bad tragic actor and the new Self of the great comic actor of the

future. The seesaw battle is a striking variation on the theme of
Romantic doubles, and it rises to a climax in a duel where the
new Self does the old Self to death amid outrageous exaggera-
tions of fencers' etiquette and to the whooping delight of carnival maskers. Thereafter, Giglio Fava is essentially dead and
only Prince Cornelio lives on. Whimsically, however, the author
makes Giglio pursue Princess Brambilla, while he refuses to
believe that she is Giacinta the seamstress, and has Giacinta
pursue Prince Cornelio, although she indignantly rejects him
whenever his bombast and preposterous chivalry identify him
as the inferior Giglio Fava. The final chapter, by way of epilogue, shows Giglio and Giacinta happily married and happily
playing leading roles—presumably under their new stage names
—with a successful *Commedia* troupe. The ultimate theme of
the story is the formation of an artist.

Some readers may experience a distressing sense of weight-
lessness in a work which so often outflies the gravitational pull
of realism. No assurance can be given them that a rational explanation underlies each mystifying episode, though they may
be certain that the author constructed his story with the support
of realistic scaffolding. Sometimes that scaffolding is visible;
sometimes a little reflection will discover it. We suggest that
Giglio, after losing his job as a tragic actor, performs in a side-
show run by the "mountebank" Celionati. Certainly he receives
a purse of ducats from time to time from Celionati, so that we
may assume a kind of "on-the-job training." That Giacinta plies
her trade in the new cause may be inferred from her receiving
similar pay from Master Bescapi. (In Hoffmann stories, the title
of Master is always reverent.) We may also infer that the side
show satire diverts audiences from the Argentina Theater, to
the ruin of the box-office-minded impresario and to the under-
cutting of *The White Moor* before that "tragedy" ever reached
the boards. The mystifying events of the Second Chapter are
best understood as hallucinations resulting from Giglio's being
"possessed" by his dream vision, though some will follow the
false clue and take them for products of that flagon at the end of
the First Chapter. The duel between the Selves, which is witnessed by crowds of people, we suggest is a brilliant piece of
acrobatics with a dummy, the live actor being dressed as the

Commedia personage Captain Pantalone and the dummy being dressed as an unmistakable Giglio Fava in the tragical role of the White Moor. The tooth which Celionati extracts from Prince Cornelio—who is Giglio, after all—is surely false theatricalism. The patient's need for vigorous physical exercise doubtless refers to the strenuous clown-acrobatics which are the antithesis of static posing for heroic declamation: exercise will cure "stiffness." Master Bescapi's "creative needle" may serve to puncture bombast.

With Celionati's telling of the experiences of his friend Ruffiamonte we have a favorite set of motifs from German Romanticism: the tale within a tale, the notion of history as cyclical, the notion of pre-existence, and the notion of Romanticism's mission to re-establish what was once won and then lost again through wrongheaded rationalism.

Melancholy King Ophioch and his silly Queen Liris are allegorical antitheses. Onesidedness brings them to grief. But the mage Hermod, an avatar of Ruffiamonte, creates the Urdar Spring of comic art, into which people gaze and laugh in sublime delight. Comic art, held as a mirror up to nature, provides those doubles, those second ironic selves, which release mankind from misery. But the Urdar Spring dried up and became a noxious swamp. A wicked demon in a black robe—and the Abbate Chiari necessarily wore a black cassock—impersonated the mage Hermod and counseled falsely as to how to restore the mirror waters. A *Commedia* performance in the final chapter of the story recreates the glorious spring.

Hoffmann, who was never in Italy, freely used the Roman carnival "finale" of Goethe's *Italian Journey* for background details. The literarily curious may wish to compare the opening of the story with the opening of Goethe's *Wilhelm Meister*. More significant would be an account of Gozzi's literary battles in the 1760's against Goldoni and the real-life Abbate Pietro Chiari. But all those elements are small details in the stupendous invention of *Princess Brambilla*.

Master Flea

Death and the police both strove mightily to keep *Master Flea* from being printed. In that struggle, Death lost out but the police were partially successful. (Wherein may lie a moral.) In any event, not until 1908, eighty-six years after composition, was this "dangerous" story published in the form intended by the author.

As chairman of a committee investigating subversive activities in the name of the Prussian government, Hoffmann had occasion to submit formal protests to his superiors concerning the unjustified arrest and detention of several prominent persons. The protests evoked counterprotest from Heinrich von Kamptz (1769–1849), Director of Police and second in charge under K. F. von Schuckmann, Minister of the Interior. In that post-Napoleonic era of political reaction, the latter was taking no chances with borderline cases, but Kamptz, the "demagogue sniffer," wanted blood and victims. Upon the arrest of the famous and controversial "Turnvater" Jahn, Kamptz published a notice in the Berlin newspapers before any trial had been held, stating that Jahn's guilt was proven. From jail Jahn proffered charges, and it was Hoffmann who summoned Kamptz, his own superior, to appear in court to answer the charges. Intervention by King Friedrich Wilhelm III in March of 1820 ruled out any such confrontation, and after the lapse of almost a year a new committee was appointed to work concurrently with the uncooperative one of which Hoffmann was chairman. Which committee was to have precedence was not clarified. Meanwhile Hoffmann's difficult position was made more difficult by the ever widening scope of Kamptz's activities. In the summer of 1821, he resigned from his committee and from government service, but it was not until December that it occurred to him to inject a caricature of Kamptz into the half-finished *Master Flea*.

Very little exaggerated from real life, Kamptz there appears as prosecutor Knarrpanti, and there the reader may investigate *him* at leisure. Possibly Hoffmann anticipated legal complications, for, if the reader will look closely, he will note that the three Knarrpanti passages are self-contained units of narrative which can be extracted from context with hardly a trace of a break. Hoffmann was also indiscreet about his story and soon all Berlin knew that a satire on Kamptz was to be expected in the next "Tale of Hoffmann." The rumor soon reached Kamptz himself, who took steps to have the government subpoena the manuscript from Wilmans Brothers, the publishers in Frankfurt-on-the-Main, a free city quite outside of Prussian jurisdiction. The Frankfurt Senate then made representations to Wilmans Brothers, who turned over not only the Knarrpanti episodes but the entire manuscript. Upon hearing this news, Hoffmann is quoted as saying: "They can all ——— ——— ———!" All the same, illness and expenses made it urgent to get the story published in order to receive pay for it. With some relief he next heard that Wilmans had ransomed the manuscript, minus the Knarrpanti sections, from the Prussian government for a sizable fee and that they were sending advance partial payment. In March of 1822, Wilmans published from a transcript. The original manuscript with the Knarrpanti sections remained in the government files to be discovered by scholars in 1908.

Meanwhile, a plea from Hippel to Prime Minister Hardenberg could not avert retaliatory action by Kamptz and Schuckmann, the latter of whom was holding the manuscript. Hoffmann's serious illness postponed action. Three months later death obviated it altogether.

Concurrently, the bedridden author, in constant pain and partially paralyzed, was dictating the final chapters of the story. At intervals his physician came to lay hot irons against the patient's spinal column to "stimulate" the dead nerves. Hoffmann asked one visitor if he noticed the smell of roast flesh in the sickroom. After the final dictation, on February 29, 1822, the author expressed to his friend Hitzig the fear that the public might blame his illness for the faults in the story.

One marvels that such circumstances permitted the bittersweet humor and the rapturous close of *Master Flea*, to say nothing of the deft and sure handling of serious thought. The ideas voiced in the work are significant ones, and though they are borrowed from other men—Friedrich Schlegel, Novalis, Schelling, and others—they were nonetheless sincerely held and skillfully manipulated. Always, however, they are expressed in terms of comedy and irony. There is no "philosophy" as such and there is no preaching.

In the early ages of the world, according to the Romantic interpretation, joyous creativity knew no bounds. With equal spontaneity, Nature expended energy in all possible varieties of experiment. The life force, having accumulated matter about one or more particles of itself, might "create" a lion; just as easily it might dissolve that lion form to "create" a flower, a cloud, a stone, a man, a centaur, a mermaid, an emerald, or, again, a lion. Form might succeed form. Nature was free and at play. Vitality was inexhaustible. Such was the Golden Age of old.

Fixed forms and restricted progressions betokened the Fall from the exuberant, childlike grace, and with the Fall came sorrow and travail. Man, evolving, learned much and raised himself admirably. In so doing, however, he came to lay undue stress on the principle of the rational mind, to the harm of his other constituent faculties, much as the joyous and credulous child becomes a problematic and doubting adolescent. Genuine adulthood must adjust childhood's values with the values of adolescence, and it must raise both to a higher power, not by a process of mere addition, but by a process of multiplication. The mission of Romanticism was not to regain the Golden Age of old, the childhood of the race, nor to undo the Age of Reason, the adolescence of the race, but to bring both into harmony within a new and greater Golden Age, the adulthood of the race. Such, in oversimplified form, is the "philosophical" premise of this story.

The characters in *Master Flea* have realistic existences in Frankfurt-on-the-Main as of 1820, but they also existed, under different names, in the Golden Age of old, and the first task of the story is to bring them to realization of their former selves. Hoffmann, like other German Romanticists, tended to believe in the reincarnation of souls, without, however, making an article of faith of it. But in the new and greater Golden Age, he saw some "souls" would be exalted by virtue of their merit while others would be reduced or even extinguished altogether, for in the present state of human life, there are petty spirits falsely aggrandized and downright negative or dead things that have wrongfully acquired the semblance of positive existence. The dream vision at the end of *Master Flea* is a grandiose setting to rights of this condition and in that setting to rights it is not difficult to discern that the Heart is king or that aggressive pseudo-intellects are reduced to mere doll-babies; the repulsive, barely living Leech is banished "below," while his accomplice, Thetel, disintegrates into sheer nothingness, for that was his essence. (He was apparently a shuttlecock.)

Against this imposing general plan, the story displays its mellow wit and vivid human portraiture. The study in contrasted "loving" and "being in love" is one of Hoffmann's finest insights, and it should be noted that he does full justice to both. No other hero of his, except Johannes Kreisler, is so expertly portrayed as is Peregrinus Tyss. We suggest that they are the tragic and comic heroes respectively of Hoffmann's art. Be it further noted that the author's concern with his hero is pedagogical, as it is in *Little Zaches* and in *Princess Brumbilla* and in numerous other instances as well. But here there is no benevolent mage to guide him. Instead, we have Master Flea, who is a delightful combination of sober entomology, a proverb about "a flea in one's ear," and Common Sense. If one looks closely, one will detect his partial provenience from Sterne's *Tristram Shandy*. George Pepusch as second hero is wholly lovable and understandable. Dörtje Elverdink is a Dostoevskian heroine before the fact, much as the Lämmerhirt family is Dickensian before Dickens, and in one brief scene in Chapter Six she anticipates both Grushenka and Nastasya Filippovna. The consummation of passion between Dörtje and George is a tremendous flight of fancy, a *Liebestod* which manages to be simultaneously funny, tragic, and beautiful. In Keats's words, they "cease upon the midnight with no pain," and, quite literally as flowers, amid an outpouring of fragrance.

The opening chapter of *Master Flea* is a masterpiece within a masterpiece. Heine called it "divine." But Heine also damned the remainder of the work as much as he had praised *Princess Brambilla*. Heine was wrong. The explanation of his uncharacteristic misjudgment may well lie in another sentence of his review: "I do not find a single line in it that is concerned with demagogic activity." In other words, he had heard rumors of the Knarrpanti episode, expected social and political satire, and felt cheated.

The suppressed Knarrpanti scandal had still another curious side effect. Duke Karl August of Weimar was mischievously amused by the highhanded goings-on in Berlin and chose to present a copy of *Master Flea* to his most distinguished courtier, the seventy-three-year-old Goethe, who, he thought, might enjoy a story set in Goethe's native Frankfurt. Of the work and its dying author, Goethe wrote in 1822: "It is undeniable that there is a certain charm from which one cannot escape in the way he has of combining the most familiar places and customary, even ordinary, situations with implausible, impossible events." The praise is grudging and head-shaking. Of the author five years dead, Goethe wrote in 1827:

What faithful participant concerned with the education of a nation has not noted with sorrow that the unhealthy works of that suffering man have been effective for long years in Germany and that healthy spirits have been inoculated with such aberrations in the guise of significantly helpful novelties.

Hoffmann satisfied neither Goethe's demand for heroic, eighteenth-century idealism nor Heine's newer demand for literature of political and social commitment. The masterpieces translated in this volume, like the rest of Hoffmann's works, were sustained by the reading public of the European continent and by certain continental intellectuals, especially Frenchmen and Russians. With love and veneration they are herewith offered to the English-speaking peoples.

Note on the English Translations of the Three Märchen

Little Zaches appeared in English under the title of *Little Zack* in E. T. A. Hoffmann's *Fairy Tales*, Boston, 1857, as translated *from the French* by Lafayette Burnham, who remarks: "The French possesses in a greater degree the ease necessary for amusing narratives, and corrects the terseness of the harsher Teutonic."

Princess Brambilla has had no English version prior to the present one.

Master Flea appeared in English under the title of *Master Flea* in Volume II of *Specimens of German Romance*, London, 1826, as translated by George Soane.

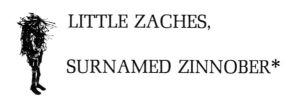

LITTLE ZACHES,

SURNAMED ZINNOBER*

A Fairy Tale
Edited by E. T. A. HOFFMANN

*One meaning of German *Zinnober* is cinnabar, an artificial red mercuric sulfide used principally to produce vermilion pigment.

FIRST CHAPTER

The little changeling. Imminent peril to a vicar's nose.
How Prince Paphnutius introduced the Enlightenment in
his country and how the Fay Rosabelverde entered an
Institute for Young Ladies.

N ot far from a pleasant village close by
the roadside, there lay a poor tattered peasant woman stretched
out on the ground that was hot from the sun's glow. Wracked
with hunger, parched with thirst, at the end of her strength, the
unhappy woman had collapsed beneath the weight of the dry
wood piled high in her basket and which she had laboriously
gathered in the forest from under the trees and brush, and since
she could hardly breathe, she fancied nothing else but that now
she was probably going to die, and thus her inconsolable misery
would suddenly be at an end. But presently she gained sufficient strength to unloosen the cords with which she had
fastened the woodbasket on her back and to drag herself slowly up onto a patch of grass that was right close by.

Now she burst forth in loud lamentations. "Must," she wailed,
"must every distress and every misery strike no one but me and
my poor husband? Are we not the only ones in the whole village who remain in constant poverty in spite of all our work, in
spite of all our sweat poured out, the only ones who barely earn
enough to stay our hunger? Three years ago when my husband found the gold pieces in the earth while he was turning
over the soil of our garden, oh yes, then we thought Luck had

finally turned in at our door and now good days would come. But what happened! Thieves stole the money, house and barn burned down over our heads, hail battered down the grain in the field, and, to brim the measure of our heart's sorrow till it ran over, Heaven punished us yet with this little changeling to which I, to the shame and mockery of the whole village, gave birth. On St. Lawrence's Day[1] the young one was two and a half years old, and he can't stand or walk on his spider's legs, and instead of talking, he snarls and meows like a cat. At the same time the wretched abortion eats like the lustiest lad of at least eight years, without its putting the least flesh onto him. God have mercy on him and on us, that we have to feed the young one fat even to our own misery and greater distress. The little runt will probably eat and drink more and more, but never work in his life! No, no, it's more than a body can bear on this earth! If only I could die—just die!" And with that, the poor woman began to weep and sob until at last, overwhelmed with grief, completely exhausted, she fell asleep.

With good right the woman might complain of the hideous changeling to which she had given birth two and a half years before. The thing which at first glance could very well have been taken for an oddly gnarled chunk of wood was actually a misshapen boy, hardly two spans tall, who had crawled down out of the basket on top of which he had been lying cater-cornered, and was now snarling and rolling about on the grass. The thing's head was stuck way down between his shoulders, a pumpkinlike growth took the place of a back, and directly beneath its chest hung the little legs as thin as hazel twigs, so that the youngster looked like a split radish. Of the face, a dull eye could not detect much, but peering more sharply, one became quite aware of the long pointed nose which protruded from black shaggy hair, and of a pair of black, glittering eyes, which, especially amid the otherwise very old and furrowed features of the face, seemed to proclaim a little mandrake.

Now that the woman, as was said before, had sunk into deep sleep over her grief and her little son had rolled himself right up beside her, it chanced that Fräulein von Rosenschön, a

[1] August 10th.

lady from the nearby Institute, came walking along the road on her way back from a stroll. She stopped, and, since she was by nature sympathetic and good, was much touched by the sight of the misery there confronting her.

"O righteous Heaven!" she began. "How much sorrow and distress there is on this earth! The poor, unhappy woman! I know she hardly has dear life in her, and so she works beyond her strength and has collapsed from hunger and travail! How I feel my own poverty and helplessness really painfully now for the first time! Oh, if only I could help the way I should like to! However, what still is left to me, the few gifts of which hostile fate was not able to rob me and could not destroy, and which are still at my command, those I shall use mightily and truly to abate this sorrow. Money, if I had it to command, would help you not at all, poor woman, and perhaps would even make your condition worse. To you and your husband both, riches are simply not given, and with one to whom riches are not given, gold pieces vanish from his pocket, he himself does not know how; he has nothing to show for them but huge vexation, and the more money pours in for him, the poorer he gets. But I know that more than all your poverty, more than all your distress, your heart is gnawed by the fact of your having borne that little monster that hangs upon you like an evil and uncanny burden which you must carry through life. Big—handsome—strong—wise: to be sure, the youngster cannot become any of those things, but perhaps he can still be helped in another way."

With that the young lady sat down on the grass and took the little fellow onto her lap. The vicious little mandrake struggled and squirmed, snarled, and tried to bite the young lady in the finger, but she said, "Quiet, quiet, little June bug!" and softly and soothingly stroked him across the head with the flat of her hand, from the forehead over and down to the nape of his neck. During the stroking the little fellow's shaggy hair gradually smoothed down until it was parted, lay tight to the forehead, and fell in pretty, soft ringlets down to his high shoulders and his pumpkinlike back. The little fellow had become quieter and quieter and finally had fallen fast asleep. Then Fräulein Rosenschön laid him carefully down in the grass close against his mother, sprinkled the latter with some spirits from a smelling bottle which she had taken from her pocket, and then withdrew with rapid step.

When the woman awoke soon thereafter, she felt wonderfully refreshed and strengthened. She felt as if she had had a solid meal and drunk a good mouthful of wine. "Aiyee!" she cried out. "How did I come by so much comfort and so much cheer in that little bit of sleep! But the sun will soon be down behind the hills. I must be off for home!" With that she was just on the point of loading on her basket, when, looking in, she missed the little fellow, who at that same moment raised himself up out of the grass and squawked piteously.

As his mother now looked around toward him, she clasped her hands together with amazement and cried, "Zaches, Little Zaches! Who has combed your hair so nicely in the meanwhile! Zaches, Little Zaches! How prettily those ringlets would become you if you weren't such a nasty, revolting youngster! Well, come on, come on! Into the basket with you!"

She was about to take hold of him and lay him crosswise over the wood, when Little Zaches kicked his legs, grinned at his mother, and meowed perfectly understandably: "I don't want to!"

"Zaches, Little Zaches!" shrieked the woman, quite beside herself. "Who has taught you how to talk in the meanwhile? Well, if you have your hair so prettily combed, and if you talk so nicely, then you must be able to walk, too."

The woman hunched the basket onto her back, Little Zaches clung to her apron, and in this way on they went toward the village.

They had to pass by the vicarage, and it so happened that the vicar was standing in his doorway with his youngest boy, a golden haired youngster of three, pretty as a picture. When *he* now saw the woman coming along with the heavy basket of wood and with Little Zaches dangling from her apron, he called out to her, "Good evening, Dame Liese, how are you? Why, you've piled on far too heavy a load, you can hardly walk with it. Come here and rest a bit on this bench in front of my door. My serving girl shall fetch you a cool drink."

Dame Liese did not wait to be asked a second time, she put

her basket down, and was just going to open her mouth to pour forth all her sorrow and distress to the reverend gentleman, when Little Zaches lost his balance at his mother's sudden turn and came flying down at the vicar's feet. The latter quickly bent down and picked the little fellow up, saying, "Ah, Dame Liese, Dame Liese, what a beautiful, charming lad you have there! It is surely a veritable blessing of Heaven to possess such a wonderfully beautiful child." And with that he took the little fellow into his arms and fondled him and did not seem to notice at all that the ill-mannered runt was snarling nastily and growling and even trying to bite the reverend gentleman in the nose.

Dame Liese was standing utterly flabbergasted before the clergyman and looking at him with wide eyes staring and didn't know what to think. "Oh, dear Mister Vicar," she finally began with a tearful voice, "a man of God like you really shouldn't be making a joke of a poor, unhappy woman whom Heaven—I hope it knows why—has punished with this repulsive changeling!"

"What crazy stuff," replied the clergyman very seriously, "what crazy stuff are you saying, dear lady, about jokes—changelings—punishment of Heaven—I don't understand you at all, and I only know that you must be totally blind if you don't love your pretty boy with all your heart. Kiss me, nice little man!"

The vicar fondled the little fellow, but Zaches snarled, "I don't want to!" and grabbed anew for the clergyman's nose.

"Just see the mischievous beast!" cried Liese in fright.

But at that same moment the vicar's boy spoke up: "Oh, father dear, you are so good, you are so nice to children, that they all cannot help but love you right from their hearts."

"Oh, just listen," cried the vicar, as his eyes shone with joy, "oh, just listen, Dame Liese, to the pretty, clever lad, your dear Zaches, to whom you are so ill-disposed. I already see you will never make anything out of the boy, be he ever so pretty and clever. Listen, Dame Liese, entrust your hopeful child to me for care and rearing. With your oppressive poverty the lad is only a burden to you, and to me it will be a joy to raise him as my own son!"

Liese simply could not, for astonishment, come to her senses, and over and over again she cried, "But dear Vicar, dear Vicar, are you really serious about wanting to take the little monstrosity in and rear him and free me from the trouble I have with the changeling?"

But the more the woman charged the vicar with the repulsive ugliness of her mandrake, the more eagerly the latter insisted that in her crazy blindness she did not deserve to be blessed by Heaven with the splendid gift of such a prodigy, until finally, very angry, he ran with Little Zaches on his arm into the house and bolted the door from the inside.

There Dame Liese stood now as though turned to stone in front of the vicar's door and simply did not know what to make of it all.

"What in the world," she said to herself, "has happened to our worthy vicar that he should so completely dote on my Little Zaches and take the simple pygmy for a pretty and clever lad? Well, God help the dear gentleman. He has taken the burden off my shoulders and loaded it onto his own. Let him look to how he will carry it! Hey! How light the woodbasket has become, now that Little Zaches is no longer sitting atop of it, and the heaviest worry is gone along with him!"

With that, Dame Liese, the woodbasket on her back, strode merrily and with good cheer on her way.

Even if I wished for the time being to pass over the matter in total silence, you, kind reader, would nonetheless probably guess that there must be something very particular about the Institute lady von Rosenschön, or, as she was also called, Rosegreenfair. For surely it was nothing other than the mysterious effect of her stroking his head and smoothing his hair that Little Zaches was regarded as a beautiful and clever child by the good-natured vicar and immediately taken in as his own. You could, dear reader, despite your excellent perspicacity, nevertheless come to false conclusions, or, to the great disadvantage of the story, even turn over many pages just to find out more about the mystical young lady from the Institute; hence it is better that I tell you at once everything that I myself know about that worthy lady.

Fräulein von Rosenschön was tall of stature, of majestic

figure, and of a manner somewhat proud and imperious. Her face, though it had to be termed supremely beautiful, made, even when she was staring ahead as usual in fixed seriousness, an odd and almost uncanny impression, which was to be attributed primarily to one very particular strange line between the eyebrows, a line about which people were not at all sure whether an Institute lady could really have such on her brow. For all of that, there were also often so much clemency and grace in her glance, especially at rose-blooming time in bright clear weather, that everyone felt captivated by a sweet and irresistible magic. When I had the pleasure of seeing the gracious creature for the first and last time, she gave the appearance of a lady in the highest and fullest bloom of her years, at the apex of the turning point, and I was of the opinion that the greatest good fortune had befallen me in beholding the lady still on precisely that peak and, in a way, to be awed by her wonderful beauty—a sight which would very soon no longer be offered. I was in error. The oldest people in the village assured me that they had known the gracious young lady for as long as they could remember, and that the lady had never looked any different, neither older nor younger, nor uglier, nor prettier, than just then. Thus, time seemed to have no power over her, and this was enough in itself to puzzle many.

But there were many other things besides at which each person, when he thought the matter over seriously, puzzled quite as much, in fact could not get over the astonishment in which he was caught. First and foremost, there was revealed very clearly in the young lady the kinship with the flowers whose name she bore. For not only was it the case that not a soul on earth could grow such magnificent thousand-petaled roses as she could, but those flowers sprang up in the utmost plenitude and splendor from the sorriest and driest thorn that she stuck into the ground. Besides, it was definitely known that on solitary walks in the woods she carried on conversations aloud with wondrous voices that seemed to come out of the trees, the bushes, and the fountains and brooks. In fact, a young huntsman had spied on her one time when she stood in the midst of the densest woodland, and rare birds with shining and variegated plumage, which were not native to the region, fluttered about her and fondled her and with their merry singing and chirping seemed to be telling her all sorts of happy things, at which she laughed and was pleased.

So it also happened that Fräulein von Rosenschön attracted the attention of all the people in the district at the time when she came to the Institute. Her admission into the Institute for Young Ladies had been ordered by the ruling prince. Hence, Baron Praetextatus von Mondschein, owner of the estate near which the Institute was located and of which he was the overseer, could raise no objections, despite the fact that he was tormented by the most ghastly doubts. In vain, for instance, had been his efforts to locate the Rosegreenfair family in Rixner's *Book of Tourneys*[2] and other chronicles. On this basis he had justifiable doubts as to the young lady's eligibility for Institute membership, since she had no family tree with thirty-two ancestors to show, and finally, quite heartbroken and with bright tears in his eyes, he begged her for Heaven's sake at least not to call herself Rosegreenfair, but Rosefair, inasmuch as there was some sense in that name and one ancestor was possible. To please him, she complied. Perhaps the resentment of the offended Praetextatus vented itself against the unfamilied young lady in one way or another and gave the first impetus to the evil talk which spread in the village more and more.

To those enchanted conversations in the forest, which otherwise did not matter, were added all kinds of dubious circumstances that passed from mouth to mouth and put the young lady's actual nature in a very ambiguous light. Mother Anne, the mayor's wife, boldly maintained that every time the young lady sneezed hard out of the window all the milk in the whole village went sour. Hardly had this been corroborated when the terrible thing happened. The schoolmaster's son Mikie had been nibbling roast potatoes on the sly in the Institute kitchen and had been caught in the act by the young lady, who smilingly shook her finger at him. At that, the youngster's mouth had frozen open exactly as if he constantly had a hot roast potato

[2] Georg Rixner's *Book of Tourneys* (Thurnierbuch) of 1530 listed the coats of arms of the most prominent families of the German aristocracy and thus constituted a kind of social register.

in it, and from then on he had to wear a hat with a broad projecting brim, because otherwise it would have rained in the poor fellow's mouth. Soon it seemed definite that the young lady had knowledge of how to conjure fire and water, how to assemble storms and hail clouds, how to braid elf locks, etc., and no one doubted the statement of the shepherd who with shuddering and horror claimed to have seen the young lady at the midnight hour rushing through the air on a broomstick with a monstrous stag beetle in front of her and blue flames shooting out from between its horns. Now everybody was in an uproar, people wanted to get their hands on the witch, and the town tribunal reached no less a decision than to get the young lady out of the Institute and throw her in the water to stand the regular test for witches. Baron Praetextatus allowed all this to go on and said smilingly to himself: "This is what happens to simple people without ancestors, people who are not of such good old stock as the Mondscheins." The young lady herself, apprised of the scandalous state of things, fled to the capital, and soon thereafter Baron Praetextatus received a royal command from the ruling prince of the country whereby he was informed that there weren't any witches and was enjoined to throw the town tribunal into jail for their greediness to watch the natatory skill of an Institute lady, and to let the other peasants and their wives know, under penalty of grievous corporal punishment, not to think evil of Fräulein Rosenschön. They repented, stood in fear of the threatened punishment, and henceforth thought well of the young lady, which had the most salutary results for both the village and the Lady Rosenschön.

In the prince's council it was perfectly well known that Fräulein von Rosenschön was none other than the formerly renowned and world-famous Fay Rosabelverde. The fact of the matter was as follows:

In the whole wide world there was formerly no more pleasant country to be found than the little princedom in which was situated the estate of Baron Praetextatus von Mondschein, in which Fräulein von Rosenschön dwelt, in short, where everything took place of which, dear reader, I am about to tell you the sequel.

Like a wonderful, magnificent garden in which the inhabitants walked as though for their pleasure, free from every oppressive burden of life, was this little country, closed in by a high mountain chain, and with its green and fragrant forests, its flowery meadows, its rustling streams and merrily plashing fountains, although there were no cities there but only friendly villages and now and again palaces standing apart by themselves. Everyone knew that Prince Demetrius ruled the country, but no one noticed the government in the least and all were thoroughly satisfied with it. Persons who loved total freedom in all their actions as well as a beautiful countryside and a mild climate, could not better select their place of stay than in this princedom, and thus it came about that various excellent fairies of the good sort, for whom warmth and freedom, as is well known, count above everything else, had, among others, settled there. To them could be attributed the fact that, in almost every village, but especially in the forests, the most delightful marvels often occurred, and that everyone, completely surrounded thus by the charm and the bliss of these wonders, fully believed in the marvelous and, without realizing it, remained for that very reason a happy and at the same time a good citizen. The good fairies, who had settled there of their own free choice and after the manner of Jinnistan, would gladly have conferred eternal life upon the excellent Demetrius. That, however, did not lie within their power. Demetrius died, and young Paphnutius succeeded him in his rule.

Even during his father's lifetime, Paphnutius had cherished an unspoken, inner sorrow over the fact that people and country were, in his opinion, being neglected and left most heinously uncared for. He decided to rule, and directly appointed as prime minister of the realm his valet Andres, who had once lent him six ducats in a tavern beyond the mountains when he had left his purse behind and thus had rescued him in great need. "I mean to rule, my good fellow!" Paphnutius exclaimed to him.

Andres read in his master's glance what was going on within him, threw himself at his feet, and solemnly declared, "Sire! The mighty hour has struck! Through you the realm rises shining forth from nocturnal chaos. Sire! Here your most faithful vassal implores you, a thousand voices of the poor unhappy people

in his heart and throat. Sire! Introduce the Enlightenment!"[3]
Paphnutius felt utterly shattered by his minister's sublime
idea. He lifted him up, clasped him impetuously to his bosom,
and said, sobbing, "Minister—Andres—I owe you six ducats
—nay, more—my happiness—my kingdom! O loyal, judicious
servant!"

Paphnutius wished to have an edict printed in big letters at
once and posted at every corner, to the effect that from this
hour forward the Enlightenment was introduced and every
man had to abide by it.

"Dearest sire!" cried Andres, however. "Dearest sire! That
isn't the way to go about it!"

"How does one go about it then, my good fellow?" said
Paphnutius and took his minister by the buttonhole and drew
him into his study, locking the door.

"You see," Andres began, once he had seated himself on a
little stool opposite his prince, "You see, gracious sir, the effect
of your princely edict on the subject of the Enlightenment
would perhaps be offset in a detestable way if we did not
combine with it a measure which seems harsh, to be sure, but
which prudence dictates all the same. Before we proceed with
the Enlightenment, that is, before we cut down the forests,
make the river passable for ships, raise potatoes, improve the
village schools, plant locusts and poplars, have the young people sing their morning and evening hymns in duet, lay out high-
ways, and give cowpox vaccinations, it is necessary to banish
from the state all persons of dangerous opinions, who lend no
ear to Reason, and who mislead the common people by downright absurdities. You have read *The Arabian Nights*, dearest
of princes, because I know that your late serene papa—may
Heaven grant him gentle rest in his grave!—used to put that
sort of accursed books in your hands when you were still using
rocking horses and eating frosted gingerbread. Well, then! From
that totally confused book, gracious sir, you are surely familiar with the so-called fairies, but you surely do not dream
that various ones of those dangerous persons have settled in

[3] A whimsical but not hostile parody of Marquis Posa's famous speech
to King Philip, culminating in the plea: "Give us freedom of thought!" in
Schiller's *Don Carlos*.

your own dear country, right here in the neighborhood of your palace, and are carrying on all sorts of mischief."

"What? What are you saying? Andres! Minister! Fairies here, in my country?" Thus cried the prince as he sank back very pale against the backrest of his chair.

"We, my most gracious sir," continued Andres, "we can rest easy as soon as we take the field with shrewdness against these enemies of the Enlightenment. Yes, I shall call them enemies of the Enlightenment, for by their misuse of your late papa's goodness they alone are to blame for the dear state's still lying prostrate in total darkness. They ply a dangerous trade in the marvelous and do not shrink from preparing, under the name of poetry, a secret poison which makes people completely unfit for service in the Enlightenment. Then they have habits that are so intolerably repugnant to the police that, on that count alone, they ought to be put up with in no cultivated state. Thus, for example, these impertinent souls have the temerity, just as the fancy takes them, to go traveling through the air with hitched-up doves, swans, and even winged horses. Now I ask you, most gracious sir, is it worth the trouble to draft and introduce a sensible excise tariff when there are people in the state who are capable of tossing untaxed goods down the chimney of any unthinking citizen, just as they like? Therefore, most gracious sir, as soon as the Enlightenment is proclaimed, away with the fairies! Their palaces will be cordoned off by the police, their dangerous goods will be taken from them, and they will be sent as vagabonds to their homeland, which, as you, most gracious sir, must know from *The Arabian Nights,* is the little land of Jinnistan."

"Is there post connection with that country, Andres?" asked the prince.

"Not at the present time," replied Andres, "but perhaps once the Enlightenment is introduced, daily service can profitably be established there."

"But, Andres," continued the Prince, "will our proceeding against the fairies not be found harsh? Will the spoiled populace not complain?"

"For that, too," said Andres, "for that, too, I have a remedy.

We won't send all the fairies away to Jinnistan, most gracious sir. We shall keep a few here in the country. But we shall not only deprive them of all means of working harm to the Enlightenment, but also apply appropriate measures to transform them into useful members of the enlightened state. If they are not willing to engage in solid marriages, then let them work at some useful business under strict supervision, knitting socks for the army in war time, or something. Mark my words, most gracious sir, it won't be long before people will no longer believe in fairies once they are walking among them, and that is the best thing. In that way, all eventual complaints will pass of themselves. As for the fairies' utensils, they will devolve upon the princely treasury, the doves and swans will be turned over to the princely kitchen for delicious roasts, and with the winged horses attempts can be made to cultivate and train them as useful beasts by clipping their wings and giving them stable feeding, which we do hope to introduce along with the Enlightenment."

Paphnutius was supremely satisfied with all his minister's proposals, and on the very next day what had been decided upon was put into effect.

The edict about the proclaimed Enlightenment shone in splendor at every corner, and at the same time the police broke into the fairies' palaces, seized their total property, and took them away prisoners.

Heaven knows how it chanced that the Fay Rosabelverde was the only one of all of them who got wind of it a few hours before the Enlightenment broke and used the time to set her swans free and to put away her magic rose wands and other valuables. She also knew that she was chosen to remain in the country, with which choice she complied, though with great repugnance.

Neither Paphnutius nor Andres could in the least understand why the fairies who were transported to Jinnistan should express such excessive joy or why they should keep asserting over and over again that they cared not a whit about all the goods which they had left behind. "When all is said and done," said Paphnutius indignantly, "when all is said and done, Jinnistan is a far prettier state than mine, and they are making fun of me as well as of my edict and my Enlightenment, which shall now really thrive!''

The geographer and the historian were summoned to give a detailed report on the country. Both agreed that Jinnistan was a sorry country, without culture, Enlightenment, erudition, locust trees, or cowpox, and did not actually exist. Worse could not befall a man or a country than not to exist at all.

Paphnutius felt reassured.

When the fine flowering grove was cut down, amid which the deserted palace of the Fay Rosabelverde used to stand, and when Paphnutius had, in exemplary fashion, vaccinated all the peasant louts in the next village, the fay waylaid the prince in the forest through which he was about to return to his castle with Minister Andres. There she so nettled him with various ways of speaking, but most particularly with some uncanny tricks which she had borrowed from the police, that he begged her in Heaven's name to be content with a place in the only, and hence the best, Institute for Young Ladies in the whole country, where she could do just as she pleased without paying any attention to the edict of Enlightenment.

The Fay Rosabelverde accepted the proposal, and in this way came to the Institute for Young Ladies, where, as was previously stated, she called herself Fräulein von Rosengrünschön, but then, at the urgent request of Baron Praetextatus von Mondschein, Fräulein von Rosenschön.

SECOND CHAPTER

Concerning the unknown people discovered by the scholar Ptolemy Philadelphus on his travels. The University of Kerepes. How a pair of riding boots went flying past the head of the student Fabian and how Professor Mosch Terpin invited the student Balthasar to tea.

In the confidential letters which the world-famous scholar Ptolemy Philadelphus,[1] while on his remote travels, wrote to his friend Rufin, there is contained the following noteworthy passage:

"You know, my dear Rufin, that I fear and shun nothing in the world so much as the burning sunrays of the day, which so consume the forces of my body and so weary and exhaust my mind that all thoughts run together in a blurred picture and I vainly strive to grasp a single clear image in my soul. Therefore, I am in the habit of resting by day during this hot season and continuing my journey by night, and thus it was that I found myself traveling last night. In the thick darkness my driver had gone astray from the right and comfortable road and had unexpectedly gotten onto the turnpike highroad. Although I was being hurled back and forth in the carriage by the rough jolts

[1] Ptolemy II, "Philadelphus," an ancestor of Cleopatra, was King of Egypt from 285 to 246 B.C. Hoffmann whimsically imitates the manner of the classical letters of Cicero or Pliny and at the same time practices the device of such eighteenth-century writers as Montesquieu (Les Lettres persanes) and Goldsmith (The Citizen of the World), whereby imaginary Oriental travelers in letters home described ironically the native land of the readers—and of the author.

17

encountered there, so that my head full of bumps was not unlike
a sack full of walnuts, I did not waken from the deep sleep
into which I had fallen until with a horrible lunge I went flying
out of the carriage onto the hard ground. The sun was shining
bright in my face, and through the turnpike standing right in
front of me I perceived the high towers of a stately city. The
driver was lamenting sorely, since not only had the thill been
broken on the big stone that lay in the middle of the road, but a
hind wheel of the carriage as well, and he seemed to be concerned little or not at all about me. I controlled my temper, as
befits a wise man, and only meekly called over to the fellow that
he was a damned rascal, that he might consider how Ptolemy
Philadelphus, the most famous scholar of his time, was sitting
on his hunkers, and that he should let thill be thill and wheel be
wheel. You know, my dear Rufin, the power that I exert over
the human heart, and thus it came about that the driver instantly ceased lamenting and helped me onto my feet with the
aid of the turnpike collector, in front of whose house the acci-
dent had happened. Fortunately I had sustained no especial injury and was able to walk on slowly down the road while the
driver laboriously dragged the broken carriage along behind.
Not far from the gate of the city which I had seen in the blue
distance, however, I met numerous people of such strange nature and of such odd dress that I rubbed my eyes to see
whether I was actually awake or whether perhaps a crazy, droll
dream were not transporting me into an alien fable-land.

"These people, whom I rightly took for inhabitants of the city
out of whose gate I saw them come, were wearing long and
very full trousers, cut in the manner of the Japanese, of expensive material—velvet, velveteen, fine cloth, and even linen in-
terwoven with many colors—richly trimmed with braiding or
pretty ribbons and lacings, and with little boys' coats that hardly covered their bellies, mostly of sun-bright colors, and only a
few in black. Their hair hung down uncombed in its natural
wildness to their shoulders and backs, and on their heads
perched odd little caps. Many had bared their throats after the
fashion of the Turks and modern Greeks, while others wore
around their neck and bosom a little piece of white linen,
similar almost to a shirt collar such as you, beloved Rufin,
must have seen in the portraits of our ancestors. Although all

these people seemed to be very young, their speech was deep and rough, every one of their movements was awkward, and many had a narrow shadow under their noses, as if a turned-up moustache were there. Out of the backs of the little coats of many there protruded a long pipe on which great silken tassels swung. Others had taken these pipes out and fastened little, or big, sometimes even very big, oddly formed heads on the bottoms of them, from which they knew how to make artificial clouds of steam arise by skillfully blowing onto the tops of them through a very slim little connecting tube. Others carried broad gleaming swords in their hands, as though about to advance upon the foe. Still others had little containers made of leather or tin hung at their waists or strapped on their backs. You can imagine, dear Rufin, that I, who seek to enrich my knowledge by careful observation of every new phenomenon, halted and fixed my eye unwaveringly on these odd people. Then they gathered around me and shouted with all their might: 'Philistine! Philistine!' and struck up a hideous laughter.

"That irritated me. For, beloved Rufin, is there anything more offensive for a great scholar than to be taken for one of that nation which many thousands of years ago was slain with the jawbone of an ass? I collected myself with my innate dignity and declared aloud to the odd people around me that I hoped I was in a civilized state and that I would address myself to the police and to the courts of justice to avenge the insult perpetrated upon me. At that they all growled, and even those who up till then had not been smoking, drew from their pockets the machines designed for that purpose and all blew thick clouds of steam in my face, clouds which, as I noticed only then, stank unbearably and dazed my senses. Then they pronounced over me a kind of curse, the words of which, beloved Rufin, I simply do not wish to repeat to you on account of their hideousness. I cannot think of them myself without profound horror. Finally, amid loud mocking laughter they left me, and it seemed to me as though the word 'hunting whip' echoed in the air![2]

[2] With only slight exaggeration, Hoffmann is describing the "old German" costume affected by aggressively nationalistic youth, especially in university circles, after the fall of Napoleon. The tough talk was intended to be the antithesis of Versailles elegance and eloquence. Everything about these "radical" youths was calculated to be anti-French.

"My driver, who had heard and seen everything, wrung his hands and said, 'O my dear master, now that what has happened *has* happened, do not on any account go into that city! No dog, as they say, would take a piece of bread from you, and constant danger would threaten—'

"I did not allow the good man to finish his speech, and I turned my steps as fast as I could go, toward the nearest village. I am now sitting in a solitary little chamber of the only inn of that village, my beloved Rufin, and writing all this to you. As far as possible I shall gather information about the strange and barbarous folk that dwell in that city. About their customs, usages, and about their language, etc., I have already gotten people to tell me many an extreme oddity, and I shall faithfully communicate everything to you. Etc., etc."

You perceive, O my beloved reader, that one can be a great scholar and yet be unacquainted with very ordinary phenomena of life and get into the oddest dreams about things known everywhere. Ptolemy Philadelphus had studied and yet did not even recognize students, did not even know that he was in the village of Hoch-Jakobsheim,[3] which, as is well-known, is near the famous University of Kerepes,[4] when he was writing his friend about an occurrence which had been transformed in his head into the strangest adventure. The good Ptolemy was startled at meeting students who were cheerily and in good spirits hiking across country for their pleasure. What anxiety would have stricken him if he had arrived an hour earlier in Kerepes and if coincidence had led him before the house of the Professor of Natural History, Mosch Terpin! He would have been surrounded by hundreds of students pouring out of the house, noisily arguing, and the like, and still odder dreams would have come into his head at seeing that confusion and thronging.

Mosch Terpin's lectures were the most frequented in all Kerepes. He was, as has been said, Professor of Natural History. He explained how it rains, thunders, lightens, why the sun

---

[3] "Upper Jamestown."

[4] "Kerepes" is the author's imaginary name for an imaginary university, though it is thought that he had Heidelberg in mind. Clemens Brentano's hilarious reports of life there were his probable source of information.

shines by day and the moon by night, how and why the grass grows, and so forth, so that any child could not but understand it. He had condensed the whole of nature into a neat little compendium so that he could conveniently manipulate it at will, and out of it he could pull an answer for any question, as out of a drawer. He first established his reputation by successfully demonstrating, after many physical experiments, that darkness derives primarily from lack of light. This gained him his incredible clientele, as well as the fact that he knew how to convert those physical experiments with much skill into clever tricks, and thus he carried on a perfectly delightful hocus-pocus.

Allow me, my gracious reader, since you know students much better than did the famous scholar Ptolemy Philadelphus, and since you know nothing of his dreamy timidity, to take you now to Kerepes, in front of the house of Professor Mosch Terpin just when he has finished his lecture. One of the students streaming out immediately catches your attention. You perceive a well-built youth of twenty-three to twenty-four, from whose dark gleaming eyes a lively, splendid, inner intelligence speaks eloquently. His glance might almost be called bold, if the visionary melancholy that lies upon his entire pale countenance did not conceal those burning rays like a veil. His coat of fine black cloth trimmed with slashed velvet is cut almost in the old German fashion, and with it the neat and dazzling white lace collar goes very well, as well as the velvet cap set upon his fine chestnut brown locks. This costume becomes him very well, because by his whole manner, by his dignity in walk and stance, by his meaningful facial formation, he really seems to belong to a fine and worthy bygone age, and hence one does not think of the affectations that are often the order of the present day in the finicky copying of misunderstood models and in equally misunderstood application to the present time. This young man who pleases you so well at first glance, beloved reader, is none other than the student Balthasar, the son of honest, well-to-do people, upright, intelligent, industrious, about whom I intend to tell you a great deal, O my reader, in the noteworthy story which I have undertaken to write.

Serious, lost in thought, as was his way, Balthasar was walking out from Professor Mosch Terpin's lecture toward the gate to betake himself, not to the fencing room, but to the pleasant grove that is situated hardly a couple of hundred steps from Kerepes. His friend Fabian, a handsome lad of cheerful looks and temperament of the same kind, ran after him and overtook him right by the gate.

"Balthasar!" cried Fabian loudly. "Balthasar, are you going out to the woods again to wander around by yourself like a melancholy Philistine when doughty lads are smartly practicing the noble art of fencing! I beg you, Balthasar, leave off your silly uncanny doings for a change and be cheerful and happy again, the way you used to be. Come on! We'll have a try at a couple of passes, and then if you still want to go out, I'll tag along with you."

"You mean well," replied Balthasar, "you mean well, and for that reason I don't want to quarrel with you for often tagging after me on highway and byway like a madman, cheating me out of many a pleasure of which you have no conception. You are one of those odd people who take everyone they see walking by himself for a melancholy fool and want to manage him and cure him in their own way, like that parasite with the worthy Prince Hamlet, who gave the little man some sound instruction when he assured him he knew nothing about playing the recorder. Naturally, I'll spare you that, dear Fabian, but I do beg you with all my heart to look up some other companion for your noble fighting with rapier and broadsword, and let me go quietly on my way."

"No, no!" cried Fabian laughing. "You won't get away from me like that, my dear friend. If you won't go to the fencing room with me, then I'll go out to the forest with you. It is a loyal friend's duty to cheer you up in your gloom. Come on then, dear Balthasar, come on then, if you won't have it any other way."

With that he took his friend by the arm and strode off vigorously with him. Balthasar clenched his teeth in silent wrath and maintained his lowering silence as Fabian went on telling one merry thing after another without stopping for breath. There was a good deal of nonsense along with the rest, as always happens in merry narration without a stop for breath.

When finally they stepped into the cool shade of the fragrant forest, as the bushes whispered as if in yearning sighs, as the wonderful melodies of the murmuring brooks and the songs of the forest birds sounded afar and awoke echoes that answered them out of the hills, then Balthasar suddenly stood still and, as he spread out his arms as if to clasp trees and bushes in loving embrace, cried out, "Oh, now I feel good again! Indescribably good!"

Fabian looked at his friend a bit astounded, like someone who can't make head or tail out of the other's words and simply doesn't know what to say.

Then Balthasar grasped his hand and with delight exclaimed, "Now doesn't your heart open up, Brother? Now don't you comprehend the blessed mystery of forest solitude?"

"I don't entirely understand you, dear Brother,"[5] replied Fabian, "but if you mean that a walk here in the forest makes you feel good, then I am completely of your opinion. Don't I also like to go walking, especially in good company, where a sensible, instructive conversation can be carried on? For example, it is a real pleasure to go across country with our Professor Mosch Terpin. He knows every little plant, every little grass, and knows how it is called by name and in what class it belongs, and he understands the wind and the weather—"

"Stop!" cried Balthasar. "I beg you, stop! You touch on something that could drive me mad if there weren't some consolation for it. The way the professor speaks about Nature rends my inmost heart. Or rather, an uncanny horror seizes me at it, as if I were looking at a lunatic who, a king and ruler in his foppish folly, caresses a straw man of his own making, imagining he is embracing his royal bride! His so-called experiments appear to me like a repulsive mockery of the divine being whose breath breathes upon us in Nature and stirs the deepest and holiest intimations within our inmost spirits. I often get the temptation to smash his glasses and his retorts and all his trash to pieces for him, except that I remember that the monkey doesn't stop playing with fire until he burns his paws.

"Look, Fabian, these feelings torment me, choke my heart in Mosch Terpin's lectures, and I may well seem to you then more serious-minded and more misanthropic than ever. At those times I feel as if the house were about to collapse over my

[5] University students addressed each other as "Brother."

head, an indescribable anguish drives me out of the city. But here—here a sweet peace quickly fills my spirit. Couched on the flowery greensward, I gaze up into the wide blue of the sky, and above me, on past the exultant forest, go the golden clouds like magnificent dreams out of a far-off world full of blessed joys. O my Fabian, then a wonderful spirit rises out of my own bosom, and I hear how it speaks in mysterious words with the bushes, with the trees, with the waves of the forest brook, and I cannot find a name for the bliss that then courses in sweet melancholy anxiety through my whole being."

"Ah," cried Fabian, "ah, that is once again the old, everlasting song about sorrow and bliss and speaking trees and forest brooks. All your poems abound in those pretty things, which fall very passably upon the ear and are profitably consumed, so long as one doesn't look for something further behind them. But tell me, my excellent Melancholicus, if Mosch Terpin's lectures actually offend and irritate you so horribly, tell me why in the world you run to every one of them, why you don't miss a single one, and then, as a matter of fact, sit there every time mute and stiff with your eyes closed like a man dreaming?"

"Don't," replied Balthasar, as he lowered his eyes, "don't ask me that, dear friend! An unknown power draws me every morning into Mosch Terpin's house. I feel my torments ahead of time, and yet I can't resist. A dark fatality sweeps me on!"

"Ha, ha," laughed Fabian aloud suddenly, "ha, ha, ha! How fine—how poetical, how mystical! The unknown power that draws you into Mosch Terpin's house lies in the deep blue eyes of the pretty Candida! That you are over your ears in love with the Professor's pretty little daughter, we have all known for a long time, and on that account we indulge you in your whims and your foolish behavior. It's never any other way with lovers. You find yourself in the first stage of lovesickness, and in your latter years of youth you must accommodate yourself to all the odd follies which we—I and many others, thank Heaven!—went through in school without a big audience of onlookers. But believe me, my beloved heart—"

Meanwhile Fabian had again taken his friend Balthasar by the arm and had walked on rapidly with him. Just now they were stepping out from the underbrush onto the broad highway that led through the middle of the forest. Then Fabian noticed a horse without a rider jogging along out of the distance, enveloped in a cloud of dust. "Hey, hey!" he cried, interrupting his own speech. "Hey, hey! There a sorry damned jade has run away and thrown her rider. We must catch her and afterwards look for her rider in the woods." With that, he took up a position in the middle of the road.

Nearer and nearer came the horse, and then it seemed as if on either side a pair of riding boots was dangling up and down in the air and as if something black were rising and moving on the saddle. Right in front of Fabian rang a long, shrill *prrr, prrr,* and at the same moment, a pair of riding boots came flying past his head and an odd little black thing came bowling along between his legs. Stock still stood the great horse and with long outstretched neck sniffed at its tiny little master, who rolled in the sand and finally with effort got onto his feet. The little pygmy's head stuck far down between his high shoulders, and with his excrescences on chest and back, with his short body and his long spider legs, he looked like an apple spitted on a fork and on which someone had carved a funny face. When Fabian now saw this odd little monster standing in front of him, he broke into loud laughter. But the little fellow defiantly pulled down over his eyes the little cap that he had picked up from the ground, and, as he bored Fabian right through with wild looks, asked in a harsh and deeply hoarse tone, "Is this the right way to Kerepes?"

Yes, sir," answered Balthasar gently and seriously, and handed the little fellow the boots which he had gathered up.

All efforts of the little fellow to pull the boots on were in vain; he tumbled over time and again and rolled groaning in the sand. Balthasar set both boots upright together, lifted the little fellow gently aloft, and, lowering him in the same manner, stuck both little feet in their too heavy and too big casings.

With proud mien, one hand set to his side and the other on his cap, the little fellow cried, "*Gratias,*[6] sir!" and walked over to the horse whose reins he seized.

However, all efforts to reach the stirrup or to climb up onto the large animal remained futile. Balthasar, still seriously and gently, walked over and lifted the little fellow to the stirrup. He

[6] (Latin): "Thanks!" Even in Hoffmann's day there was some survival of student Latin in university circles.

probably took too strong a swing, because at the same instant as he was sitting mounted above, he also was lying down below again on the other side.

"Not so hastily, dearest M'sieu!" cried Fabian, as once again he burst forth in ringing laughter.

"The Devil is your dearest M'sieu!" shrieked the little fellow, quite infuriated, as he clapped the sand out of his clothes. "I am a student, and if you are one likewise, then it is grounds for challenge the way you are laughing in my face like an idiot, and tomorrow you will have to fight me in Kerepes!"

"Thunderation!" cried Fabian, still laughing. "Thunderation! That's a lad of spirit, an everybody's man, for courage and true going by the code."

And with that he picked the little fellow up in spite of all his wrigglings and strugglings and set him on the horse, which immediately jogged off, merrily whinnying, with its little master. Fabian was holding both his sides and on the point of bursting with laughter.

"It is cruel," said Balthasar, "to laugh at a person whom Nature has injured in such a horrible way as it has that little horseman there. If he really is a student, you will have to fight him, and with pistols too, even if it is contrary to all academic customs, since he cannot handle either rapier or broadsword."

"How solemnly," said Fabian, "how solemnly, how gloomily you are taking all this again, my dear friend Balthasar. It never occurred to me to laugh at a deformed person. But tell me, is a gristly little hop-o'-my-thumb like that to get on a horse when he can't see past its neck? Is he to stick his little feet in such damnably big boots? Is he to wear a tight-fitting kurtka with a thousand braids and tassels and tufts? Is he to wear an amazing velvet cap like that? Is he to assume such a haughty, defiant manner? Is he to squeeze out such barbarous hoarse sounds? Is he to do all these things, I ask you, without being rightly laughed at as a consummate ass? But I must go in, I must see the to-do when this cavalier of a student arrives on his proud steed! There is nothing to be done with you today anyway. Farewell!"

Posthaste Fabian ran through the woods back to the city.

Balthasar left the open road and lost himself in the densest undergrowth, and there he sank down on a mossy seat, seized, indeed overwhelmed, by the bitterest emotions. It could well be that he really loved the lovely Candida, but he had locked that love in the innermost depths of his soul, away from all people, away even from himself, as a deep, tender secret. And now when Fabian had spoken of it without concealment, so frivolously, he felt as if rough hands in overbearing insolence were tearing away the veils from the sacred image which he had not ventured to touch, and as if the saint must now be forever angry with *him*. Yes, Fabian's words seemed to him an abominable mockery of his entire being, his sweetest dreams.

"So," he cried out in the excess of his annoyance, "so you look upon me as a lovesick ass, Fabian! For a fool who runs to Mosch Terpin's lectures in order to be under the same roof with the beautiful Candida for an hour at least, who roves solitary around the woods to think up miserable poems to the Beloved and to write them more wretchedly still, who ruins trees by cutting ridiculous names into their smooth bark, who can't produce a single sensible word in the presence of the girl but only sighs and moans and makes lachrymose faces as if he were suffering from cramps, who wears against his bare breast dried-up flowers that she wore at her bosom, or even the glove that she lost—in short, one who commits a thousand childish follies! And for that, Fabian, you tease me, and for that all the lads are probably laughing at me, and for that I am perhaps the object of mockery together with the inner world that has opened up for me. And the gracious, lovely, glorious Candida—"

As he pronounced that name, something went through his heart like a burning dagger's thrust. Alas! At that moment an inner voice whispered very audibly to him that he really did go to Mosch Terpin's house only for Candida's sake, that he did make poems to the Beloved, that he did carve her name in tree bark, that he did lapse silent in her presence, that he did sigh, moan, wear against his breast dried-up flowers that she had lost, and that, besides, he really was falling into all the follies that Fabian could ever reproach him with. Not until now had he actually felt how unspeakably he did love the beautiful Candida, but at the same time too he realized that the purest, most fervent love, oddly enough, took on a somewhat preposterous appearance in external life—a fact which was probably to be attributed to the profound irony that Nature has inserted into all human affairs. He might be right, but meanwhile it was wholly wrong for him to begin to get angry about it. Dreams which formerly encompassed him were lost, the voices of the forest sounded to him like mockery and derision. He ran back to Kerepes.

"Mister Balthasar—*mon cher* Balthasar!" someone called to him. He raised his glance and stopped as though halted by magic, for Professor Mosch Terpin was coming toward him with his daughter Candida on his arm. Candida greeted the statuelike youth with the cheerful, friendly ease characteristic of her. "Balthasar, *mon cher* Balthasar," cried the professor, "you are indeed the most industrious and the dearest to me of my auditors! O my dear fellow, I notice that you love nature with all her marvels, just as do I, who simply dote on her! Surely you have been botanizing again in our little woods. Found anything profitable?—well! Let us get better acquainted. Come and visit me—welcome any time—we can experiment together. —have you seen my air pump yet? Well, *mon cher*, tomorrow evening there is gathering at my house a friendly circle who will consume tea and bread-and-butter sandwiches and divert themselves with pleasant conversation. Increase it by the addition of your worthy person. You will meet a very attractive young man who comes especially recommended to me. *Bon soir, mon cher* —good evening, my excellent fellow, *au revoir—auf Wiedersehen*—you are coming to the lecture tomorrow? Well, *mon cher—adieu!*"

Without waiting for Balthasar's answer, Professor Mosch Terpin walked away with his daughter.

Balthasar in his confusion had not dared to raise his eyes, but Candida's glances burned into his heart, he felt the exhalation of her breath, and sweet shudders made his inmost being quiver.

All his annoyance was taken from him. He gazed full of rapture after the lovely Candida until she disappeared amid the arbor walks. Then he returned slowly to the forest in order to dream more magnificently than ever.

THIRD CHAPTER

How Fabian did not know what to say. Candida and maidens who are not permitted to eat fish. Mosch Terpin's literary tea. The young prince.

A s he took the cross-path diagonally through the forest, Fabian had the intention of arriving ahead of the odd little pygmy who had gone jogging away from him. He had miscalculated, for, emerging from the bushes, he perceived far off in the distance how another stately horseman had joined the little fellow and how both were now riding in through the gate of Kerepes.

"Hm!" said Fabian to himself. "If the nutcracker on his big horse has arrived before me, I am still getting there in time for the spectacle that will be produced with his coming. If the odd thing is really a student, let them direct him to the Winged Steed, and if he stops there with his shrill *prrr-prrr* and throws his riding boots first and himself after them, and acts wild and defiant when the grooms laugh—well!—then the crazy farce will be finished!"

As Fabian now reached the city, he expected to meet nothing but laughing faces on the way to the Winged Steed. But such was not the case. All the people were walking by, calmly and earnestly. Just as earnestly, several academics who had gathered there were strolling back and forth talking together on the square in front of the Winged Steed. Fabian was convinced that the little fellow must not have come in here at least, and then, casting a glance through the inn gate, he saw that the little fellow's perfectly recognizable horse was just being led to stable. He now ran over to the first of his acquaintances that came along and inquired whether a very odd, curious pygmy had not ridden up. The one whom Fabian asked knew quite as little about it as the others, to whom Fabian now recounted what had befallen him and the hop-o'-my-thumb who claimed to be a student. They all laughed heartily but assured him that such a thing as he described had by no means arrived. Two very stately cavaliers *had* dismounted, however, at the Winged Steed Inn barely ten minutes before.

"Was one of them riding the horse which was just taken to stable?" asked Fabian.

"Absolutely," replied one, "absolutely. The one who was riding that horse was of somewhat small stature but of elegant physical build, pleasing features, and had the prettiest curly hair you ever could see. What's more, he showed himself a most excellent horseman, for he swung down from his horse with an agility and a dignity, like the first equerry of our ruling prince."

"And," cried Fabian, "and did not lose his riding boots and did not tumble at your feet?"

"God forbid!" they all replied with one voice. "God forbid! What are you thinking of, Brother? A capital horseman like that little fellow!"

Fabian simply did not know what to say. But there was Balthasar coming down the street. To him rushed Fabian, drew him aside, and related how the little pygmy who had encountered them outside the gate and fallen off his horse, had just arrived here and been taken by everyone for a handsome man with elegant physical build and for a most excellent horseman.

"You see," replied Balthasar, earnestly and calmly, "you see, dear Brother Fabian, not everyone attacks with loveless mockery unfortunate persons abused by Nature."

"But good Lord in Heaven," Fabian interrupted him, "here there is no question of mockery and lovelessness, but only of whether a three-foot-high little fellow who looks not unlike a radish, is to be termed a handsome, well-built man."

Balthasar had to confirm Fabian's statement, as far as the stature and appearance of the little student were concerned. The others asserted that the little cavalier was a pretty and well-built man. To which Fabian and Balthasar continued to maintain on the contrary that they had never seen a more repulsive dwarf. It remained at that, and they all parted full of puzzlement.

Late evening came on and the two friends betook themselves together to their residence. Then it came out, Balthasar himself did not quite know how, that he had met Professor Mosch Terpin, who had invited him for the following evening.

"Oh, you lucky fellow!" cried Fabian, "Oh, you super-lucky fellow! There you will see and hear and talk with your sweetheart, the pretty Mamsell Candida!"

Balthasar, deeply offended anew, tore himself loose from Fabian and started to go out. But he reconsidered, stopped, and fighting down his irritation by force, said, "You may be right, dear Brother, in taking me for a ridiculous fool in love. Maybe I really am. But this ridiculousness is a deep and painful wound dealt to my spirit, and one which, touched incautiously, could arouse me in rather vehement pain to all sorts of madness. Therefore, Brother, if you are really fond of me, don't mention the name Candida to me any more!"

"You're taking," replied Fabian, "you're taking the matter, my dear friend Balthasar, terribly tragically again, and in your condition nothing else is to be expected. But in order not to get into all kinds of hateful dissension with you, I promise that the name Candida shall not pass my lips until you yourself give me an occasion for it. For today, merely allow me to say that I foresee all kinds of vexation into which your love state will plunge you. Candida is a very pretty, splendid girl, but she does not suit your melancholy, visionary temperament at all. If you get to know her better, her innocent, cheerful nature will seem to you a lack of poetry, which you find missing everywhere. You will get into all sorts of odd reveries, and the whole thing will end tumultuously with horrible imaginary pain and considerable despair. Besides, I, as well as you, am invited for tomorrow to our professor's, who will entertain us with very pretty experiments. Now good night, fablelike dreamer! Sleep, if you can sleep before such an important day as tomorrow!"

With that, Fabian left his friend, who was sunk in deep meditation. Not without reason might Fabian foresee all sorts of moments of declamatory unhappiness which could come about with Candida and Balthasar, for both their natures and temperaments seemed in fact to offer plenty of occasion for such.

Candida was, as everyone had to admit, as pretty as a picture, with eyes that beamed right into your heart and with rather pouting rosy lips. Whether her hair, which she could do up quite fantastically in curious braids, was to be termed more blond or more brown, I have forgotten, but I do recall very well this odd characteristic: that it kept getting darker and darker the longer you looked at it. Tall and slender of build, light of movement, the girl was graciousness and charm itself, even in jolly surroundings, and with so much physical charm one was very willing to overlook the fact that her hands and feet could perhaps have been built smaller and daintier. Moreover, Candida had read Goethe's *Wilhelm Meister,* Schiller's poems, and Fouqué's *Magic Ring,*[1] and had forgotten again almost everything contained in them. She played the piano quite passably, sometimes even sang to her own accompaniment; she danced the newest françaises and gavottes, and she wrote out the laundry lists with a fine legible hand. If you insisted on finding fault with something about the dear girl, it was perhaps that she spoke somewhat too low, laced her stays too tight, rejoiced too long in a new hat, and ate too many cupcakes at tea. For extravagant poets, there was frankly a good deal more about the pretty Candida that was not right, but what all don't they ask for? First of all, they want the young lady to get into a state of somnambulistic rapture over everything they utter, to sigh deeply, roll her eyes, and occasionally too to faint a trifle, or even to go blind for a moment at the peak of the most feminine femininity. Then the aforesaid young lady must sing the poet's songs to the melody that streams forth from her heart, yet she must instantaneously be taken ill over it, and even write poems herself, yet be very ashamed when that fact comes out, although the lady has written with her own hand

---

[1] *Der Zauberring,* a chivalric romance of 1813 by Hoffmann's friend and the then very popular Romantic author, Baron de la Motte-Fouqué.

with delicate lettering on very fine scented paper and passed them to the poet's own hand, who then on his own account becomes ill with rapture over them—something for which he is not to be blamed. There are poetical ascetics who go still further and find it contrary to all feminine tenderness for a girl to laugh, to eat, to drink, and to dress prettily according to the fashion. They almost resemble Saint Jerome, who forbids maidens to wear earrings or to eat fish. They are to feed, so the saint ordains, only on some prepared grass, be continually hungry without feeling it, to wrap themselves in coarse, badly sewn garments which conceal their forms, and especially, to choose as their companion a female person who is serious-minded, pale, sad, and a little dirty!

Candida was through and through a cheerful, artless creature, and therefore she liked nothing better than a conversation that moved upon the light and airy pinions of the most spontaneous humor. She laughed heartily at everything funny; she never sighed, except when rain spoiled the walk she had been hoping for, or when, in spite of all precautions, her new shawl had got a spot on it. At the same time, if there was genuine occasion for it, a deep inner sentiment did peep through, which never degenerated into shallow sentimentality, and thus the girl might well suit me and you, beloved reader, for we do not belong to the fantastical. With Balthasar, it could well be otherwise. But soon it must come to light to what extent the prosaic Fabian had correctly prophesied.

That Balthasar could not sleep all night long for sheer uneasiness, for indescribable sweet apprehension—what was more natural than that? Completely possessed by the image of the Beloved, he sat down at the table and wrote down a sizable number of nice, well-sounding lines of verse, which portrayed his state in a mystical tale of the love of the Nightingale for the Red Rose. These he intended to take along to Mosch Terpin's literary tea and let fly with them at Candida's unguarded heart, whenever and however such might be possible.

Fabian smiled a little when, in keeping with the appointment, he arrived at a specified hour to call for Balthasar and found him more elegantly dressed than he had ever seen him before. He had on a notched collar with the finest Brussels lace around it, and his short coat with slit sleeves was of slashed velvet. Along with these, he was wearing French boots with high pointed heels and silver fringe, an English hat of the finest plush, and Danish gloves. Thus he was completely dressed in the German fashion, and the costume became him exceptionally well, especially since he had had his hair nicely curled and had combed up his little upturned moustache.

Balthasar's heart fluttered with rapture as Candida met him at Mosch Terpin's house, completely dressed in the costume of the old German maiden, amicable, charming in glance and word, in her entire being, just as people were accustomed to see her always. "My utterly sweet young lady!" sighed Balthasar from the depths of his heart as Candida, sweet Candida herself, handed him a cup of steaming tea.

But Candida looked at him with shining eyes and said, "Here are rum and maraschino, zwieback and pumpernickel, dear Mr. Balthasar. Please help yourself to whatever you like."

But instead of looking at or reaching for rum or maraschino, zwieback or pumpernickel, the inspired Balthasar could not avert his gaze full of painful melancholy of the most heartfelt love away from the lovely maiden, and he struggled for words that would express from the bottom of his heart what he was feeling just then.

Just then, however, the Professor of Aesthetics, a big, husky man, seized him from behind with a mighty fist, turned him around so that he spilled more tea on the floor than was seemly, and cried out in a thunderous voice, "Dear Lucas Cranach,[2] don't swill any more of that vile water, you will ruin your stomach utterly. In the other room there, our valiant Mosch has set up a battery of the handsomest bottles of noble Rhine wine, and we are going to fire them right away!" He dragged the unhappy youth away.

There Mosch Terpin came to meet them out of a side room, leading by the hand a small, very odd little man and crying loudly, "Here, ladies and gentlemen, I present to you a youth highly gifted with the rarest qualities, who will have no difficulty in winning your good will and your esteem. This is young Mr. Zinnober, who arrived only yesterday at our university and

[2] Lucas Cranach, 1472–1553, a famous German painter.

who intends to study law." Fabian and Balthasar recognized at first glance the curious little pygmy who had come dashing up to them outside the gate and had fallen from his horse.

"Shall I," said Fabian softly to Balthasar, "shall I challenge the mandrake to blowpipe or to cobbler's puncheon? After all, I can't use any other weapons against this fearful opponent."

"Shame on you," replied Balthasar, "shame on you for making fun of the helpless man, who, as you hear, possesses the rarest qualities, and in *that* way makes up in intellectual worth for what Nature denied him in the way of physical advantages." Then he turned to the little fellow and said, "I hope, dearest Mr. Zinnober, that your fall from your horse yesterday has not had any ill effects?"

But Zinnober, bracing himself from behind on a small cane he was carrying in his hand, rose on tiptoe so that he almost reached to Balthasar's waist, threw his head way back, looked up with wildly glittering eyes, and said in an oddly growling bass voice, "I don't know what you mean or what you are talking about, sir! Fall from a horse? *I*, fall from a horse? Apparently you do not know that I am the best horseman there can be, that I never fall from my horse, that I was on campaign as a volunteer with the cuirassiers, and that I gave equestrian instruction to officers and men at the riding academy! Hm, hm, fall from a horse, *I*, fall from a horse!"

With that he was about to turn quickly away, but the cane on which he was braced, slipped, and the little fellow went tumbling over and over at Balthasar's feet. Balthasar reached down toward the little fellow to help him up and in so doing unintentionally touched his head. Then the little fellow let out a piercing scream so that it echoed through the whole room and the shocked guests started up from their seats. People gathered around Balthasar and everybody asked at once why in Heaven's name he had screamed so horribly.

"Do not take it amiss, dear Mr. Balthasar," said Professor Mosch Terpin, "but that was a somewhat odd joke. Apparently you wanted to make us think that someone here was stepping on a cat's tail."

"Cat! Cat! Away with the cat!" shrieked a lady with weak nerves and straightway collapsed in a faint. And with the cry of

"Cat! Cat!" a couple of elderly gentlemen, who suffered from the same idiosyncrasy, rushed out the door.

Candida, who had emptied her entire smelling salts bottle onto the fainted lady, said softly to Balthasar, "But what mischief you are causing with your odious, piercing meow, dear Mr. Balthasar!"

The latter did not know what was happening to him. Fiery red in his whole face for annoyance and shame, he could not produce a single word, not even to say that it was little Mr. Zinnober and not *he*, who had squealed so hideously.

Professor Mosch Terpin saw the youth's intense embarrassment. He approached him in friendly fashion and said, "Now, now, dear Mr. Balthasar, just be calm. I observed everything. Bending down to the floor, hopping on all fours, you did a splendid imitation of the mishandled and furious tomcat. Usually, I just love that sort of natural history game, but here at a literary tea—"

"But," exploded Balthasar, "but most excellent Professor, it really wasn't I!"

"All right, all right," the professor cut him short. Candida stepped over to them. "Do," said the professor to the latter, "do console our good Mr. Balthasar for me, he is completely embarrassed at all the mischief that has been brought about."

The kindly Candida felt heartily sorry for poor Balthasar, who stood before her all confused and with downcast glance. She extended her hand to him and with a charming smile whispered, "They are really funny people to be so terribly afraid of cats."

Balthasar pressed Candida's hand to his lips with fervor. Candida allowed the soulful glance of her heavenly eyes to rest upon him. He was transported to the highest heaven and thought no more about Zinnober and the cry of cats.

The tumult was over and peace was restored. The lady with the weak nerves was sitting at the tea table enjoying sundry zwiebacks which she was dipping in rum and was assuring people that spirits menaced by hostile powers were thereby restored, and that after panic followed yearning hope. And the two elderly gentlemen also returned, between whose legs a fleeing tomcat actually had scooted, and, like numerous others, they were looking for the gaming table.

Balthasar, Fabian, the Professor of Aesthetics, and several young men sat down with the ladies. Mr. Zinnober meanwhile had moved up a footstool and by means of it had climbed up onto the sofa, where he was now sitting between two ladies and casting proud, glittering looks about him.

Balthasar thought the right moment had come to go ahead with his poem about the love of the Nightingale for the Red Rose. With proper modesty, such as is the usage among young poets, he said that, if he did not have to fear rousing weariness and boredom, and if he might rely on the kind consideration of the esteemed assemblage, he would be willing to venture reading a poem, the most recent offspring of his Muse.

Since the ladies had already adequately covered everything new that had happened in the city, since the girls had appropriately talked over the latest ball at the president's and even had reached agreement on the standard shape of the latest hats, and since the men could not count on any further food or drink short of two hours, Balthasar was unanimously invited not to withhold that splendid enjoyment from the company.

Balthasar drew forth the neatly written manuscript and read.

His own work, which had indeed poured forth from genuine poetic talent in full strength and vivid life, inspired him more and more. His delivery, rising to ever greater heights of passion, displayed the inner fire of the loving heart. He quivered with delight as soft sighs and many a soft "Ah!" from the ladies and many an exclamation of "Splendid! Excellent! Heavenly!" from the men convinced him that his poem had swept them all away.

At last he finished. Then they all cried, "What a poem! What thoughts! What imagination! What beautiful lines! What musical language! Thank you, thank you, dearest Mr. Zinnober, for the divine pleasure!"

"What? What?" cried Balthasar.

But no one paid any attention to him. They rushed over to Zinnober who was puffing himself up like a little turkey over on the sofa and who was growling in a repulsive voice, "Oh, please! Oh, please! You will have to put up with it. It's just a little thing I tossed off in haste just last night!"

But the Professor of Aesthetics shrieked, "Excellent—divine Zinnober! Friend of my heart, after me you are the first poet on the face of the earth! Come to my bosom, beautiful soul!" With that he swept the little fellow up off the sofa and petted him and kissed him.

Zinnober evinced some very unruly behavior at this. He pommeled the professor's fat belly with his little legs and squawked, "Let me go! Let me go! You're hurting me! You're hurting—hurting—I'll scratch your eyes out! I'll bite your nose in two!"

"No," cried the professor as he put the little fellow back down on the sofa, "no, gracious friend, don't carry modesty too far!"

Mosch Terpin had now stepped over from the gaming table, and he took Zinnober's little hand, pressed it, and said very seriously, "Excellent young man! Not too much, no, rather not enough did they tell me about the lofty genius that animates you."

"Which one," cried the Professor of Aesthetics again in full enthusiasm, "which one of you maidens is going to reward the magnificent Zinnober with a kiss for his poem, which expresses the innermost emotion of purest love?"

Then Candida rose and with full ardor in her cheeks approached the little fellow, knelt down, and kissed him on his hideous mouth with the blue lips.

"Yes!" shrieked Balthasar now, as though suddenly seized with madness. "Yes! Zinnober, divine Zinnober, you composed the profound poem about the Nightingale and the Red Rose, you deserve the magnificent reward you have received!" And with that he dragged Fabian into the side room and said, "Do me the kindness and look straight at me and then tell me frankly and honestly whether or not I am the student Balthasar, whether you are really Fabian, whether we are in Mosch Terpin's house, whether we are in a dream, or whether we are crazy. Tweak my nose or shake me, just so I wake up out of this accursed sorcery!"

"Why," replied Fabian, "why carry on so out of pure jealously because Candida kissed the little fellow? You must confess after all that the poem the little fellow read really was excellent."

"Fabian!" cried Balthasar in the tone of the profoundest astonishment. "What are you saying?"

"Why, yes," continued Fabian, "why, yes, the little fellow's poem was excellent and I concede him Candida's kiss. All the way around, there seems to be a lot to the odd little man that is worth more than a handsome figure. But as far as his figure is concerned, it strikes me as just as repulsive now as at the beginning. During the reading of the poem, inner inspiration did lend beauty to his features, so that frequently he did seem to me to be a charming, well-built youth, despite the fact that he hardly reached higher than the table. Give up your useless jealousy and make friends with him as one poet to another!"

"What!" shouted Balthasar, full of anger. "What! Make friends yet with the damned changeling whom I'd like to strangle with these hands?"

"This way," said Fabian, "this way you shut yourself away from all reason. But let us go back into the drawing room, where something new must be happening, since I hear loud cries of applause."

Mechanically Balthasar followed his friend back into the drawing room.

As they stepped in, Mosch Terpin was standing alone in the middle, stark astonishment on his face and still in his hand the instrument with which he had performed some physical experiment. The whole company had gathered around little Zinnober, who, with his cane braced under him, was standing on tiptoe acknowledging with haughty glances the applause pouring in upon him from all sides. People turned back to the professor, who was performing another very nice trick. Hardly had he finished when again everyone turned to the little fellow, crying, "Splendid! Excellent, dear Mr. Zinnober!"

Among the company was young Prince Gregor, who was studying at the university. The prince was of the most charming appearance you could ever see, and yet his behavior was so noble and unconstrained that his high lineage and his habitual movement in the most aristocratic circles were clearly expressed in it. Prince Gregor was now the one who did not leave

Zinnober's side and who kept praising him beyond all measure as the most magnificent poet and as the most skilled physicist. It was an odd group formed by those two standing together. Beside the splendid figure of Gregor, the tiny little man stood out very oddly as, with his nose stuck way up, he could barely support himself on his thin legs. The glances of all the ladies were directed, not at the prince, but at the little fellow, who kept rising on tiptoe and sinking back again and thus swayed back and forth like a Cartesian Devil.[3]

Professor Mosch Terpin stepped up to Balthasar and said, "What do you say to my protégé, to my dear Zinnober? There is a good deal to the man, and now that I look at him closely, it dawns on me what an extraordinary case he may represent. The parson who brought him up and who recommended him to me expresses himself very mysteriously about his ancestry. But just observe his noble dignity, his aristocratic, unconstrained behavior. He is surely of princely blood, perhaps even a king's son!"

At that instant it was announced that supper was ready. Zinnober staggered clumsily over to Candida, awkwardly seized her hand, and led her toward the dining room.

In total fury the unhappy Balthasar ran through the dark night, right through wind and rain, for home.

---

[3] A kind of children's toy, made of colored glass, usually in the shape of a devil, that floated upright in water.

FOURTH CHAPTER

How the Italian violinist Sbiocca threatened to throw
Mr. Zinnober into the bass viol, and how Referendary
Pulcher could not get appointed to the Foreign Office.
Concerning customs officials and marvels retained for
the house. Balthasar's enchantment by a cane-head.

O n a jutting, mossy stone in the most
isolated part of the forest, Balthasar was sitting and looking
pensively down into the depths, where a stream rushed and
foamed between rocky cliffs and dense underbrush. Somber
clouds were passing and dipping down behind the hills. The
rustling of the trees and of the waters produced a sound like a
muffled whine, and intermittently birds of prey screamed as
they soared up out of the dark brush into the broad space of the
sky and flung themselves in pursuit of the fleeing masses of
cloud.

To Balthasar, it seemed as though he were hearing the disconsolate lament of Nature in the wonderful voices of the forest, as though he himself must perish amid that lament, as
though his entire being were but the sensation of the deepest,
most insuperable pain. His heart was at the point of bursting for
sadness, and as frequent tears fell from his eyes, it seemed as if
the spirits of the sylvan stream gazed up to him and lifted
snow-white arms aloft out of the waves to draw him down into
the cool riverbed.

Then through the air, from the far distance, came bright and
cheerful horn calls and laid themselves consolingly against his

heart, and yearning awoke in him, and with it sweet hope. He looked around, and as the horn calls went on sounding, the green shade of the forest no longer seemed sad to him, the rustling of the wind and the whispering of the bushes no longer seemed full of lamentation. He found words.

"No!" he exclaimed, jumping up from his seat and gazing into the distance with shining glance. "No, all hope has not vanished! It is only too certain that some dark mystery, some evil magic has entered disquietingly into my life, but I shall break that magic, though I perish in the attempt! When finally, swept away and overwhelmed by the emotion that was on the verge of bursting my heart, I confessed my love to the lovely, sweet Candida, did I not read my happiness in her looks, did I not feel it in the pressure of her hand? But just as soon as that damned little monster puts in an appearance, all love is turned to *him*. On him, on that accursed abortion, Candida's eyes hang, and sighs of yearning escape from her bosom when the clumsy youth goes near her or so much as touches her hand. There must be something mysterious about him, and if I believed in silly nursemaids' tales, I would declare the youth was bewitched and could, as they say, put a charm on people. Is it not insane that everybody mocks and laughs at the deformed, utterly hapless manikin, and then again, once the little fellow steps among them, cry him up as the wisest, most learned, in fact the best-looking gentleman of a student that there is in our midst? What am I saying? Don't I almost feel the same way myself? Doesn't it often seem to me too as though Zinnober were clever and handsome? Only in Candida's presence the magic has no power over me; then Mr. Zinnober is and remains a stupid, repulsive mandrake. Nevertheless, I shall resist the hostile force! A dark intimation lies deep within my soul that something unexpected will put a weapon in my hand against this evil demon!"

Balthasar sought the way back to Kerepes. Walking along between a double row of trees, he noticed on the highway a small, loaded, traveling carriage out of which someone was waving to him in a friendly manner with a white handkerchief. He stepped up and recognized Mr. Vincenzo Sbiocca, the world-famous violin virtuoso, whom he esteemed beyond measure for his superb and expressive playing and from whom he had been taking lessons for the last two years.

"Lucky," cried Sbiocca as he leaped out of the carriage, "lucky, my dear Mr. Balthasar, my loyal friend and pupil, lucky that I still meet you here and can bid you a cordial farewell."

"What!" said Balthasar. "What, Mr. Sbiocca! You're not leaving Kerepes, where everybody honors and esteems you, where no one can compare with you?"

"Yes," replied Sbiocca, as all the fire of inner anger came into his face, "yes, Mr. Balthasar, I am leaving a place where all the people are foolish, a place that is like a huge insane asylum. You were not at my concert yesterday, since you had gone out walking in the country, otherwise you could have supported me against the raging people to whom I succumbed."

"What happened? In a thousand Heaven's names, what happened?" cried Balthasar.

"I play," Sbiocca continued, "the most difficult concerto by Viotti.[1] It is my pride and joy. You have heard me do it and it never left you uninspired. Yesterday, I well may say, I was very particularly in a good mood—*anima,* I mean, in cheerful spirits —*spirito alato,* I mean. No violin player in the whole wide world, not even Viotti himself could have matched my playing. When I finished, applause bursts forth in all its frenzy— *furore,* I mean—as I had expected. Fiddle under my arm, I step out to offer my most courteous thanks. But! What do I see! What do I hear! Without paying the slightest attention to me, everybody is pushing toward the corner of the hall shouting, 'Bravo! Bravissimo! Divine Zinnober! What playing! What execution, what expression, what skill!' I run over, I push my way through—and there stands a three-span-tall, misshapen fellow growling in an unpleasant voice, 'Oh, please! Oh, please! I played with the best talent I have, I really am by this time the leading violinist in Europe and the other parts of the known world.' 'A thousand devils!' screamed I, 'who did the playing, I or that angleworm there?' And when the little fellow

---

[1] Giovanni Battista Viotti, 1753–1824, "the father of modern violin playing," and a prolific composer. At the time of our story's composition, he was the director of the Paris Opéra.

kept on growling 'Oh, please! Oh, please!' I start to go after him
and grab him, using full fingering. But then they pitch onto me
and talk crazy stuff about envy, jealousy, and begrudging. Meanwhile somebody shouts, 'And what composition!' and with one
voice they all shout after him, 'And what composition! Divine
Zinnober! Sublime composer!' More furious than before, I
screamed, 'Is everyone crazy? Possessed? The concerto was by
Viotti, and I—I—the world-famous Vincenzo Sbiocca, played it!'
But then they hold me fast, talk about Italian madness—
rabbia, I mean—about strange attacks, take me by force into a
side room, treat me like an invalid, like a madman. It isn't long
before in rushes Signora Bragazzi and collapses in a faint. It had
gone with her the same as with me. As soon as she finished her
aria, the hall rang with 'Brava! Bravissima, Zinnober!' and
everybody was screaming that there was no singer on earth any
more except Zinnober, and there he was growling his damned
'Please! Please!' again. Signora Bragazzi is in bed with a fever
and will soon expire. I, for my part, am taking refuge in flight
from these insane people. Farewell, dearest Mr. Balthasar! If
by chance you see Signorino Zinnober, be so kind as to tell
him he had better not turn up anywhere in a concert where I
am present. Otherwise I would certainly grab him by his beetle-
legs and slam him through the F-hole in the bass viol, and there
he could play concerti and sing arias to his heart's content for
the rest of his life. Farewell, my beloved Balthasar! And do not
give up the violin!"

With that, Mr. Vincenzo Sbiocca embraced the thunderstruck
Balthasar and got back into his carriage, which rolled swiftly
on its way.

"Wasn't I right?" said Balthasar to himself. "Wasn't I right?
That uncanny object, that Zinnober, is bewitched and he is
putting a spell on people."

In the next instant a young man went rushing past, pale,
distracted, madness and despair in his face. Balthasar's heart
sank. In the youth he thought he had recognized one of his
friends, and he swiftly ran into the forest in pursuit of him.
Hardly had he run twenty or thirty steps, when he caught sight
of Referendary Pulcher, who had halted underneath a big tree
and with glances directed toward heaven was saying, "No! I

cannot endure this shame any longer! Every hope of my life
is gone! Every prospect points only toward the grave! Farewell, life—world—hope—beloved—'' And with that, the desperate referendary wrenched a pistol from his bosom and
pressed it to his forehead.

With the swiftness of lightning, Balthasar rushed up to him,
hurled the pistol far away out of his hand, and cried, "Pulcher!
For Heaven's sake, what is the matter? What are you doing?"

For a few minutes the referendary could not get back his
senses. He had collapsed half fainting on the grass and Balthasar had sat down beside him and was speaking words of
comfort as best he could, without knowing the cause of Pulcher's desperation.

A hundred times Balthasar had asked what had happened to
the referendary so awful that it had roused in him the black
thought of suicide. Then finally Pulcher fetched a deep sigh
and began, "You know, dear friend Balthasar, of my distressed
situation. You know how I had all my hopes set on the position of confidential courier which is open at the Ministry of
Foreign Affairs. You know with what zeal and with what dili-
gence I had prepared for it. I had handed in my dissertation,
which I learned to my joy had received the minister's fullest
approval. With what confidence I appeared this morning for
the oral examination! In the room I found a little, misshapen
fellow whom you probably know under the name of Mr. Zinnober. The Legation Counselor entrusted with the examination
met me in friendly fashion and told me that Mr. Zinnober had
also applied for the same position which I wished to obtain,
and that hence he would examine us *both*. Then he whispered
softly in my ear, 'You have nothing to fear from your com-
petitor, my dearest Referendary. The work handed in by little
Zinnober is wretched.'

"The examination began. Not one of the counselor's questions did I leave unanswered. Zinnober didn't know anything.
Absolutely nothing. Instead of answering, he kept growling and
squawking incomprehensible stuff that nobody understood, and
a couple of times when he was impolitely swinging his legs, he
fell off the high stool, so that I had to help him back up again.
My heart was quivering with satisfaction. The friendly glances

that the counselor kept casting toward the little fellow, I took for bitterest irony.

"The examination was over. No one can describe my terror, it seemed to me as if a sudden lightning bolt were hurling me fathoms deep into the ground, when the counselor embraced the little fellow and said to him, 'Magnificent man! What knowledge, what comprehension, what sagacity!' And then to me, 'You have greatly disappointed me, Referendary Pulcher. Why, you don't know anything! And—don't take it amiss, but the cheek you must have had in coming to the examination, runs counter to all propriety, counter to all decorum! Why, you couldn't even stay on your stool, you fell right off, and Mr. Zinnober had to help you up. Diplomatic personnel must be very properly sober and self-possessed. Adieu, Referendary!'

"I still was taking all this for a mad illusion. I ventured to go to the minister. He called upon me to state how I could presume to importune him with my call after the way I had conducted myself at the examination; he knew everything already. The post for which I had competed was already given to Mr. Zinnober. Thus some hellish power has robbed me of all hope, and I intend to make a voluntary sacrifice of my life which has fallen prey to that dark fatality. Leave me!"

"Never!" cried Balthasar, "Listen to me first!"

He now related everything he knew about Zinnober since his first appearance outside the gate of Kerepes; how he had fared with the little fellow at Mosch Terpin's house; what he had just now heard from Vicenzo Sbiocca. "It is only too certain," he said then, "that back of all the doings of this unholy monstrosity lies some mystery, and believe me, friend Pulcher, some infernal enchantment is at work. And so it is merely a question of challenging him with a firm mind. Victory is assured if we just have the courage. Therefore, no desponding, no overhasty decision. Let us go after this little witch's brat together!"

"Witch's brat," cried the referendary with enthusiasm, "yes, witch's brat, that little fellow is an out-and-out damned witch's brat, that's sure! But Brother Balthasar, what is the matter with us? Are we in a dream? Witchcraft, magic spells, hasn't all that been over and done with for a long time? Didn't Prince

Paphnutius introduce the Enlightenment years ago and banish all crazy, disorderly stuff and everything incomprehensible from the country? And yet this sort of accursed contraband is supposed to have sneaked in? Confound it! This ought to be reported right away to the police and to the customs officials! But no, no. Only the madness of the people or, as I am almost afraid, vast bribery is to blame for our misfortunes. This accursed Zinnober is said to be immeasurably wealthy. Recently he was standing in front of the mint and people were pointing their fingers at him and crying, 'Look at pretty little money-daddy, he owns all the shiny gold that's stamped in there.' "

"Be still," replied Balthasar. "Be still, friend Referendary, there's no compelling the monster with gold. There is something else back of it. It's true that Prince Paphnutius introduced the Enlightenment for the welfare and betterment of his people and posterity, but many a marvelous and incomprehensible thing is still left. Right on our doorsteps, I feel, several charming miracles have been retained. For example, from paltry seed-kernels still grow the highest, grandest trees, and even the manifold sorts of fruit and grain with which we cram our bodies. Grant, too, that the multicolored flowers and insects bear the most resplendent hues on their petals and wings, and even inscriptions of the utmost strangeness, about which no man knows whether they are oil, or *gouache,* or water color, and no devil of a penmanship teacher can read the fine running hand, to say nothing of copying it! Ho, ho! Referendary, I tell you, peculiar things go on within me sometimes! I lay my pipe aside and pace back and forth in my room, and a curious voice whispers that I am myself a miracle, that the enchanter Microcosmos is at work inside of me and driving me on to all sorts of crazy stunts. But, Referendary, then I run out and gaze into Nature and understand everything the flowers and the waters say to me, and the blessed joy of heaven envelops me!"

"You're talking in delirium," cried Pulcher.

But Balthasar, paying him no heed, stretched out his arms toward the far distance, as if seized by the most ardent yearning. "Listen!" cried Balthasar, "Just listen, O Referendary! What celestial music resounds through the forest in the rustling of the evening wind! Do you hear how the fountains more strongly lift their song? How the bushes and the flowers join in with lovely voices?"

The referendary cocked his ear to catch the sound of the music that Balthasar was talking about. "As a matter of fact," he began, "as a matter of fact, there are tones wafting through the forest that are the most delightful, the most magnificent that I have ever heard in my life and that penetrate deep into my soul. But it is not the evening wind, nor the bushes, nor the flowers, that are singing this way, but rather it seems to me as if someone were in the distance touching the deepest throated bells of a glass harmonica."[2]

Pulcher was right. The full chords swelling louder and ever louder as they sounded closer and closer by, really did resemble the tones of a glass harmonica, the size and power of which, however, must have been unheard of.

As the friends now walked on ahead, a spectacle presented itself, so magical that they stopped dead with amazement as though rooted to the ground. A short distance off, a man was driving slowly through the forest, dressed almost in the Chinese manner, except that he was wearing on his head a huge puffy cap with resplendent feathers. His vehicle resembled an open seashell of glittering crystal, and both high wheels seemed of like material. As the wheels turned, there were produced the magnificent glass harmonica tones which the friends had already heard in the distance. Two snow-white unicorns with golden harnesses drew the chariot, on which, in lieu of a coachman, sat a silver pheasant, holding the golden reins in its beak. On the back sat a large rose beetle, which, by the fanning of its

---

[2] The glass harmonica of this passage is to be understood as Hoffmann's fanciful "adaptation" of the actual glass harmonica invented by Benjamin Franklin, the instrument for which Mozart composed the *Adagio* (K 617 A), the fragment of the *Adagio* (K 616), both for glass harmonica alone, and the *Quintet* (K 617) for viola, cello, flute, oboe, and glass harmonica. All are late works, the *Quintet* bearing the date of May 23, 1791. In *Die Frau ohne Schatten* Richard Strauss scored the call of the unborn children for glass harmonica, but in this case, as in others, the celesta is substituted because of the unavailability of the intended instrument. Franklin's glass harmonica produced its ethereal tones by means of glass discs of graduated sizes mounted on spindles in a trough of water; the player touched the spinning wet discs with gloved fingers to produce the sounds.

shimmering wings seemed to blow coolness down upon the man in the seashell. As he drove up opposite the strangers he bowed to them in friendly fashion. At that moment, from the glittering head of the long cane which the man was holding in his hand, there fell upon Balthasar a ray of light such that he felt a burning sting deep in his heart and with a muffled "Oh!" cringed with pain.

The man gazed at him, smiled, and beckoned in more friendly way than before. As soon as the magic vehicle disappeared amid the dense undergrowth, even while the harmonica tones were still dying away, Balthasar, completely beside himself with rapture and delight, fell upon his friend's neck and cried, "Referendary, we are saved! There is the man who will break Zinnober's infamous magic!"

"I don't know," said Pulcher, "I don't know what I do feel at this moment, whether I am awake or dreaming. But this much is certain, an unknown feeling of bliss is running through me, and hope and comfort are returning to my soul."

FIFTH CHAPTER

How Prince Barsanuph breakfasted on Leipzig larks and
Danziger Goldwasser, got a butter stain on his cashmere
trousers, and promoted Privy Secretary Zinnober to
Special Privy Counselor. The picture books of Prosper
Alpanus. How a butler bit the student Fabian in the
finger, and how the latter wore a coat with a train and
was ridiculed for it. Balthasar's flight.

It can no longer be kept a secret that the
Minister of Foreign Affairs, by whom Mr. Zinnober had been
appointed Privy Courier, was a descendant of that Baron Praetextatus von Mondschein who sought in vain in the tourney
books and chronicles for the family tree of the Fay Rosabelverde. His name, like that of his ancestor, was Praetextatus
von Mondschein. He had the most delicate upbringing and
the most pleasing manners, never confused "who" and "whom"
or "like" and "as," wrote his name in French letters and had a
legible handwriting generally, and sometimes even worked
himself, primarily when the weather was bad. Prince Barsanuph, a successor to the great Paphnutius, loved him tenderly
because he had an answer for every question, bowled with the
prince during recreational hours, had a splendid knowledge of
money negotiation, and was on the lookout for his equal at
the gavotte.

It befell that Baron Praetextatus von Mondschein had invited
the prince to a breakfast of Leipzig larks and a little glass of
Danziger Goldwasser. When he arrived at Mondschein's house
he found, among other agreeable diplomatic gentlemen in the
entrance hall, little Zinnober, who, braced on his cane, glit-

tered at him with his little eyes and then, without taking any further note of him, stuck in his mouth a roast lark which he had just snitched from the table.

As the prince caught sight of the little fellow, he smiled at him graciously and said to the minister, "Mondschein, who is the clever, pretty, little man you have in your house? Surely he is the one who composed the well-styled and beautifully written reports that I have been getting from you for some time?"

"Precisely so, gracious sir," replied Mondschein. "Destiny brought him to me as the most intelligent and able worker in my office. His name is Zinnober, and I recommend the splendid young man very particularly to your grace and favor, my dearest Prince! He has been with me only for a few days."

"And for just that reason," spoke up a good-looking young man who had meanwhile come up, "and for just that reason, as Your Excellency will permit me to observe, he has not yet turned in anything. The reports which had the good fortune to be noticed with favor by you, my most Serene Prince, were composed by me."

"What are you saying?" angrily asked the prince.

Zinnober had shoved in close by the prince and was smacking his lips with greed and appetite as he consumed the lark. And the young man really was the one who had composed those reports.

All the same the prince cried, "What are you saying? Why, you haven't so much as touched a pen yet, have you? And the fact that you are eating roast larks right up close to me so that, as I observe to my great annoyance, my new cashmere trousers already have a butter stain on them, and the fact that you are so indecorously smacking your lips in the process—yes! all that adequately demonstrates your total unsuitability for any diplomatic career. You go right on home and don't let me see you again unless you bring me a proper stain remover to use on my cashmere trousers. Perhaps then I will be in a forgiving mood again." Then to Zinnober: "Youths like you, worthy Zinnober, are an ornament to the state and deserve to be singled out with honor. You are, my excellent fellow, Special Privy Counselor!"

"Thank you kindly," growled Zinnober as he swallowed

down the last bite and wiped his snout with both his little hands. "Thank you kindly. I'll handle the business as I feel like it."

"Gallant self-confidence," said the prince, raising his voice, "Gallant self-confidence gives evidence of the inner strength that must be inherent in a worthy statesman."

And with that dictum the prince took a dram of Goldwasser which the minister himself handed to him and which pleased him very well.

The new counselor had to be seated between the prince and the minister. He consumed an incredible quantity of larks and drank Malaga and Goldwasser at random and growled and snarled between his teeth and carried on terrifically with his little hands and feet, because he could hardly get his pointed nose up over the table.

When the breakfast was over, both the prince and the minister cried out, "He is an angel of a man, this Special Privy Counselor!"

"You look," said Fabian to his friend Balthasar, "you look so cheerful, your glance is lit with particular fire. Do you feel happy? Ah, Balthasar, you may be dreaming a beautiful dream, but I must wake you from it. It is a friend's duty."

"What is the matter with you? What has happened?" asked Bathasar, confounded.

"Yes," Fabian continued, "yes, I must tell you. Only, control yourself, my friend. Consider that perhaps no misfortune in the world could hit you more painfully than this one, and yet none is easier to overcome. Candida—"

"In Heaven's name!" cried Balthasar in horror, "Candida! What is the matter with Candida? Has she gone—is she dead?"

"Be calm," Fabian went on, "be calm, my friend. Dead Candida is not, but as good as dead to you. Know, then, that little Zinnober has become Special Privy Counselor and is as good as engaged to the beautiful Candida, who, God knows how, is reported to be completely infatuated with him."

Fabian thought Balthasar would now burst forth in frantic, despairing lamentations and curses. Instead, he said with a quiet smile, "If it is nothing more than that, there isn't any misfortune that could trouble me."

"You don't love Candida any more?" asked Fabian, full of astonishment.

"I love," replied Balthasar, "I love that heavenly child, that splendid girl, with all the fervor, with all the ecstasy that can be kindled in a young man's bosom! And I know—ah, I know that Candida loves me in return, that only an unholy magic spell holds her in thrall. But soon I shall dissolve the bonds of that witchery, soon I shall annihilate the monster that has deluded the poor thing."

Balthasar now informed his friend in detail about the wonderful man whom he had encountered in the strange vehicle in the forest. He concluded by saying that, as a ray had flashed from the head of that enchanted creature's cane against his heart, the firm conviction had dawned on him that Zinnober was nothing but a witch's puppet whose power that man would annihilate.

"But," cried Fabian when his friend had finished, "but, Balthasar, how can you hit on such crazy, odd stuff? The man you are taking for an enchanter, is none other than Doctor Prosper Alpanus,[1] who lives at his country house not far from the city. True, the strangest rumors are spread abroad about him, so that he might be considered almost a second Cagliostro,[2] but for them he is himself to blame. He loves to surround himself in mystical darkness and to assume the appearance of a man acquainted with the most profound knowledge of Nature, who commands unknown powers, and with all of that he has the most bizarre ideas. His carriage, for example, is so oddly constituted that a person of vivid and fiery imagination like you, my friend, may well be brought to the point of taking it for an apparition out of some mad fairy tale. So listen to me. His cabriolet has the shape of a seashell and is silver all over. Between the wheels a barrel organ has been placed, which plays of itself as soon as the carriage moves. What you took for a silver pheasant was certainly his little white-uniformed jockey, just as you certainly mistook the pleats of the outspread sunshade for the wing covers of a rose beetle. He has

---

[1] An actual Italian physician named Prosper Alpinus lived from 1553 to 1617.

[2] Giuseppe Balsamo, 1743–1795, who called himself Alexander Count Cagliostro, was a notorious adventurer, alchemist, and swindler.

big horns screwed onto both his white ponies so that they will look really fabulous. For the rest, it is correct that Doctor Alpanus carries a handsome Spanish cane with a magnificent glittering crystal like a knob on the top of it, and about its strange effect a lot of fabulous things are told, or rather, invented. The eye is supposed to be hardly able to bear the ray from that crystal. If the doctor covers it over with a thin veil and one then looks fixedly at it, the image of the person that one bears in his inmost thoughts is supposed to appear on the outside of it, as in a concave mirror."

"Indeed?" Balthasar interrupted his friend. "Indeed? Is that what they tell? What else do they say about Doctor Prosper Alpanus?"

"Oh," replied Fabian, "don't ask me to talk a great deal about those mad pranks and things. You well know that even nowadays there are fantastic people who, contrary to sound Reason, still believe in all the so-called wonders of silly nursery tales."

"I will confess to you," continued Balthasar, "that I am forced to post myself among the party of those fantastic people without sound Reason. Silver-painted wood is no gleaming, transparent crystal, a barrel organ does not sound like a glass harmonica, a silver pheasant is no jockey, and a sunshade no rose beetle. Either the wonderful man whom I met was not the Doctor Prosper Alpanus you are talking about, or else the doctor really does rule over extraordinary mysteries."

"To," said Fabian, "to cure you completely of your peculiar dreams, it would be best for me to take you straight out to Doctor Prosper Alpanus. Then you will perceive for yourself that the doctor is a very ordinary physician and that he by no means travels with unicorns, silver pheasants, and rose beetles."

"You voice," retorted Balthasar as his eyes lit up with a bright flashing, "you voice the devoutest wish of my soul, my friend. We'll start out immediately."

Soon they were standing in front of the closed grille gate of the park, in the middle of which was situated the country house of Doctor Alpanus.

"How do we get in?" said Fabian.

"I imagine we knock," replied Balthasar, and he took hold of the metal knocker installed close by the lock.

As soon as he lifted the knocker, there began a subterranean murmur like distant thunder, and it seemed to die away in the deepest depths. The grille gate swung slowly open, and they entered and walked on through a long, broad alley of trees through which they glimpsed the villa.

"Do you detect," said Fabian, "anything extraordinary or magical here?"

"I should think," replied Balthasar, "that the way the grille gate opened was not so totally ordinary, and then I just can't explain how everything here appeals to me as being so wonderful, so magical. Are there far and wide such magnificent trees as right here in this park? Indeed, many a tree and shrub seems, with its gleaming trunk and emerald leaves, to belong to an unknown foreign land."

Fabian noticed two frogs of uncommon size which had been hopping along on either side of the travelers all the way from the grille gate.

"A beautiful park," cried Fabian, "with such vermin in it!" He stooped down to pick up a little stone which he intended to throw at the merry frogs. Both of them jumped into the bushes and looked at him with shining human eyes. "Wait! Wait!" cried Fabian, and aimed at the one and threw. At that moment, however, an ugly little woman sitting by the path croaked, "You big bully, don't throw your stones at honest people that have to earn their little bit of bread here in the garden by sour toil."

"Come on, come on," murmured Balthasar horrified, for he had indeed observed how the frog had taken on the form of the old woman. A glance into the bushes convinced him that the other frog had turned into a little man who was busy pulling weeds.

In front of the villa was a fine, large lawn, on which both the unicorns were grazing, while the most glorious chords resounded through the air.

"Do you see? Do you hear?" said Balthasar.

"I don't see anything," replied Fabian, "except two little

white ponies eating grass. And as for what you hear in the air, they are apparently aeolian harps suspended."³

The grand but simple architecture of the moderately large, one-story villa delighted Balthasar. He gave the bell-pull a tug, the door opened at once, and a large bird, ostrichlike and all shiny golden-yellow, stood before the friends as a butler.

"Now just look," said Fabian to Balthasar, "now just look at the crazy livery! If you wanted to give the fellow a tip afterwards, does he have a hand to put it into his vest pocket?"

And with that he turned to the ostrich, seized it by the gleaming down that was ruffled at its throat like a rich jabot underneath its beak, and said, "Announce us to the doctor, my charming friend." The ostrich, however, said nothing but "Quirrrr," and bit Fabian in the finger. "What the deuce!" cried Fabian, "the fellow is turning out to be a damned bird!"

At the same moment an inner door opened and the doctor himself advanced to meet the friends. A little, thin, pale man! On his head he was wearing a small velvet cap from underneath which beautiful hair poured down in long curls, a long Indian garment of earthen yellow, and little red laced boots; whether they were trimmed with variegated fur or with the gleaming plumage of a bird could not be determined. Upon his countenance lay peace, good-naturedness itself. It did seem odd, however, that when you looked at him close by and very sharply, it was as if from his face an even smaller face were looking out, as from a glass watchcase.

"I glimpsed," Prosper Alpanus now said softly and somewhat drawlingly with a pleasant smile, "I glimpsed you, gentlemen, from the window. I also knew beforehand, at least as far as you are concerned, dear Mr. Balthasar, that you would be coming to see me. Follow me, please."

Prosper Alpanus conducted them to a high, circular room with sky-blue curtains hung all around. The light came down through a window set above in the dome and cast its rays on the shiny, polished marble table, which was supported by a sphinx and which stood in the middle of the room. Otherwise there was absolutely nothing out of the ordinary to be observed in the place.

³ A stringed instrument suspended in air where every breeze elicits random tones. Here a very large one is suspended from the trees.

"What can I do for you?" asked Prosper Alpanus.

Then Balthasar pulled himself together, narrated what had happened with little Zinnober, beginning with his first appearance in Kerepes, and he concluded with the assertion, just as the firm conviction had dawned on him, that he, Prosper Alpanus, was the benevolent mage who would put a stop to Zinnober's infamous and repugnant wizardry.

Prosper Alpanus remained silent and deep in thought. Finally, after a few minutes had passed, he began in a solemn and somber tone, "After all that you have told me, Balthasar, there can be no doubt but that there is something mysterious about little Zinnober. But first, one has to know the enemy that one has to fight, and know the cause of which one wishes to destroy the effect. It is to be surmised that little Zinnober is none other than a mandrake root. But we shall investigate immediately."

With that, Prosper Alpanus gave a tug at one of the silken bell-pulls that hung suspended about from the ceiling of the room. A drapery rustled open, great folio volumes all in gilded bindings became visible, and a dainty, airily light stairway of cedar wood unrolled downwards. Prosper Alpanus ascended these stairs and from the uppermost shelf extracted a folio, which he laid on the marble table after carefully dusting it off with a large shock of glittering peacock feathers.

"This work," he then said, "treats of mandrake men, which are all illustrated in it. Perhaps you will find your hostile Zinnober among them, in which case he is delivered into our hands."

As Prosper Alpanus opened the book, the friends glimpsed a number of neatly illuminated copper plates representing the most astounding misshapen manikins with the maddest caricatures of faces that you could ever have seen. But as soon as Prosper touched one of these little men on the page, the creature came alive, leaped out, and hopped and cavorted drolly about on the marble table and snapped its fingers and with its crooked legs did the most beautiful pirouettes and entrechats and in so doing sang "Quirr, quapp, pirr, papp," until Prosper took it by the head and placed it back in the book, where it forthwith smoothed itself down and flattened itself out into the colored picture.

In the same fashion all the pictures in the book were gone

over, but no sooner would Balthasar be ready to cry, "This is the one! This is Zinnober!" than, on closer examination, he was obliged to concede to his sorrow that this little man was by no means Zinnober.

"That is odd enough," said Prosper Alpanus when the book was done. "But," he continued, "Zinnober may perhaps be an earth spirit. Let us look."

Then with uncommon agility he skipped once again up the cedar stairs, fetched another folio, dusted it tidily off, laid it on the marble table, and opened it, saying, "This work treats of earth spirits. Perhaps we'll catch Zinnober in this book."

Once again the friends glimpsed a quantity of neatly illuminated copper plates representing the repulsively ugly, brownish-yellow monsters. And as Prosper Alpanus would touch them, they would set up whimpering, squeaking lamentations and finally come crawling clumsily forward and roll about, growling and moaning on the marble table, until the doctor pressed them back into the book again.

Nor had Balthasar found Zinnober among these either.

"Odd. Extremely odd," said the doctor, and sank into mute meditation.

"The Beetle King," he then went on, "the Beetle King can't be the one, because he, as I definitely know, is occupied elsewhere just now. Nor the Spider Marshal, because the Spider Marshal, though ugly, is nevertheless sensible and able, and lives by the labor of his own hands without appropriating the work of others. Odd, very odd."

He was silent again for a few minutes, so that there could be heard all sorts of wonderful voices sounding, now in individual tones, now in full, swelling chords.

"You have very nice music everywhere all the time, dear Doctor," said Fabian.

Prosper Alpanus seemed to take no notice of Fabian at all. He only looked Balthasar in the eye, first stretching out both arms toward him and then moving his finger tips toward him as though sprinkling him with invisible droplets.

At last, the doctor took both Balthasar's hands and said with friendly seriousness, "Only the purest consonance of the psychic principle in the law of dualism can favor the operation which I shall now undertake. Follow me."

The friends followed the doctor through several rooms, which contained nothing noteworthy except for some odd animals that were busy with reading, writing, painting, and dancing, until a pair of double doors opened and the friends stepped up before a thick drapery, behind which Prosper Alpanus disappeared and left them in profound darkness. The drapery rustled open, and the friends found themselves in what seemed to be an oval room where a magical semidarkness prevailed. Upon observation of the walls, it was as if the prospect lost itself in green groves and flowery meadows, with plashing fountains and brooks as far as the eye could see. The mysterious fragrance of an unknown aroma undulated up and down and seemed to waft the sweet tones of the glass harmonica now one way, now the other. Prosper Alpanus appeared dressed entirely in white like a Brahman, and in the middle of the apartment he set a large round crystal mirror, over which he cast a veil.

"Step up," he said in a muffled and solemn voice, "step up before this mirror, Balthasar. Fix your thoughts firmly on Candida. With your whole soul, *will* her to show herself to you in the moment which now exists in space and time."

Balthasar did as bidden, while Prosper Alpanus stood behind him and with both hands described circles around him.

A few seconds had elapsed when a bluish mist welled from the mirror. Candida, lovely Candida, appeared in her lovely form with all the fullness of life! But beside her, close beside her was sitting the repulsive Zinnober, pressing her hands, kissing her—and Candida was holding one arm around the monster and caressing him. Balthasar started to scream aloud, but Prosper Alpanus seized him hard by both shoulders and the scream choked in his bosom.

"Be calm," said Prosper softly, "be calm, Balthasar. Take this cane and direct blows against the little fellow, but without moving from the spot where you are."

Balthasar did so and to his pleasure perceived how the little fellow cringed, fell over, and rolled on the gound. In his fury he leaped forward, whereat the image melted into fog and mist, and Prosper Alpanus wrenched the wild Balthasar back by force, crying loudly, "Stop! If you smash the magic mirror we shall all be lost! Let us go back to the bright light."

At the doctor's bidding, the friends left the apartment and stepped into an offensively bright room.

"Heaven," cried Fabian, drawing a deep breath, "Heaven be thanked that we are out of that accursed apartment. The close air has all but crushed the heart out of me, and then all those absurd parlor tricks that I loathe from the bottom of my soul!"

Balthasar was about to reply when Prosper Alpanus came in.

"It is," said he, "it is now definite that the misshapen Zinnober is neither a mandrake nor an earth spirit, but an ordinary human being. But there is a mysterious magic power at work which I have not yet succeeded in recognizing, and for that reason I cannot yet be of any help. Come to see me soon again, Balthasar, and then we shall see what further is to be done. Till we meet again."

"So," said Fabian, stepping right up to the doctor, "so it's a magician you are, Doctor! And for all your magical arts you can't even get after that miserable little Zinnober? Do you know that I consider you an arrant charlatan, you and your colored pictures, puppets, magic mirrors, and all your crazy junk? Balthasar here, he is in love and he writes poetry; you can talk him into all kinds of stuff. But with me you will have a hard time! I am an enlightened man and I simply will not tolerate marvels!"

"Have that," replied Prosper Alpanus as he laughed harder and more cordially than anyone would have believed him capable of, judging by his total person, "have that as you will. But —if I am not exactly a magician, I do, however, have a command of clever tricks."

"Probably out of Wiegleb's *Magic*[4] or something!" cried Fabian. "Now there you will find your master in our Professor Mosch Terpin, and you will be no match for him, because that honest man is always showing us that everything happens naturally, and he doesn't surround himself with such myster-

---

[4] Johann Christian Wiegleb's *Instruction in Natural Magic*, 1782, was one of Hoffmann's favorite books in childhood.

ious business as you do, Doctor. Now I most submissively take my leave of you."

"Aiyee!" said the doctor. "You are not going to part from me, surely, in such anger?"

And with that he stroked Fabian gently down both arms several times from shoulder to wrist, so that the latter felt decidedly strange and he cried out uneasily, "What are you doing to me, Doctor?"

"Go, gentlemen," said the doctor. "You, Mr. Balthasar, I hope to see again very soon. The remedy will soon be found!"

"You still won't get any tip, my friend," cried Fabian to the golden-yellow butler on the way out, and grabbed him by the jabot. But again the butler said nothing but "Quirrr," and once again bit Fabian in the finger.

"Brute!" cried Fabian and took to his heels.

The two frogs did not fail to accompany the two friends courteously as far as the grille gate, which opened with low thunder and closed again.

"I simply," said Balthasar as he walked along the highway behind Fabian, "I simply don't know, Brother, what curious coat you put on today, with such horribly long coattails and such short sleeves."

Fabian perceived to his astonishment that his short jacket had grown down to the ground behind, while in contrast the sleeves, usually unnecessarily long, had shrunk back up as far as the elbows.

"Thunderation, what is this!" he cried and pulled and tugged at the sleeves and wiggled his shoulders. That seemed to help, but now as they were going in the city gate, the sleeves shrank up and the coattails grew down until, all pulling and tugging notwithstanding, the sleeves were way up to the shoulders, exposing Fabian's naked arms, and until he had a train dragging after him that stretched out longer and longer. All the people were stopping and laughing their heads off, the street urchins were running in packs of a dozen exulting and jubilating at the long robe and making Fabian fall down. And every time he picked himself up again, not one shred of the train was missing. No, it had gotten still longer. Wilder and wilder became the laughter, the jubilation, and the shouting, until finally Fabian, half insane, rushed into an open house. Immediately the train disappeared.

Balthasar had no time to be astonished at Fabian's strange enchantment, for Referendary Pulcher seized him, drew him off into a remote street, and said, "How is it possible that you are not already gone? That you can still allow yourself to be seen here, when the beadle is out after you with a warrant for your arrest?"

"What is this? What are you talking about?" asked Balthasar, full of astonishment.

"So far," continued the referendary, "so far did the insanity of jealousy sweep you away, that you violated the right of privacy by breaking into Mosch Terpin's house, attacking Zinnober in the presence of his fiancée, and beating the misshapen runt half to death!"

"Please!" cried Balthasar. "All day long I haven't been in Kerepes. These are shameless lies."

"Oh, be quiet, be quiet!" Pulcher interrupted him. "Fabian's crazy, senseless idea of putting on a gown with a train has saved you. No one is paying any attention to you now. Just escape the disgraceful arrest, and then we'll fight the rest out later. You mustn't go back to your quarters any more. Give me the key, and I will forward everything to you. Off to Hoch-Jakobsheim!"

And with that the referendary swept Balthasar off through the outlying sidestreets, out the gate, and toward the village of Hoch-Jakobsheim, where the famous scholar Ptolemy Philadelphus was writing his noteworthy book about the unknown tribe of students.

SIXTH CHAPTER

How Special Privy Counselor Zinnober had his hair dressed in his garden and how he took a dew bath in the grass. The Order of the Greenspotted Tiger. A stage costumer's lucky inspiration. How Fräulein von Rosenschön spilled coffee on herself and how Prosper Alpanus assured her of his friendship.

Professor Mosch Terpin was floating in pure bliss. "Could," he said to himself, "could a luckier thing have happened to me than that the excellent Special Privy Counselor should come to my house as a student? He marries my daughter, he becomes my son-in-law, and through him I win the favor of the excellent Prince Barsanuph and follow up the ladder that my magnificent little Zinnober is now climbing. True, it does often seem incomprehensible to me myself how the girl, my Candida, can be so completely infatuated with the little fellow. Women generally tend to look more to a handsome exterior than to particular intellectual gifts, and sometimes when I get to looking at this special man, it seems to me as though you couldn't exactly call him handsome—even *bossu*[1]—quiet! Sh! Sh! The walls have ears—he is the prince's favorite. He will climb higher and higher—higher up—and he is my son-in-law!"

Mosch Terpin was right. Candida expressed the most pronounced inclination toward the little fellow, and if here and there someone who had not been beguiled by Zinnober's strange magic let it be understood that the Special Privy Coun-

[1] French for "hunchbacked."

selor was an accursed, misshapen thing, she immediately spoke about the wonderously beautiful hair with which Nature had endowed him.

When Candida talked that way, however, no one smiled more maliciously than Referendary Pulcher.

The latter trailed Zinnober's every step, and in this he was loyally supported by Privy Secretary Adrian, the very same young man whom Zinnober's magic had almost elbowed out of the minister's office and who regained the prince's favor only by virtue of the excellent stain remover with which he provided him.

Special Privy Counselor Zinnober inhabited a handsome house with a still more beautiful garden, in the middle of which was an open space surrounded by dense shrubbery, where the most magnificent roses bloomed. It had been observed that every ninth day Zinnober got up softly at dawn, no matter how bitter it might be for him to do so, dressed himself without any assistance from his servant, went down into the garden, and disappeared among the shrubbery which surrounded that spot.

Pulcher and Adrian, sensing some mystery, and having learned through his valet that Zinnober had visited this spot nine days before, made bold one night to climb the garden wall and conceal themselves in the bushes.

Hardly had morning dawned when they saw the little fellow coming along, sneezing and wheezing because, since he was walking through a flower bed, the dewy stalks and shrubs kept hitting him about the nose.

As he came to the lawn by the roses, a sweet sounding breeze blew through the bushes and the scent of the roses became more pervasive. A beautiful veiled lady with wings on her shoulders flew softly down, seated herself on the dainty chair that stood in the midst of the rosebushes, and with the gentle words, "Come, my dear child," took the little Zinnober and ran a golden comb through his long hair which fell in waves down his back. That seemed to comfort the little fellow greatly, for he blinked his little eyes and stretched his little legs way out and growled and purred almost like a tomcat. This had been going on for perhaps five minutes when once again the magical lady ran one finger along the little fellow's scalp, and Pulcher and Adrian observed a narrow, gleaming, fire-colored streak on Zinnober's head. Then the lady said, "Farewell, my sweet child. Be good, be as good as you can." The little fellow said, "Adieu, little mother. I am good enough. You don't have to repeat that so often." The lady slowly rose and vanished in the air.

Pulcher and Adrian were frozen rigid with astonishment. Just as Zinnober was about to walk away, the referendary jumped out and cried loudly, "Good morning, Special Privy Counselor! Oh, how beautifully you have had your hair dressed!"

Zinnober looked around and started to run away as soon as he caught sight of the referendary. Clumsy and weak as he was on his little legs, however, he stumbled and fell in the high grass, which closed its stems over him, and he lay in a bath of dew. Pulcher ran up and helped him onto his feet, but Zinnober snarled at him, "Sir, how do you come to be here in my garden! Get the devil out of here!" And with that he skipped and ran into the house as fast as he could.

Pulcher wrote Balthasar about this wonderful occurrence and promised to redouble his surveillance of the little magical monster. Zinnober seemed inconsolable at what had befallen him. He had himself put to bed and so moaned and groaned that the news of his having suddenly been taken ill soon reached Minister Mondschein and Prince Barsanuph.

Prince Barsanuph immediately dispatched his physician in ordinary to the little favorite.

"My most excellent Special Privy Counselor," said the physician in ordinary as he was taking his pulse, "you are immolating yourself for the state. Strenuous work has put you in a sickbed, continuous thinking has caused you this unspeakable suffering, you must understand that. Your face looks very pale and sunken, but your worthy head is frightfully hot. Ah, ah! But no inflammation of the brain? Could the welfare of the state have brought on a thing like this? Hardly possible. Allow me, however—"

The physician in ordinary may well have observed that same red streak on Zinnober's head that Pulcher and Adrian had discovered. After he had tried several magnetic strokes[2] from a

[2] Hypotism, then termed "magnetism," was the rage in 1818.

distance and several times had breathed upon the patient, at which the latter whimpered and whined, he started to pass his hand over his head and accidentally touched it. Foaming with rage, Zinnober rose up and to the physician in ordinary who had just bent down over him, dealt such a telling slap with his long bony little hands that it echoed through the whole room.

"What," shrieked Zinnober, "what are you doing to me? Why are you fussing around my head? I am not sick at all, I am well, perfectly well! I'm getting up right away and going to the minister's meeting. Get out of here!"

The physician in ordinary hurried away, completely alarmed. But when he told Prince Barsanuph what had happened to him, the latter exclaimed with delight, "What zeal for the service of the state! What dignity! What loftiness of behavior! What a man, this Zinnober!"

"My dearest Special Privy Counselor," said Minister Praetextatus von Mondschein to the little Zinnober, "how magnificent it is of you to come to the meeting in disregard of your illness. In the important matter touching the court of Kakatukk I drew up a memorandum *myself*, and I am requesting *you* to present it to the prince, because your intelligent delivery exalts the whole document, and then the prince will recognize me as its composer." (The memorandum by virtue of which Praetextatus wished to shine had been composed by none other than Adrian.)

The minister betook himself, together with the little fellow, to the prince. Zinnober drew from his pocket the memorandum which the minister had given him and began to read. But since it just wouldn't go right and since he kept muttering and buzzing incomprehensible things, the minister took the paper out of his hands and read it himself.

The prince seemed completely delighted. He kept expressing his approval and crying again and again, "Fine! Well said! Splendid, striking!"

As soon as the minister had concluded, the prince walked straight over to little Zinnober, lifted him up, pressed him to his bosom, right against the place where the great star of the Greenspotted Tiger hung, and, as many tears streamed from his eyes, kept stammering and sobbing, "No! Such a man—such a

genius! Such zeal! Such love! It is too much—too much!" Then
with more composure, "Zinnober, I hereby elevate you to be my
minister! Be faithful and true to the fatherland, remain a good
servant of the Barsanuphs by whom you are honored—and
loved." And now turning with a vexed look toward his minister:
"I notice, dear Baron von Mondschein, that your powers have
been declining for some time. Repose on your estates will be
salutary for you. Farewell!"

Minister von Mondschein withdrew, murmuring incomprehensible words between his teeth and casting looks full of
sparks at Zinnober, who, braced on his cane behind him, raised
himself on tiptoe in his fashion and peered about proudly and
boldly.

"I must," the prince now said, "I must, my dear Zinnober,
decorate you at once commensurately with your high merit.
Therefore, receive from my hands the Order of the Greenspotted Tiger."

Around Zinnober's neck the prince started to hang the sash
of the Order, which he had had quickly handed to him by the
valet. But because of Zinnober's misshapen stature the sash
absolutely would not fit in the normal way. Now it improperly
worked its way up, and then again it improperly sagged.

The prince was very particular about this, as about other such
matters which involved the most essential welfare of the state.
The badge of the Order of the Greenspotted Tiger, which was
affixed to the sash, had to come between the hip bone and the
base of the spine, three-sixteenths of an inch diagonally up from
the latter. That could not be managed. The valet, three pages,
and the prince all lent a hand, but all their efforts were in vain.
The treacherous sash kept slipping back and forth and Zinnober
began to squawk irritably, "What are you fussing so terribly
for around my body! Let the stupid thing hang the way it will,
I am the minister now anyway, and minister I shall remain!"

"What," said the prince angrily, "what do I have Order Counselors for, when in the matter of sashes they have such crazy
contrivances that run counter to my will? Patience, dear Minister Zinnober, this shall be changed presently!"

At the prince's command, the Council on Orders now had to
assemble—it had as auxiliary members two philosophers as

well as a natural scientist who happened to be passing through
on his way back from the North Pole[3]—to discuss the question
of how the sash of the Greenspotted Tiger could most adroitly
be fitted to Minister Zinnober. To gather strength for this important discussion, it was enjoined upon all members not to
think for a week beforehand, and, the better to enforce this and
yet remain active in the service of the state, to busy themselves
with the accounting system. The streets in front of the palace
where the Order Counselors, the philosophers, and the natural
scientist were to meet in session were strewn thick with straw,
so the clatter of carriages would not disturb the wise men, and
for the same reason it was not allowed to beat drums, make
music, in fact, not even to talk aloud in the vicinity of the palace.
In the palace itself everybody tiptoed around in thick felt shoes
and communications were made by signs.

Seven days, from early morning till late at night, the sessions
lasted, and still no decision was to be thought of.

The prince, thoroughly impatient, sent time and time again to
have them told in the Devil's name to think of something sensible. But that didn't help at all.

The natural scientist had explored Zinnober's makeup as far
as possible, had taken the length and width of his humpback,
and submitted the most exact calculations of them to the Counselor on Orders. He was also the one who finally suggested:
why didn't they bring in the stage costumer for consultation?

Odd as this suggestion might seem, it was nevertheless accepted unanimously in the anxiety and distress in which they
all found themselves.

The stage costumer, Mr. Kees, was an excessively skillful and
artful man. As soon as the difficult case was laid before him, as
soon as he had looked over the natural scientist's calculations,
he was ready with the most splendid method of how the sash of
the Order could be brought to stay in normal position. Namely,
a certain number of buttons were to be set front and back and
the sash of the Order buttoned to them. The attempt was
successful beyond measure.

---

[3] A whimsical allusion to Hoffmann's friend and fellow Romanticist,
Chamisso, who had just returned from his three-year voyage around the
world.

The prince was delighted and approved the suggestion of the Counselor on Orders to divide the Order of the Greenspotted Tiger henceforth into various classes according to the number of buttons with which it was bestowed. For example, Order of the Greenspotted Tiger with Two Buttons, with Three Buttons, etc. As a very special distinction which no other person could aspire to, Minister Zinnober received the Order with twenty faceted buttons, because precisely twenty buttons were required by the odd shape of his body.

Costumer Kees received the Order of the Greenspotted Tiger with Two Gold Buttons, and since the prince, despite his fortunate inspiration, considered him a bad tailor and hence did not wish to be tailored by him, he was named Actual Chief Costumer to the Prince.

From the window of his villa, Doctor Prosper Alpanus was gazing pensively down into the park. He had busied himself all night long with drawing Balthasar's horoscope, and by doing so had brought out many things that related to the little Zinnober. Most important for him, however, was what had occurred to the little fellow in the garden when Adrian and Pulcher eavesdropped on him. Prosper Alpanus was just on the point of calling to his unicorns and having them bring up the seashell because he wished to go to Hoch-Jakobsheim, when a carriage came clattering up and stopped in front of the grille gate of the park. Word was brought that the Institute lady von Rosenschön wished to see the doctor.

"Very welcome," said Prosper Alpanus, and the lady came in. She was wearing a long black gown and was covered with a veil like a matron. Prosper Alpanus, seized by an odd premonition, took his cane and allowed the glittering rays of its head to fall upon the lady. Then it was as if rushing lightning bolts darted around her, and there she stood in a transparent white garment, shining dragonfly wings on her shoulders, and red and white roses in her hair. "Ah, ah," breathed Prosper, and put his cane inside his dressing gown. Immediately the lady was standing there in her former costume.

Prosper Alpanus amicably invited her to have a chair. Fräulein von Rosenschön now said how long it had been her intention to seek out the doctor in his country house in order to make the acquaintance of a man whom the whole district reported as a highly gifted and benevolent sage. Surely he would grant her plea to add the near-by Institute to his professional roll, since the elderly ladies there were often poorly and in want of help. Prosper Alpanus politely replied that he had, as a matter of fact, long since given up his practice, but that he would, as an exception, visit the Institute ladies when necessary; and then he inquired whether perhaps she herself, Fräulein von Rosenschön, were not suffering from some malady. The young lady assured him that only now and again did she feel a rheumatic twinge in her limbs when she had been chilled by the morning air, but that she was now quite sound, and began some noncommittal topic or other. Prosper inquired whether, since it was still early morning, she would perhaps take a cup of coffee. Miss Rosenschön opined that young ladies of the Institute never disdained such. The coffee was brought, but, try as Prosper would to pour it, the cups remained empty, though the coffee was pouring out of the coffeepot. "Ah, ah," smiled Prosper Alpanus, "this is unruly coffee, my dearest young lady. Would you just pour the coffee yourself?"

"With pleasure," replied the young lady, and picked up the pot. But though not a drop poured from the pot, the cup got fuller and fuller, and the coffee went streaming across the table and onto the dress of the Institute lady. She quickly put the coffeepot down, and immediately all the coffee had vanished without a trace. Both of them, Prosper Alpanus and the young lady from the Institute, looked at each other silently now with odd looks.

"You were," the lady now began, "you were, Doctor, surely occupied with a very attractive book as I entered."

"Indeed," replied the doctor, "this book does contain very noteworthy things."

With that, he started to open the little book with gilded binding which lay before him on the table. But that was effort wasted, for with a loud clip-clop the book kept shutting itself again. "Ah, ah," said Prosper Alpanus, "would *you* have a try at the stubborn thing, my worthy young lady?"

He handed the lady the book, which, as soon as she touched it, opened of itself. But all the pages came loose and expanded to giant folio size and went rustling about the room. Startled, the young lady fell back. Now the doctor slammed the book shut with vehemence, and all the pages disappeared.

"But," Prosper Alpanus now said with a soft smile as he rose from his seat, "but, my dearest and most gracious young lady, why do we waste time with such base parlor tricks, for they are nothing but vulgar parlor tricks that we have been playing up to now. Let us rather proceed to higher things."

"I wish to leave!" cried the young lady and rose from her chair.

"Ah," said Prosper Alpanus, "that may not be so easily done without my assent, for, gracious lady, I must tell you that you are now totally in my power."

"In your power," cried the young lady angrily, "in your power, Doctor? Silly notion!"

And with that she spread out her silken gown and sailed up to the ceiling as the most beautiful mourning cloak butterfly. But immediately, Prosper Alpanus went buzzing and whirring after her as a doughty stag beetle. Completely faint with weariness, the mourning cloak fluttered down and ran across the floor as a little mouse. But the stag beetle went meowing and hissing in pursuit as a grey tomcat. The mouse rose anew as a gleaming hummingbird, and then there arose all sorts of strange voices round about the villa, and all sorts of wonderful insects came buzzing up, strange forest birds along with them, and a golden net spun itself about the windows. All of a sudden there stood in the middle of the room the Fay Rosabelverde, radiant in all her splendor and dignity, in a gleaming white garment, with a diamond girdle about the middle of it, and red and white roses in her dark curls. Confronting her was the mage in gold-embroidered robe, a shining crown upon his head, and in his hand the cane with the fire-darting knob.

Rosabelverde stepped up to the mage, but as she did so a golden comb fell out of her hair and smashed as if it were made of glass upon the marble floor.

"Alas for me! Alas for me!" cried the fay.

Suddenly, the Institute lady von Rosenschön was again sitting in her long black dress by the coffee table, and opposite her was Doctor Prosper Alpanus.

"I fancy," said Prosper Alpanus very quietly, as without hindrance he poured out the most magnificent steaming mocha coffee into the Chinese cups, "I fancy, my dearest and gracious lady, we both now sufficiently know where we stand with one another. I am very sorry that your beautiful comb was smashed on my hard floor."

"Only my own clumsiness," replied the young lady, sipping her coffee with delight, "is at fault. One must take care not to drop anything on this floor, for, if I am not in error, these stones are inscribed with the most wonderful hieroglyphs which many might think only ordinary veins of marble."

"Outworn talismans, my gracious lady," said Prosper, "outworn talismans, that's what these stones are, nothing more."

"But, dearest Doctor," cried the young lady, "how is it possible that we have not known each other from time immemorial, that our paths have not crossed one single time?"

"Different upbringing, dear lady," replied Prosper Alpanus, "different upbringing is solely to blame for that. While you, as the most promising girl in Jinnistan, were able to give yourself over entirely to your own abundant nature and to your happy genius, I was immured as a gloomy student in the pyramids and was listening to lectures by Professor Zoroaster, an old fogy but one who knew a whale of a lot. In the reign of the worthy Prince Demetrius, I took up residence in this pleasant little country."

"What?" said the young lady. "And you weren't expelled when Prince Paphnutius introduced the Enlightenment?"

"Not at all," answered Prosper. "On the contrary, I succeeded in concealing my true self by taking the pains to demonstrate very particular knowledge relative to matters of the Enlightenment in all sorts of writings which I spread abroad. I demonstrated that it can never thunder and lighten without the prince's will, and that we owe fine weather and a good harvest solely and simply to the exertions of his noblesse, which deliberates very wisely in the inner chambers on those things while the common folk have been plowing and sowing in the fields outside. Prince Paphnutius promoted me at that time to Upper Privy Enlightenment President, a position which I abandoned, together with my disguise, as a heavy burden, once the storm was over. Secretly I was as useful as I was able to be. That is to say, what we, you and I, my gracious lady, term genuinely useful. Are you aware, my dearest young lady, that I was the one who forewarned you of the invasion of the Enlightenment Police? That I was the one whom you can thank for the retention of the nice little items that you were showing me before? Good heavens, dear Institute lady, do have a look outside these windows! Do you no longer recognize the park in which you so often walked for your pleasure and spoke with the friendly spirits that live in the bushes and flowers and springs? I salvaged this park by my knowledge. It still stands there as in the time of old Demetrius. Prince Barsanuph, thank Heaven, doesn't bother much about enchantment. He is an affable gentleman and lets everybody alone, lets everybody practice magic to his heart's content, as long as he isn't too obvious about it and pays his taxes properly. So I live here, as you, dear lady, live in your Institute, happily and without a care."

"Doctor," cried the young lady as the tears gushed from her eyes, "Doctor, what are you saying! What clarifications! Yes, I do recognize this grove where I used to enjoy the most blissful happiness! Doctor! Noblest of men, to whom I owe so much! And you can persecute my little protégé so harshly?"

"You were," replied the doctor, "you were, my dearest young lady, carried away by your native kindliness and squandered your gifts on an unworthy person. Your kind help notwithstanding, Zinnober is and always will be a little deformed rascal, who, now that the golden comb is broken, is delivered up totally into my hands."

"Have mercy, O Doctor!" implored the young lady.

"But just be so kind as to look at this," said Prosper, holding out Balthasar's horoscope which he had drawn.

The young lady took it, then, full of sorrow, cried, "Yes! If that is the way things stand, I must yield to the higher power. Poor Zinnober!"

"Confess, my dearest young lady," said the doctor, smiling, "confess that ladies often do take pleasure in what is most bizarre, impetuously and recklessly pursuing the inspiration born of the moment and not heeding any painful derangement of other circumstances. Zinnober must pay the penalty for his fate. But *then* he shall achieve unmerited honor. Therein I do homage to your might, your goodness, and your virtue, my very worthy and most gracious young lady."

"Splendid, excellent man," cried the young lady, "remain my friend!"

"Evermore," replied the doctor. "My friendship and my heart-felt attachment to you, lovely Fay, will never fail. Apply with assurance to me in all dubious occasions of life, and—have coffee with me as often as you think of it."

"Farewell, my most worthy mage. Never shall I forget your clemency, never shall I forget this coffee." So spoke the young lady, and, overcome with sincere emotion, she rose to depart.

Prosper Alpanus accompanied her to the grille gate, while all the wonderful voices of the forest resounded in the loveliest fashion.

Instead of the young lady's carriage, there stood before the gate the doctor's crystal seashell with its team of unicorns, and at the rear the rose beetle expanded his shining wings. On the box sat the silver pheasant holding the golden reins in its bill, and it looked at the young lady with knowing eyes.

The Institute lady felt herself taken back to the most blessed time of her splendid fairy life as the carriage, magnificently sounding, went rushing through the scented forest.

SEVENTH CHAPTER

How Professor Mosch Terpin investigated Nature in the princely wine cellar. Mycetes Beelzebub. The student Balthasar's despair. Advantageous influence of a well-ordered country house upon domestic happiness. How Prosper Alpanus handed Balthasar a tortoiseshell snuffbox and rode away.

Balthasar, who was in concealment in the village of Hoch-Jakobsheim, received from Referendary Pulcher in Kerepes a letter which went as follows:

"Our affairs, good friend Balthasar, are going worse and worse. Our enemy, the loathsome Zinnober, has become Minister of Foreign Affairs and has received the great Order of the Greenspotted Tiger with Twenty Buttons. He has soared up to become the prince's favorite and accomplishes everything he desires. Professor Mosch Terpin is completely beside himself; he puffs himself up in stupid pride. Through the intercession of his future son-in-law he has received the post of General Director of all affairs of Nature in the state, a post which brings him much money and a host of other emoluments. As appointed General Director, he examines and revises solar and lunar eclipses as well as the weather predictions in the state-authorized calendars, and in particular investigates Nature in the capital and its surrounding district. By virtue of this occupation he receives from the princely forests the rarest birds and the most uncommon animals, which, in order to investigate their natures, he roasts and tears apart. In the same way he is now writing—at least he so alleges—a treatise on why wine tastes different from water and manifests different effects. This treatise he will dedicate to his son-in-law. Zinnober has arranged for Mosch Terpin to be allowed to study every day in the princely wine cellar on account of this treatise. Already he has studied up half a hogshead of old Rhine wine as well as several dozen bottles of champagne and has now gotten to a cask of Alicante. The cellar master is wringing his hands! This is a great advantage for the professor, who, as you know, is the biggest gourmand on earth, and he would be leading the coziest life in the world if he didn't often have to go out in the country after a hailstorm has devastated the fields in order to explain to the princely tenants why it hailed, so the dull devils will get a bit of knowledge and can prevent such things in the future and not always be requesting remission of their leases on account of something for which no one is to blame but themselves.

"The minister can not get over the beating you gave him. He has vowed vengeance on you. You will never again be allowed to let yourself be seen in Kerepes. He is also persecuting me, because I eavesdropped on his mysterious way of having his hair dressed by a winged lady. As long as Zinnober remains the prince's favorite I shall not be able to apply for any decent position. My evil star will have it that I am forever running into the monster where I least expect it and in a manner that is sure to be fatal for me. Recently the minister was in the Zoological Museum Room in full state, with sword, star, and sash of the Order, and braced himself on his cane, as his habit is, swaying on tiptoe next to the glass case where the rarest American monkeys stand. Strangers inspecting the collection came up, and one of them, catching sight of the little mandrake, called out loudly, 'Oh! what a charming monkey! What a cute animal! The ornament of the whole collection! Oh, what's the name of that pretty little monkey? What country does he come from?'

"Then the collection curator spoke up very seriously, touching Zinnober's shoulder as he did so, 'Yes, a very fine specimen, an excellent Brazilian, the so-called Mycetes Beelzebub, *Simia Beelzebub Linnei: niger, barbatus, podiis caudaque apice brunneis*, a howler monkey—'[1]

"'Sir!' the little fellow snorted at the curator. 'Sir, I think you

---

[1] Chamisso furnished these scientific designations at Hoffmann's request.

are mad or else possessed by nine devils. I am no *Beelzebub caudaque*, no howler monkey, I am Zinnober, Minister Zinnober, Knight of the Greenspotted Tiger with Twenty Buttons!'

"I was standing not far off, and, if it had cost my life on the spot, I could not hold myself, I burst out in heehaws of laughter.

" 'Are you here, too, Mr. Referendary?' he snarled at me, red fire glowing in his witch-eyes.

"God knows how it was, but the strangers kept right on taking him for the prettiest and rarest monkey they had ever seen and absolutely wanting to feed him filberts that they were taking out of their pockets. Zinnober became so completely beside himself that he gasped in vain for breath and his little legs failed him. His valet was summoned and had to lift him up in his arms and carry him down to the carriage.

"I can't explain to myself why this story gives me a gleam of hope. It is the first injury to be sustained by that little bewitched monster.

"This much is certain, that Zinnober recently came back from his garden early one morning very perturbed. The winged lady must not have turned up, for his beautiful curls are a thing of the past. The say his hair hangs unkempt down his back and that Prince Barsanuph told him: 'Do not neglect your appearance so much, dearest Minister. I shall send you my hairdresser.' To which Zinnober then very politely stated that he would kick the fellow out of the window if he came. 'Great soul! There is no getting near you!' said the prince, and wept bitterly as he said it.

"Farewell, dearest Balthasar. Do not give up all hope, and keep well hidden so they don't catch you."

In complete despair at what his friend had written, Balthasar ran deep into the forest and burst forth in loud lamentations.

"I am supposed to hope," he cried, "I am supposed to hope even now when every hope has vanished, when all stars have set, and dismal, dismal night enshrouds me in desolation? Unholy fate! I succumb to the dark power which has entered destructively into my life! It was madness to hope for rescue from Prosper Alpanus, from that same Prosper Alpanus who lured me astray with his hellish arts and got me driven out of Kerepes by letting the blows which I was supposed to deal to his mirror image fall on Zinnober's actual back. O Candida! If I could just forget that heavenly child! But mightier, stronger than ever the spark of love glows within me. Everywhere I see the lovely form of the Beloved, yearning with sweet smile and stretching out her arms to me. I know you do love me, lovely, sweet Candida, and precisely that is my hopeless, mortal sorrow, that I cannot rescue you from the unholy enchantment in which you are involved. Treacherous Prosper! What did I do to you that you should delude me so cruelly?"

Deep twilight had come on, and all the colors of the forest were fading into muted grey. Then it was as if a particular radiance like flaming sunset fires shone through tree and shrub, and a thousand tiny insects rose humming in the air with the beat of rustling wings. Shining rose beetles darted back and forth, and in among them fluttered gorgeous butterflies, strewing fragrant pollen about them. The whispering and humming turned into soft, sweet, murmuring music, which laid itself comfortingly against Balthasar's shattered heart. Above him the radiance glittered with rays even more strong. He looked up and to his amazement saw Prosper Alpanus hovering there upon a wonderful insect which was not unlike a dragonfly resplendent in its most magnificent colors.

Prosper Alpanus lowered himself toward the youth, at whose side he sat down, while the dragonfly flew up into a clump of bushes and joined in the song which was resounding through the whole forest.

With the wonderfully shining flowers which he was carrying in his hand, he touched the youth's brow, and directly fresh courage to live was kindled in Balthasar's inmost being.

"You do," said Prosper Alpanus in a soft voice, "you do me great wrong, dear Balthasar, in describing me as cruel and treacherous at the moment when I have succeeded in mastering the enchantment which is destroying your life, and when, the more swiftly to find you and console you, I get on my favorite little steed of many colors and ride to you, provided with everything that is needed for your welfare. But nothing is bitterer than the pangs of love, nothing equals the impatience of a spirit desperate with love and yearning. I forgive you, for things went no better with me when, some two thousand years ago I loved

an Indian princess named Balsamine and in my despair tore out
the beard of the magician Lothos, who was my best friend. On
that account, as you see, I don't wear one, so the like may not
happen to me.

"But this would decidedly be the wrong place to relate all this
at length to you, for every lover wants only to hear about *his*
love, which he believes the only one worth talking about, just
as every poet likes to hear only *his* verses.

"To the point then! Know that Zinnober is the hapless offspring of a poor peasant woman and that his real name is Little
Zaches. He assumed the proud name of Zinnober only out of
vanity. The Institute lady von Rosenschön, or more correctly
the famous Fay Rosabelverde, for that lady was none other,
found the little monster by the wayside. She thought she would
make up for all that Nature, like a stepmother, had denied the
little fellow if she endowed him with the odd and mysterious
gift whereby everything of excellence that was thought, said, or
done in his presence by someone else should be attributed to
him, indeed whereby, in the company of well-educated, sensible,
intelligent people, he too should pass for well-educated, sensible, and intelligent, and always be unfailingly considered as
the most perfect of the sort with which he was in conflict.

"This odd spell is embodied in three gleaming, fiery red hairs
that traverse the little fellow's scalp. Any touching of these
hairs, or of his head anywhere, cannot fail to be painful and
even injurious to the little fellow. Therefore the fay caused his
naturally thin and straggling hair to fall down in thick, lovely
curls which, while protecting the little fellow's head, at the
same time conceal that red streak and intensify the magic spell.
Every nine days the fay herself dressed the little fellow's hair
with a magical golden comb, and that dressing of the hair coun-
teracted any venture designed to undo the spell. But the comb
itself was destroyed by a powerful talisman which I was able to
foist upon the good fay when she was visiting me.

"It is now a matter of pulling out those three fire-colored
hairs, and he will sink back into his former nothingness. For you,
my dear Balthasar, this disenchantment is reserved. You have
courage, strength, and adroitness, and you will carry the thing
out as is proper. Take this little polished glass, get up close to

little Zinnober wherever you find him, direct your sharp glance
at his head through this glass, and the three red hairs will be
clear as anything to you where they grow across the little fellow's head. Grab him hard, pay no attention to the piercing cat-
screams that he will send up, tear out those three hairs with one
yank, and burn them on the spot. It is necessary to get the hairs
with *one* yank and to burn them *immediately*, otherwise they
could still cause all sorts of harmful effects. Therefore direct
your most preeminent attention to getting an adroit and firm
hold on the hairs and to attacking the little fellow precisely
when there is a fire or a candle close at hand."

"O Prosper Alpanus," cried Balthasar, "how ill have I de-
served this goodness and this magnanimity by my distrust! How
I feel in the depths of my bosom that now my suffering is
coming to a close and that all the happiness of heaven is opening its golden doors to me!"

"I love," continued Prosper Alpanus, "I love youths who,
like you, my Balthasar, bear love and yearning in their pure
hearts, in whose inmost beings still re-echo those magnificent
chords which belong to that distant land full of divine wonders,
which is my native country. The happy persons thus endowed
with this inner music are the only ones whom one can term
poets, although many are abused with that name who grab up
the first bass viol that comes to hand, scrape away at it, and
take for splendid music out of their own hearts the muddled
racket of the strings that groan under their fists. I know you feel,
my beloved Balthasar, I know you feel sometimes as though
you understood the murmuring fountains, the rustling trees,
yes, as if the flaming sunset spoke to you in comprehensible
words. Yes, my Balthasar, in those moments you really do
understand the wonderful voices of Nature, for out of your
own inner self arises the divine tone which is kindled by the
wonderful harmony of the deepest essence of Nature. Since
you play the piano, O poet, you will know that once a tone is
struck, its related tones sound in its wake. This law of Nature
serves for more than a shallow metaphor. Yes, O poet, you
are a far better man than many take you for, to whom you have
read aloud your attempts to put the inner music on paper with
pen and ink. These attempts are of little value. But you struck
it lucky with the narrative form when you wrote out with

pragmatic breadth and detail the story of the love of the
Nightingale for the Red Rose—a story which occurred beneath
my own eyes. That is a very nice piece of work."
Prosper Alpanus paused. Balthasar looked at him in astonishment with large eyes and did not know what to say to the fact
that Prosper would designate as a historical essay the poem
which he himself looked upon as the most fantastic he had ever
written.

"You may," continued Prosper Alpanus, as a gracious smile
irradiated his face, "you may perhaps be astonished at my
speech, you may find a lot of things about me odd in general.
Consider, however, that in the judgment of all rational people I
am a person who may appear only in fairy tales, and you, beloved Balthasar, know that such persons can behave curiously
and talk nonsense just as they like, particularly, however, when
underneath it all there is something which is not exactly to be
spurned.

"But now further. If the Fay Rosabelverde so zealously embraced the cause of the misshapen Zinnober, you, my Balthasar, are now wholly and entirely my beloved protégé.
Hear, therefore, what I have thought of for you to do. The
magician Lothos visited me yesterday. He brought me a thousand greetings, but also a thousand complaints, from the Princess Balsamine, who has awakened from sleep and in the sweet
tones of the *Chartah Bhade*[2] that magnificent poem which was
our first love, stretches out yearning arms toward me. My old
friend, Minister Yuchi, also beckons in a friendly fashion to me
from the polar star. I must be off to farthest India.

"My country house which I am vacating, I wish to see in the
possession of none other than yourself. Tomorrow I shall go to
Kerepes and have a formal deed of gift made out, in which I
shall pose as your uncle. If Zinnober's magic spell is once un-
done, and if you go before Professor Mosch Terpin as the owner
of an excellent country estate and a considerable fortune, and
if you sue for the hand of the beautiful Candida, he will grant
you everything with full joy.

[2] More properly the *Shastra Bhade,* a Hindu poem about which Hoffmann
had read in Schubert's *Views of the Nightside of Natural Science.* In the
same book there is mention of the identification of the polar star by a
very early Chinese Minister Yuchi.

"But still further. If you move with Candida into my country house, the happiness of your marriage is assured. Beyond the beautiful trees grows everything that a household requires. Besides the most magnificent fruits, the finest cabbage and such excellent tasty vegetables as cannot be found far and wide. Your wife will always have the first green salad, the first asparagus. The kitchen is so arranged that the pots never boil over and no dish spoils, even if sometimes you might be gone for a whole hour past the time for eating. Carpets, chair and sofa cushions, are of such a kind that, with the utmost clumsiness of servants, it is impossible to get a spot on them. Likewise no porcelain or glass will break, even if the servants went to the greatest pains to throw them onto the hardest floor. And finally, every time your wife washes, there is the finest, brightest weather out on the big meadow behind the house, though all around it may be raining and thundering and lightning. In brief, my Balthasar, things have been arranged so you can enjoy domestic happiness at the side of your lovely Candida quietly and undisturbed.

"But now it really is time for me to be getting home and starting preparations for my present journey together with my friend Lothos. Farewell, my Balthasar!"

With that Prosper whistled once or twice to the dragonfly, which came buzzing down immediately. He put the bridle on and swung himself into the saddle. But just as he was flying off, he stopped suddenly and turned back to Balthasar.

"I had all but forgotten your friend Fabian," he said. "In a fit of roguish whimsy I punished him too harshly for his impertinence. This snuffbox contains something that will console him."

Prosper handed Balthasar a small, highly polished, tortoise-shell snuffbox, which he immediately put in his pocket, along with the little lorgnette which he had first received from Prosper for the disenchantment of Zinnober.

Prosper Alpanus went rustling away through the shrubbery, as the voices of the forest resounded stronger and more charmingly.

Balthasar returned to Hoch-Jakobsheim with all the bliss and all the delight of sweetest hope in his heart.

EIGHTH CHAPTER

How Fabian was taken for a sectarian and an agitator on account of his long coattails. How Prince Barsanuph stepped behind the fire screen and cashiered the General Director for Natural Affairs. Zinnober's flight from Mosch Terpin's house. How Mosch Terpin tried to ride forth on a butterfly and become emperor, but then went to bed.

In the very earliest dawning light, when roads and streets were still deserted, Balthasar stole into Kerepes and immediately ran to see his friend Fabian. As he knocked at the door of the room, a sick, faint voice called, "Come in."

Pale, disfigured, hopeless sorrow on his face, Fabian was lying on the bed.

"For Heaven's sake!" cried Balthasar, "For Heaven's sake, friend, speak! What has happened to you?"

"Ah, friend," said Fabian in a broken voice, as with effort he sat up, "it's all over with me, all over. The accursed wizardry which I know the vengeful Prosper Alpanus has instigated against me, is plunging me into destruction."

"How is that possible?" asked Balthasar. "Wizardry, magic —you didn't use to believe in such things."

"Ah," continued Fabian in a tearful voice, "ah, I believe in everything now, in wizards and witches and earth spirits and water spirits, in the Rat King and the Mandrake Root—in anything you will. Anybody who has had the creature tread on his neck the way I have, will give in all right. You remember the hellish scandal with my coat as we were coming back from

Prosper Alpanus'? Yes, if it had only stopped at that! But just take a look around my room, dear Balthasar!"

Balthasar did so, and all around the walls he preceived untold numbers of dress coats, morning coats, kurtkas of every possible cut and of every possible color.

"What!" he cried. "Are you planning to start a clothing store, Fabian?"

"Don't joke," retorted Fabian, "don't joke about it, dear friend. I had all these clothes made up by the most famous tailors, always hoping to escape at last from the unholy perdition that clings to my coats, but it is no use. As soon as I have been wearing for just a few minutes the handsomest coat that fits me as if I had been poured into it, the sleeves shrink up to my shoulders and the coattails dangle six elbow-lengths long. In desperation I had that spencer made with Pierrot sleeves a mile long; 'Now shrink, you sleeves,' thought I, 'just stretch, you coattails, and everything will come out right.' But—it was exactly the same as with the other coats in a few minutes! All the skill and all the craft of the mightiest tailors accomplished nothing against the accursed enchantment. That I was hooted and jeered wherever I turned up, goes without saying, but soon my undeserved stubbornness in continuing to appear in such a bedeviled coat, gave rise to quite different opinions. The least of these was that women blamed me as infinitely vain and absurd because, contrary to all propriety, I insisted on letting myself be seen with completely bare arms, apparently because I thought they were very beautiful. The theologians, however, were soon crying me down as a sectarian, their only point at issue being whether I was to be reckoned with the sect of the Sleevists or of the Coattailists; they were in agreement that both sects were extremely dangerous, since both proclaimed total freedom of the will and made bold to think as they wished. Diplomats took me for a contemptible agitator. They claimed that by my long coattails I was trying to rouse dissatisfaction among the people and make them refractory toward the government, and that I belonged to a secret society whose emblem was the short sleeve. For a long time they claimed to have found traces of the Shortsleevists, who were as much to be feared as the Jesuits, in fact more so, because they were everywhere trying to introduce poetry which is harmful to the state and because they doubted the infallibility of princes. In short, the matter got more and more serious, until the rector called me in. I foresaw my misfortune if I put on a coat, and so I appeared in my vest. At which the man got angry, said I was ridiculing him, and thundered at me that I was to appear before him in a sensible, respectable coat within one week, and if I didn't, he would mercilessly pronounce expulsion over me. Today is the last day of the reprieve. Oh, miserable that I am! O accursed Prosper Alpanus!"

"Hold on!" cried Balthasar "Hold on, dear friend Fabian, don't find fault with my dear, cherished uncle who has made me the gift of an estate. Nor is he so angrily disposed toward you, although I must confess he has too harshly punished the impudence you displayed toward him. But I bring you help! He sends you this little snuffbox, which is supposed to put an end to all your sufferings."

With that Balthasar drew from his pocket the little tortoiseshell snuffbox that he had received from Prosper Alpanus and handed it to the disconsolate Fabian.

"What," said the latter, "what good is the silly piece of junk supposed to do me? How can a little tortoiseshell snuffbox have any effect on the tailoring of my coats?"

"That I don't know," replied Balthasar, "but my dear uncle could not and would not deceive me. I have the utmost confidence in him. So just open up the snuffbox, dear Fabian, and we'll see what it contains."

Fabian did so, and out of the snuffbox poured forth a splendidly made black morning coat of the finest material. Neither Balthasar nor Fabian could keep from loud exclamations of the utmost amazement.

"Ha! I understand you," cried Balthasar enthusiastically. "Ha! I understand you, my Prosper, my cherished uncle! This coat will fit, it will dissolve all enchantment."

Fabian put on the coat without further ado, and what Balthasar had surmised actually came true. The handsome garment fitted Fabian as none had ever fitted him before, and there was no thought of shrinking sleeves or of self-extending coattails.

Absolutely beside himself with joy, Fabian decided to run

over immediately in his new, well-fitting coat to see the rector and smooth matters over.

Balthasar now told his friend in detail how everything had gone with Prosper Alpanus, and how the latter had placed in his hands the means of putting an end to the unholy monstrosity of that misshapen dwarf. Fabian, who had become a completely new man now that all doubts had left him, lauded Prosper's lofty nobility beyond measure and offered to lend a helping hand in Zinnober's disenchantment. At that moment Balthasar glimpsed from the window his friend, Referendary Pulcher, who was very gloomily just about to sneak around the corner.

At Balthasar's bidding, Fabian stuck his head out of the window and motioned and called to the referendary to come on up right away.

As soon as Pulcher stepped in he cried, "What a magnificent coat you have on, dear Fabian!" But the latter said that Balthasar would explain everything to him and he himself went running out to see the rector.

And now, after Balthasar had told the referendary everything in detail about what had happened, the latter said, "It's high time the repulsive monster was killed. I want you to know that today he is celebrating his solemn engagement to Candida, and the vain Mosch Terpin is giving a great banquet, to which he has invited the prince himself. We'll make our way into the professor's house right during the party and attack the little creature. There won't be any lack of candles in the room for the instantaneous burning of his malignant hairs."

Many another thing the friends had discussed and arranged with each other when Fabian came in, his face radiant with joy.

"The power," he said, "the power of the coat that poured out of the tortoiseshell snuffbox has stood the test magnificently. As soon as I stepped into the rector's office, he smiled with satisfaction. 'Ha!' said he to me, 'Ha! I notice, my dear Fabian, that you have recovered from your odd aberration. Well, hotheads like you are easily led to extremes. I never did look on your actions as religious fanaticism—rather misguided patriotism—penchant for the unusual, based on the example of heroes of antiquity. Yes, I won't dispute it, such a handsome, well-fitting coat! Blessed is the state, blessed is the world, when high-hearted youths wear coats like this, with such becoming sleeves and coattails. Remain true, Fabian, remain true to such virtue, to such sterling character: thence springs true, heroic greatness!' The rector embraced me, while fervent tears came into his eyes. I don't know myself how I came to take out the little tortoiseshell snuffbox from which the coat had materialized and which I had thrust into the pocket of it. 'May I?' asked the rector, extending his thumb and forefinger. Without knowing whether there was tobacco in it or not, I flipped open the box. The rector reached in, snuffed, seized my hand, pressed it hard, tears ran down his cheeks, and he said with deep emotion, 'Noble youth! A lovely pinch of snuff! Everything is forgiven and forgotten. Dine with me this noon at my home!'–You see, friends, all my suffering is at an end, and if we succeed today, and there is no reason to expect otherwise, in the disenchantment of Zinnober, then you too will be happy from now on!'"

In the drawing room illuminated with a hundred candles stood little Zinnober in an embroidered scarlet coat, the great Order of the Greenspotted Tiger with Twenty Buttons around him, sword at his side, plumed hat under his arm. Beside him stood the lovely Candida adorned as a bride, radiant in all her grace and youthfulness. Zinnober had taken her hand, which from time to time he pressed to his lips, grinning and smiling repulsively as he did so. Each time a deeper blush overspread Candida's cheeks, and she kept gazing at the little fellow with an expression of most fervent love. That was downright horrible to behold, and only the hallucination that put everybody under Zinnober's magic spell could be blamed for the fact that people, in their fury at Candida's unholy involvement, didn't grab the little witch's brat and throw him into the hearthfire. The company had gathered in a circle around the pair, but at a respectful distance. Only Prince Barsanuph was standing near Candida and making an effort to cast around significantly gracious glances, to which, meanwhile, no one paid any special attention. Everyone had eyes only for the bridal couple and hung on every word from Zinnober's lips. From time to time, he would snarl out a few incomprehensible words, followed each time by a soft "Ah!" of supreme admiration breathed by the company.

The moment had come for the engagement rings to be exchanged. Mosch Terpin entered the circle with a salver on which the rings glittered. He cleared his throat. Zinnober rose on tiptoe as high as possible—he almost reached to the bride's elbow. Everyone was standing in the most tense expectation—when suddenly, strange voices are heard, the doors of the room are flung open, Balthasar makes his way in, Pulcher with him, Fabian too! They break through the circle. "What is this? What do these outsiders want here?" everybody shouts at once.

Prince Barsanuph screams in horror, "Mutiny! Rebellion! Guards!" and jumps behind the fire screen. Mosch Terpin recognizes Balthasar, who has pushed in close to Zinnober, and shouts, "Student! Are you mad? Have you lost your senses? How can you presume to force your way into this engagement ceremony! People! Guests! Servants! Throw this rude fellow out the door!"

But without paying the slightest heed to anything whatsoever, Balthasar has already taken out Prosper's lorgnette and through it is directing his fixed gaze at Zinnober's head. As though struck by an electric ray, Zinnober sets up a shrill catlike screaming so the whole room echoes with it. Candida falls in a faint into a chair. The tightly closed circle of the company scatters. Plain to Balthasar's eye lies the gleaming, fire-colored streak of hair, he leaps upon Zinnober, grabs him, as he thrashes his little legs and struggles and scratches and bites.

"Grab him! Grab him!" cries Balthasar, and Fabian and Pulcher hold the little fellow so he cannot move or stir. Surely and carefully, Bathasar seizes the red hairs, tears them out of the head with one yank, runs to the fireplace, and throws them in the fire; they blaze up with a crackle, a deafening thunderclap falls, and everybody wakens from a dream. There stands little Zinnober, who with effort has picked himself up off the floor, shouting abuse and scolding and commanding that the insolent disturbers of the peace who have attacked the sacred person of the Prime Minister of the state should be grabbed immediately and thrown into the deepest dungeon.

But everyone is asking everyone else, "How did that little somersaulting chap get in here all of a sudden? What does the little monster want?" And as the hop-o'-my-thumb keeps right on raging and stamping his little feet and shouting intermittently, "I am Minister Zinnober! I am Minister Zinnober! The Greenspotted Tiger with Twenty Buttons!" everybody bursts out in crazy laughter. The little fellow is surrounded, the men pick him up and toss him back and forth like a toy ball, one Order button after another snaps off—his hat is lost—his sword—his shoes. Prince Barsanuph comes out from behind the fire screen and steps into the midst of the tumult. Then the little fellow screams hoarsely, "Prince Barsanuph—Serene Highness—save your minister—your favorite—help—help—the state is in danger—the Greenspotted Tiger—they're hurting me—they're hurting me—!"

The prince casts a wrathful glance at the little fellow and then strides swiftly toward the door. Mosch Terpin intercepts him, and is grabbed by him and pulled into a corner, where the prince says to him, his eyes glittering with anger, "You have the audacity to try to play a stupid farce here with your prince, the Father of your Country? You invite me to the engagement ceremony between your daughter and my worthy Minister Zinnober, and instead of my minister, I find here a revolting abortion of a creature that you have stuck into resplendent clothes. Know, sir, that I would strongly suspect that it was a treasonable prank if you were not a completely ridiculous person who belongs in a madhouse. I hereby relieve you of your office as General Director for Natural Affairs and forbid all further studying in my wine cellar! Adieu!"

With that he stormed out.

But Mosch Terpin, quivering with rage, went plunging after the little fellow, grabbed him by the long tousled hair, and ran with him toward the window. "Down with you," he shrieked, "down with you, infamous, wretched abortion who have so disgracefully deceived me and robbed me of all my life's happiness!"

He was on the verge of hurling the little fellow out the open window, but the curator of the zoological museum room, who was also present, ran over with lightning speed, grabbed the little fellow, and wrested him from Mosch Terpin's fists.

"Stop!" said the curator, "Stop, Professor! Do not wrongfully appropriate princely property. That is no monster, that is the *Mycetes Beelzebub, Simia Beelzebub,* that escaped from the museum."

"*Simia Beelzebub! Simia Beelzebub!*" went up the cry from all sides amid resounding laughter.

But scarcely had the curator gotten the little fellow into his arms and taken a good look at him, when he cried out in annoyance, "What do I see! Why, this isn't *Simia Beelzebub,* this is a nasty, loathsome mandrake-man. Ugh! Ugh!"

And with that he threw the little fellow into the middle of the room. Amid the loud mocking laughter of the company the little fellow ran screeching and growling out the door—down the steps—and on, on toward his own house, without being noticed by a single one of his servants.

Meanwhile, as all this was taking place in the drawing room, Balthasar had gone off to the private room where he had heard the fainting Candida had been taken. He threw himself at her feet, pressed her hands to his lips, called her by the sweetest names. Finally she revived with a deep sigh, and when she caught sight of Balthasar, she exclaimed full of rapture, "Have you finally, finally come, my beloved Balthasar! Oh, I all but perished from yearning and the sorrow of love! And always I heard the tones of the Nightingale to whose sound the Red Rose poured forth its heart's blood!"

Now, ignoring everything around her, she related how a hideous, evil dream had enmeshed her, how it had seemed to her as though an ugly monster had laid itself upon her heart, to which she was compelled to give her love because she could not do otherwise. The monster was capable of dissembling himself so that he resembled Balthasar; and whenever she had thought vividly of Balthasar, she had known that the monster was not Balthasar; but then, in some incomprehensible way it had seemed to her again as though she were compelled to love the monster precisely for Balthasar's sake.

Balthasar cleared up as much for her as could be done without completely bewildering her already overwrought senses. Then, as often happens between lovers, there followed a thousand assurances and a thousand pledges of eternal love and loyalty. And as they did so, they embraced each other and clasped each other to their hearts with the fervor of sincerest tenderness and were completely engulfed in all the bliss and all the rapture of the highest heaven.

Mosch Terpin came in, wringing his hands and lamenting, and with him came Pulcher and Fabian, who kept offering consolation, but in vain.

"No!" cried Mosch Terpin, "No! I am a totally ruined man! No longer General Director for Natural Affairs in the state. No more study in the princely cellar—the prince's disfavor—I intended to become a Knight of the Greenspotted Tiger with at least Five Buttons. All is lost! What will His Excellency, the worthy Minister Zinnober, say, when he hears that I mistook for him a nasty monster, the *Simia Beelzebub cauda prehensili*, or whatever it was, I don't know! O Lord, his hatred will fall upon me, too—Alicante! Alicante!"

"But, dearest Professor," the friends consoled him, "revered General Director, just consider that there isn't any more Minister Zinnober! You made no mistake at all. The misshapen dwarf deceived you as he deceived all of us, by virtue of the magic gift which he had received from the Fay Rosabelverde!"

Balthasar now related how everything had happened from the beginning. The professor listened and listened until Balthasar had finished, and then he cried, "Am I awake? Am I dreaming? Witches—wizards—fays—magic mirrors—kindred sympathies —am I supposed to believe in this nonsense?"

"Ah, dearest Professor," interrupted Fabian, "if for a time you had worn a coat with short sleeves and long tails the way I did, you would believe in anything so it would be a joy to behold!"

"Yes," cried Mosch Terpin, "yes, that is just how it was— yes!—a hexed monster deluded me—I am no longer standing on my feet—I'm floating up to the ceiling—Prosper Alpanus is coming to fetch me—I'm riding on a butterfly—I'm having my hair dressed by the Fay Rosabelverde—by the Institute lady

von Rosenschön—and am becoming Prime Minister—King—
Emperor—!"

And with that he ran around the room shouting and exulting
so that everyone feared for his wits, until he collapsed exhausted in an armchair. Then Candida and Balthasar approached
him. They spoke of how they loved each other so fervently,
so beyond all measure, of how they simply could not live without one another, and it was downright melancholy to hear.
Wherefore even Mosch Terpin actually wept a little. "Anything," he said sobbing, "anything you wish, children! Marry,
love one another—starve together, because I'm not giving Candida one groschen of dowry."

Speaking of starving, Balthasar smilingly said that he hoped
to surprise the professor tomorrow, that there could never very
well be any talk of that, because his Uncle Prosper Alpanus had
sufficiently taken care of him.

"Do that," said the Professor dully, "do that, my dear son, if
you can, and tomorrow. Because, if I am not to fall into insanity,
if my head is not to split apart, I must go to bed at once!"
He actually did so on the spot.

NINTH CHAPTER

Embarrassment of a loyal valet. How old Liese plotted a rebellion and how Minister Zinnober slipped during flight. In what a remarkable way the prince's physician in ordinary explained Zinnober's sudden death. How Prince Barsanuph mourned, ate onions, and how the loss of Zinnober continued to be irreplaceable.

Minister Zinnober's carriage had waited in vain almost all night in front of Mosch Terpin's house. Time and again people assured the driver that His Excellency must have left the party long ago, but he insisted on the contrary that that was quite impossible, since His Excellency would not very well have run home on foot through the rain and storm. When finally all the lights were out and the doors shut, the driver had to go on with the empty carriage. But at the minister's house he immediately woke the valet and asked in heaven's name whether, and by what means, the minister had come home.

"His Excellency," replied the valet softly into the driver's ear, "His Excellency returned yesterday in the late twilight, that much is certain, and is lying in bed sleeping. But! O my good driver! In what manner! I will tell you everything, but let your lips be sealed. I am a lost man if His Excellency finds out that I was the one in the dark corridor. I will lose my position, for His Excellency, though he may be short of stature, possesses an extraordinary amount of ferocity, becomes easily excited, loses his self-control in anger, and just yesterday drew his bare sword on a nasty mouse that ventured to skip through His Excellency's bedchamber, and ran the animal through and through again. All right! So, in the twilight I put on my little coat and start to sneak over very quietly to the tavern for a game of trick-track, when something comes sliding and gliding up the stairs toward me, and in the dark corridor runs between my legs, plops down on the floor, and raises a piercing catlike scream, and then grunts like—O God! Driver! keep your mouth shut, noble man, or I am lost!—come a little closer—and then grunts the way our gracious Excellency grunts when the cook has burned the leg of veal or something else in the state is not right with him."

These last words the valet, with upraised hand, had spoken into the driver's ear. The driver fell back, pulled a dubious face, and cried, "Is it possible!"

"Yes," continued the valet, "it was beyond any doubt our gracious Excellency that ran between my legs in the corridor. Then I distinctly heard His Grace pushing chairs in the rooms and opening the doors of one room after another until he finally got to his bedchamber. I didn't dare to follow him, but a couple of hours later I sneaked up to his bedchamber door and listened. There was his dear Excellency snoring just the way he usually does when great things are in the offing. Driver! 'There are more things in heaven and earth than our philosophy dreams of.' I heard a melancholy prince say that once on the stage; he went around in black and was terribly scared by a man all dressed in grey cardboard. Driver, something or other astounding happened yesterday that drove His Excellency home. The prince was at the professor's; perhaps he voiced this or that—some cute little reform—and now the minister is hard at it, he has run out on the engagement and is beginning to work for the welfare of the government. I could tell by the snore, yes, great things, decisive things will happen. O Driver, maybe sooner or later we'll all be letting our pigtails grow again.[1] But, dear friend, let us go down and, like loyal servants, listen at the door of the bedchamber to see whether His Excellency is still lying quietly in his bed working out his inner thoughts."

The two of them, the valet and the driver, sneaked down to the door and listened. Zinnober was purring and sawing and

---

[1] As in the case of aristocratic gentlemen's hair styles before 1789.

whistling in the strangest key-progressions. Both servants stood in mute awe, and the valet said, with profound emotion, "Our gracious minister is, after all, a great man."

With the first light of dawn, a mighty din arose downstairs in the minister's house. An old peasant woman, pitifully clad in a long since faded Sunday outfit had forced her way into the house and asked the butler to take her immediately to her little boy, to Little Zaches. The butler had signified to her that His Excellency, Lord Minister von Zinnober, Knight of the Greenspotted Tiger with Twenty Buttons, lived in this house and that no one on the servant staff was known by name or nickname as Little Zaches. But then the woman had shrieked with absolutely insane joy that the Lord Minister Zinnober with Twenty Buttons, that was her dear little boy, Little Zaches. At the woman's shrieking and at the thunderous cursing of the butler, everybody in the house had come running, and the din was getting worse and worse. When the valet came down to disperse the people who were so shamelessly disturbing His Excellency during his morning rest, they threw the woman out of the house as being insane.

On the stone steps leading to the house across the way the woman now sat down and sobbed and lamented because the ill-mannered folk inside there wouldn't let her in to see the child of her heart, Little Zaches, who had become Minister. Gradually a lot of people gathered around her, to whom she repeated over and over again that Minister Zinnober was none other than her son, to whom she had given the name of Little Zaches when he was young. Thus, in the end, the people did not know whether they should take the woman for insane or whether they should suspect that there really was something to the matter.

The woman did not avert her eyes from Zinnober's window. Then all of a sudden, she gave forth a shrill laugh, clapped her hands, and shouted jubilantly, "There he is, there he is, my heart's little man, my little kobold. Good mornig, Little Zaches! Good morning, Little Zaches!"

All the people looked up, and when they perceived little Zinnober in his embroidered scarlet gown with the sash of the Order of the Greenspotted Tiger draped around him, standing at the window, which went all the way to the floor so that his entire figure could plainly be seen through its large panes, they laughed exceeding and made noise and shouted, "Little Zaches! Little Zaches! Hey! Just look at the little baboon in his finery— the crazy monster—the little mandrake—Little Zaches! Little Zaches!"

The butler and all of Zinnober's servants ran out to see what the people were laughing at and jubilating over so excessively. But scarcely had they caught sight of their master when they shouted with the craziest laughter, even worse than the mob, "Little Zaches! Little Zaches! Mandrake—hop-o'-my-thumb —mandrake root!"

Only now did the minister seem to realize that the crazy mischief in the street was directed at none other than himself. He threw the window up, gazed down with eyes glittering in anger, shouted, raged, did funny leaps for fury, threatened them with the guard, the police, stockade, imprisonment.

But the more His Excellency raved in anger, the worse the tumult and laughter became. They began to throw stones at the unlucky minister—fruit—vegetables—whatever they could get their hands on. He was forced to go in.

"God in Heaven!" cried the valet in horror. "Why, the repulsive little monster was looking out from His gracious Excellency's window! How is that? How did that little witch's brat get into the room?" With that he ran up, but as before, he found the minister's bedchamber tightly locked. He ventured to knock softly. No answer.

Meanwhile, Heaven knows how it came about, a muffled murmuring had begun among the mob to the effect that the ridiculous little monster up there was really Little Zaches, who had assumed the proud name of Zinnober and made his way up by all sorts of abominable lies and deceits. Louder and louder the voices rose. "Down with the little beast! Down with him! Knock the minister's jacket off of Little Zaches! Put him in a cage! Show him for money at the fair! Give him a coat of gold paint and give him to the children for a toy! Let's go up! Let's go up!"

And with that, the people stormed the house.

The valet was wringing his hands in despair. "Rebellion!

Riot! Excellency, get up! Save yourself!" Thus he shouted. But there was no answer. Only a low moaning was to be heard. The doors of the house were broken in. Amid wild laughter the people were pounding up the stairs.

"Now's the time!" said the valet, and rammed with all his might against the door of the private apartment till, ringing and clattering, it burst from its hinges. No Excellency! No Zinnober to be found!

"Excellency! Most gracious Excellency! Don't you hear the rebellion? Excellency! Most gracious Excellency! Where the— God forgive me my sin—where may it please you to be found?"

Thus shouted the valet in wild despair, running through the rooms. But no reply. Not a sound, except for the mocking echo rebounding from the marble walls. Zinnober seemed to have vanished without a trace, without a sound.

Outside it had become quieter. The valet heard the deep, sonorous voice of a woman talking to the crowd, and as he looked out the window he saw the people gradually with-drawing from the house, muttering softly among themselves and casting dubious glances up toward the windows as they went.

"The rebellion seems to be over," said the valet. "Now His gracious Excellency will probably come out of his hiding place."

He went back to the sleeping apartment, surmising that the minister would probably be found there.

He peered around, and then, out of a suspended vessel of handsome silver that always used to stand right next to the dressing table because the minister prized it highly as a precious gift from the prince, he became aware that two thin little legs were sticking straight out.

"God! God!" cried the valet in horror, "God! God! If I am not deceived, those little legs there belong to His Excellency, the Lord Minister Zinnober, my gracious master!" He went over and, trembling all over with the horror of the shock as he looked down, he cried, "Excellency! Excellency! In God's name, what are you doing? What are you after down there in the depths?"

But since Zinnober remained silent, the valet realized the

danger in which Excellency hung and that it was high time to set all respect aside. He seized Zinnober by his little legs and pulled him out. Alas, His little Excellency was dead—quite dead. The valet broke forth in loud lamentation. The coachman and the servant corps hurried up. They ran for the prince's physician in ordinary. Meanwhile the valet dried his poor, unlucky master off with clean handkerchiefs, put him into bed, and covered him with silken cushions, so that only the little shriveled face remained visible.

Now in stepped Fräulein von Rosenschön. She had first, Heaven knows by what means, calmed the crowd. Now she walked over to the departed Zinnober, followed by old Liese, Little Zaches's natural mother. Zinnober was better looking, as a matter of fact, in death than he had ever been in his whole life. The tiny eyes were shut, the little nose was very white, the mouth was drawn a little awry in a gentle smile, but, above all, his dark brown hair fell down in the most beautiful curls. The young lady passed her hand over the little fellow's head, and at that instant a red streak shone forth with a dull gleam.

"Ah!" cried the young lady as her eyes shone for joy, "Ah, Prosper Alpanus! Noble master, you keep your word. His fate has been atoned, and with it all shame!"

"Oh," said old Liese. "oh, dear God! Why, that isn't my Little Zaches. He never looked that pretty. Then I have had my trip to the city for nothing after all, and you did not give me good advice at all, gracious young lady!"

"Complain not, old woman," replied the young lady. "Had you but followed my advice properly and not made your way into this house before I got here myself, you would be better off in every way. I repeat, the little fellow lying dead there in that bed is truly and surely your son, Little Zaches."

"Well," cried the woman, with gleaming eyes, "well, if that little Excellency there is actually my child, then I must fall heir to all the beautiful things standing about here, the whole house and everything there is in it?"

"No," said the young lady. "That is all over now. You missed the proper moment to win the money and the property. To you, as I said straightaway, to you riches simply are not given."

"Then may I not," continued the woman, as the tears came

to her eyes, "then may I not as least take my poor little man in my apron and carry him home? Our pastor has such a lot of pretty stuffed birds and squirrels, he shall have my Little Zaches stuffed, and I will put him up on the cupboard, just as he is in his red coat with the wide sash and with the big star on his breast, as an eternal memorial."

"That," cried the young lady almost with annoyance, "that is a very silly idea. It absolutely will not do!"

Then the woman began to sob and complain and lament. "What do I," she said, "get out of it now, that my Little Zaches achieved high dignity and great wealth? If he had only stayed with me, I would have brought him up in my own poverty and he would never have fallen into that accursed silver thing; he would still be alive, and perhaps I would have had joy and blessing from him. If I carried him around in my woodbasket, people would have felt pity and tossed me many a pretty piece of money. But now—"

Steps were heard in the anteroom. The young lady pushed the old woman out, with the instruction to wait for her downstairs at the door and the promise that as they drove away she would entrust her with an unfailing remedy which would end all her distress and all her misery at once.

Now Rosabelverde stepped up close to the little fellow once again and with a softly tremulous voice of deep pity said, "Poor Zaches! Stepchild of Nature! I meant well toward you. It may well have been folly for me to think that the lovely external gift which I bestowed upon you would cast its rays into your inner being and waken a voice that would unfailingly tell you, 'You are not the person people take you for, but strive to be like the one on whose pinions you soar, O you who are lame and unfledged.' But no inner voice was wakened. Your dull, dead spirit was not able to lift itself up, you did not abate your stupidity, your vulgarity, and your unruliness. Alas! Had you been only a tiny bit less of a little uncouth lout, you would have avoided this shameful death. Prosper Alpanus has seen to it that people will now again find you in death what, through my power, you seemed to be in life. If perhaps I see you again as a little June bug, or as a nimble mouse, or as an agile squirrel, it will give me pleasure. Sleep well, Little Zaches."

As Rosabelverde left the room, the prince's physician in ordinary entered with the valet.

"For God's sake!" cried the physician as he caught sight of the dead Zinnober and convinced himself that all remedies would be futile to bring him back to life, "for God's sake, how did this happen, valet?"

"Oh," replied the latter, "Oh dear Doctor, the rebellion, or the revolution, it's all one and the same whatever you call it, was raging and carrying on frightfully outside in the anteroom. His Excellency, fearful for his precious life, was surely trying to slip into the dressing table, and slipped, and—"

"And so," said the doctor solemnly and with emotion, "and so he died from the fear of dying."

The door flew open and in rushed Prince Barsanuph with a pale countenance, and behind him seven gentlemen of the bedchamber, paler still.

"Is it true, is it true?" cried the prince. But as soon as he caught sight of the little fellow's corpse, he staggered back and with eyes raised to heaven said in a tone of deepest sorrow, "O Zinnober!" And the seven gentlemen of the bedchamber cried after their prince, "O Zinnober!" and in imitation of the prince they produced their pocket handkerchiefs from their pockets and held them to their eyes.

"What a loss," began the prince after a pause of soundless grief, "what an irreplaceable loss for the state! Where to find a man to wear the Order of the Greenspotted Tiger with Twenty Buttons which such dignity as my Zinnober? Physician in ordinary, you could let *this* man die on me! Tell me, how did it come about, how could it have happened, what was the cause, what did this excellent man die of?"

The physician in ordinary observed the little fellow very carefully, took his former pulse at several places, passed his hand over his head, then, clearing his throat, began, "My most gracious lord, if I were satisfied with floating on the surface, I could say that the minister died of the total absence of breath, that this absence of breath was caused by the inability to draw breath, and that this inability was in turn occasioned by the element and the humor into which the minister plunged. I could say that, in this way, the minister died a humorous death. But far from me be such shallowness, far from me be the mania for trying to explain on the basis of contemptible physical principles everything that finds its natural, irreversible foundation only in the domain of the purely psychic. My most gracious Prince, let man's word be free! [2] The minister found the earliest seed of death in the Order of the Greenspotted Tiger with Twenty Buttons!"

"What!" cried the prince as he glared at the physician in ordinary with eyes aglow with anger. "What! What are you saying! The Order of the Greenspotted Tiger with Twenty Buttons which the deceased, to the welfare of the state, wore with so much grace, with so much dignity? *That* the cause of his death? Prove that to me, or—Gentlemen of the Bedchamber, what do you say to this?"

"He must prove it, he must prove it, or—" cried the seven pale gentlemen of the bedchamber.

And the physician in ordinary went on, "My best and most gracious Prince, I shall prove it, but no *or!* The matter is as follows: the heavy emblem of the Order on the sash, but most particularly the buttons on the back detrimentally affected the ganglia of the spinal cord. Simultaneously the star of the Order caused a pressure on that tangled snarl of a thing between the tripod[3] and the superior mesentery artery, which we call the solar plexus and which controls the labyrinthine weft of the nervous plexus. This controlling organ stands in the most diverse relationship to the cerebral system, and naturally the attack upon the ganglia was also inimical to the latter. But is not the free control of the cerebral system the prerequisite of consciousness, of the personality, as an expression of the most perfect concentration of the totality in a single focus? Is the life process not the activity in both spheres, in both the gangliar and the cerebral system? Well, suffice it to say that that attack disturbed the functions of the psychic organism. First came gloomy ideas of unappreciated sacrifices for the state by the painful wearing of that Order, and the like. Ever more insidious

[2] Again, as in the First Chapter, a parody of the phrase, "Give us freedom of thought!" which Marquis Posa addresses to King Philip in Schiller's *Don Carlos.*

[3] "Tripod" whimsically indicates the three-pronged celiac artery.

became his condition, until finally the total disharmony of gangliar and cerebral systems brought on a total cessation of consciousness and a total surrender of the personality. This condition we indicate by means of the word 'death.' Yes, most gracious lord, the minister had already surrendered his personality, and consequently was dead as a doornail when he plunged into that fatal vessel. Thus, his death had, not a physical, but rather an unfathomably profound psychic cause."

"Physician," said the prince with impatience, "physician, you have been rattling on for half an hour and I'll be damned if I understand one syllable of it. What do you mean with your 'physical' and 'psychic'?"

"The physical principle," the physician resumed, "is the prerequisite of purely vegetable life, whereas the psychic, on the other hand, determines the human organism, which finds its driving wheel only in the mind, in the capacity for cognition."

"I still," cried the prince in supreme annoyance, "I still don't understand you, incomprehensible man!"

"I mean," said the doctor, "I mean, Your Serene Highness, that the physical relates merely to purely vegetable life without powers of cognition, as in the case with plants, whereas the psychic relates to the powers of cognition. Now, since the latter predominates in the human organism, the physician must always begin with the powers of cognition, with the mind, and look upon the body as but the vassal of the mind, which must obey as soon as the ruler will have it to."

"Ho, ho!" cried the prince. "Ho, ho, physician, never mind! Cure my body and leave my mind alone; I've never yet noticed any inconveniences from that. Altogether, physician, you are a confused man, and if I weren't standing here at my minister's deathbed and weren't moved, I know what I would do! Now, Gentlemen of the Bedchamber, let us shed a few more tears here at the catafalque of the deceased and then get to dinner."

The prince held his handkerchief to his eyes and sobbed, the gentlemen of the bedchamber did likewise, and then they all walked away.

In front of the door stood old Liese, who had hanging over her arm several strands of the most beautiful yellow onions that you ever saw. The prince's glance accidentally fell upon the

produce. He stopped, the sorrow disappeared from his countenance, he smiled gently and graciously, and said, "I've never
seen such beautiful onions in all my life. They must have a
wonderful flavor. Are your wares for sale, good woman?"

"Oh yes," replied Liese with a deep curtsy, "Oh yes, Your
most gracious Serene Highness. I eke out a meager living from
the sale of onions, as well as I can. These are as sweet as pure
honey. Would you like some, most gracious lord?"

With that she handed the prince a strand of the finest, shiniest
onions. He took it, smiled, smacked his lips a bit, and then cried,
"Gentlemen of the Bedchamber, lend me your pocketknife, one
of you." The knife being provided, the prince neatly and tidily
peeled an onion and tasted a bit of the pulp.

"What flavor, what sweetness, what strength, what fire!" he
cried as his eyes flashed with delight, "and at the same time it
seems as though I were seeing the deceased Zinnober standing
before me, beckoning to me and whispering to me, 'Buy some,
eat of these onions, my Prince. The welfare of the state requires it!' "

The prince pressed a couple of gold pieces into old Liese's
hand, and the gentlemen of the bedchamber had to cram all the
strands of onions into their pockets. Further, he ordained that
nobody but Liese should have the onion concession for the
princely luncheons. And thus Little Zaches's mother, without
becoming exactly rich, did escape from all distress and all misery, and it was certain that a secret magic charm of the good
Fay Rosabelverde helped her to it.

Minister Zinnober's funeral was one of the most magnificent
that had ever been seen in Kerepes. The prince and all the
Knights of the Greenspotted Tiger followed the bier in profound
mourning. All bells were rung, and even the two small mortars,
which the prince had acquired at heavy cost for fireworks displays, were fired. Citizens, common folk, everybody wept and
lamented because the state had lost its best prop and never
again probably would there come to the helm of government a
man of the deep understanding, the depth of soul, the gentleness, the unflagging zeal for the commonweal, that Zinnober
had been.

As a matter of fact, the loss continued to be irreplaceable, for never again was a minister found whom the Order of the Greenspotted Tiger with Twenty Buttons was said to suit as well as it had the unforgettable deceased Zinnober.

LAST CHAPTER

Melancholy requests of the author. How Professor Mosch Terpin calmed himself and how Candida could never become irritable. How a rose beetle buzzed something in Prosper Alpanus's ear, how the latter took his farewell, and how Balthasar led a happy marriage.

It has come to the point, beloved reader, when he who is writing these pages for you, must take his leave of you, and melancholy and anxiety overcome him as he does so. There is still a very, very great deal that he knows about the remarkable deeds of the little Zinnober, and, inasmuch as he was irresistibly moved in his inner being to tell the story at all, he would have taken real pleasure in relating all the rest besides to you, O my reader. But, looking back over all the events as they happened in the nine chapters, he feels that so many marvelous, mad things were contained there, things contrary to sober Reason, that, by piling up still more of the same, he would run the risk of completely spoiling the whole business for you, beloved reader, by misusing your forbearance. In the melancholy and anxiety that suddenly choked his heart as he wrote down the words, "Last Chapter," he requests you to be so kind as to regard with cheerful and dispassionate mind, indeed to make friends with the odd creatures which the poet owes to the inspiration of the ghostly spirit named Phantasus, to whose bizarre and whimsical nature he surrendered himself, perhaps too much. Do not hold it against either of them, the poet or the whimsical spirit. If you, beloved reader, have now and again really smiled inwardly at many a thing, then you were in *that* mood which the writer of these pages desired, and then, he believes, you will give him credit for a good deal.

Actually, the story could have ended with the tragic death of little Zinnober. But is it not more pleasant when, instead of a sad funeral, there is a happy wedding at the end?

Briefly, then, let our thought be of the lovely Candida and of the happy Balthasar.

Professor Mosch Terpin was ordinarily an enlightened man of worldly experience who, consonant with the wise dictum *nil admirari,* had for many, many years been in the habit of finding nothing in the world astonishing. But now it came about that, abandoning all his wisdom, he was compelled to be ever more and more amazed, so that finally he complained that he no longer knew whether he was actually the Professor Mosch Terpin who formerly directed Natural Affairs in the state, and whether he was still really walking about on his good feet and with his head up.

First, he was amazed when Balthasar introduced to him as his uncle Doctor Prosper Alpanus and the doctor produced for him the deed of gift by token whereof Balthasar became owner of a country house an hour's distance from Kerepes, together with forests, fields, and pastures, and when, hardly believing his eyes, he saw valuable effects itemized in the inventory, even to gold and silver ingots whose value far transcended that of the riches in the princely treasury. Then he was again amazed when he looked through Balthasar's lorgnette at the magnificent casket in which Zinnober lay, and it suddenly seemed to him as if there had never been a Minister Zinnober, but rather only a little, uncouth, unruly pygmy whom people had erroneously taken for a sensible, wise minister.

But the supreme degree of Mosch Terpin's amazement was reached when Prosper Alpanus guided him around the country villa, showed him his library and other very useful things, and even made several very pleasant experiments with strange plants and animals.

It began to dawn on the professor that there was nothing at all to his own investigations of Nature and that he was sitting in the midst of a magnificent world of many colors, as though in the middle of an egg. This thought distressed him so much that finally he broke down and cried like a baby. Balthasar immediately led him to the spacious wine cellar, where he glimpsed shining casks and gleaming bottles. He could study better there, Balthasar said, than in the princely wine cellar, and he would have plenty of opportunity for investigating Nature in the beautiful park.

Whereupon the professor was consoled.

Balthasar's wedding was celebrated at the villa. He and his friends Fabian and Pulcher were all astonished at Candida's lofty beauty and at the magic charm of her apparel and her whole being. And it really was magic that invested her, for the Fay Rosabelverde, who, forgetting all her resentment, attended the wedding as the Institute lady von Rosenschön, had herself arranged her trousseau and adorned her with the most beautiful and magnificent roses. Now it is well-known that a garment must fit well when a fairy has taken a hand to it. Moreover, Rosabelverde had presented the lovely bride with a splendidly glittering necklace which exerted a magic effect in that, once she had put it on, she would never be annoyed about trifles— a poorly tied ribbon, an unsuccessful hair ornament, a spot on the linen, and the like. This quality, conferred upon her by the necklace, caused a particular grace and cheerfulness to be spread upon her whole countenance.

The bridal couple stood in the highest heaven of bliss and— so superbly was Alpan's wise and secret magic working—they had not yet had a word or a glance for the friends of their heart who were assembled. Both Prosper Alpanus and Rosabelverde saw to it that the finest marvels made the wedding day splendid. Sweet tones of love resounded everywhere from bushes and trees, while there arose shimmering tables laden with the most glorious foods and crystal goblets from which the noblest wine streamed forth, pouring the warmth of life through the veins of all the guests.

Night had come on, and then flaming rainbows arched over the entire park, shimmering birds and insects were seen flying up and down, which, whenever they shook their wings, sent a million sparks flying to form all kinds of lovely shapes in constant change, shapes which danced and pranced in the air and vanished in the shrubbery. And all the while, the music of the forest resounded more strongly, and the night wind came up, mysteriously murmuring and breathing sweet fragrances.

Balthasar, Candida, and their friends recognized Alpan's mighty magic, but Mosch Terpin, half tipsy, laughed aloud and said that behind everything was none other than that devil of a fellow, the prince's scene designer and fireworks operator.

Piercing bell tones sounded. A gleaming rose beetle flew down, lighted on Prosper Alpanus's shoulder, and seemed to be buzzing something softly into his ear.

Prosper Alpanus rose from his seat and said earnestly and solemnly, "Beloved Balthasar—lovely Candida—my friends—the time has come, Lothos calls, I must depart."

Whereupon he went over to the bridal couple and spoke softly with them. Both Balthasar and Candida were very touched, Prosper seemed to be giving them all sorts of good instructions, and he embraced both of them with fervor.

Then he turned to Fräulein von Rosenschön and likewise spoke softly to her. Apparently she was giving him commissions in affairs of magic and of fairies, which he was willingly receiving.

Meanwhile, there had descended through the air a little crystal carriage with a team of two shimmering dragonflies and with a silver pheasant for a driver.

"Farewell! Farewell!" cried Prosper Alpanus. He climbed into the carriage and floated away over the flaming rainbow until his vehicle seemed at last like a little glittering star in the upper air, which finally hid itself beyond the clouds.

"Lovely Mongolfiere!"[1] snored Mosch Terpin, and, overcome with the power of the wine, sank into deep sleep.

Balthasar, mindful of the instructions of Prosper Alpanus and making good use of the possession of the wonderful country house, did indeed become a good poet, and since the other particularities never failed, which Prosper had vaunted in the property for the lovely Candida's sake, and since Candida never removed the necklace which the Institute lady von Rosenschön gave her as a wedding gift, it could not be otherwise but that

---

[1] *Mongolfiere* was the name of the first balloon, invented in 1783 by brothers, Joseph Michel and Jacques Etienne Montgolfier.

Balthasar, in all bliss and splendor, led the happiest marriage that any poet ever led with a young and pretty wife.

And thus the fairy tale about Little Zaches surnamed Zinnober now actually comes wholly to a happy

END.

PRINCESS BRAMBILLA

A *Capriccio* in the Style of Jacques Callot
by E. T. A. HOFFMANN

FOREWORD

The fairy tale, *Little Zaches, Surnamed Zinnober* (Berlin, F. Dümmler, publisher, 1819), contains nothing beyond the loose and coarsely woven realization of a whimsical idea. The author, meanwhile, has been not a little astonished to come upon a review in which this jest, which had been tossed off lightly for the amusement of the moment and with no further pretensions whatsoever, was dissected with a solemn and grave mien, and in which was cited every source from which the author was supposed to have drawn. As a matter of fact, this latter point was agreeable to him, inasmuch as he thereby found occasion to look up those sources for himself and enrich his knowledge.

To anticipate all misunderstandings now, the Editor of these pages announces in advance that *Princess Brambilla* is no more a book for people who like to take everything seriously and gravely, than *Little Zaches* was. To the kind reader who might perhaps be willing and ready to forgo seriousness for a few hours and surrender to the pert and capricious sport of a hobgoblin who is perhaps often overimpudent—the Editor humbly addresses the plea not to lose sight of the basis for the whole thing, namely Callot's fantastically caricatured drawings, and also to keep in mind what a musician might expect from a *capriccio*.

Let it signify what the Editor was aiming at and not what he actually accomplished, when he recalls that remark of Carlo Gozzi (in the Preface to *Il Re de' geni*), to the effect that a

113

whole arsenal of absurdities and ghost paradings will not suffice to breathe a soul into a fairy tale, for such is achieved only by a profound motivation and by a guiding idea drawn from some philosophical view or other of life.

Berlin, in September, 1820.

FIRST CHAPTER

Magical effects of a sumptuous gown on a young milliner. Definition of an actor who plays lovers' roles. Concerning the *smorfia* of Italic maidens. How a respectable little man sitting in a tulip is devoted to learning and how respectable ladies weave nets between asses' ears. The mountebank Celionati and the tooth of the Assyrian prince. Sky blue and pink. Pantalone and the wine bottle with the wonderful contents.

Twilight came on. In the convents the bells rang for the Ave. Then the lovely, pretty child, Giacinta Soardi by name, cast aside the sumptuous gown of heavy red satin, on the embroidery of which she had been busily working, and looked down with annoyance from the high window into the narrow alley devoid of people.

Old Beatrice, meanwhile, was carefully gathering up the colorful masquerade costumes of all sorts from where they lay on tables and on chairs about the little room and was hanging them up in proper order. Arms akimbo, she then stood there in front of the open wardrobe and said with a smirk, "This time, Giacinta, we really have been industrious. It seems as if I were looking at half of the merry world of the Corso here before my eyes. Besides, Master Bescapi has never put in such sumptuous orders with us before. Well, he knows that our beautiful Rome will really light up again this year in merriment, splendor, and magnificence. Just you watch, Giacinta, how the celebration will start up tomorrow on the first day of our carnival! And tomorrow—tomorrow Master Bescapi will shake a whole handful of ducats in our laps. Just you watch, Giacinta! But what ails you, child? You hang your head, you are cross, out of temper? And tomorrow is carnival!"

Giacinta had sat down on the workbench and, with her head propped on one hand, was staring down at the floor without paying any attention to the old woman's words. But when the latter simply would not stop chattering about the forthcoming merriment of the carnival, she began, "Oh, do be quiet, old woman, do be quiet about a time which may be merry enough for others but which brings me nothing but annoyance and boredom! What good does my working day and night do me? What good do Master Bescapi's ducats do us? Are we not bitterly poor? Don't we have to worry to see that the earnings from these days will last to feed us wretchedly enough the whole year through? What is left for our enjoyment?"

"What," replied the old woman, "what has our poverty got to do with the carnival? Didn't we go running about last year from morning till late in the night, and didn't I look fine and stately as a *dottore*?[1] And I had you on my arm and you were darling as a gardeneress! Hee, hee! And the handsomest masks ran after you and spoke to you in sugar-sweet words. Now, wasn't that fun? And what's to keep us from trying the same thing again this year? All I have to do is give my *dottore* costume the brushing up it needs and all traces of the nasty confetti that it had thrown at it will vanish, and your gardeneress costume is still hanging there, too. A couple of new ribbons, a couple of fresh flowers, and what more do you need for you to be pretty and smart?"

"What are you saying," cried Giacinta, "what are you saying, old woman? I should venture out in those pitiful rags? No! A fine Spanish dress that fits tight above and then falls in rich, thick folds downward, full sleeves slashed and with magnificent lace sticking out, a little hat with pertly swinging plumes, a belt, and a necklace of glittering diamonds—that's the way Giacinta would like to go out onto the Corso and get out in front of the Ruspoli Palace. How the cavaliers would crowd around: 'Who is

[1] "The Doctor" was a stock figure of the *Commedia dell'Arte,* a pompous dullard in black robe, black or flesh-colored half-mask, and with cheeks daubed bright red. At carnival time many people chose to go masking in costumes of the *Commedia dell'Arte* clowns.

the lady? Surely a countess—a princess!' Pulcinella himself would be seized with awe and would forget his wildest pranks."

"I listen," the old woman said, "I listen to you in great astonishment. Tell me, since when has such an accursed devil of pride gotten into you? Well, if your mind runs so very high that you want to compete with countesses and princesses, then go and get yourself a lover who can dig right into the purse of Fortunatus[2] for the sake of your beautiful eyes, and turn Signor Giglio out, the have-not, who no sooner finds a couple of ducats in his pocket than he squanders them on scented pomades and knickknacks and who still owes me two paoli[3] for freshly laundering his lace collar."

In the course of this speech the old woman had fetched the lamp and lighted it. As the bright glow now fell upon Giacinta's face, the old woman noticed that bitter tears were welling from her eyes.

"Giacinta!" cried the old woman. "In the name of all the saints, Giacinta, what ails you? What is the matter? Oh, child, I didn't mean it so bad as all that. Just be still, don't work so hard, the dress will be done all right by the proper time."

"Oh," said Giacinta, without looking up from the work which she had resumed, "oh, it's the dress, the nasty dress, I think, that has filled me with all sorts of silly ideas. Tell me, old woman, have you ever in your life seen a dress to compare with this one in beauty and splendor? Master Bescapi has indeed outdone himself. A particular spirit ruled over him when he cut this magnificent satin. And then the splendid lace, the shining braid, the precious gems that he gave us for the trimming. I'd give anything to know who the lucky woman is who will be adorned with this goddess's gown."

"What," the old woman interrupted the girl, "what is that to us? We do the work and we get our money. But it is true that Master Bescapi acted so mysteriously, so oddly—well, it must be at least a princess who wears this dress, and though I'm not usually curious, I would like to have Master Bescapi

[2] Fortunatus, the folk-tale character, had a purse whose supply of coins never diminished, no matter how much he spent.
[3] A small silver coin of the Papal States.

tell me her name, and tomorrow I'll keep at him until he does."

"Oh, no, no!" cried Giacinta, "I don't want to know. I would rather imagine that no mortal will ever don this dress and that I am working on a mysterious attire for a fairy. In fact, I already feel as though all sorts of tiny faces were looking out at me from the shining gems and smiling and whispering, 'Sew, swiftly sew for our beautiful queen! We will help you, we will help you!' And as I intertwine the lace and the braiding I seem to see lovely little elves skipping about amid gnomes in golden armor, and—oh!''

Giacinta gave a little scream. Just as she was sewing the bodice braiding, she had pricked her finger so hard that the blood was spurting out of it like a fountain.

"Heaven help us!'' shrilled the old woman, "Heaven help us! The beautiful gown!'' And she took the lamp and cast some light, and plentiful drops of oil spilled over.

"Heaven help us, the beautiful gown!'' cried Giacinta, half fainting with terror.

But despite the fact that both blood and oil had spilled on the dress, neither the old woman nor Giacinta could discover the slightest trace of a stain.

Now Giacinta went sewing away again until with a joyous "Finished! Finished!'' she jumped up and held the dress high aloft.

"Oh, how beautiful,'' cried the old woman. "oh, how splendid, how magnificent! No, Giacinta, never have your dear hands produced anything like this. And do you know, Giacinta, it seems to me as if the dress were exactly your size, as if Master Bescapi had taken the measurements from nobody else but you?''

"And why not?'' answered Giacinta, blushing deeply. "You are dreaming, old woman. Am I as tall and slender as the lady for whom this dress must be intended? Take it! Take it and keep it carefully till tomorrow. Heaven grant that no nasty stain will be found by daylight! What would we poor things do? Take it!''

The old woman hesitated.

"To tell the truth," continued Giacinta, looking at the dress, "to tell the truth, as I worked along, it often seemed to me as if this gown must fit me. I would be slim enough in the waist, and as for the length—"

"Giacinta," cried the old woman with eyes shining, "Giacinta, you read my mind, and I yours. Wear this gown whoever may, princess, queen, or fairy, it makes no difference, my Giacinta must first be adorned with it."

"Never," said Giacinta. But the old woman took the gown from her hands, hung it carefully over the chair back, and began to undo the girl's hair, which she then did up again in elegant fashion. Then from the wardrobe she fetched the little hat adorned with flowers and plumes, which at Bescapi's bidding were to be fixed up to match the garment, and fastened it to Giacinta's chestnut curls.

"Child, how darling the little hat becomes you. But now, down with your bodice!" Thus cried the old woman and began to disrobe Giacinta, who in her lovely modesty was unable to offer any further objections.

"Hm," murmured the old woman, "this gently arched neck, this lily bosom, these alabaster arms, the Venus of Medici does not have any more beautifully formed, Giulio Romano[4] has not painted more magnificent ones. I'd like to know what princes would not envy my sweet child for them!"

But now as she put the magnificent gown on the girl, it seemed as if invisible spirits were attending her. Everything went smoothly and right, every pin was instantaneously in place, every fold adjusted itself as though by its own will, and it was not possible to imagine that the gown could have been made for anyone but Giacinta.

"O all you saints," cried the old woman when Giacinta stood before her arrayed in such splendor, "O all you saints, I don't think you're my Giacinta at all—oh!—oh!—how beautiful you are, my most gracious Princess! But wait, wait! We must have it bright, we must have it all bright in the room!"

And with that the old woman fetched forth all the holy candles that she had saved up from the festivals of the Blessed

4 Giulio Romano (1492–1546) was a disciple of Raphael.

Virgin and lit them, so that Giacinta stood there bathed in radiant splendor.

In astonishment at Giacinta's lofty beauty, and still more at the gracious and at the same time noble manner in which she paced back and forth in the room, the old woman clapped her hands and cried, "Oh, if only someone, if only the whole Corso could see you!"

At that moment the door flew open, Giacinta fled with a cry toward the window, and two steps into the room, a young man stopped, rooted to the spot as if frozen into a statue.

You, much beloved reader, may observe the young man at your leisure while he stands there, soundless and motionless. You will find that he can scarcely be twenty-four to twenty-five years old and that he is of a very nice and pretty appearance. For just that reason his attire seems to merit being called odd, because, though every article of it is blameless in color and cut, the totality absolutely does not go together but rather presents a gaudily clashing play of colors. Besides, despite the fact that it is all neatly kept, a certain paltriness is apparent. A glance at the lace collar shows that it is his only change, and one of the plumes fantastically adorning the hat perched tilting on his head shows that they are precariously held together by needle and thread. You perceive, kind reader, that the young man so garbed cannot be other than a rather vain actor whose merits are not to be rated too highly. And that is what he actually is. In a word, it is the very Giglio Fava who still owes old Beatrice two paoli for a laundering of his lace collar.

"Ha! What do I see?" Giglio Fava finally began, as bombastically as if he were standing on the stage of the Argentina Theater. "Ha! What do I see? Is it a dream that deludes me anew? No! It is her very self, the divine one. I may presume to address her with bold words of love! O Princess! O Princess!"

"Don't be an oaf," cried Giacinta, turning quickly around, "and save your comedy for the days ahead!"

"Don't I know," replied Giglio with a forced smile after catching his breath, "don't I know that it is you, my lovely Giacinta? But tell me, what is the meaning of this magnificent costume? Indeed you have never seemed so charming to me. I should like never to see you otherwise."

"So?" said Giacinta in anger. "Then your love is for my satin gown and for my plumed hat?"

And with that she slipped swiftly into the next room and presently emerged again in her customary clothing, with all adornment removed. Meanwhile, the old woman had put out the candles and given the impertinent Giglio a good dressing down for spoiling Giacinta's pleasure in a dress that was intended for some fine lady and for having been ungallant enough to suggest besides that such magnificence was capable of heightening Giacinta's charms and making her appear more gracious than usual. Giacinta vigorously fell in with this lecture, until poor Giglio, all submission and repentance, finally gained enough calm to permit him at least to be heard as he assured them that a strange coincidence of very special circumstances was the basis for his astonishment.

"Let me tell you," he began, "let me tell you, my lovely child, my sweet life, about what a fabulous dream occurred to me last night when I threw myself on my couch weary and all worn out from the role of Prince Taer,[5] which, as you know and as the world knows, I play with surpassing excellence."

"I thought I was still on stage and that I was quarreling with that filthy skinflint of an impresario, who was stubbornly refusing me an advance of a couple of lousy ducats. He was heaping all kinds of stupid reproaches on me. Then, the better to defend myself, I started to make a fine gesture, but my hand unexpectedly caught the impresario's right cheek, so that out came the sound and melody of a sharp slap. With no more ado, the impresario went after me with a big knife, I stepped back, and as I did so my handsome prince's cap fell on the floor, the very cap which you, my sweet hope, so nicely trimmed with the handsomest plumes that were ever plucked off an ostrich. In full fury, that monster, that barbarian fell upon it and stabbed the poor thing with the knife until it writhed whining in death at my feet. I wanted to—I had to avenge the ill-fortuned thing. With my mantle thrown over my left arm and my princely sword drawn, I went after the pitiless murderer. But he quickly fled into a house and from the balcony shot down at me with

[5] Prince Taer is "the blue monster" and the hero of Carlo Gozzi's comedy, *The Blue Monster (Il mostro turchino)*.

Truffaldino's musket.[6] It was odd, how the blaze of the fire-arm stopped and shone upon me like glittering diamonds. And as the smoke cleared away more and more, I observed that what I had thought was the blaze from Truffaldino's musket was nothing other than the precious jewels on the little hat of a lady. O all ye gods! All ye saints of Heaven together! A sweet voice said—no, sang!—no, breathed the fragrance of love in sound and tone: 'O Giglio! My Giglio!' and I saw a creature amid such divine charm of love, in such lofty graciousness, that the withering sirocco of fervent love went through all my veins and nerves and the fiery flood hardened into lava erupted from the volcano of my blazing heart. 'I am,' said the goddess as she drew near me, 'I am Princess—' "

"What!" Giacinta angrily interrupted the ecstatic youth. "What! You dare to dream about someone besides me? You dare to fall in love upon beholding a silly stupid dream image shot from Truffaldino's musket?"

And now there was a tempest of reproaches and complaints and words of abuse and imprecations, and all poor Giglio's avowals and asseverations that the dream princess had been dressed exactly as he had just encountered his Giacinta, would do absolutely no good at all. Even old Beatrice, not usually disposed to take the part of Signor Have-not, as she called Giglio, felt herself overcome with pity and did not leave the headstrong Giacinta alone until she forgave her lover for the dream, on the condition that he should never again mention a word about it. The old woman fixed a good dish of macaroni, and Giglio produced a bag of candy and a phial of actually quite drinkable wine out of his coat pocket, for, contrary to the dream, the impresario had really advanced him a couple of ducats.

"I see after all that you do think of me, good Giglio," said Giacinta as she thrust a candied fruit into her mouth. Giglio was even allowed to kiss the finger that the nasty needle had wounded, and all bliss and happiness returned once more.

But once you are dancing with the Devil, the prettiest capers won't help you. For it was that evil demon that prompted Giglio,

[6] Truffaldino was a stock clown of the *Commedia dell'Arte* and a variant form, at least in the eighteenth century, of the more familiar Arlecchino (Harlequin). He often carried a musket and played a hunter.

after he had drunk a couple of glasses of wine, to speak as
follows:

"I wouldn't have believed that you, my sweet life, could be
so jealous of me. But you are right. I am very good-looking and
gifted by Nature with all sorts of agreeable talents. But more
than that, I am an actor. A young actor who divinely plays
princes in love the way I do, with the proper oh's and ah's, is a
walking romance, a plot on two feet, a love song with lips for
kissing and arms for embracing, an adventure sprung from the
binding into life, standing before the eyes of the most beautiful
girl when she shuts the book. Hence it comes that we exert an
irresistible magic on the poor women who are infatuated with
everything in and about us, in our temperament, in our eyes, in
our imitation jewels and plumes and ribbons. Neither rank
nor place makes any difference, laundresses or princesses, it's
all the same. Now I will tell you, my lovely child, that, if certain
mysterious intimations do not deceive me, if an evil illusion is
not misleading me, the heart of the most beautiful princess
has really flamed forth with love for me. If that has happened,
or if it is yet to happen, you will not blame me, my fairest
hope, if I do not leave unmined that vein of gold that opens for
me, if I neglect you a bit, you poor little thing of a milliner—"

Giacinta had been listening with ever-increasing interest and
had come closer and closer to Giglio, in whose shimmering eyes
the night's dream image was mirrored. Now she quickly
jumped up and gave the blessed lover of the most beautiful
princess such a box on the ear that all the fiery sparks from that
fateful musket of Truffaldino's skipped before his eyes, and
then she swiftly ran into the bedroom. All further pleas and im-
plorings were of no use.

"Just go on home, she has her smorfia,[7] and then it's no
use," said the old woman, and lighted the troubled Giglio down
the narrow stairs.

There must be something very peculiar about the smorfia,
about the oddly moody and somewhat fearless nature of
young Italic girls, for connoisseurs maintain unanimously that
out of precisely that nature arises a wonderful magic of such
irresistible charm that the captive, instead of ripping his bonds

---

[7] Smorfia (Italian): "a sour face, a grimace," hence "a pet, a fit of
sulkiness."

asunder with impatience, involves himself ever more tightly, and that the vilely rejected *amante,* instead of beginning an everlasting *addio,* only sighs and implores all the more fervently, just as it says in that folk ditty, *Vien quà, Dorina bella, non far la smorfiosella!*[8]

He who thus speaks to you, beloved reader, surmises that that pleasure out of displeasure can flower only in the happy south, but that such a lovely bloom cannot grow from more peaceable matter up here in the north. At least in the place where he lives, he would not liken that pretty "smorfiosity" to the state of mind he has often observed in young girls just escaped from childhood. If Heaven has vouchsafed them pleasing features, they twist them out of shape in unseemly fashion. Everything in the world is either too narrow or too wide for them; there is no suitable place here below for their little figures; they endure the torment of a too narrow shoe sooner than a friendly, or even a clever, remark, and take it horribly amiss that all the youths and men in the precincts of the city are mortally in love with them, which they nevertheless think to themselves anyway without getting angry over it. For this soul-state of the tender sex there is no expression. In boys, the substratum of bad manners included in that concept is reflected, as in a concave mirror, at that period which the uncivil schoolmasters designate as "the smart aleck age."

And yet poor Giglio, under a curious strain as he was, was not to be blamed for dreaming, even while awake, of princesses and wonderful adventures. That very day, while he was walking down the Corso,[9] outwardly half and half but inwardly totally and completely Prince Taer, many adventurous things had actually befallen him.

By the church of San Carlo, just where the Via Condotti intersects the Corso, in the midst of the booths of the sausage vendors and macaroni cooks, it happened that the *ciarlatano*[10] whom all Rome knew, Signor Celionati by name, had set up his platform and to the crowd gathered around him was babbling fantastic nonsense about flying cats, jumping earthlings, man-

---

[8] *Amante* (Italian): "lover," i.e., the young male lead in a play. *Addio* (Italian): "Farewell." (Italian): "Come hither, pretty Dorina, don't play the sulky one!"

[9] The principal boulevard of Rome.

[10] *Ciarlatano* (Italian): "charlatan, mountebank."

drake roots, and so on, and in the process sold many an arcanum for hopeless love and toothache, for lottery tickets and the gout. Then far off in the distance was heard a curious music of cymbals, pipes, and drums, and the crowd scattered and poured rushing down the Corso toward the Porta del Popolo, shouting, "Look! Look! Hey! Has the carnival already started? Look! Look!"

The crowd was right, for the procession that was moving slowly up the Corso from the Porta del Popolo could not properly be taken for anything else but the strangest masquerade that anybody had ever seen. On twelve little snow-white unicorns with golden hooves sat creatures enveloped in red satin robes, daintily blowing on silver pipes and beating on cymbals and little drums. Almost in the manner of the mendicant friars, only eyeholes were cut out of the robes and they had golden braid stitched around them, which stood out oddly enough. Whenever the wind lifted slightly the robe of one of the small riders, a bird's foot stuck out with diamond rings adorning the claws. Behind these twelve charming musicians two mighty ostriches were pulling along a shiny gold tulip mounted on a wheeled frame. Inside sat a little old man with a long white beard, clad in a robe of silver material, and with a silver funnel cocked like a cap on his reverend head. Through an enormous pair of spectacles on his nose the old man was reading very attentively in a huge book that he had open in front of him. He was followed by twelve richly clad Moors armed with long pikes and short sabers, who, every time the little old man turned a page in the book, emitting as he did so a very high, sharply piercing *Kurri—pire—ksi—li—iii*, sang with mighty booming voices: *Bram—bure—bil—bal—Ala monsa Kikiburra—son—ton!* Behind the Moors, on twelve chargers whose color seemed to be pure silver, rode twelve figures almost as completely hooded as the musicians, except that their robes were richly embroidered with pearls and diamonds on a silver background and their arms were bared to the shoulders. The amazing plumpness and beauty of these arms adorned with most magnificent bracelets should already have divulged that the most beautiful ladies must be concealed underneath the robes. Moreover, as she rode, each one was very busily weaving nets, for which purpose large velvet cushions were fastened between the ears of the chargers. Next followed a large coach which seemed made all of gold and which was drawn by eight of the handsomest mules adorned with golden caparisons, each one led by diamond-studded bridles in the hands of little pages daintily clad in jerkins of colored feathers. The animals could shake their stately ears with indescribable dignity, and then tones like those of a harmonica[11] were heard, at which both the animals and the pages who led them raised an appropriate cry which harmonized in the most pleasing fashion.

The crowd pressed around and tried to peep inside the coach, but they saw nothing but the Corso and themselves, for the windows were all mirrors. Many a one looking at himself in this way fancied for a moment he was sitting inside the magnificent coach himself and thus was quite beside himself with delight, as was the whole crowd, as they were greeted with uncommon niceness and politeness by a little and extremely pleasant Pulcinella, who was standing on top of the carriage roof. Amid the general and most extravagant jubilation hardly any attention was paid to the rest of the gleaming retinue, which consisted of other musicians, Moors, and pages dressed like the previous ones, but among whom there were also to be found monkeys, clad tastefully in the most delicate colors, which danced along on their hind legs with telling mimicry and vied with one another at turning somersaults. So passed the fantastic show down the Corso, through the streets, as far as the Piazza Navona, where it halted before the palace of Prince Bastianello di Pistoja.

The double doors of the palace flew open, suddenly the jubilation of the crowd fell silent, and amid the deathly stillness of profound amazement there was witnessed the marvel that then took place. Up the marble steps and through the narrow gate they all went, unicorns, horses, mules, coach, ostriches, ladies, Moors, and pages, without any difficulty, and a thousand-voiced "Ah!" filled the air as the gate closed with a thunderous noise after the last four-and-twenty Moors had marched in in spruce ranks.

---

[11] Not the mouth organ, but again the curious instrument encountered at the end of the Fourth Chapter of *Little Zaches*; see p. 48.

After vainly gaping long enough, and when everything inside the palace remained quiet and silent, the crowd had a good mind to storm the abode of the fairy tale, and were dispersed only with difficulty by the sbirri.[12] Then they all poured back up the Corso. In front of the church of San Carlo the abandoned Signor Celionati was still standing on his platform, shouting and raging horribly: "Stupid people! People, why are you running, why are you chasing around in mad folly and deserting your good old Celionati? You should have stayed here and heard from the mouth of the wisest of men, of the most experienced of philosophers and experts, what there was to all of that which you saw with wide eyes and open mouths like foolish boys! But I shall still proclaim it all to you. Hear! Hear who it was that rode into the Pistoja Palace. Hear, hear who it is that is having the dust shaken out of sleeves inside the Pistoja Palace!" These words suddenly arrested the swirling mass of the crowd, which now thronged up to Celionati's platform and gazed up at him with curious looks.

"Citizens of Rome!" Celionati began now oratorically, "citizens of Rome! Exult, jubilate, throw aloft your caps or whatever else you may be wearing on your heads! To you a great blessing has befallen. For into your walls has come the world-famous Princess Brambilla from far-off Ethiopia, a miracle of beauty and at the same time so rich in immeasurable treasures that without any difficulty she could have the entire Corso paved with the most magnificent diamonds and gems. Who knows what she will do for your pleasure? I realize that there are very many among you who are no asses, but are versed in history. And they will know that the Most Serene Princess Brambilla is a great-granddaughter of the wise King Cophetua[13] who built Troy, and that her great-uncle, the great King of Serendippo,[14] a friendly gentleman, here in front of San Carlo and

---

[12] Sbirri (Italian): "men-at-arms, policemen."

[13] The African King Cophetua married the beggar maid Penelophon in the ballad, Cophetua and the Beggar Maid. See Percy's Reliques of Ancient English Poetry.

[14] Serendippo is Sarandib or Serendip, the names European travelers gave to the island of Ceylon. Horace Walpole coined the word "serendipity" after reading the fairy tale, The Three Princes of Serendip (letter to Mann, January 28, 1754).

in your midst, ye beloved children, often used to overindulge in macaroni. If I add further that the high Lady Brambilla was held at the baptismal font by none other than the Queen of Tarot, Tartagliona by name,[15] and that Pulcinella[16] taught her how to play the lute, then you know enough to set you beside yourselves for joy. Do so, people! By virtue of my secret lore and by virtue of white, black, yellow, and blue magic, I know that she has come because she thinks she will find among the masks of the Corso her heart's friend and her betrothed, the Assyrian Prince Cornelio Chiapperi, who left Ethiopia to have a molar tooth extracted here in Rome—an operation which I successfully performed for him. Behold it here before your eyes!"

Celionati opened a small golden box, took forth a very long, pointed, sharp tooth, and held it aloft. The crowd shrieked aloud for joy and delight and eagerly purchased the replicas of the princely tooth which the charlatan now offered for sale.

"You see," Celionati then continued, "you see, good people, after the Assyrian Prince Cornelio Chiapperi had endured the operation with steadfastness and meekness, he himself lost himself, he did not know how. Search, people! Search, people, for the Assyrian Prince Cornelio Chiapperi, search for him in your rooms, chambers, kitchens, cellars, wardrobes, and drawers! Whoever finds him and brings him back unharmed to Princess Brambilla will receive a finder's reward of five times one hundred thousand ducats. That is the price Princess Brambilla has put on his head, not counting the pleasant and no small amount of sense and acumen in it. Search, people, search! But

[15] In Carlo Gozzi's comedy, The Little Green Bird (L'Augellino bel verde), Tartagliona is a Queen; she is also the queen of the tarot deck of cards.

[16] Pulcinella was one of the stock clowns of the Commedia dell'Arte. His shape and costume varied. He might be hunchbacked or potbellied, or both; his white linen blouse and his trousers were many sizes too large; from his leather belt might dangle either a wooden sword or a big wallet, and his headgear might be either a white skullcap or an outlandish hat or, in Naples, a conical cap. In the latter seventeenth century he acquired, in France, rooster feathers as adornments to his hat and huge buttons down the front of his blouse. In England his guise and manners developed into the character of Punch; in Germany, by a separate development, he turned into the stupid, guzzling clown known as Hans Wurst ("Jack Sausage") or as Hans Pickelhering ("Jack Pickle Herring").

will you be able to discover the Assyrian Prince Cornelio
Chiapperi even if he is standing right in front of your noses?
Yes! Will you be able to discern the Most Serene Princess
even if she walks close in front of you? No! That you will not
be able to do, unless you avail yourselves of the spectacles
which the wise Indian mage Ruffiamonte himself has ground.
And from pure compassion and love of neighbor I will provide
you with those insofar as you do not spare the paoli."

And with that the charlatan opened a chest and produced a
quantity of disproportionately large spectacles.

If the crowd had already scuffled sharply for the princely
molar teeth, the same was now done much more sharply for
the spectacles. From scuffling, it came to thrusts and blows
until finally, in good Italic fashion, knives were flashing so that
the sbirri had to intervene once again and disperse the people
as they had done before in front of the Pistoja Palace.

While all this was going on, Giglio Fava, lost in profound
dreams, was still standing in front of the Pistoja Palace and
staring at the walls which had engulfed, in a totally inexplicable
way, the strangest of all masquerade processions. It struck him
as amazing that he could not master a certain uncanny and yet
sweet sensation which had taken total possession of his inner
being, and as even more amazing that he deliberately made an
association between the fantastic procession and the dream
about the princess who threw herself into his arms as she
flashed forth in the lightning of the musket fire, and a premonition dawned within him to the effect that none other than his
dream figure had sat in the coach with the mirror windows. A
gentle tap on the shoulder woke him from his reveries. The
ciarlatano was standing before him.

"Hey," began Celionati, "hey, my good Giglio, it wasn't nice
of you to leave me and not buy any princely molars or any magic
spectacles."

"Get along," replied Giglio, "get along with your childish
nonsense and the crazy stuff you chatter to the crowd in order
to get rid of your useless wares!"

"Ho, ho!" continued Celionati. "Just don't be so stuck on
yourself, my young gentleman! I wish you had many an excellent arcanum from among my wares, which you are pleased to

term useless, most particularly the talisman which would give you the power to be an excellent, a good, or at least a tolerable actor, inasmuch as it continues to please you to perform most wretchedly in tragedies at the present time!"

"What?" cried Giglio, thoroughly provoked. "What? Signor Celionati, you presume so far as to take me for a wretched actor? —I who am the idol of Rome?"

"Puppet," replied Celionati very calmly, "puppet, you only imagine that. There isn't a word of truth in it. If at times a particular spirit has welled up in you to make you successful in several roles, today you will irrevocably lose the little approval or fame you gained thereby. For, you see, you have completely forgotten your prince, and if his image perhaps still stands in your heart, it has become colorless, mute, and rigid, and you are not capable of summoning it to life. Your whole mind is filled with a curious dream image, which you fancy drove in the glass coach into the Pistoja Palace there. Do you observe that I see into your inner being?"

Blushing, Giglio lowered his eyes. "Signor Celionati," he murmured, "you are indeed a very strange person. Wondrous powers must be at your disposal to allow you to divine my most secret thoughts. And then again your clownish carryings on in front of the crowd—I can't make any sense of that. And yet— give me one of your big pairs of spectacles."

Celionati burst into loud laughter. "That's the way," he cried, "that's the way with all you people! As long as you run around with a clear head and a healthy stomach, you believe in nothing except what you can touch with your own hands; but let an attack of spiritual or physical indigestion get you, and you reach greedily for whatever anyone offers you. Ho, ho! That *professore* who hurled his excommunication at my and all the sympathetic remedies in the world, sneaked off the next day in morosely pathetic earnest to the Tiber, and, as an old beggar woman had counseled him, threw his left slipper into the water because he thought that by so doing he would drown the evil fever which was troubling him so badly; and that wisest signor of all wise signori wore blue gentian powder[17] in a lappet of his

---

[17] A volatile substance, perhaps like bicarbonate of soda.

coat in order to play badminton better. I know, Signor Fava, that you want to see Princess Brambilla, your dream image, through my spectacles. But you won't succeed in that for the time being! Meanwhile take them and try."

Full of curiosity, Giglio seized the splendid, gleaming, outsized spectacles that Celionati proffered him, and gazed in the direction of the palace. Wondrously enough, the walls of the palace seemed to turn into transparent crystal. But nothing but a many-colored and indistinct blur composed of all sorts of odd figures presented itself to him, and only at intervals did an electric ray twitch through his heart, proclaiming the lovely dream image which seemed to be trying in vain to wrest itself loose from the mad chaos.

"All the mean devils in hell ram down your throat!" screamed a fearful voice right beside the fascinated Giglio, who simultaneously felt himself grabbed by the shoulders. "All mean devils down your throat! You will be my ruination! The curtain goes up in ten minutes, you have the first scene, and here you stand like a weak-witted fool gaping at the old walls of the empty palace!"

It was the impresario of the theater where Giglio was playing, who had run all over Rome in the sweat of death-agony looking for the vanished *primo amoroso*[18] and who had finally found him where he least expected to.

"Wait a minute!" cried Celionati and likewise grabbed poor Giglio by the shoulders rather strongly as the latter, like a driven post, was not to be budged, "Wait a minute!" And then more softly, "Signor Giglio, it is possible that you will see your dream image tomorrow on the Corso. But you would be a great fool if you decked yourself all out in a beautiful costume. That would rob you of seeing your beauty. The more fantastic, the more hideous, the better! A doughty nose that would support my spectacles with dignity and tranquillity of soul! For you mustn't forget *them!*"

Celionati let go of Giglio, and in a trice the impresario went rushing off with his *amoroso* like a stormy wind.

The very next day Giglio did not fail to procure a costume which, in accordance with Celionati's advice, seemed to him

---

[18] *Primo amoroso:* (Italian) "leading man" (literally, "first lover").

fantastic and hideous enough. An odd cap adorned with two tall rooster feathers, a mask with a red hooked nose of unreasonable length and sharpness outdoing all excesses of the most extravagant noses, a jerkin with thick buttons not unlike Brighella's,[19] and a broad wooden sword—Giglio's self-renunciation in donning all these ceased when, first of all, full pantaloons reaching down to his slippers were supposed to conceal the handsomest pedestal on which a *primo amoroso* ever stood or walked. "No!" cried Giglio. "No! It is not possible that Her Serene Highness sets no store by well-proportioned stature, that she would not be repulsed by such vile disfigurement. I shall imitate the actor who, when he was playing the blue monster in a hideous makeup in Gozzi's play, let the daintily formed hand with which nature had endowed him stick out from under his colored tiger paw and thus won the ladies' hearts *before* his transformation! What his hand was to him, my foot is to me!" And with that, Giglio put on a pair of pretty sky-blue silk breeches with dark red bows, and to go with them pink stockings and white shoes with airy, dark red laces, all of which probably looked pretty enough but which clashed rather oddly with the rest of his costume.

Giglio did not believe other than that Princess Brambilla would step forth to meet him in full splendor and magnificence, surrounded by the most resplendent retinue. But when he saw nothing of the sort, he recalled that, inasmuch as Celionati had said he would be able to view the princess only by means of the magic spectacles, some odd disguise was signified in which the beauty was concealed.

Giglio went up and down the Corso scanning every feminine mask, disregarding all chaffing, until he finally arrived in a more remote area.

---

[19] The *Commedia dell'Arte* clown named Brighella was, in the sixteenth century, a lean, sly knave, lecherous, drunken, and utterly untrustworthy. Under more than a dozen variant names in the eighteenth century he acquired more amiable traits and attained his ultimate avatar as the Figaro of Beaumarchais, Mozart, and Rossini.

Oddly enough, Hoffmann seems here not to be describing a Brighella at all, but rather the left-hand figure in the first of the Callot engravings that accompanied his text of *Princess Brambilla* and which is reproduced with the present translation.

"My best Signor, my dear, best Signor!" he heard someone growl at him.

Standing before him was a fellow who outdid anything he had ever seen in the way of mad comicality. The mask with its pointed beard, spectacles, and gypsy hair, as well as the body posture, bent forward with crooked back and right foot advanced, seemed to indicate a Pantalone.[20] On the other hand, the hat coming to a peak in front and adorned with two rooster feathers would not go with such. Jerkin, breeches, and the little wooden sword at his side apparently belonged to the worthy Pulcinella.[21]

"Best Signor," said Pantalone—we shall call the masked figure by that name in spite of the altered costume—to Giglio, "my best Signor! A lucky day that gives me the satisfaction and the honor of beholding you! Mightn't you belong to my family?"

"As much," replied Giglio, bowing very politely, "as much as that would delight me, inasmuch as you, my best Signor, please me beyond all measure, I really don't know in what way any relationship—"

[20] The details are exact for the Commedia dell'Arte clown named Pantalone, who represented a duped father, husband, or master, a retired merchant, and a frequent victim of Cupid. His tight-fitting clothes were normally red, his cloak was either red or black, and he usually wore Turkish slippers. He is the "lean and slipper'd Pantaloon" of Shakespeare's As You Like It, II, 7.

[21] For Pulcinella, see note 16. We are to understand that the mask addressing Giglio is half Pantalone, half Pulcinella, but Hoffmann seems to be indulging in caprice, for he is clearly describing the right-hand figure of the Callot plate reproduced at the end of this chapter and in Callot's original that figure is very legibly labeled "Scapino." Moreover, Scapino — Molière's Scapin — was not a Pulcinella but one of the many variant forms of Brighella.

The reader may be grateful for the hint that this mask who is talking to Giglio is Giglio's own future actor-self.

At Celionati's advice, Giglio had obtained the wholly suitable costume of a Brighella (or of a Captain Zerbino), but, misguided by his old vanity, he donned only the upper half of it in order to display his handsome legs in sky-blue breeches, pink stockings, and white shoes. Thus he is half dandy and half Commedia clown. The Pantalone–Pulcinella (or Scapino) who is the future Giglio first greets him as a possible kinsman, then denounces and disowns him because of the dandified lower half of him. The desired "vision" of Princess Brambilla is, for the same reasons of unworthiness, reduced to a grotesque illusion which, the author hints, may be produced by consumption of alcohol.

"Heavens!" Pantalone interrupted Giglio, "Heavens! Dearest Signor, have you ever been in Assyria?"

"A dim recollection," answered Giglio, "hovers before me to the effect that I once started on a journey there but got only as far as Frascati,[22] where the rascal of a *vetturino*[23] overturned the carriage with me in it in front of the gate, so that this nose—"

"Heavens!" cried Pantalone, "Then it is true? This nose, these rooster feathers—My dearest Prince, O my Cornelio! But I see you are turning pale with joy at having found me again—O my Prince! Just a swallow, one single swallow!"

And with that, Pantalone lifted up the big demijohn that was standing in front of him and handed it to Giglio. And at that moment, faint reddish vapor rose from the bottle and condensed to form the lovely countenance of Princess Brambilla. And the lovely little image rose upwards, but only waist-high, and stretched out its little arms to Giglio.

The latter, beside himself with rapture, cried, "Oh, rise all the way up so that I can see you in your beauty!"

Whereupon a deep voice rumbled in his ears, "You cowardly coxcomb with your sky blue and your pink, how dare you try to pass yourself off as Prince Cornelio! Go home and sleep it off, you hick!"

"Brute!" Giglio flared up.

But maskers surged and thronged between them, and without a trace vanished Pantalone, together with his bottle.

---

[22] Frascati, a town just a few miles southeast of Rome (ancient Tusculum).
[23] Vetturino: (Italian) "driver."

SECOND CHAPTER

Concerning the odd circumstances, once amid which, one stubs one's toes on jagged stones till they are sore, gives up speaking to distinguished people, and bangs one's head against closed doors. Influence of a dish of macaroni on love and enthusiasm. Ghastly torments of Actors' Hell and Arlecchino. How Giglio did not find his girl but was overpowered by tailors and let blood. The prince in the candy box and the lost beloved. How Giglio wanted to be Princess Brambilla's knight because a flag had sprouted from his back.

B e so kind, beloved reader, as not to get angry when he who has undertaken to tell you the fantastic story of Princess Brambilla exactly as he found it indicated in Master Callot's bold pen strokes, forthrightly says that he expects you will surrender yourself willingly to the marvelous at least until the final words of this little book, and even that you will believe a little something of it. But perhaps at the moment when the fairy-tale vision took up quarters in the Pistoja Palace, or when the princess rose up out of the bluish vapor of the wine bottle, you exclaimed: "Crazy, silly stuff!" and disregarding the pretty copper plates, you threw the book away? In that case, everything I am about to say in order to win you over to the side of the strange enchantments of the Callot *capriccio* comes too late, and that would indeed be bad enough for both me and Princess Brambilla! But then again, you may perhaps have hoped that the author only shied at some crazy image that suddenly crossed his path and made a detour into the wild underbrush, and that, once having come to his senses, he would rein back again onto the broad, level way, and that idea enabled you, kind reader, to go on reading. Good luck!

Now I can tell you, kind reader, that from time to time I have succeeded—perhaps you know this from your own experience, too—in seizing upon fairy-tale adventures precisely at the moment when they were about to vanish into nothingness, airy phantoms of the excited mind that they are, and in giving them a form such that every eye endowed with vision for such, actually saw them alive and even, for that reason, believed in them. Thence may derive my spirit for carrying on further, and in public, my spiritual association with all sorts of fantastic figures and with many rather mad images, and even for inviting the most earnest people to this odd and colorful society, and you, well-beloved reader, will hardly be able to take this spirit for excessive spiritedness but rather, for only the forgivable effort to lure you forth from the narrow sphere of humdrum wont and to give you pleasure in a wholly unique way in that alien region which, in the last analysis, is included in the realm which in real life and existence the human mind rules with free volition.[1]

But if all this is disallowed, I can only appeal, amid the anxiety that has befallen me, to very serious books in which similar things are advanced and against the total credibility of which one cannot raise the slightest doubt. As for the Princess Brambilla's procession which passed, together with all its unicorns, horses, and other vehicles, without hindrance through the narrow portals of the Pistoja Palace, there was already talk in *Peter Schlemihl's Odd History,* whose composition we owe to that gallant world-circumnavigator Adalbert von Chamisso,[2] of a certain agreeable "Man in Grey" who performed a stunt which puts that bit of magic to shame. Namely, as is well known, he produced upon request: court plaster, a telescope, a carpet, a tent, and finally horses and carriage, all quite comfortably and without hindrance out of one and the same coat pocket. As far as the princess is concerned, however—

But enough. It remains only to say that in life we often stand suddenly in front of the open gate of a wonderful, magic realm,

---

[1] The variations on the word "spirit" are attempts to parallel the author's threefold pun on *Mut, gemütlich,* and *Übermut.*

[2] Chamisso is the same French émigré turned Prussian nobleman mentioned in connection with *Little Zaches.* His enormously popular story of Peter Schlemihl was published in 1814; his journey around the world as an exploring natural scientist occupied the years 1815–1818.

that glimpses are vouchsafed us into the innermost household of the mighty spirit whose breath wafts mysteriously about us in the strangest premonitions. You, however, beloved reader, could perhaps assert with full right that out of that gate you had never seen such a mad *capriccio* issue as I claim to have beheld. Therefore, I shall rather inquire of you whether in all your life there has never risen within you a strange dream whose origin you could not put down either to an upset stomach or to the spirit of wine or of fever? Rather it was as if the lovely magic form, which otherwise spoke to you only in distant intimations, had overpowered your entire inner being in a mystic marriage with your mind, and in your shy desire of love, you did not venture so much as to embrace the sweet bride who in all her gleaming splendor had entered into the drab and gloomy workshop of your thoughts; but *it* opened up in shimmering light before the radiance of the magic form, and all longing, all hope, the ardent desire to clasp the ineffable, woke and stirred and sprang alive in glowing lightning fires, and you wanted to perish in unspeakable anguish and be nothing but *her*, nothing but that lovely magic form. Did it help you to waken from the dream? Did the nameless rapture not remain with you, which like a trenchant pain bores through your soul in external life? And everything around you seemed void, dreary, colorless? And you fancied that only that dream was your true existence, while what you had formerly considered as your life was only the misunderstanding of your befuddled mind? And all your thoughts converged like rays into the focus which, as a chalice of fire composed of supreme ardor, kept your sweet secret hidden from the blind and muddled activity of the everyday world? Hm! In such dreamy moods as that, one stubs one's toes on jagged stones until they are sore, forgets to take off one's hat to distinguished people, bids friends a "Good morning" at the dead of midnight, and knocks one's head against the first house door he comes upon because he forgets to open it; in short, the mind wears the body like an uncomfortable garment which is in every way too broad, too long, and too clumsy.

Into such a state now fell the young actor Giglio Fava, as for several days in succession he sought to discover the slightest news of Princess Brambilla. All the wonderful things he encountered on the Corso seemed to him only the continuation of that dream which had brought to him the lovely creature whose image now rose up from the bottomless sea of longing in which he himself wished to perish and be dissolved. Only his dream was life, all else was insignificant, empty nothingness. Thus, one can imagine that he also neglected the actor. He did more than that: instead of speaking the words of his role, he talked about his dream image, about Princess Brambilla, and in the confusion of his thoughts, vowed he would overwhelm the Assyrian prince so that he himself might become the prince, and thus lost himself in a labyrinth of confused and rambling speeches. Everyone was forced to look upon him as insane, the first one to do so being the impresario, who finally fired him with no further ado. And his meager income vanished completely away. The few ducats which the impresario tossed him out of pure charity at farewell, could last only a brief time, and the bitterest want was approaching. Once that would have caused Giglio great worry and anxiety; now he gave it no thought, floating as he was in a heaven where earthly ducats are not required.

As for the ordinary requirements of life Giglio, never dainty, satisfied his hunger in passing at one of the *fritteroli*[3] which, as you know, maintain their eating places on the open sidewalk. Thus it chanced that the idea occurred to him one day to have a good dish of macaroni which was sending forth its steamy fragrance from the booth. He stepped up. But when he pulled out his purse to pay for the meager dinner, he was no slight bit confounded by the discovery that not one single *baiocco*[4] was left in it. Just at that moment, however, there was a lively self-assertion on the part of the corporeal principle by which the spiritual one is held in vile durance here on earth, be the latter however proud. Giglio felt uncommonly hungry, as had never happened before when he had consumed a good helping of macaroni while he was filled with the sublimest thoughts, and he assured the proprietor that he just happened not to be carrying any money to pay for the dish that he intended to eat, but that he would certainly pay for it the next day. The proprietor

---

[3] *Fritteroli*: (Italian) "booths serving hot foods cooked in oil."
[4] *Baiocco*: (Italian) "farthing."

laughed in his face and said if he didn't have any money he could still satisfy his appetite; all he had to do was to leave the fine pair of gloves he was wearing, or his hat, or his cape. Only now did poor Giglio clearly see the sorry state in which he found himself. He saw himself soon as a tattered beggar, spooning up the soup served by the convents. But he felt a sharper slash into his heart as, roused from his dream, he now noticed Celionati, who was at his usual stand in front of the church of San Carlo entertaining the crowd with his nonsense and who, as he glanced across, threw him a look in which he thought he read the utmost contempt. Dissolved into nothingness was the lovely dream image, vanished was every last sweet intimation. He was sure the infamous Celionati had lured him astray by all sorts of devilish magical tricks and, manipulating his silly vanity in mockingly malicious joy, had hoaxed him in the most ignoble fashion with Princess Brambilla.

Wildly he ran off. He was no longer hungry. His only thought was of how he could get revenge on the old wizard.

He himself did not know what strange emotion it was that shot through all his anger and all the fury in his heart and compelled him to stop as if an unknown magic spell suddenly arrested him. "Giacinta!" arose the cry from within him. He was standing in front of the house where the girl lived and whose steep stairs he had so often climbed in the secretive twilight. He recalled how the treacherous dream image first roused the girl's irritation, how he had then left her and had not seen her again, nor thought of her any more, how he had lost his beloved and plunged into want and misery, all because of Celionati's crazy, unholy hoaxing. Completely dissolved in grief and sorrow, he could not recover his senses until finally the decision forced its way forward to go up here and now and win back Giacinta's favor, cost what it might.

No sooner said than done. But now as he knocked at Giacinta's door, everything within remained quiet as a mouse. He put his ear to the door, but not a breath was to be heard. Then he mournfully called out Giacinta's name several times, and when no answer was forthcoming he began a most moving avowal of his folly. He assured her that the Devil himself, in the form of the accursed quack Celionati, had tempted him, and passed from that to the most extreme asseverations of his profound remorse and his fervent love.

Then a voice shouted up from below: "I'd like to know what donkey is groaning his lamentations here in my house and howling ahead of time when it is still a long way till Ash Wednesday!"

It was Signor Pasquale, the fat landlord, who was toiling his way up the stairs, and when he caught sight of Giglio he called out to him, "Ah! Is it you, Signor Giglio? But tell me what evil spirit is forcing you to whine an 'Oh and Alas' role from some silly tragedy into that empty room?"

"Empty room?" shrieked Giglio. "Empty room? In the name of all the saints, Signor Pasquale, tell me, where is Giacinta? Where is she, my life, my all?"

Signor Pasquale stared into Giglio's face and then said quietly, "Signor Giglio, I know how things stand with you. All Rome has learned how you had to retire from the stage because you've gone off your rocker. Go to a doctor, go to a doctor, have a couple of pounds of blood drained off, stick your head in cold water!"

"If," cried Giglio vehemently, "if I am not crazy yet, I will be if you don't tell me this instant what has become of Giacinta."

"Don't," Signor Pasquale calmly continued, "don't try to tell me, Signor Giglio, that you wouldn't be informed as to how Giacinta left my house a week ago and how old Beatrice followed her."

But now as Giglio in full fury shouted, "Where is Giacinta?" and grabbed the fat landlord hard as he did so, the latter bellowed "Help! Help! Murder!" so that the whole house was roused. A brawny lout of a porter came running up, grabbed poor Giglio, carried him down the stairs, and threw him out of the house with adroitness as if he had a doll-baby in his paws.

Paying no heed to his hard fall, Giglio picked himself up and ran through the streets of Rome, now indeed driven by semi-madness. Just as the clocks were striking the hour at which he used to have to hurry to the theater, a certain instinct born of habit brought him precisely there and into the actors' dressing room. Only then did he recollect where he was, but it was only to be struck with the most profound astonishment when, there

in the place where tragic heroes decked out in silver and gold
and stalking about in total solemnity used to rehearse the highfalutin verses with which they intended to stun the audience
and put them in *furore*,[5] he saw himself surrounded by Pantalone and Arlecchino, Truffaldino and Colombina, in short, by all
the masks of the Italian comedy and pantomime. He stood there
as if pegged down to the floor, and stared wide-eyed around like
someone who has suddenly awakened from sleep and sees himself surrounded by a strange, mad company wholly unknown
to him.

Giglio's confused and sorrow-distorted appearance may have
stirred some pangs of conscience in the impresario's heart,
thus transforming him suddenly into a very cordial and gentle-
souled man.

"You are amazed," he said to the youth, "you are amazed
probably, Signor Fava, to find everything here so completely
different from what it was when you left it? I must confess to
you that all the grandiose plots with which my theater used to
plume itself began to inspire much boredom in the audiences
and that that boredom attacked me myself all the more because
of the fact that on account of it my purse fell into the miserable
state of real consumption. Now I have turned all that tragic
stuff out and given my theater over to the free jesting and
sprightly fun of our maskers, and feel quite well for having done
so."

"Ha!" cried Giglio with burning cheeks. "Ha! Signor Impresario, just confess that the loss of me ruined your tragedy. With
the fall of the hero, the crowd which his breath animated also
fell into dead nothingness?"

"We shan't," replied the impresario smiling, "we shan't look
too closely into that! But you seem to be in bad humor, and so I
beg you to go down and watch my pantomime. Perhaps it will
cheer you up, or perhaps you will change your mind and you
will again become mine, although in a completely different way.
For possibly it might be the case that—but just go along, just
go along! Here is a mark. Visit my theater as often as you like!"

Giglio did as bidden, more from dull indifference toward
everything around him than for the pleasure of actually seeing
the pantomime.

[5] *Furore:* (Italian) "frenzied enthusiasm."

Not far distant from him two masks were standing engaged in eager conversation. Several times Giglio heard his name mentioned, and that roused him from his torpor. He stole nearer, pulling up his cape over his face as far as his eyes in order to listen without being recognized.

"You are right," the one was saying, "you are right, Fava is to blame for our not seeing any more tragedies in this theater. But I would by no means attribute that fault, as you do, to his withdrawal from the stage, but rather to his appearance on the stage."

"How do you mean?" asked the other.

"Well," continued the first one, "I for my part have always considered this Fava as the most wretched actor that ever was, despite the fact that he only too often succeeded in rousing *furore*. Does the youthful tragic hero consist of a pair of flashing eyes, shapely legs, a pretty costume, colored feathers on his cap, and excellent ribbons on his shoes? In fact, when Fava used to come forward from backstage with such measured dancer's steps, and when he used to leer toward the loges, disregarding all his fellow actors and actresses, and pausing in an oddly studied pose to give the fair ones time to admire him, then he really did seem to me like a young, silly, many-colored barnyard rooster strutting in the sun and enjoying himself. And then when he rolled his eyes, sawed the air with his hands, rising now on tiptoe and then again folding up like a jackknife, and reeled off the verses jerkily and badly in a hollow voice, tell me, what sensible human heart could really be moved? But that's the way we Italians are. We want what is overdone, what affects us powerfully for a moment, and which we despise as soon as we see that what we took for flesh and blood is only a lifeless puppet which was pulled by ingenious wires from the outside and which deceived us with its curious movements. That's the way it would have gone with Fava. Little by little he would have died off miserably if he hadn't hastened his earlier death himself."

"It seems to me," the other began, "it seems to me you judge poor Fava much too harshly. When you blame him for being vain and affected, when you maintain that he never acted his role but only acted himself and that he strained for success in ways that were not exactly praiseworthy, you may very well be right. But he was to be termed a very nice talent, and the fact that he finally fell into wild madness must after all claim our pity, all the more so, in fact, since the strain of acting is probably the cause of his madness."

"Don't," replied the first, laughing, "don't you believe it! Wouldn't it seem to you that Fava went mad from pure vanity of love? He thinks a princess is in love with him, and he is now chasing her on highway and byway. And along with that, he has become impoverished by pure shiftlessness, so that today he had to leave his gloves and hat behind at the *fritteroli* to pay for a dish of tough macaroni."

"What are you saying?" cried the other. "Is it possible that such crazy things exist? But in one way or another we ought to bestow a little something on poor Giglio, who did after all give us pleasure many an evening. That dog of an impresario, into whose pockets he played many a ducat, ought to look after him and at least not let him starve."

"That isn't necessary," said the first, "for a little purse filled with ducats has been slipped him by Princess Brambilla, who knows of his madness and of his distress, the way women not only find all folly of love forgivable but even pretty, and they only too willingly surrender themselves to pity."

Mechanically, involuntarily, as the stranger spoke these words, Giglio reached for his pocket and did indeed feel the little purse full of jingling gold which he was supposed to have received from the dream Princess Brambilla. Something like an electrical shock darted through all his limbs. With horror blowing icy-cold over him, he could find no room for joy in this welcome marvel which would instantly rescue him from his sorry plight. He saw himself as the plaything of unknown powers. He started to rush at the strange mask, but at that moment realized that both masks who had been carrying on that fateful conversation had vanished without a trace.

Giglio just did not dare to draw the purse from his pocket and convince himself more cogently of its existence, as he feared the illusion would melt away to nothingness in his hands. But now as he surrendered entirely to his thoughts and gradually became quieter, he imagined that all he had been inclined to take for a trick played by prankish magic powers might turn out to be a hoax which the fantastic and capricious Celionati might be pulling from the deep dark background by means of strings invisible only to him. He realized how, in the crush of the human throng, the strange man could very well have planted the little purse on him and that all he had said about Princess Brambilla could be just the continuation of the hoax begun by Celionati. Now, as the whole enchantment was about to change over quite naturally within him into the ordinary and be resolved, he felt the recurrence of all the pain occasioned by the wounds which the sharp critics had mercilessly dealt him. Actors' Hell can have no more hideous torment than attacks on their vanity, dealt right to their hearts. The very exposure to attack of that point, the feeling of nakedness, increases the pain of blows amid increased vexation and makes the victim really feel that he has been hit, try as he may to swallow the pain and to alleviate it by any appropriate means. Thus, Giglio could not elude the odious picture of the young, silly, many-colored barnyard rooster strutting in the sun and enjoying himself, and he vexed himself and grieved over it enormously, precisely because, against his will, he was perhaps compelled in his inner heart to acknowledge that the caricature was really based on the original image.

With Giglio in this irritated mood, it could hardly be otherwise but that he scarcely saw the stage and paid no attention to the pantomime, although the hall frequently rang with the laughter, the applause, and the shouts of joy of the spectators.

The pantomime portrayed nothing other than the love adventures of the excellent Arlecchino and the sweet and pertly lovely Colombina, as those adventures are repeated in hundreds and hundreds of variations. Already rich old Pantalone's charming daughter had refused the hand of the flashingly adorned cavalier, of the wise *dottore*, and stoutly declared she absolutely would not love and marry anyone but the little nimble man with the swarthy face and with the jerkin patched together out of a thousand shreds; already Arlecchino had fled with his loyal girl and, protected by a mighty magic, had happily escaped the persecutions of Pantalone, or Truffaldino, of the *dottore*, and of the cavalier. It was at this point that finally Arlecchino, making love to his sweetheart, was supposed to be surprised by the *sbirri* and dragged off to jail along with her. And this did now happen. But just at the moment when Pantalone and his cohorts were about to jeer at the poor couple, when Colombina, all sorrow amid a thousand tears, was begging on her knees for her Arlecchino, the latter swung his wooden sword and from all sides, out of the earth, out of the air, came very pretty, shining people of the most beautiful appearance, who bowed deeply before Arlecchino and led him off in triumph together with Colombina. Pantalone, frozen with amazement, sinks down completely exhausted on a stone bench which happens to be there in the jail and invites the cavalier and the *dottore* to be seated also. All three discuss what now can possibly be done. Truffaldino comes up and stands behind them, sticks his head in curiously between them, and refuses to budge, although copious boxes on the ear are raining from all sides. Now they start to get up, but they are enchanted fast to the bench, which that very instant sprouts a pair of mighty wings. Amid loud cries for help, the whole company flies off through the air on the back of a monstrous vulture.

And now the jail is transformed into a spacious columned hall adorned with flower garlands and in the middle of it is erected a high and richly ornamented throne. Pleasant music of drums, pipes, and cymbals is heard. A magnificent procession approaches. Arlecchino is being carried by Moors on a palanquin, Colombina follows him in a splendid triumphal chariot. Both are conducted to the throne by richly clad ministers, Arlecchino raises his wooden sword as a scepter, everyone kneels to do him homage, and even Pantalone and his cohorts are glimpsed on their knees among the reverent crowd. Arlecchino rules, a mighty emperor, with his Colombina, over a beautiful, magnificent, resplendent realm!

As the procession came on stage, Giglio cast a glance upward, and for sheer wonder and amazement could not turn his eyes away as he perceived all the persons from the retinue of Princess Brambilla, the unicorns, the Moors, the net-making ladies on muleback, and the others. Nor was the venerable scholar and statesman missing from his shiny gold tulip; he looked up from his book as he went by and seemed to nod in a friendly manner to Giglio. Only, instead of the closed mirror-coach of the Princess, Colombina drove along in the open triumphal chariot.

From Giglio's inner self a dim premonition sought to rise, to the effect that this pantomime might well stand in some mysterious connection with all the marvelous things that had befallen him. But, just as a dreamer tries in vain to hold the images that rise up from within his own ego, Giglio too was unable to form a distinct idea as to how that connection could be possible.

In the nearest café Giglio convinced himself that Princess Brambilla's ducats were no illusion but rather of sound ring and stamp. "Hm!" he thought, "Celionati slipped me this little purse out of great mercy and compassion, and I will pay him back the debt as soon as I shine again on the Argentina—which cannot help but come about since only the fiercest envy and the most pitiless intrigue dares cry me down as a bad actor!"

The suspicion that the money must have come from Celionati was well-founded. In fact, the old man had already helped him out of great distress several times. And yet it did strike him as odd that he should find embroidered on the dainty purse the words: "Remember your dream image!" He was gazing pensively at the inscription when someone shouted in his ear: "So I find you at last, you traitor, you faithless rogue, you monster of falsity and ingratitude!" A shapeless *dottore* had grabbed him and now, without a by-your-leave, sat down beside him and was continuing with all sorts of imprecations.

"What do you want of me? Are you crazy? Insane?" So cried Giglio, but now the *dottore* removed the ugly mask from its face and Giglio recognized old Beatrice. "In the name of all the saints!" cried Giglio, beside himself. "Is it you, Beatrice? Where is Giacinta? Where is that sweet and lovely child? My heart is breaking with love and longing! Where is Giacinta?"

"Just ask," replied the old woman in a surly tone, "just ask, wretched, infamous man! In jail is where poor Giacinta is, and pining away her youthful life, and you are to blame for everything. For if she hadn't had her little head full of you, if she could have waited for the evening hour, she wouldn't have pricked her finger when she was sewing the trimming on Princess Brambilla's gown, and then the nasty spot wouldn't have gotten onto it, and then the worthy Master Bescapi—may Hell consume him!—could not have demanded that she make the damage good, and when she couldn't do so because we couldn't raise all that money that he asked, he wouldn't have had her put in jail. You could have gotten help. But that's where Master Actor Good-for-nothing got cold feet—"

"Stop!" Giglio interrupted the garrulous old woman. "It is your fault for not running to me and telling me everything. My life for that lovely girl! If it weren't midnight, I would run over to that vile Bescapi's—these ducats—and my girl would be free within the hour. But what difference if it is midnight! Off, off, to save her!"

And with that Giglio went racing off. The old woman's mocking laughter followed him.

But just as in our overhaste to do something we forget our main concern, so it did not occur to Giglio until he had run breathless through the streets of Rome, that he should have inquired from the old woman about Bescapi's residence, since it was totally unknown to him. Fate, however, or Chance, would have it that when he got to the Spanish Square he was standing right in front of Bescapi's house, as he cried out: "Where the devil does this man Bescapi live?" Immediately an unknown person took him by the arm and led him into the house, saying that Master Bescapi lived precisely there and that he could very probably pick up the masquerade costume which he had perhaps ordered. Once in the room, the man asked him, since Master Bescapi was not at home, to point out the costume he had selected; perhaps it was a simple *tabarro*[6] or something—

But Giglio grabbed the man by the neck—he was nothing more than a very worthy tailor's apprentice—and talked so much and so confusedly about a bloodstain and jail and payment and instantaneous liberation that the apprentice, completely motionless and flabbergasted, stared him in the eye, without being able to make one syllable of reply.

"Damned rascal, you just won't understand me! Bring me your master, the devilish cur, right away!" shouted Giglio and grabbed the apprentice.

---

[6] *Tabarro*: (Italian) "cloak."

But then things went exactly as they had gone at Signor Pasquale's house. The apprentice bellowed so that from all sides the servants came pouring in. Bescapi himself rushed in. But as soon as he caught sight of Giglio, he shouted, "In the name of all the saints, it is the insane actor, poor Signor Fava. Grab him, men, grab him!"

Now they all rushed at him, overpowered him easily, tied him hand and foot, and laid him down on a bed. Bescapi walked up to him. Him Giglio deluged with a thousand bitter reproaches about his greed and about his cruelty, and talked much about Princess Brambilla's gown, about a bloodstain, about payment, and so on.

"But do be calm," said Bescapi gently, "but do be calm, dearest Signor Giglio, dismiss the phantoms that are tormenting you! In a few minutes everything will seem very different to you."

What Bescapi meant by that was soon manifest, for in came a surgeon and tapped a vein of Giglio's, despite all the latter's resistance. Exhausted by all the events of the day and by the loss of blood, poor Giglio sank into a deep sleep not unlike a faint.

When he awoke it was deep night all around. Only with effort could he recall what had happened to him last. He felt that he had been untied, but because of his languor he still could not move or stir about very much. Through a crack, apparently in a door, a faint ray of light finally fell into the room, and it seemed to him as if he could hear a deep breathing, and then again a soft whispering, which finally turned into comprehensible words: "Is it really you, my beloved Prince? And in this condition? So small, so small, that I think you would have room in my candy box! But do not think that I esteem you and respect you any the less for that, for do I not know you are a stately and gracious gentleman and that I am only dreaming all of this now? But be so kind as to show yourself to me tomorrow, even if it is as no more than a voice. If you but cast your eyes upon me, your poor handmaiden, then it could not fail to come about, because formerly—" Here the words again became an indistinguishable whisper. There was something uncommonly sweet and lovely about the voice, and Giglio felt shaken with a mysterious shudder. But when he tried to listen very sharply, he was again lulled to deep sleep by the whispering, which was almost like the plashing of a nearby fountain.

The sunlight was shining brightly into the room when a gentle shake woke Giglio from his sleep. Master Bescapi was standing in front of him and, as he took his hand, was saying with a good-natured smile, "You feel better now, don't you, dearest Signor? Yes, the saints be praised! You do look a little pale, but your pulse is regular. Heaven guided you to my house in your bad seizure and permitted me to perform a small service for you, whom I look upon as the most splendid actor in Rome and whose loss has thrown us all into deepest mourning."

Bescapi's final words were frankly a powerful ointment for wounds sustained. Meanwhile, however, Giglio began earnestly and somberly enough: "Signor Bescapi, I was neither ill nor insane when I entered your house. You were hardhearted enough to send my lovely fiancée, poor Giacinta Soardi, to jail because she was unable to pay you for a splendid gown which she had spoiled—no! which she had made holy!—by dropping rosy ichor upon it from a needle prick of her most delicate finger. Tell me instantly what you are asking for the gown. I will pay the amount and then we shall go at once and set the lovely child free from the jail where she is languishing on account of your greed." With that, Giglio got out of the bed as fast as he could and from his pocket produced the purse of ducats which he was determined to empty completely if need be.

But Bescapi stared at him wide-eyed and said, "But how can you think up such crazy stuff, Signor Giglio? I don't know one word about any gown that Giacinta is supposed to have spoiled for me, not one word about a bloodstain or about putting anybody in jail!"

But now as Giglio once again recounted everything as he had heard it from Beatrice, and in particular as he very minutely described the gown which he himself had seen at Giacinta's house, Master Bescapi opined that it was only too obvious that the old woman had made a fool of him, because there was absolutely nothing to the whole pretty story, as he could positively avow, and what was more, he had never given any such gown as Giglio claimed to have seen to Giacinta to work on. Giglio could not mistrust Bescapi's words, since it was beyond comprehension that he should not have accepted the money he had offered him, and he became convinced that here too a mad enchantment was at work, in which he was involved. What was there left to do but leave Master Bescapi and to wait for random chance to lead him to the arms of the lovely Giacinta, with whom he was now once again passionately in love.

In front of Bescapi's door stood a person whom he could have wished a thousand miles away, namely, old Celionati. "Ah!" he greeted Giglio laughingly, "ah! You are really a good soul after all, trying to give away the ducats flung to you by the benevolence of Fate, and for the sake of your sweetheart who is, as a matter of fact, no longer your sweetheart."

"You," replied Giglio, "you are a horrible, cruel person! Why are you interfering in my life? Why are you trying to get control of my being? You parade an omniscience, which probably does not cost you much effort, you surround me with spies who lurk about my every step, you incite everybody against me! It's you I have to thank for the loss of Giacinta, of my job, by a thousand tricks—"

"That," cried Celionati, laughing loudly, "that would be worth the effort, badgering that way the highly important person of the ex-actor, Mister Giglio Fava! But really, my son Giglio, you do need a guardian to guide you to the right path and conduct you to your goal."

"I am of age," said Giglio, "and I beg you Mister *Ciarlatano,* just to leave me alone."

"Ho, ho!" answered Celionati. "Not so high and mighty! What if I intended the good and best for you, what if I meant your highest happiness on earth, what if I stood as intermediary between you and Princess Brambilla?"

"O Giacinta, Giacinta! Oh, unhappy man that I am, I have lost her! Was there ever a day that brought me blacker misfortune than yesterday?" Thus cried Giglio, beside himself.

"Now, now," said Celionati soothingly, "the day wasn't so totally unlucky after all. The good advice you got at the theater could be very wholesome for you, once you were reassured that you really didn't leave your gloves, hat, and cape behind for the sake of a dish of tough macaroni. And then you saw the most magnificent performance, which may be called the best in the world because it expressed the most profound things without recourse to words. And then in your pocket you found the ducats that you needed."

"From you! From you, I know," Giglio interrupted him.

"Even if that were actually true," continued Celionati, "it wouldn't alter the case any. Suffice it to say that you got the gold, got yourself back on a good footing with your stomach, luckily chanced upon Bescapi's house, got yourself treated to a much needed and very useful bloodletting, and finally slept under the same roof with your beloved."

"What are you saying?" cried Giglio. "What are you saying? With my beloved? Under the same roof with my beloved?"

"That is how it is," replied Celionati. "Just look up."

Giglio did so and a hundred lightning flashes pierced his heart as he glimpsed his lovely Giacinta on the balcony, daintily adorned and prettier and more alluring than he had ever seen her, and with old Beatrice behind her. "Giacinta! My Giacinta, my sweet life!" he called up in a voice full of yearning. But Giacinta cast a scornful glance down at him and left the balcony, old Beatrice following her.

"She's still sticking to her accursed smorfiosity," said Giglio impatiently, "but that will be overcome."

"Hardly," spoke up Celionati, "for, my good Giglio, you probably don't know that, at the same time as you went pursuing Princess Brambilla in your bold way, a handsome, stately prince was wooing your donna and, as it appears—"

"All the devils of hell!" cried Giglio, "that old Satan of a Beatrice has pandered the poor thing off. But I'll poison the wretched woman with rat poison and I'll thrust a dagger into the accursed prince."

"Give that all up!" interrupted Celionati. "Give that all up, good Giglio. Just go along home and have a little more blood let when evil thoughts come to you. God be your guide. We shall doubtless see each other again on the Corso."

With that Celionati hurried away across the street.

Giglio stood as if rooted there, cast furious glances at the balcony, grit his teeth, and muttered the most ghastly imprecations. But now as Master Bescapi stuck his head out the window and politely asked him to come on in and wait until the new crisis that seemed to be approaching passed off, he spat out, "Damned procurer!" at him, whom he thought to be also conspiring against him and in the plot with the old woman, and ran wildly away.

On the Corso he met several former cronies with whom he went into a nearby wine tavern in order to drown all his annoyance, all his pangs of love, and all his misery in the heat of a fiery Syracusan vintage.

Usually that sort of decision is just not the most advisable, for the very heat that consumes the annoyance has a way of blazing up out of control and setting fire to everything within that one keeps otherwise away from the flame. But with Giglio, it succeeded very well. In cheerful and pleasurable conversation with the actors and in glorying in all sorts of recollections and merry adventures of the theater, he really did forget all the misfortunes that had befallen him. At parting, they agreed to appear that evening on the Corso in the maddest costumes imaginable.

The costume which he had already worn once seemed adequately preposterous to Giglio, only this time he did not disdain the odd full-length trousers, and in addition he now wore his cape impaled on a rod behind him so that it almost looked as if a flag were growing out of his back. In this getup he went roving the streets and gave himself up to extravagant merriment, mindful neither of his dream image nor of his lost sweetheart.

But he stopped as though rooted to the ground when, not far from the Pistoja Palace, a tall and stately figure approached him clad in the very magnificent gown in which Giacinta had once surprised him, or more correctly, in which he had glimpsed his dream image in clear and actual life. Like lightning it shot through all his limbs, and yet he himself did not know how it happened that the constriction of the heart and the anguish of love's yearning, which usually paralyze the mind when the lovely image of the beloved stands suddenly before one, now vanished in the cheerful courage of a joy such as he had never before felt. Right foot forward, chest out, shoulders back, he immediately threw himself into the most decorative pose in which he had ever tragedized his most extraordinary speeches,

doffed his *biretta*[7] with the long pointed rooster feathers from off his stiff wig, and, maintaining the grating tone that suited his disguise and staring fixedly through his great spectacles at Princess Brambilla—for there was no doubt but that it was she— began: "The loveliest of the fays, the loftiest of the goddesses walks upon the earth; the jealous wax of a mask conceals the triumphant beauty of her countenance, but from the radiance shed about her a thousand lightning flashes dart and penetrate the bosoms of age and of youth; aflame with love and rapture, all do homage to the celestial one."

"From what," replied the princess, "from what highfalutin tragedy did you cull this beautiful manner of speaking, Mister Pantalone Capitano, or whoever it is you claim to be? But tell me rather what triumphs are signified by the trophies that you are so proudly carrying at your back?"

"Those are no trophies," cried Giglio, "for I am still fighting for the victory! It is the banner of hope and of yearning desire to which I am sworn, and the distress signal of unconditional surrender that I have set up, which is meant to waft 'Have mercy!' out of those folds to you. Accept me as your knight, O Princess! Then I shall fight and triumph and wear trophies to the glory of your favor and your beauty."

"If you want to be my knight," said the princess, "then arm yourself as befits you. Cover your head with the menacing battle helmet, take up the real broadsword. Then I will believe in you."

"If you will be my lady," answered Giglio, "Rinaldo's Armida,[8] then be so to the fullest. Put aside this ostentatious finery which infatuates me, which captivates me like perilous magic. This gleaming bloodstain—"

"Are you out of your mind!" cried the princess quickly, and leaving Giglio standing there, she swiftly walked away.

To Giglio it seemed as though it had not been he at all who had been speaking to the princess, as though he had spoken quite involuntarily what he himself did not even understand. He was close to believing that Signor Pasquale and Master Bes-

---

[7] *Biretta:* (Italian) "cap."

[8] In Tasso's poem, *Jerusalem Delivered,* the Crusader knight Rinaldo succumbs to the enchantments of the sorceress Armida.

capi were right in thinking he was a little crazy. But now his extravagant merriment returned as he saw a troop of maskers coming along who in the maddest caricatures represented the most distorted offspring of Fantasy and in whom he immediately recognized his cronies. He joined the hopping and dancing crowd, shouting as he did so: "Go it! Go it! Mad hobgoblin rout! Move, you mighty impish spirits of sauciest mockery! I am all yours now, and you may look upon me as one of your own!"

Among his cronies Giglio thought he recognized also the old man out of whose bottle Brambilla's form had arisen. Before he knew it, he felt himself scizcd by him, spun round in a circle, and into his ears the old man shrilled: "I've got you, brother! I've got you!"

THIRD CHAPTER

Concerning blonds who presume to find Pulcinella boring and insipid. German and Italian senses of humor. How Celionati, sitting in the Caffè Greco, maintained he was not sitting in the Caffè Greco but was making Parisian rappee by the shores of the Ganges. Wonderful tale of King Ophioch who ruled in the land of Urdargarten and of Queen Liris. How King Cophetua married a beggar maid, an aristocratic princess chased after a bad actor, and Giglio girded on a wooden sword but then made a detour around a hundred maskers on the Corso until he finally stopped because his Self had begun to dance.

You blonds! You blue-eyed fellows! You haughty young men at whose 'Good evening, my pretty child!' spoken in a resounding bass voice, the boldest wench takes fright. Can your blood, frozen as it is in eternal frost of winter, ever thaw out in the wild gale of the *tramontana*[1] or in the ardor of a love song? Why boast of your mighty lust for life, of your vivid spirits, when you don't have any sense in you for the maddest, jestingest jest of all jests, such as our blessed carnival offers in fullest measure? When you dare to find even our excellent Pulcinella often boring and insipid, and when you say the most delightful abortions that laughing mockery ever bore are the offspring of a deranged mind?!"

So spoke Celionati in the Caffè Greco[2] where, according to custom, he had gone in the evening and sat down among the German artists who were in the habit of patronizing this house in the Strada Condotti at the same hour and who had just launched into a sharp criticism of the grotesqueries of the carnival.

[1] *Tramontana:* (Italian) "north wind."
[2] The Caffè Greco, located where the Via Condotti opens into the Spanish Square, was a favorite meeting place for Germans traveling in Italy.

157

"How," spoke up the German painter Franz Reinhold, "how can you talk like that, Master Celionati! That doesn't fit in at all with what you usually say in favor of the German mentality and nature. True, you have always reproached us Germans for asking of every joke that it should mean something besides the joke itself, and I will grant you that point, though in a wholly different sense from what you intend. God be your comfort if you should credit us with the stupidity of tolerating irony only if it is allegorical! Then you would be in great error. We see quite clearly that pure jest as such is far more at home among you Italians than among us. I should like, however, to make quite clear to you the distinction I make between your sense of humor and ours, or more properly, between your sense of irony and ours. Now, we were just talking about the mad, grotesque figures running around the Corso; there at least I can more or less make a comparison. When I see a mad fellow like that moving the people to laughter by hideous grimaces, it seems to me as if an archetype, which had become perceptible to him, were speaking though *he* did not understand the words and, as happens in real life when one is struggling to grasp the sense of strange and incomprehensible speech, as if he were involuntarily imitating the gestures of the speaking archetype, although in an exaggerated way on account of the effort it requires.

"Our sense of humor is the speech of the archetype itself, which sounds from within us and inevitably determines the gesture according to that deep-seated principle of irony, just as the submerged rock forces the brook flowing over it to produce rippling waves on its surface. Don't think, Master Celionati, that I have no sense for the farcical which is contained only in the external manifestation and which receives its motivation only externally, or that I do not credit your nation with superior powers of evoking that farcical element into life. But forgive me, Celionati, if I also maintain that a jot of kindly sentiment has to be added to the farcical if it is to be tolerated at all and which I miss in your comic personages. The kindly sentiment which keeps our humor pure is lost in the principle of obscenity which activates your Pulcinella and a hundred other masks of the sort, and then, through all the grotesques and farces there is visible the horrible, ghastly fury of rage, of hatred, and of despair which drives you to madness and murder. When on that carnival day each one carries a candle and each tries to blow out the other's candle, and when the whole Corso, amid the maddest, most extravagant jubilation and the most resounding laughter, quivers with the frenzied cry, 'Ammazzato sia, chi non porta moccolo!' [3] Believe me, Celionati, when I am completely swept away by the insane merriment of the people and blow on all sides of me harder than anyone else and shout 'Ammazzato sia!', uncanny shudders run through me, in the face of which that kindly sentiment peculiar to our German mentality simply cannot survive."

"Kindly sentiment!" said Celionati with a smile. "Kindly sentiment! But tell me, my kindly and sentimental German, what you think of our stage masks, of our Pantalone, Brighella, Tartaglia?"

"Oh," answered Reinhold, "I think those masks open a mine of the most delicious humor, of the most striking irony, of the freest—I might almost say the most impudent—whimsy, although I think they lay better claim to the various external manifestations of human nature than to human nature itself. Or, more briefly and more concisely, lay better claim to men than to man. Moreover, I beg you, Celionati, not to look upon me as insane for doubting somewhat that the men endowed with the most profound sense of humor are to be found among your nation. The invisible church[4] knows no distinction between nations; it has its members everywhere. And, Master Celionati, I may as well tell you that for this long time you and your whole being and conduct have seemed to me most peculiar. The way you carry on in front of the populace as the most fantastic ciarlatano, and then the way you again take pleasure in our company, forgetting everything Italian and delighting us with wonderful stories that penetrate deep into our souls, and then again babbling on and storifying till you enmesh us and hold us ensnared in the strange bonds of magic. The people are indeed right when they decry you as a wizard, but I, for my part, merely think that you belong to the invisible church,

---

[3] Italian for "Slaughter anybody not carrying a taper!"
[4] The invisible church of true artists everywhere.

which numbers some very odd members even if all of them have grown from one torso."

"What," cried Celionati vehemently, "what can you think of me, Mister Painter, what can you think of me, suspect of me, imagine of me? Are you all then so sure that I am sitting here among you and uselessly chattering useless stuff about things which none of you understand in the slightest unless you have gazed into the bright mirror waters of the Urdar Spring[5] or unless Liris has smiled at you?"

"Ho, ho!" they all cried in a medley, "now he's getting around to his old leaps, to his old leaps—on, Mister Wizard! On!"

"Is there any sense among these people?" cried Celionati simultaneously, as he brought his fist down upon the table so violently that everybody suddenly fell silent. "Is there any sense among these people?" he went on more calmly. "What leaps? What dances? I merely ask how you happen to be so convinced that I am actually sitting here among you, carrying on all sorts of conversations that you think you hear with your corporeal ears, though perhaps only a tricksy spirit of the air is teasing you? Who will guarantee you that the Celionati whom you're trying to talk into thinking that Italians don't understand anything about irony, is not strolling right now beside the Ganges, picking fragrant flowers to make Parisian rappee[6] for the nostrils of some mystic idol? Or walking among the dark and gruesome tombs at Memphis to discuss with the most ancient of kings the matter of the little toe of his left foot for medicinal use by the proudest princess on the Argentina stage? Or that he isn't sitting by the Urdar Spring in profound conversation with his closest friend, the mage Ruffiamonte? But hold on! I will actually pretend that Celionati is sitting here in the Caffè Greco and I will tell you about King Ophioch, Queen Liris, and the mirror waters of the Urdar Spring, if you would like to hear about such matters."

"Tell us," said one of the young artists, "do tell us, Celionati. I can see already that this will be one of your stories that are

---

[5] In Norse mythology, the Urdar Spring, so named for one of the three Norns (Fates), lies at the foot of the World Ashtree.

[6] Snuff.

crazy and fantastic enough, but which are very pleasant to hear all the same."

"Just so long," began Celionati, "just so long as none of you thinks I am going to dish out nonsensical fairy tales and none of you doubts but that everything did happen just as I am going to tell it! All doubt will be obviated when I assure you that I have everything from the lips of my friend Ruffiamonte, who is himself in a way the chief personage of the story. It was hardly a couple of centuries ago that we were talking at length about the Urdar Spring as we were walking through the fires of Iceland looking for a talisman born of the flood and the fire. So, ears open! Minds open!"

Here, then, well beloved reader, you must put up with hearing a story which seems to lie outside the area of those events which I have undertaken to relate for you and which stands as an objectionable episode besides. But, just as it often happens that one suddenly arrives at the destination which had been lost from sight by vigorously following the road which seemed to be leading one astray, so it may perhaps also be that this episode is only apparently a wrong path and will lead straight to the core of the main story. Listen, therefore, O my reader, to the wonderful

Story of King Ophioch and Queen Liris

A very long, long time ago, one might almost say in a time that more or less directly followed upon the time primeval the way Ash Wednesday follows Shrove Tuesday, young King Ophioch ruled over the land of Urdargarten. I do not know whether the German Büsching[7] has described the land of Urdargarten with any geographical exactitude, but this much is certain, as the mage Ruffiamonte has assured me a thousand times, that it belonged among the most blessed lands that ever were or ever will be. It had such luxuriant meadow grass and stands of clover that the most finicky kine did not yearn

[7] Anton Friedrich Büsching, geographer, director of Berlin secondary schools, and composer of A New Description of the Earth, published from 1754 to 1792.

beyond their beloved fatherland, as well as imposing forests with trees and plants and superb game and such sweet fragrances that the morning wind and the evening wind just could not get their fill of fondling them. Wine there was, and oil, and fruits of every sort in plenty. Silver-bright streams flowed through the whole land, mountains bestowed largess of gold and silver, mountains which like truly wealthy men clothed themselves very simply in muted gray, and whoever took just a few pains could scrape the most beautiful jewels out of the sand to use, if he chose, for dainty shirt buttons or vest buttons. If, apart from the capital, which was built of marble and alabaster, there was a lack of proper cities of brick, this was due to the lack of culture which did not yet allow people to realize that it is better, after all, to sit in an armchair and be protected by sturdy walls than to dwell in a lowly hut surrounded by rustling bushes beside a murmuring brook and run the risk of having this or that immodest tree hang its leafy branches in through the windows and like an uninvited guest put its word in everywhere, or of having grapevine and ivy playing the wallpaperhanger. Add to this the fact that the inhabitants of the land of Urdargarten were the most excellent patriots, uncommonly loved their king even when he was not right in plain sight, and called out "Long may he live!" on days other than his birthday, and King Ophioch must have been the happiest monarch under the sun. And that he could have been, if only he, and not just he but a great many persons in his country who could be reckoned among the most wise, had not been beset by a certain odd melancholy which would not allow any joy to exist in the midst of all this splendor. King Ophioch was a sensible youth of good judgment and of clear understanding, and he even had poetic sense. This would seem wholly incredible and inadmissible, if it were not conceivable and to be excused on the basis of the epoch in which he lived.

In King Ophioch's soul there may well still have been echoes of that wonderful primeval time of supreme joy when Nature, cherishing and fostering man as her dearest offspring, provided him with an immediate vision of all being and with a comprehension of the highest ideal and of the purest harmony. For often it seemed to him as if lovely voices spoke to him in the mysterious rustling of the forest, in the whispering of the bushes and springs, and as if shimmering arms stretched down from the golden clouds to clasp him, and his heart swelled with ardent yearning. But then again everything would disappear in confused and disordered ruins, the dark and fearful demon would fan him with icy pinions, the same demon who had parted him from his mother, and he saw himself helpless and abandoned by her in her anger. The voice of the forest and of the distant mountains, which usually woke his longing and the sweet intimation of past joy, died away in the mockery of that dark demon. But the hot and searing breath of that mockery roused in King Ophioch's soul the illusion that the demon's voice was the voice of his angered mother who was now seeking to annihilate her own degenerate child.

As we have said, many people in the land understood King Ophioch's melancholy and, understanding it, were themselves seized by it. Most people, however, did not understand that melancholy, least of all the whole state council, who remained healthy to the good of the kingdom.

In this healthy condition, the state council fancied they realized how nothing could rescue King Ophioch from his brooding unless he should be given a pretty, thoroughly cheerful, and contented spouse. Eyes were turned upon Princess Liris, the daughter of a neighboring king. Princess Liris was, in fact, as beautiful as a king's daughter can possibly be thought to be. Despite the fact that everything around her and everything that she saw passed across her mind without a trace, she did laugh constantly, and since no one in the land of Hirdargarten—that was the name of her father's kingdom—could give a reason for this merriment any more than in the land of Urdargarten any reason could be given for King Ophioch's melancholy, the two royal souls seemed on that very account to be made for one another. Moreover, it was the princess's sole pleasure, which really took the form of pleasure, to make nets while surrounded by her ladies-in-waiting, who also had to make nets, just as King Ophioch could find contentment only in stalking the beasts of the forest in total solitude. King Ophioch had not the slightest objection to the spouse proposed for him. The whole marriage seemed to him an indifferent matter of state business, the management of which he entrusted to his ministers who were so eagerly busying themselves about it.

The consummation of the marriage was presently fulfilled amid all the magnificence possible. Everything went off splendidly and successfully except for one little mischance. The court poet at whose head King Ophioch threw the nuptial hymn with which he was about to present him fell into unhappy madness on the spot as a result of fright and anger and imagined himself to be a poetic temperament, a notion which then hindered him from composing any more and which made him unfit for further service as a court poet.

Weeks and moons passed, but no sign of an altered spiritual state manifested itself in King Ophioch. His ministers, who were uncommonly pleased by the laughing Queen, nevertheless continued to comfort the people and themselves by saying: "It will come."

But it didn't come. Every day King Ophioch became more somber and more sad than he had been, and, what was worst of all, a profound aversion was growing up within him against the laughing queen. The latter did not seem to notice this at all, although indeed it could never be fathomed whether she noticed anything whatsoever in the world outside the meshes of her nets.

It befell that King Ophioch, while on a hunt one day, got into a wild and rugged district of the forest where there rose into the air a tower of black stone, old as creation, as if it had sprouted from the cliff. There was a muffled roaring in the treetops and from the deep stone chasm came answering voices howling in the most heartrending sorrow. In this grisly spot King Ophioch's bosom was stirred wondrously. But it seemed to him as if a gleam of hope for reconciliation shone in those horrible sounds of profoundest misery and as if he no longer heard the mocking anger, no, only the moving lament of his mother for her lost and degenerate child, and this lament seemed to give him comfort that his mother would not be angry forever.

As King Ophioch was standing there lost in thought that way, an eagle swooped up and hovered about the ramparts of the tower. Involuntarily King Ophioch seized his crossbow and sped an arrow at the eagle. But instead of hitting it, the arrow lodged in the bosom of a venerable old man whom King Ophioch only then perceived on the ramparts of the tower.

Horror came over King Ophioch as he realized that the tower was the observatory which, as the story had it, the old kings of the land used to climb on mysterious nights and, as sacred intermediaries between the people and the mistress of all being, proclaimed the will and the sayings of the mighty one to the populace. He perceived that he was at the spot which everyone carefully avoided because it was said that the aged mage Hermod stood upon the ramparts of the tower sunken in a thousand-year sleep, and if he were wakened from that sleep, the anger of the elements would boil up, they would enter into combat with one another, and everything would be destroyed in that conflict.

Utterly overwhelmed, King Ophioch was on the point of collapse, when he felt himself gently tapped, and there before him stood the mage Hermod, holding in his hand the arrow that had pierced his bosom. As a gentle smile brightened the solemn and reverend features of his countenance, he said, "You have wakened me from a long, visionary sleep, King Ophioch! I thank you. For it happened at the proper hour. It is now time for me to go to Atlantis and receive from the hand of the high and mighty queen the gift which she promised me as a token of reconciliation and which will take away the annihilating barb, O King, from the sorrow that is rending your heart.

"Thought destroyed contemplation, but from the prism of the crystal into which the fiery flood poured in marriage strife with the antithetic poison, contemplation streams forth newborn, itself an embryo of thought.[8]

"Farewell, King Ophioch. In thirteen moons times thirteen you shall see me again, and I shall bring you the fairest gift from your reconciled mother, a gift which will dissolve your sorrow in supreme joy, a gift in whose presence will melt the icy prison in which your spouse Queen Liris has so long been held captive by the most hostile of all demons. Farewell, King Ophioch."

With these mysterious words the old mage left the young king and disappeared into the depths of the forest.

If King Ophioch had previously been sad and melancholy, he now became much more so. Firmly rooted in his soul were the

[8] These intentionally obscure words are couched in alchemists' terms reminiscent of *Faust*, lines 1040–1049.

words of the aged Hermod. He repeated them for the court astrologer, who was supposed to interpret their incomprehensible meaning to him. The court astrologer, however, declared there was no meaning at all in them, for there was neither prism nor crystal, at least none such as any apothecary knew, composed of fiery flood and antithetic poison; and as for the thought and newborn contemplation that occurred in Hermod's confused discourse, they must remain incomprehensible because no astrologer or philosopher of any honest training would have anything to do with the senseless speech of the rude era to which the mage Hermod belonged. King Ophioch was not only completely dissatisfied with this evasion but flew at the astrologer in great anger, and it was a good thing that he did not happen to have anything at hand to throw at the unfortunate court astrologer's head the way he had thrown that hymn at the court poet. Ruffiamonte maintains that, though there is nothing about it in the chronicle, it is nevertheless certain from folk tradition in Urdargarten that on this occasion King Ophioch called the court astrologer—an ass.

But now that those mystic words of the mage Hermod would not leave the soul of the melancholy young king, he finally decided to find out their significance for himself, cost what it might. On a tablet of black marble, therefore, he caused to be engraved in letters of gold the words: "Thought destroyed contemplation," and the rest of what the mage had gone on to say, and had the tablet set into the wall of a remote and gloomy room of his palace. In front of that tablet he then set himself down on a soft cushioned seat, propped his head in his hand, and, contemplating the inscription, gave himself over to profound meditation.

It befell quite by chance that Queen Liris came into the room where King Ophioch was with his inscription. Despite the fact that she burst out in loud laughter, as was her habit, so that the walls rang, the king seemed absolutely not to notice his dear and cheerful spouse at all. He did not avert his fixed stare from the tablet of black marble. At last Queen Liris also directed her gaze thereat. Scarcely had she read the mysterious words when her laughter fell silent and she sank down wordless on the seat beside the king. After both King Ophioch and Queen

Liris had stared for some time at the inscription, they both began to yawn harder and harder, closed their eyes, and sank into such a profound deathlike sleep that no human skill could wake them from it. People would have taken them for dead and conveyed them to the royal crypt with the customary ceremonies of the land of Urdargarten, had there not been infallible signs of continuing life, such as their faint respiration, their beating pulse, and the color of their faces. Since there was no lack of successors at the time, the state council decided to rule in the stead of the slumbering King Ophioch, and they went about this so skillfully that no one so much as surmised the monarch's lethargy.

Thirteen moons times thirteen had passed since the day when King Ophioch had had the important colloquy with the mage Hermod, and then there was a spectacle more magnificent than any the inhabitants of the land of Urdargarten had ever beheld.

The great mage Hermod came riding along on a fiery cloud surrounded by elemental spirits of both sexes and alighted upon the multihued carpet of a lovely fragrant meadow, while all the harmonies of all of Nature resounded in mystic chords through the air. Above his head there seemed to hover a gleaming star whose fiery glow the eye could not bear to behold. That was a prism of shimmering crystal which, as the mage lifted it high aloft, melted in drops of lightning into the earth to come surging up instantaneously as the merry plash of the most splendid silvery spring.

Everyone crowded around the mage. As the earth spirits dived into the deep and cast up flashing metal flowers, the fire and water spirits surged amid the mighty streams of their elements, the air spirits went rushing and blustering about as if they were fighting and struggling in a jolly tournament. The mage got back in his chariot and spread out his broad mantle. Then a dense mist rose and concealed everything, and when it disappeared, there over the spirits' combat area a magnificent mirror of water had formed, clear as the sky, encircled by glittering minerals and wonderful herbs and flowers, and in its midst the fountain merrily gushed, dispersing the foam-edged waves around as if in mischievous prankish play.

At the same moment as the mage Hermod's mysterious prism

melted into a spring, the royal pair wakened from their long enchanted sleep. Both King Ophioch and Queen Liris hurried up, impelled by irresistible curiosity. They were the first to gaze into the waters. And now as they perceived the gleaming blue sky, the bushes, the trees, the flowers, the whole of Nature, and their very selves in inverted reflection in the infinite depths, it was as if dark veils were rolled up. A splendid new world full of life and joy became clear before their eyes, and with the recognition of that world there was kindled within their hearts a rapture they had never known and never dreamed of before. Long did they gaze, and then they rose, looked at one another, and *laughed*—for one must term "laughter" the physical expression of inner satisfaction as well as of joy at victory by inner spiritual strength. Had not Queen Liris's total transformation of mind been attested by the transfiguration of her countenance, a transformation which now, for the first time conferred a truly heavenly charm upon those fine features, everyone would have had to deduce it anyway from the way she laughed. This laughter was so sky-high away from the laughter with which she used to annoy the king that many shrewd people claimed it really was not she who was laughing but another wonderful being hidden within her. It was the same way with King Ophioch's laughter.

And now when both had laughed in such unique fashion, they exclaimed simultaneously: "Oh, we lay in oppressive dreams in waste and inhospitable alien lands, and we have awakened in our native country! Now we recognize ourselves in ourselves and are no longer orphaned children!"

Then they fell into each other's arms with the expression of the most sincere love. During this embrace everybody who could crowd up gazed into the water. Those who had been infected by the king's melancholy and gazed into the mirror waters, felt the same effects as the royal couple; those who had been merry anyway, however, remained in their former condition. Numerous physicians found the water ordinary, without mineral adjunct, just as many philosophers counseled absolutely against gazing into the watery mirror, because man, when he sees himself and the world upside down, can easily get dizzy. There were even some from the most educated classes of

the realm who maintained there was no Urdar Spring at all—
for king and people immediately christened the splendid water
that had risen from Hermod's mysterious prism the "Urdar
Spring." King Ophioch and Queen Liris both fell at the feet of
the great mage Hermod who had brought them joy and salva-
tion and thanked him in the finest words and phrases at their
disposal. The mage Hermod lifted them up with polite dignity,
clasped first the queen and then the king to his bosom, and
promised to let himself be seen from time to time on the observatory tower on future critical occasions, because he had the
welfare of the land of Urdargarten very much at heart. King
Ophioch absolutely insisted on kissing his noble hand, but that
he would not allow, but rather, rose instantly into the air. From
aloft he cried down in a voice that sounded like heavily struck
metal bells and spoke these words:

"Thought destroys contemplation, and man, once torn from
his mother's breast, staggers in confused illusion, in blind
numbness, without a homeland, until thought's own mirror
image provides thought itself with the awareness that it exists
and that it rules as master in the deepest and richest shaft that
the maternal queen had opened for it, even if it must also obey
as a vassal."

End of the Story of King Ophioch and Queen Liris

Celionati fell silent and the youths also remained sunk in the
silence of contemplation to which they had been moved by the
old *ciarlatano's* tale, which they had imagined would be quite
different.

"Master Celionati," Franz Reinhold finally broke the stillness,
"Master Celionati, your tale smacks of the *Edda*, of the *Voluspá*,
of the Somskritt, of I don't know what all old mystical books.[9]
But if I have understood you aright, the Urdar Spring whereby the inhabitants of the land of Urdargarten were made happy
was none other than what we Germans call humor, that wonderful power of thought born of the most profound contemplation

[9] Oldest of Icelandic poem collections is the *Edda*, its opening piece
being the *Voluspá*, a poem about the beginning and the end of the world.
"Somskritt" is an old-fashioned spelling of Sanskrit, the language of
ancient India.

of Nature and capable of creating its own ironic double, in whose odd tomfooleries he recognizes his own tomfooleries and—I retain the bold word—the tomfooleries of all existence here below, and takes his delight in them. But as a matter of fact, Master Celionati, you have shown by your myth that you have understanding for the humor of others besides that of your carnival. I shall henceforth count you among the invisible church, and I shall bend my knee before you, like King Ophioch before the great mage Hermod, for you are also a mighty wizard."

"What," cried Celionati, "what are you saying about a fairy tale, about a myth? Have I related nothing else, did I intend to relate to you anything other than a pretty story out of the life of my friend Ruffiamonte? You must know that he, my intimate friend, *is* the great mage Hermod who cured King Ophioch of his melancholy. If you won't believe me, you can ask him himself about it all, for he is here and resides in the Pistoja Palace."

Scarcely had Celionati mentioned the Pistoja Palace when everyone recalled that most fantastic of all maskers' processions which had moved into that palace a few days ago, and now they stormed the queer *ciarlatano* with a hundred questions about what there was to it, since they assumed that he, as a fantast, must be better informed than any one else about the fantastic things that had gone on in that procession.

"Without any doubt," cried Reinhold, laughing, "without any doubt the handsome old man in the tulip who was poring over the sciences was your intimate friend, the great mage Hermod or the black-magic artist Ruffiamonte?"

"That," replied Celionati, calmly, "that is the case, my good son. However, it may not yet be the time to say very much about who is residing in the Pistoja Palace. Now, if King Cophetua married a beggar maid, then the great and mighty Princess Brambilla can probably also go chasing after a poor actor."

With that remark Celionati left the coffeehouse, and nobody knew or even had an inkling of what he meant by those final words. But since this was often the case with Celionati's remarks, no one took any special pains to reflect upon them further.

While all this was going on at the Caffè Greco, Giglio was chasing up and down the Corso in his crazy costume. As Princess Brambilla had desired, he had not omitted to don a hat which, with its high projecting brim, looked like a siege helmet and to arm himself with wooden broadsword. His entire being was full of the lady of his heart, but he himself did not know how it could be that it now seemed to him nothing at all unusual or a dreamlike happiness to win the love of the princess, or that in his insolent pride be believed in the inevitability of her becoming his, because she could not do otherwise. And this thought kindled in him a mad merriment which found its outlet in the most exaggerated grimaces, before which he himself cringed with an inner horror.

Princess Brambilla was nowhere to be seen, but Giglio, completely beside himself, went shouting: "Princess! Little dove! Child of my heart! I'll find you yet! I'll find you yet!" and ran like crazy round and round a hundred maskers until a dancing couple caught his eye and enthralled his total attention.

A clownish fellow who was dressed like Giglio to the last detail and who was indeed, as to height, posture, and so forth, his second self, was playing a guitar and at the same time dancing with a very daintily dressed lady who was playing the castanets. If the sight of his dancing double turned Giglio to stone, his heart flamed up anew as he looked at the girl. He thought he had never beheld so much grace and beauty. Every one of her movements betrayed the inspiration of a very special pleasure, and it was precisely that inspiration which lent an ineffable charm to the wild wantonness of her dance.

It could not be denied that by the very mad contrast of the dancing pair there was created a ludicrousness which could not help but move everyone to laughter in the midst of their adoring admiration for the lovely girl. But it was just this feeling, mixed of the most antithetical elements, that kindled within him that same inspiration of a strange and ineffable pleasure by which the girl and the clownish fellow were possessed. A premonition was beginning to dawn on Giglio as to who the dancing lady might be, when a masker at his side said, "That is Princess Brambilla, and she is dancing with her beloved, the Assyrian Prince Cornelio Chiapperi."

FOURTH CHAPTER

Concerning the utilitarian invention of sleep and dreams and what Sancho Panza thinks about the matter. How a Württemberg official fell down stairs and Giglio could not see through his Self. Rhetorical fire screens, double balderdash, and *The White Moor.* How old Prince Bastianello di Pistoja sowed orange pips on the Corso and defended masks. The *beau jour* of homely girls. News of the black-magic witch Circe who tied knots, as well as of the pretty snakeweed that grows in flowery Arcadia. How Giglio stabbed himself from sheer despair, then sat down to table, helped himself without bashfulness, but then wished the princess "Good night."

In a thing which calls itself a *capriccio* but which is as near to a fairy tale as if it were one itself, it should not be surprising to you, well beloved reader, if there is to be found a good deal of bizarre hobgoblinery and dreamlike delusion of the kind the human spirit harbors and cherishes, or, more correctly, if the scene of action is often shifted to the inner selves of the characters. Might that not be just the proper scene, after all? Perhaps you, O my reader, share my opinion to the effect that the human spirit is itself the most wonderful fairy tale that can possibly be. What a magnificent world lies enclosed within our bosoms! No solar orbit hems it in, the inexhaustible wealth of the total visible creation is outweighed by its riches! How dead, how beggarly, how blind as a mole our lives would be if the World Spirit had not equipped us hirelings of Nature with that unfailing diamond mine in our hearts whence in radiance and luster shines forth the wonderful realm that has become our possession! Gifted indeed are those who are clearly aware of that possession! More highly gifted still and blessed are they to be called who are able not only to view the gems of their inner Perus but also know how to bring them forth, cut them, and draw from them a more splendid fire.

Now Sancho held that God should honor the man who invented sleep; he must have been a clever fellow.[1] Much more should he be honored who invented dreams. Not the dreams that rise from our inner selves only when we lie beneath the soft blanket of sleep. No, but that dream which we go on dreaming all our lives, which often takes the oppressive weight of the terrestrial upon its pinions, in the presence of which every bitter grief and every inconsolable lament for cheated hopes falls silent, because it is itself a ray of Heaven in our bosoms that has gleamed forth and with infinite yearning proclaims fulfillment.

These thoughts, well beloved reader, occurred to him who has undertaken to present to you the bizarre *capriccio* about Princess Brambilla, at the moment when he was just going to set about describing the noteworthy state of mind that befell the disguised Giglio Fava when the words were whispered to him: "That is Princess Brambilla, and she is dancing with her beloved, the Assyrian Prince Cornelio Chiapperi." Authors seldom have the self-control to keep from their readers what they think about this or that stage of affairs to which their heroes have arrived. All too willingly they act as a chorus for their own books and term as reflection everything that is not necessary to the story but which can nevertheless stand as a pleasing flourish. So, let the thoughts with which this chapter has begun stand as a pleasing flourish. For as a matter of fact they were as little necessary to the story as they were to the description of Giglio's state of mind, which was by no means so odd or unusual as might be thought from the running start the author has taken.

In short, then! No less a thing occurred to Giglio Fava as he heard those words than that he instantly took himself to be the Assyrian Prince Cornelio Chiapperi who was dancing with Princess Brambilla. Any able philosopher of any solid experience will be able to explain all this so easily that fifth graders cannot help but understand the experiment with the inner mind. Such a psychologist will hardly be able to do better that cite the case of the Württemberg official in Mauchardt's

[1] A reference to *Don Quixote*, Part II, chapter 68.

Repertorium of Empirical Psychology[2] who fell downstairs while drunk and then pitied his secretary, who was accompanying him, for having fallen so hard. "To judge," the psychologist then goes on to say, "from everything we have heard up to now about this Giglio Fava, he is suffering from a condition wholly comparable to that of inebriation and, in a sense, a kind of spiritual drunkenness brought on by the nervous strain of certain eccentric ideas about his Self, and inasmuch as actors in particular are very much inclined to this kind of intoxication—etc."

So Giglio took himself to be the Assyrian Prince Cornelio Chiapperi. And if this was nothing unusual, it would still be more difficult to explain whence came the rare and never-before-felt joy that penetrated his inner being with flaming ardor. Louder and louder he struck upon the strings of his guitar, madder and more wanton became the grimaces and leaps of the wild dance. But his Self stood opposite him, and dancing and leaping in exactly the same way and making just such faces as he did, kept dealing him blows through the air with his wooden broadsword. Brambilla had vanished.

"Aha!" thought Giglio, "none but my Self is to blame for my not seeing my fiancée, the princess. I cannot see through my Self, and my accursed Self is trying to attack me with a dangerous weapon, but I shall play and dance it to death; only then will I be myself and the princess be mine!"

During the course of these somewhat confused thoughts, Giglio's leaps kept getting more frenzied, but at that moment his Self's wooden sword hit his guitar so hard that it smashed in a thousand pieces and Giglio ungently fell over backwards to the ground. The bellowing laughter of the crowd that had gathered around the dancers woke Giglio from his reverie. In his fall, his spectacles and mask had fallen off, people recognized him, and a hundred voices shouted, "*Bravo, bravissimo, Signor Giglio!*" Giglio picked himself up and rushed away, for it suddenly occurred to him that it was highly improper for a tragic actor to have given the people a grotesque exhibition. Arriv-

[2] Immanuel David Mauchardt's (1764–1826) *Allgemeine Repertorium für empirische Psychologie und verwandte Wissenschaften*, Volume I, under the heading of "Loss of personality in drunkenness."

ing at his residence, he threw off the crazy mask, wrapped himself in a *tabarro* and returned to the Corso.

In wandering back and forth he finally came up in front of the Pistoja Palace, and here he felt himself suddenly seized from behind, and a voice whispered to him, "If gait and stance do not deceive me, it is you, my worthy Signor Giglio Fava?" Giglio recognized Abbate[3] Antonio Chiari. At the sight of the abbate he suddenly recalled the whole splendid former time when he was still playing tragic roles and then, when he had removed his cothurni,[4] he used to sneak up the narrow stairs to his lovely Giacinta. Abbate Chiari—perhaps a forebear of the celebrated Chiari who feuded with Count Gozzi and was forced to lay down his weapons[5]—had from his youth displayed no small energy of mind and fingers in the composition of tragedies which were, inventionwise, stupendous and which were pleasing and gracious insofar as their execution was concerned. He carefully avoided having any ghastly event actually take place before the eyes of the spectators except under mild and conciliatory circumstances, and all horrors of any hideous action he so involved in the sticky glue of so many fine words and phrases that the audiences took the sweet pap without any horror and never got the taste of the bitter kernel. He could even advantageously make use of the flames of hell as a cheerful backdrop by placing in front of them the chrism-drenched fire screen of his rhetoric, and into the smoky waves of Acheron he poured the rose water of his Martellian verses[6] to make the infernal river flow gently and smoothly and become a

[3] *Abbate* or *abate* (Italian): "priest" or an unordained ex-seminarian who is allowed to wear ecclesiastical garb.

[4] The high shoes worn by tragic actors on the Greek and Roman stages of antiquity.

[5] Pietro (not Antonio) Chiari (1711–1785) was denounced by Count Gozzi as "the most bombastic and highfalutin writer of the century" and forced to retire from the theater in 1762. By coincidence, his name "Chiari" is the Italian word for "clear," so that it lends itself very well to Hoffmann's caricature of a shallow eighteenth-century rationalist writing genteel tragedies in the vein of a second-rate Voltaire. Gozzi's plays are, of course, the very core of the repertory of Princess Brambilla's troupe.

[6] The name of Pier Jacopo Martello (1665–1727) was attached to a fourteen-syllable verse type used by the real Chiari and other tragedy writers.

poet's river. Things like that please a lot of people and so it was no wonder that Abbate Antonio Chiari was to be termed a beloved poet. And if, besides, he had a special knack for writing what are called grateful roles, it could hardly be otherwise but that the poetic abbate also became the idol of actors. Some witty Frenchman or other has said that there are two sorts of balderdash, one which readers and hearers do not understand and a second and higher kind which the creator—poet or novelist—does not understand.[7] To this latter and more sublime variety belongs the dramatic balderdash of which most of the so-called grateful roles in tragedy consist. Applauded most are the speeches full of resounding statements which neither the hearer nor the actor understands and which the poet himself did not understand. Creating such balderdash, that was what the Abbate Chiari understood superbly, just as Giglio Fava possessed a particular flair for reciting it and for making such faces and getting into such frightfully contorted postures as he did so that on that very account the audiences cried aloud in tragic rapture. Both Giglio and Chiari stood, therefore, in an extremely pleasing mutual relationship and respected each other beyond measure. It just could not be otherwise.

"It's a good thing," said the abbate, "it's a good thing that I finally come upon you, Signor Giglio! Now I can find out from your very self all the things that people have been feeding me as crumbs now and again about your deeds and doings, and crazy and silly enough that all is, too. Tell me, they've been giving you a rough time of it, haven't they? That ass of an impresario drove you off the stage because he took for insanity the inspiration my tragedies inspired in you, because you didn't want to speak any other verses but mine. It is wicked, as you know. The brainless man has completely given up tragedy and puts nothing on his stage but those ridiculous mask-pantomimes which mortally revolt me. Therefore not one of my tragedies will that most simple-minded of all impresarios accept any more, though I can assure you, Signor Giglio, as an honorable man, that in my best works I have succeeded in showing the Italians what a tragedy really is. As for the ancient tragedians,

[7] Hoffmann paraphrases a remark of Nicolas Boileau-Despréaux (1636–1711).

I mean Aeschylus, Sophocles, etc.—you no doubt have heard of them—it goes without saying that their harsh, uncouth manner is totally unaesthetic and to be excused only on the score of the childhood status of art at that time, but remains wholly indigestible to us. Nor will there be much talk any more either about Trissino's *Sophonisbe* and Speroni's *Canace,*[8] those products of our older poetic era which have been touted as masterpieces because of incomprehension, when once my plays have educated the people in the starkness and overwhelming power of the genuinely tragic, which is produced by expression. Only for the moment it is odious that not a single theater will produce my plays since your former impresario, the rascal, has switched horses. Just wait! *Il trotto d'asino dura poco.*[9] Your impresario will presently fall on his face, together with his Arlecchino and Pantalone and Brighella and all the rest of the vile offspring of base delirium, and then—indeed, Signor Giglio, your retirement from the stage was a dagger-thrust to my heart, for no actor on earth has done so much toward grasping my very original, unheard-of ideas, as you have—but let us get out of this wild mob which is deafening me. Come with me to my residence. There I shall read you my latest tragedy, which will occasion you the greatest astonishment you have ever felt. I have entitled it *Il Moro bianco* (*The White Moor*). Do not be put off by the oddness of the name. It reflects completely the extraordinary, the unheard-of quality of the play."

With the garrulous abbate's every word, Giglio felt further withdrawn from the tense state in which he had found himself. His whole heart warmed with joy when he thought of himself once more as a tragic hero declaiming the incomparable verses of the Abbate Antonio Chiari. Very urgently he asked the poet whether there was a really fine and grateful role in the *Moro bianco* which he could play.

"Have I," replied the abbate in some heat, "have I ever created any but grateful roles in any tragedy? It is a misfortune

[8] Giangiorgio Trissino (1478–1550) wrote the tragedy *Sofonisba* (1515), the first Renaissance play based on "Aristotle's rules" and the beginning of the long classical tradition usually thought of as French. Sperone Speroni's *Canace* (1546) followed in the same tradition.

[9] Italian for "A donkey's trot does not last long."

that my plays cannot be acted by masters right down to the smallest role. In the *Moro bianco,* there is a slave who, just before the beginning of the catastrophe, speaks the lines:

Ah! giorno di dolori! crudel inganno!
Ah signore infelice, la tua morte
mi fa piangere e subito partire![10]

He then actually departs swiftly and does not appear again. The role is slight in scope, I confess, but you can trust me, Signor Giglio, that it takes almost a lifetime for the best actor to deliver those lines in the spirit in which I felt them and composed them and in which they must inevitably enchant the audience and sweep them away to the maddest rapture."

In the course of this conversation both the abbate and Giglio had come to the Via del Babuino[11] where the abbate lived. The stairs they climbed were so like a chicken roost that, for a second time, Giglio thought vividly of Giacinta and wished in his heart he would chance upon that lovely girl rather than upon the abbate's *White Moor.*

The abbate lighted two candles, moved up an armchair to the table for Giglio, drew forth a rather corpulent manuscript, sat down opposite Giglio, and very solemnly began: *Il Moro bianco, tragedia,* etc.

The first scene began with a long monologue by some important personage of the play who spoke of the weather, of the hoped-for yield of the impending grape harvest, and then stated observations on the inadmissibility of fratricide.

Giglio himself could not understand how it was that the abbate's verses, which he had formerly considered stupendous, today seemed so trivial, so silly, and so boring. Indeed, although the abbate read everything with the ringing and mighty voice of the most exaggerated eloquence so that the walls quivered, Giglio nevertheless fell into a dreamy state in which oddly there came to mind everything that had happened to him since the

---

[10] Italian for "Ah, day of sorrows! Cruel deception! Ah, ill-fortuned lord, thy death makes me weep and depart forthwith."

[11] Italian for "Street of the Baboon," the actual name of the street leading to the Spanish Square in Rome.

day the Pistoja Palace received into itself that most fantastic of all masked processions. Abandoning himself wholly to these thoughts, he sank deep back into the recess of the armchair, crossed his arms, and allowed his head to sink further and further down upon his chest.

A stout blow on his shoulder wrenched him from his dreamy thoughts. "What!" angrily shrieked the abbate who had jumped up and dealt him the blow, "what! I do believe you are asleep! You don't want to hear my *Moro bianco*? Ha! Now I understand everything. Your impresario was right to drive you away, for you have turned into a miserable scamp without sense or understanding for the highest in poetry. Do you realize that your fate is now decided, that you will never again be able to rise out of the slime in which you have sunk? You went to sleep over my *Moro bianco*. That is a crime never to be atoned for, a sin against the Holy Ghost. Go to the Devil!"

Giglio was very startled by the abbate's extravagant anger. Humbly and plaintively he represented to him that it took a strong, firm soul to grasp his tragedies, but that as far as he, Giglio, was concerned, his entire inner being was crushed and bruised by the events, some of them oddly spectral, some of them unfortunate, in which he had been involved these latter days.

"Believe me," said Giglio, "believe me, Signor Abbate, a mysterious fate has taken hold of me. I am like a broken zither, incapable of receiving harmonious sound into me or of giving forth harmonious sound out of me. If you fancied I went to sleep during your magnificent verses, this much is certain, that a morbid, uncontrollable drowsiness so overcame me that even the most powerful speeches in your incomparable *White Moor* seemed flat and tedious to me."

"Are you mad?" shrieked the abbate.

"But don't get so angry," continued Giglio, "I honor you, after all, as the supreme master whom I have to thank for my entire art, and I have come to you for advice and help. Permit me to relate to you everything that has befallen me, and support me in my supreme distress. Arrange it so that I may stand in the sunlit radiance of the fame in which your *White Moor* will shine and so that I may recover from the worst of all fevers!"

The abbate was soothed by this speech of Giglio's and allowed himself to be told everything, about the crazy Celionati, about Princess Brambilla, etc.

When Giglio had finished, the abbate, after allowing himself a few moments for profound meditation, began in a solemn and serious voice: "From all you have told me, Giglio my son, I rightly gather that you are completely innocent. I forgive you, and so that you may perceive that my magnanimity and my goodness of heart are boundless, be yours through me the supreme good fortune that can befall you in your earthly course: accept the role of the *Moro bianco,* and may the most ardent longing of your heart for the highest things be gratified when you enact it. But, O my son Giglio, you lie in the traps of the Devil. An infernal cabale against the highest things in the poetic art, against my tragedies, against me, is trying to use you like a lifeless instrument. Have you never heard about old Prince Bastianello di Pistoja who used to live in that old palace where the masked blackguards went in and who, many years ago now, vanished from Rome without a trace? Well, that old Prince Bastianello was a pretty foolish chap and peculiar in a foolish way in all he said and did. For instance, he claimed to be the offspring of a royal line of a far-off and unknown country and to be three or four hundred years old, although I myself knew the priest who had baptized him here in Rome. He often used to talk about visits he received in a mysterious fashion from his family, and, as a matter of fact, the most fantastic characters were often suddenly seen in his house, and they disappeared again just as suddenly as they had appeared. Is there anything more easy than to dress servants and maids in a strange way? For that was all those characters were which the stupid populace gaped at full of astonishment, and they took the prince for something very special, in fact even for a wizard. He did foolish things enough, and this much is certain, that once at carnival time he strewed orange pips in the middle of the Corso, out of which cute little *pulcinelle*[12] sprang up, to the jubilation of the crowd, and he said those were the sweetest fruits of the Romans. But why should I bore you with this crazy nonsense of the prince's and not rather tell

[12] Italian for "little clown puppets."

you straight off what it is that makes him the most dangerous man there is?

"Can you imagine it! The accursed old man had as his aim to undermine all good taste in literature and art. Can you imagine it, especially insofar as the theater is concerned, he took up the defense of masks and was going to concede validity only to the ancient tragedy, and then he talked about a variety of tragedy such as only an unhinged brain could dream up. Actually, I never did rightly understand what he wanted, but it practically amounted to his maintaining that the supremely tragic must be produced by a particular kind of jest. And—no, it is unbelievable, it is all but impossible to say—my tragedies—you understand?—*my* tragedies he said were uncommonly funny, although in a different way, because the tragic oratory in them involuntarily parodied itself. But what can absurd ideas and opinions accomplish? If the prince had only been satisfied with that! But as a matter of fact, as a matter of cruel fact, his hatred passed over to me and my tragedies! Still, before you came to Rome, the most horrible thing happened to me. The most magnificent of my tragedies—I will not count the *Moro bianco* —*Lo spettro fraterno vendicato,*[13] was being given. The actors outdid themselves. Never had they so grasped the inner significance of my words, never had they been so genuinely tragic in movement and posture. Let me take this occasion to tell you, Signor Giglio, that in the matter of your gestures and particularly of your postures, you are still somewhat behind. Signor Zechielli, my tragic actor of the time, was capable of spreading his legs, rooting his feet to the ground, standing firm, raising his arms in the air, and then turning his body little by little until he could face back toward the rear, and thus in gesture and facial play appear to the audience with the dual effect of a Janus. A thing like that frequently has the most striking effect, but it must be done each time I write: 'He begins to despair.' Put that in your pipe and smoke it, my good son, and take the trouble to despair like Signor Zechielli!

[13] Italian for *The Fraternal Shade Avenged*. This imaginary title may parody the popular German "fate tragedies" of Hoffmann's day, such as Adolf Müllner's *Guilt*. They were the immediate offspring of the "Gothic novel."

"Now! I return to my *spettro fraterno.* The performance was the most excellent I ever saw, and yet with every speech of my hero the audience burst out in uncontrolled laughter. When I glimpsed Prince Pistoja in the loge intoning that laughter every time, I had no doubt at all but that he was the one who—God knows on account of what hellish wile and guile—was doing me that frightful wrong. How glad I was when the prince disappeared from Rome! But his spirit lives on in that accursed old *ciarlatano,* in that crazy Celionati, who has already tried, though in vain, to make my tragedies ludicrous on the marionette stage. It is only too certain that Prince Bastianello is also haunting Rome again, for that is the significance of the crazy masquerade's moving into his palace. Celionati is laying snares for you in order to harm me. He has already succeeded in getting you off the boards and in destroying your impresario's tragedy. Now you are supposed to be diverted entirely from art by having all sorts of crazy stuff put in your head, phantom princesses, grotesque specters, and the like. Take my advice, Signor Giglio, you just stay home, drink more water than wine, and study with the greatest care my *Moro bianco,* which I will give you to take along. Only in the *Moro bianco* is there comfort and peace, and then fortune, honor, and fame to be sought and found for you. Farewell, Signor Giglio!"

Next morning Giglio started to do as the abbate had bidden him, namely, to study the excellent tragedy of the *Moro bianco,* but he just could not bring himself to it because all the letters on every page melted away before his eyes into the shape of the lovely and charming Giacinta Soardi.

"No!" cried Giglio finally with impatience, "No! I can't stand it any longer, I must go and see her, that lovely girl. I know she still loves me, and in spite of all her *smorfia,* she won't be able to conceal it when she sees me again. Then maybe I shall get rid of this fever which that accursed fellow Celionati has hexed me with, and from the mad hurly-burly of all these dreams and fancies I shall arise newborn, as the *Moro bianco,* like the phoenix from its ashes! Bless you, Abbate Chiari, you have led me back to the right path!"

Immediately Giglio dressed up in his best to betake himself to Master Bescapi's residence, where his girl, so he thought,

was now to be found. In the act of stepping forth from his door
he suddenly felt the effects of the *Moro bianco* which he had
meant to read. Like a stark fever chill, tragic oratory struck him.

"What," he cried, as he thrust his right foot far forward,
threw his shoulders back, and stretched forth both arms,
spreading his fingers wide apart as though to ward off a ghost,
"what if she no longer loved me? If, lured by the magic illusions of the Orcus of the genteel world, intoxicated by the
Lethe potion of oblivion in cessation of thought of me, she
has actually forgotten me? If a rival—ghastly thought which
black Tartarus bore from chasms pregnant with death! Ha!
Despair—murder and death! Out with thee, lovely friend, who
dost atone all shame in rosy fire of blood, who givest peace and
consolation and—*vengeance!*"

These last words Giglio bellowed so the whole house shook.
Simultaneously he reached for the naked dagger lying on the
table and thrust it home.

But it was only a stage dagger.

Master Bescapi seemed not a little astonished when Giglio
inquired for Giacinta. He claimed to know absolutely nothing
about her having ever lived in his house, and all Giglio's asseverations of having seen her on the balcony a few days before
and spoken with her, did not avail in the least. Rather, Bescapi cut the whole conversation off and asked with a smile
how the recent bloodletting had agreed with Giglio. As soon
as Giglio heard bloodletting mentioned, he ran headlong away.

As he was going across the Spanish Square he saw an old
woman striding along ahead of him, toiling under the weight
of a covered basket, and he recognized her as old Beatrice.
"Ha," he murmured, "you shall be my guiding star, I am going
to follow you." Not a little astonished was he that the old
woman stole rather than walked toward the street where Giacinta used to live, when she stopped in front of Signor Pasquale's house and set down the heavy basket. At that moment
she caught sight of Giglio, who had been following close behind her.

"Ha!" she cried aloud, "Ha! my sweet Mister Good-for-nothing, so you finally put in an appearance again? Now you are a
handsome, loyal lover, chasing around from pillar to post

where you don't belong and forgetting your girl in the fine and merry time of the carnival! Now just help me carry up this heavy basket and then you can see whether Giacinta has saved up yet a few boxes on the ear for you to steady your wobbly head."

Giglio heaped the bitterest reproaches on the old woman for fobbing him off with the silly lie that Giacinta was in jail. The old woman, on the other hand, claimed not to know the slightest thing about it and maintained that Giglio was only imagining all that; Giacinta had never left her room in Signor Pasquale's house, and had been busier during the carnival than ever before. Giglio rubbed his brow and tweaked his nose, as if trying to wake himself from sleep.

"It is only too certain," he said, "that either I am in a dream now, or I have been dreaming the wildest dream all the time."

"Be so kind," the old woman interrupted him, "be so kind as to take hold! By the weight on your back you will best be able to judge whether you are dreaming or not."

With no further ado, Giglio shouldered the basket and climbed the narrow stairs with the most remarkable emotions in his heart.

"What in the world do you have in this basket?" he asked the old woman who was walking up ahead of him.

"Stupid question!" replied the latter. "I suppose you never realized before that I have been to market to buy things for my little Giacinta? And besides, we are expecting guests today."

"Guests?" asked Giglio in a long-drawn tone.

But at that moment they had reached the top. The old woman bade Giglio set the basket down and go into the room, where he would find Giacinta.

Giglio's heart was pounding with fearful expectation and sweet anxiety. He knocked softly and opened the door. There sat Giacinta, busily working as usual, at the table, which was piled high with flowers, ribbons, and all sorts of materials.

"Ah!" cried Giacinta as she looked at Giglio with flashing eyes. "Ah! Signor Giglio, where do you come from again? I thought you had left Rome long ago?"

Giglio found his girl so beyond all measure pretty that he stood there in the doorway completely nonplussed and incapable of any word. There actually seemed to be a very particular magic of grace shed over her whole person. A higher flush glowed on her cheeks, and her eyes—yes, her eyes especially—flashed, as we have said, right into Giglio's heart. All that could be left to say was that Giacinta was having her *beau jour*. Since this French expression is no longer admissible nowadays, let it be merely remarked in passing that *beau jour* was not only the exact phrase but also appropriate. Every nice young lady of a little beauty, or even of passable homeliness, whether impelled to it from within or from without, has a right to think with more animation than usual: "I am pretty as a picture just the same!" and to be convinced with that magnificent thought and with the sublime contentment of her inner being that her *beau jour* came of its own accord.

At last, quite beside himself, Giglio threw himself on his knees at his girl's feet and seized her hand with a tragic: "My Giacinta! My sweet life!" But all of a sudden he felt a deep needle-thrust pierce his finger so that he jumped up for pain and felt obliged to execute a few hops with a cry of "Devil! Devil!" Giacinta burst into hearty laughter, but then said very quietly and calmly, "You see, dear Signor Giglio, that was for your rude and violent behavior. Otherwise it was very nice of you to call on me, because soon you may not be able, perhaps, to see me this way without any ceremony. I permit you to stay. Sit down there on the chair opposite me and tell me how things have been going with you this long time and what fine new roles you are playing, and the like. You know I like to hear about those things, and if you don't fall into your accursed tearful rhetoric that Signor Abbate Chiari has hexed onto you—may God not withhold him from everlasting bliss on that account! —you are tolerably pleasant to listen to."

"My Giacinta," said Giglio in the pain of love and of the needle-prick, "my Giacinta, let us forget all the torment of separation! They have come back, the sweet and blessed hours of happiness and love—!"

"I don't know," Giacinta interrupted him, "I don't know what silly stuff you are talking. You speak of the torment of separation, and I can assure you that I for my part, if I ever really did think you had separated from me, have felt nothing over it, least of all any torment. If you call blessed hours the ones in which you strove to bore me, I don't think that they will ever come back again. But confidentially, Signor Giglio, you have many things about you that please me, oftentimes you have not been undear to me, and so I shall permit you to see me in the future as often as it may come about, although the circumstances which forbid all intimacy and which require a distance between us, may impose some constraint upon you."

"Giacinta!" cried Giglio, "What strange words!"

"Nothing strange," replied Giacinta, "is involved here. Just sit calmly down, good Giglio. This is perhaps the last time that we shall be so intimate with one another—but you may count on my favor always. For, as I said, I shall never withdraw the goodwill that I have borne you."

Beatrice came in with a couple of plates in her hand whereon lay the most delicious fruit; she also had a quite conspicuous bottle clutched under her arm. The contents of the basket seemed to have been disclosed. Through the open door Giglio saw a cheerful fire crackling on the hearth, and the kitchen table was full and loaded down with all sorts of dainties.

"Giacinta, child," said Beatrice, smirking, "if our little meal is to do the guest proper honor, I shall have need of some more money."

"Take as much as you need, old woman," answered Giacinta as she handed the old woman a small purse out of whose meshes pretty ducats glinted.

Giglio froze, as in the purse he recognized the twin of the purse which, as he could not help but think, Celionati had stuck into his own pocket and whose ducats were on the wane. "Is this an illusion of hell?" he shouted, swiftly snatched the purse from the old woman's hand, and held it close before his eyes. But he sank back in the chair, completely overcome when on the purse he read the legend: "Remember your dream image!"

"Aha!" the old woman growled at him as she took back the purse which Giglio was holding out to her with outstretched arm, "Aha! Mister Have-not! Such a sight must throw you completely into astonishment and amazement? But listen to the lovely music and feel pleasure at it." And with that she rattled the purse so the gold in it rang, and left the room.

"Giacinta," said Giglio, wholly dissolved in inconsolable grief, "Giacinta, what a ghastly, horrible mystery. Pronounce it! Pronounce my death!"

"You are the same old Giglio still," replied Giacinta as she held toward the window the fine needle between her pointed fingers and skillfully thrust the silver thread through the eye. "It has become so commonplace with you to go into ecstasies over everything that you walk around in one continuous tragedy with still more tedious oh's and ah's and alas's! There is no question here of ghastly and horrible things, and if you could possibly be nice and not gesticulate like a half-insane person, I should like to tell you about a lot of things."

"Speak! Give me my death!" muttered Giglio to himself with a half-choked voice.

"Do you remember," began Giacinta, "do you remember, Signor Giglio, what you once told me—it's no very long time ago—about the miracle of a young actor? You termed such an excellent hero a walking adventure of love, a living romance on two feet, and I don't know what all besides. Now I shall make the claim that a young milliner, on whom Heaven bestowed a pretty figure, a nice face, and above all that inner magical power by which a girl first really takes on the form of an actual girl, is to be termed a still greater marvel. Such a nestling of kindly Nature is truly a lovely adventure hovering in the air, and the narrow stairway up to her is the heavenly ladder that leads up to the kingdom of childishly daring dreams of love. She is herself the fragile mystery of feminine adornment which casts a lovely spell over you men, now in the shimmering splendor of wanton color, now in the mild light of white moonbeams, rosy mist, and blue fragrances of evening. Lured by yearning and desire, you approach the wonderful mystery, you see the mighty fairy in the midst of her magical equipment; but then, at the touch of her little white finger, every point of lace becomes a net of love and every bow she ties becomes a snare in which you are entrapped. And in her eyes is mirrored all the delicious folly of love, which there recognizes itself and in itself finds heart-warming joy. You hear your own sighs re-echo from the inmost being of the beloved, but softly and graciously, as the yearning echo calls the lover from far-off magic mountains. Rank and

class are of no account. To the wealthy prince as to the poor
actor, the little room of the charming Circe is the flowery and
blooming Arcadia amid the inhospitable desert of his life and
the place to which he flees for refuge. And if a little snakeweed
also blooms amid the beautiful flowers of that Arcadia, what
does it matter? It is of the seductive variety that blossoms
magnificently and smells more fragrant still."

"Oh, yes," Giglio interrupted Giacinta, "oh, yes, and out of
the very blossom darts the little beast whose name the prettily
blooming and sweetly smelling herb bears, and suddenly stings
with its tongue like a sharp needle."

"Every time," Giacinta continued, "any strange man who has
no business being in that Arcadia, oafishly pokes his nose in."

"Nicely put," Giglio went on, full of annoyance and wrath,
"nicely put, my lovely Giacinta! I really have to admit that during the time I have not seen you you have gotten clever in a
wonderful way. You philosophize about yourself in a manner
that astonishes me. Apparently you are uncommonly pleased
with yourself as an enchanting Circe in the charming Arcadia
of your garret room, which Master Costumer Bescapi does not
cease to supply with all the necessary magical equipment."

"It may be," Giacinta went on to say very calmly, "it may be
that things are going with me exactly as with you. I too have had
all sorts of pretty dreams. But, my good Giglio, all I said about
the nature of a pretty milliner, take half of that at least for jest,
for roguish teasing, and apply it all the less to me since here
is perhaps my last job of millinery work. Don't be startled, my
good Giglio! But it is very easily possible that on the last day
of the carnival I shall exchange this shabby dress for a purple
mantle and this little bench for a throne!"

"Heaven and Hell!" cried Giglio, jumping up and hitting his
forehead with his clenched fist, "Heaven and Hell! Death and
corruption! Then it's true what that deceitful rascal whispered
in my ear? Ha! Open, flame-spewing abyss of Orcus! Arise,
black-plumaged spirits of Acheron! Enough!"

Giglio passed on into the ghastly monologue of despair from
some tragedy or other of the Abbate Chiari's. Giacinta had mem-
orized this monologue down to the last verse from Giglio's having declaimed it a hundred times before, and without looking

up from her work she prompted the despairing lover with every word whenever he got stuck here or there. Finally he drew his dagger, thrust it into his heart, fell so that the room resounded, got up again, dusted himself off, wiped the sweat from his brow, and asked with a smile: "That shows the master, eh, Giacinta?"

"Absolutely," replied Giacinta without budging, "absolutely. You tragedized excellently, good Giglio. But now, I think, we shall sit down to supper."

Old Beatrice had meanwhile set the table, carried in a couple of wonderful smelling dishes, and placed the mysterious phial alongside of gleaming crystal glasses. As soon as Giglio caught sight of this he seemed beside himself.

"Ha! The guest, the prince—what is happening to me? Heaven! I wasn't playing a role, I really was in despair—yes, you have plunged me in sheer and total despair, faithless deceiver, serpent, basilisk, crocodile! But, vengeance! vengeance!" And with that he flourished the stage dagger which he had picked up off the floor.

But Giacinta, who had thrown her sewing down on the sewing table and stood up, took him by the arm and said, "Don't be an oaf, good Giglio. Give that murder weapon to old Beatrice for her to whittle into toothpicks and sit down with me to supper. For, when all is said and done, you are the only guest I have been waiting for."

Suddenly placated, patience itself, Giglio allowed himself to be led up to the table, and in *that* fray did himself no further violence.

Giacinta went on very calmly and cheerfully telling about her impending happiness and assured Giglio over and over again that she absolutely would not fall into excessive pride and forget Giglio's face entirely, but rather that if he were to show himself to her even from afar, she would most certainly remember him and would pass him many a ducat so he would never lack for rosemary-colored stockings and perfumed gloves. Into Giglio's head, once he had drunk a few glasses of wine, came once again the whole wonderful fable of Princess Brambilla, and he amicably assured her in turn that he highly esteemed Giacinta's kind and heartfelt thoughts; but as far as the pride and the ducats were concerned, he would not be able to make any use of them inasmuch as he, Giglio, was himself on the verge of jumping with both feet into a princedom.

He now related how the most aristocratic and the wealthiest princess in the world had already selected him for her cavalier, and how he hoped to be able to say *vale* forever to the wretched life he had been leading up to now, as the spouse of his princely lady even before the end of the carnival. Giacinta seemed immensely pleased at Giglio's good fortune, and both now chatted on very contentedly about their future time of joy and riches.

"I only hope," said Giglio finally, "that the kingdoms which we are to rule over in the future will just border on each other, so we can maintain the relationship of good neighbors. But if I am not mistaken, the princedom of my adored princess lies on beyond India, just to the left in the direction of Persia as you go around the earth."

"What a shame," replied Giacinta, "'I too shall probably have to go very far away, because the kingdom of my princely consort is said to be right near Bergamo. But it can probably be arranged just the same for us to be and to remain neighbors."

Both Giacinta and Giglio agreed that their future realms would absolutely have to be moved to the neighborhood of Frascati.

"Good night, dear Princess," said Giglio.

"Sleep well, dear Prince," answered Giacinta.

And thus they parted amicably and peaceably as evening came on.

FIFTH CHAPTER

How Giglio arrived at a wise decision at a time of total aridity of the human mind, pocketed the purse of Fortunatus, and cast a proud glance at the humblest of all costumers. The Pistoja Palace and its marvels. A reading by the sage from the tulip. King Solomon the Spirit-Prince and Princess Mystilis. How an old mage threw on a black nightgown, put a sable cap on his head, and with his beard unkempt, delivered prophecies in bad verse. Unfortunate fate of a greenhorn. How the kind reader does not find out in this chapter what ensued upon Giglio's dance with the unknown beauty.

As it says in some book or other ponderous with worldly wisdom, everyone who is endowed with imagination of his own is supposed to suffer from a mental derangement that is forever rising and falling like flood and ebb. The time of the former, when the waves come rushing higher and stronger, is the time of descending night, while the morning hours over the cup of coffee directly after waking pass for the lowest point of the ebb. The book therefore also gives the sensible advice to make use of that moment of clearest and most resplendent sobriety for the most important concerns of life. Only in the morning, for example, should one get married, read bad reviews, make a will, beat a servant, etc.

It was in that fine ebb time, when the human mind is permitted enjoyment of total aridity, that Giglio Fava was shocked by his folly and simply did not know himself why he had not long since been able to do the thing for which the invitation, so to speak, had been shoved right under his nose.

"It is only too obvious," he thought to himself in the cheerful awareness of full rationality, "it is only too obvious that old Celionati is half insane and that he not only takes uncommon pleasure in that insanity but is also definitely out to involve other quite sensible people in it. But it is also quite as obvious that the most beautiful and wealthiest of all princesses, the divine Brambilla, rode into the Pistoja Palace, and—O Heaven and earth! can that hope very well deceive, confirmed as it is by intimations, dreams, and by the roselike lips of the most charming of all masks, that she has directed the sweet love-ray of her heavenly eyes upon fortunate me! Veiled and unrecognized behind the closed lattice of a loge she glimpsed me when I was playing some prince or other, and her heart was mine! Can she then very well approach me by a direct path? Does the lovely creature not need intermediaries, confidants, to spin the thread which will finally be tied in the sweetest of knots? Be that as it may, Celionati is undoubtedly the one who is supposed to lead me to the princess's arms. But instead of proceeding right along the direct path, he plunges me head over heels into a whole ocean of madness and hoaxing, tries to talk me into believing that, disguised in a caricature of a costume, I have to go on looking on the Corso for the most beautiful of princesses, tells me about Assyrian princes, about magicians—away, away with all that crazy stuff, away with the insane Celionati! What is to prevent me from dressing myself up nicely and walking right into the Pistoja Palace and throwing myself at the feet of Her Most Serene Highness? O Lord, why didn't I do that yesterday —day before yesterday?"

It was disagreeable for Giglio, as he now scanned his best wardrobe in haste, that he could not get around admitting to himself that his plumed cap minutely resembled a plucked barnyard rooster, that his triple-dyed jerkin shone with all the colors of the rainbow, that his cape all too plainly betrayed the skill of the tailor who had challenged the wear of time with the most desperate darnings, and that his well-known blue silk breeches and his pink stockings themselves were autumnally faded. Woebegone, he reached for the purse which he believed all but emptied and—found it teeming in glorious plenitude.

"Divine Brambilla," he exclaimed with rapture, "divine Brambilla, indeed I do remember you, I do remember my lovely dream image!"

It can be imagined that with that pleasant purse, seemingly a kind of purse of Fortunatus, in his pocket, Giglio immediately ran through all the shops of the used clothes dealers and tailors to procure himself an outfit as grand as any stage prince had ever donned. Nothing they showed him was rich or splendid enough. Finally he made up his mind that no outfit could possibly satisfy him except one created by Bescapi's master hand, and he betook himself to him at once. When Master Bescapi had heard Giglio's request he exclaimed, his face all sunlight, "O my best Signor Giglio, there I can help you," and conducted the purchase-bent customer to another room. But Giglio was not a little astonished to find here no other costumes than those of the complete Italian *Commedia* and, outside of those, the maddest caricatures of masks. He thought Master Bescapi had misunderstood him and rather vehemently described the rich aristocratic attire in which he wished to be adorned.

"O Lord," cried Bescapi sadly. "O Lord! What is this again? My dearest Signor, I don't believe that certain seizures are again—"

"If you," Giglio impatiently interrupted him as he rattled the purse with its ducats, "if you are going to sell me a costume of the kind I want, Master Costumer, well and good; if not, call it a day!"

"Now, now," said Master Bescapi speaking very meekly, "just don't get angry again, Signor Giglio! Oh, you don't know how well I mean by you! Oh, if you only had a little, just a little sense!"

How dare you, Master Costumer!" cried Giglio angrily.

'Ah," continued Bescapi, "if I am a master costumer, I should like to be able to fit you to a costume with the proper measure, one that would be appropriate and serviceable. You are hastening to your ruin, Signor Giglio, and I regret that I cannot repeat to you all the things which the wise Celionati has told me about you and about your future destiny."

"Ho, ho!" said Giglio. "The *wise* Signor Celionati, the fine Mister Mountebank, who pursues me in every possible way, who is trying to do me out of my finest happiness because he hates my talent and me, because he opposes the seriousness of loftier natures, because he would like to turn everything into the preposterous hoax of brainless mockery! O my good Master Bescapi, I know everything, the worthy Abbate Chiari has disclosed all that fraud to me. The abbate is the most splendid person and the most poetic nature you can find, for he has created *The White Moor* for me, and no one else in the whole wide world, I tell you, can play the White Moor except me."

"What are you saying?" cried Master Bescapi, laughing loudly. "Has the worthy abbate—may Heaven call him soon to the assemblage of loftier natures!—has he washed a Moor white with the water of tears which he causes to flow so abundantly?"

"I ask," said Giglio, suppressing his anger with difficulty, "I ask you once again, Master Bescapi, whether you want to sell me a costume or not, of the kind I want and in exchange for my full-weight ducats?"

"With pleasure," replied Bescapi very happily. "With pleasure, my best Signor Giglio!"

Whereupon the master opened up a closet in which there hung the richest and most magnificent costumes. Giglio's eye immediately caught a complete outfit which was indeed very rich, although it struck the eye as somewhat fantastical on account of its curious variegated coloring. Master Bescapi opined that this costume came high and would probably be too expensive for Giglio. But when Giglio insisted on buying the outfit, fetched forth his purse, and challenged the master to set whatever price he would, then Bescapi declared he absolutely could not let the costume go, because it was already intended for a foreign prince, namely for Prince Cornelio Chiapperi.

"What!" cried Giglio, all enthusiasm, all ecstasy. "What! What are you saying! Then the costume is made for me and no one else. Fortunate Bescapi! It is precisely Prince Cornelio Chiapperi who is standing before you and who has found his inmost being, his very Self, in your house!"

As Giglio spoke these words, Master Bescapi swept the costume down from the wall, called one of his apprentices, and ordered him to carry the basket into which he swiftly crammed everything for the Most Serene Prince.

"Keep," cried the master as Giglio started to pay him, "keep your money, my most revered Prince! You are doubtless in a hurry. Your most submissive servant will get his money in due time; perhaps the White Moor will defray the small outlay. God shield you, my excellent Prince!"

Giglio cast a proud glance at the master, who was bobbing and ducking in the daintiest of repeated bowings and scrapings, thrust his Fortunatus purse into his pocket, and made off with the handsome princely raiment.

The costume fitted so superbly that Giglio in his most exuberant joy pressed a shiny ducat into the hand of the costumer's apprentice who had helped him change clothes. The apprentice begged him to give him a couple of good paoli instead, because he had heard that the gold of stage princes was not worth anything and that their ducats were only buttons or playing chips. Giglio threw the too clever lad out the door.

After Giglio had practiced the fairest and most gracious gestures for a while in front of the mirror, after he had thought of the fantastical speeches of lovesick heroes and gained the total conviction that he was utterly irresistible, he confidently betook himself to the Pistoja Palace as evening twilight was beginning to set in.

The unlocked door yielded to the pressure of his hand and he entered into a spacious columned vestibule where the stillness of the grave prevailed. As he gazed about in astonishment there arose from the deepest recesses of his being hazy images of the past. It seemed to him as though he had been here before, but since absolutely nothing would assume a distinct form within his soul, and since all effort to focus those images remained futile, he was overcome with a fear and an anxiety which robbed him of all his courage to pursue his adventure any further.

In the very act of leaving the palace, he all but collapsed on the floor from shock as his Self, enveloped as if in mist, suddenly stepped toward him. He quickly perceived, however, that what he had taken for his double was his image reflected in a dark wall mirror. And yet at that very moment it also seemed to him as though a hundred sweet and tiny voices whispered: "O Signor Giglio, how handsome you are, how superbly beautiful!" In front of the mirror Giglio threw out his chest, lifted his head, put his left hand to his hip, and as he raised his right one cried out oratorically: "Courage, Giglio, courage! Your good fortune is certain, make haste to seize it!" With that he began to stalk up and down with bolder and bolder tread, to clear his throat, and to cough. But quiet as the grave all still remained, not a living soul was to be heard. Then he tried to open this door and that door which must lead into the various rooms. All were locked tight. What else could he do but climb the broad marble stairs that wound gracefully upwards on either side of the vestibule?

When he arrived at the upper corridor, whose adornment corresponded to the simple elegance of the whole, it seemed to Giglio as if he could hear the tones of a strange and odd-sounding instrument in the far distance. Cautiously he stole forward and presently noticed a dazzling ray of light falling into the corridor through the keyhole of the door opposite him. Now he also discerned that what he had taken for the tone of an unknown instrument was the voice of a man speaking, and a very curious sound that voice had, too, for now it was as if a cymbal were being struck, and then again as if someone were blowing on a deep, hollow pipe. As Giglio came up to the door it opened softly, softly of itself. Giglio stepped in and stood rooted to the spot in profoundest astonishment.

Giglio found himself in a mighty hall, the walls of which were covered with purple-speckled marble and from the high dome of which was suspended a lamp whose radiant flame cast glowing gold over everything. At the rear a sumptuous drapery of cloth-of-gold formed a canopy beneath which, upon a dais five steps up, stood a gilded armchair with colored tapestries. On it was sitting the little old man with the long white beard and dressed in a robe of silver material. It was he who had, inside that gold-gleaming tulip, been poring over books of learning during Princess Brambilla's entrance procession. As on that occasion, he was wearing a silver funnel on his reverend head; as on that occasion, he had a monstrous pair of spectacles sitting on his nose; as on that occasion, he was reading, though now in a loud voice, the very voice which Giglio had heard from a distance, from a great book which lay open in front of him on the back of a kneeling Moor. At either side like mighty men-at-arms stood the ostriches, taking turns at turning the pages with their beaks for the old man whenever he had finished a given page.

Round about in a semicircle sat perhaps a hundred ladies, wondrously beautiful as fays and clad as richly and as magnificently as the latter are known to be. All were busily making nets. Upon a little altar of porphyry in the middle of the semicircle and in front of the old man, stood two odd little dolls in the posture of persons in profound sleep and with crowns upon their heads.

As Giglio recovered somewhat from his astonishment, he wished to make his presence known. But scarcely had he formed the thought of speaking when he felt the sharp blow of a fist upon his back. To his no small shock he only now perceived the row of Moors armed with long pikes and short sabers in whose midst he was standing and who had their blazing eyes fixed upon him and were showing their ivory teeth. Giglio realized that patience would be the best thing to practice here.

What the old man was reading to the net-making ladies, however, went approximately as follows:

"The fiery sign of Aquarius stands above us, the dolphin is swimming toward the east upon rushing waves and spouting pure crystal from his nostrils into the misty flood. It is time for me to tell you of the great mysteries that befell and of the wonderful riddle whose solution will save you from miserable destruction.

"Upon the ramparts of the tower stood the mage Hermod observing the courses of the constellations. Then four old men wrapped in cloaks whose color was like that of the fallen leaves came walking through the forest and up to the tower, and as they arrived at the foot of the tower they raised a mighty cry of lamentation: 'Hear us! Hear us, great Hermod! Be not deaf to our imploring, awake from your profound sleep. Had we but the strength to bend King Ophioch's bow, we would shoot an arrow through your heart as he did, and you would have to descend and could not stand up there in the storm wind like an unfeeling lout! But, most worthy old man, if you will not wake up, we have a few catapults ready and we are going to knock at your bosom with a few good-sized stones to stir the human emotion enclosed within there. Wake up, splendid old man!'

"The mage Hermod gazed down, bent over the battlement, and in a voice which sounded like the muffled raging of the sea or the howl of the approaching hurricane, said: 'You people down below there, don't be asses! I am not asleep and I am not to be wakened with arrows and stones. I almost know what you want, good folk. Wait a bit and I will come right down. You can be picking a few strawberries meanwhile, or playing tag on the grassy stones. I'll be right down.'

"When Hermod had come down and seated himself on a large rock covered with the soft and many-hued carpet of the most beautiful moss, the eldest of the men—he seemed to be the eldest on account of his white beard that grew down to his waist—began thus: 'Great Hermod, you surely know beforehand everything I am about to say, and better than I myself. But so that you may see that I know it, too, I must tell you.'

" 'Speak,' said Hermod, 'speak, O youth, and gladly will I listen; for what you just said proves that keen comprehension, if not profound wisdom, dwells with you although you hardly went to elementary school.'

" 'You know,' continued the speaker, 'you know, great mage, that one day in the council there was talk of holding every vassal under obligation to contribute a specified quantity of wit annually to the main storehouse of humor to feed the poor in case of famine or spell of thirst, and that during that discussion King Ophioch suddenly said: "The moment at which a man topples over is the first one in which his true self rises upright." You know that no sooner had King Ophioch spoken these words than he actually toppled over and did not rise again, because he was dead. And since it chanced that Queen Liris also closed her eyes at that same moment, never to open them again, the State Council found itself in no small embarrassment as to the succession to the throne, inasmuch as the royal pair totally lacked descendants. The court astronomer, a subtle man, hit at last upon a method of prolonging the wise rule of King Ophioch in the land for many years to come. He proposed, namely, to proceed just as in the case of a well-known Spirit-Prince, King Solomon, whom the spirits obeyed long after he had died. In accordance with this proposal the master cabinet-maker to the court was brought into the State Council. He constructed a dainty pedestal of boxwood, and after King Ophioch's body had been properly stuffed with the most excellent spices, this pedestal was shoved under his rump so that he sat up very stately there; by means of a secret pull-cord, the end of which hung down like a bell-pull in the conference chamber of the great council, his arm was manipulated so that he swung his scepter back and forth. No one doubted but that King Ophioch lived and ruled. Strange things now happened concerning the Urdar Spring. The waters of the lake which it had formed remained bright and clear. But whereas all who gazed into it used to feel a special pleasure, there now were many who showed irritation and anger when they saw all Nature and themselves reflected in it, because it was against all dignity, indeed against all human reason and all arduously gained wisdom, to behold things upside down, especially one's own Self. More numerous and ever more numerous became those who finally maintained that the mists of the clear lake befuddled the mind and transformed seemly gravity into folly. In annoyance they now threw all sorts of nasty stuff into the lake until it lost its mirror brightness and became duller and duller and finally looked like a nasty swamp. This, O wise mage, has worked much harm across the country, for the most aristocratic people now hit each other in the face and imagine that such is the true irony of the wise. The greatest harm, however, befell yesterday, when things went with King Ophioch exactly as with that Spirit-Prince. Unnoticed, the nasty bore-worm had eaten through the pedestal and suddenly in the best part of his reign His Majesty toppled over right in front of a lot of people who had crowded into the throne room, so that his demise could no longer be concealed. I myself, great mage, was just pulling the scepter-string, which, as His Majesty keeled over, broke in such a way that it hit me across the face so that I have had enough of scepter pulling to last me a lifetime. You, O wise Hermod, have ever faithfully espoused the cause of the land of Urdargarten. Say, what shall we do in order to have a worthy successor take over the regime so that the Lake of Urdar may be clear and bright again?'

"The mage Hermod sank into profound meditation. Then he spoke: 'Tarry nights nine times nine; then from the Lake of Urdar there shall bloom forth the queen of the land. Meanwhile, however, rule the land as best you can.'

"And it came to pass that rays of fire rose up over the swamp which had formerly been the Urdar Spring. But those were the fire spirits gazing into it with burning eyes, and from the depths the earth spirits squirmed up. From the dried-up bed, however, there bloomed forth a beautiful lotus flower in the chalice of which lay a lovely slumbering child. That was Princess Mystilis, who was carefully removed from her beautiful cradle and elevated to be regent over the land by those four ministers who had fetched the information from the mage Hermod. The said four ministers assumed guardianship over the princess and sought to foster and keep the dear child to the limit of their powers. But into great distress they fell when the princess, once she was old enough to be able to talk properly, began to speak a language that no one understood. From far and wide knowers of tongues were invited by letter to investigate the princess's speech, but perverse and horrible Fate would have it that the wiser and the more erudite these knowers of tongues were, the less they understood the child's speech, which nevertheless sounded very sensible and comprehensible. Meanwhile, the lotus bud had again closed up its chalice, but around it, in tiny fountains, spurted the crystal of purest water. The ministers were overjoyed at the sight, since they could hardly believe otherwise but that the fair mirror waters of the Urdar Spring would soon be flashing in the place of the swamp. As to the matter of the princess's speech, the wise ministers determined, as they should have done long since, to seek counsel from the mage Hermod.

"When they had come into the eerie darkness of the mysterious forest and the masonry of the tower was already visible through the dense underbrush, they came upon an old man who was sitting on a rock pensively reading in a great book and whom they could not help taking for the mage Hermod. Against the cool of the evening Hermod had thrown a black dressing

gown around him and put on a sable cap which did not become
him ill at all but rather gave him a foreign and somewhat
sinister look. It also seemed to the ministers as if Hermod's
beard had become untidy, for it was like tangled brush. When
the ministers had submissively presented their request, Hermod
rose, flashed the ferocious glitter of his eyes upon them so that
they all fell right to their knees, and then burst into laughter
that shrilled and rang through the whole forest until the animals
rushed frightened and fleeing through the bushes and the fowl,
shrieking in mortal anguish, went whirring up from the thickets.
The ministers had never seen the mage Hermod in this somewhat wild mood or talked with him that way before, and they
became uneasy; meanwhile they waited in respectful silence to
see what the great mage would do. But the mage sat back down
on the big rock, opened his book, and with a solemn voice
read:

> There lies a black stone in a shadowed hall
> Where once engrossed in sleep a royal pair
> With mute, pale death on brow and cheek all fair
> Awaited magic power's mighty call.
>
> And buried deep beneath that stone there lies
> A thing that all life's pleasures will adorn;
> For Mystilis of bloom and blossom born
> It will flash forth as a most precious prize.
>
> The colored bird will then in nets be caught
> That fairy skill with tender hands shall weave.
> Illusion fades, the mists depart and leave,
> The foe himself shall his own death have wrought.
>
> For better vision now remove your glasses!
> For better hearing now prick up your ears,
> If you seek honest ministers' careers;
> But you are lost if you persist in being asses!

"With that the mage clapped the book shut with such vehemence that it resounded like a heavy peal of thunder and all the
ministers fell over backwards. When they recovered, the mage
had vanished. They agreed that many things must be endured

for the sake of the fatherland; otherwise it would be intolerable to have this rude fellow of a stargazer and sorcerer calling the foremost pillars of the state asses for a second time. Besides, they were astonished themselves at the wisdom with which they saw through the mage's riddle.

"Once back in Urdargarten, they went instantly to the hall where King Ophioch and Queen Liris had spent thirteen moons times thirteen in sleep, raised the black stone which had been set in the middle of the floor, and deep in the earth discovered a small but superbly carved box of the finest ivory. This they put into the hands of Princess Mystilis, who immediately pressed a spring so that the lid flew up and she could take out the pretty and dainty netting that was in the box. But hardly did she have the netting in her hands when she laughed aloud for joy and then said very plainly: 'Grandmother had put this in my cradle, but you rogues stole the trinket from me and wouldn't have given it back again if you hadn't fallen on your faces in the forest!' Whereupon the princess began at once to make nets most diligently. The ministers were just on the point of executing a common leap of joy from sheer delight when the princess suddenly became rigid and shriveled up into a dainty little porcelain doll. If the ministers' joy had been great at first, their sorrow was all the greater now. They wept and sobbed until they could be heard through the whole palace Then all of a sudden one of them, absorbed in thought, stopped, dried his eyes with both lappets of his robe, and spoke thus: 'Ministers! Colleagues! Comrades ! I almost think the great mage is right, and we are—well, let us be what we may. Has the riddle been solved? Has the many-colored bird been caught? The netting is the net woven by delicate hands, in which he must be caught.'

"At the ministers' behest the most beautiful ladies of the realm, real fays in charm and grace, were now assembled, and they were obliged to make nets incessantly while clad in the most splendid adornment. But what good did it do? The many-colored bird did not show up. Princess Mystilis remained a porcelain doll, the spouting fountains of the Urdar Spring dried up more and more, and all the vassals of the realm fell into the bitterest ill-humor.

"Then it came to pass that the four ministers sat down in

near desperation by the swamp which once had been the beautiful mirror-clear Lake of Urdar, burst forth in loud lamentation, and in the most moving appeals implored the mage Hermod to have pity on them and on the poor land of Urdar. A muffled groan rose from the depths, the lotus flower opened its chalice, and from it emerged the mage Hermod, who with angry voice spoke thus: 'Unhappy, blinded creatures, it was not I with whom you spoke in the forest, it was the evil demon, it was Typhon[1] himself, who mocked you in a shimmering illusion of magic and who conjured up the unholy secret of the box with the netting. But to his own harm he spoke more truth than he intended. Let the delicate hands of fairy ladies make nets, let the many-colored bird be caught, but listen to the actual riddle, the solution to which will also dissolve the enchantment upon the princess.' "

Thus far the old man had read when he stopped, rose from his seat, and addressed the little dolls that stood on the porphyry altar in the middle of the circle, saying:

"Good and excellent royal pair, dear Ophioch, most honored Liris, disdain no longer to follow us upon the pilgrimage in the comfortable traveling costumes I have given you. I, your friend Ruffiamonte, shall fulfill what I promised!"

Then Ruffiamonte looked about the circle of ladies and said, "It is now time to lay aside your weaving and recite the mystic dictum of the great mage Hermod as he delivered it from the chalice of the wonderful lotus flower."

While Ruffiamonte beat time with a silver staff whose heavy blows fell loudly upon the open book, the ladies, having left their seats and formed a close circle around the mage, recited in chorus the following:

Where is the land whose blue and sunny skies
Will kindle earth's delight to glorious bloom?
Where is the city whose hilarious cries
In happy time deliver gloom from gloom?
Where are the merry forms of fantasy
That fill a world shrunk to an egg's small room?

[1] Typhon (or Set-Typhon) was the Egyptian god of drought, hence opposed to the life-giving principle of water.

Where does it rule, this light hobgoblinery?
Who is the Self who from the Self gives birth
To Non-Self, rends its heart, and painlessly
Authenticates the rapture of high mirth?

Land, city, world, and Self are found; the Self
Beholds the world in total clarity
From which it boldly disengaged itself;
Touched by displeasure's dull asperity
It skirts the follies that the senses feel;
The inner mind in potent verity,
The master's wondrous needle will reveal
That realm, and by mad roguish pranks redeem
What seemed base, on it set the noble seal,
He who will wake the pair from their sweet dream.

Hail then to fair and far-off Urdar Land!
Its Spring shines clear and mirror-bright,
Sprung are the fetters that the Demon spanned,
And from the depths rise raptures into light.
How every bosom with delight now plays!
To joy is every grief transformed outright.
What gleams there in the shadowed woodland ways?
Ha, from afar, what jubilation wild!
The queen, she comes! Arise and give her praise!
She found the Self! and Hermod is reconciled!

Now the ostriches and the Moors raised a confused cry, and
through it were to be heard numerous other strange bird-sounds
squawking and peeping. But louder than any cried Giglio who,
wakened as from a state of insensibility, suddenly gained full
possession of himself and to whom it seemed as if he were in
some sort of grotesque play. "In the name of a thousand Heavens, what is this? Make an end of this crazy, mad stuff! Be
sensible for once and just tell me where to find Her Highness
the Princess, the most splendid Brambilla! I am Giglio Fava, the
most celebrated actor on earth, and Princess Brambilla loves
me and will bring me to high honor—but listen to me! Ladies,
Moors, ostriches, don't let silly stuff be chattered at you! I know

far better than that old man there, for I am the White Moor and
no one else!"

As the ladies finally became aware of Fava they set up a pro-
longed, shrill laughter and rushed at him. Giglio himself did not
know why a frightful terror suddenly came over him and why
he sought with all his might to escape from the ladies. But he
would not have succeeded in doing so had he not managed to
spread out his cloak and flutter up into the high dome of the hall.
Now the ladies shooed him back and forth and threw large ker-
chiefs at him until he sank down exhausted. Then the ladies cast
the meshes of a net over his head and the ostriches brought up
a stately golden birdcage in which Giglio was relentlessly im-
prisoned. At that moment the lamp went out and everything
disappeared as though by a stroke of magic.

Since the birdcage was standing by a large open window,
Giglio could look down into the street, but since the people had
gone pouring into the playhouses and inns, the street was completely empty and devoid of people, so that poor Giglio,
cramped in his narrow confinement, found himself in dismal
solitude.

"Is this," he broke forth in lamentation "is this the happiness
I dreamed of? Is this what there is to the delicate and wonderful
mystery which is hidden in the Pistoja Palace? I saw them, the
Moors, the ladies, the little old chap in the tulip, the ostriches,
I saw them just as they moved in through the narrow gate. Only
the mules and the feathered pages were missing. But Brambilla
was not among them. No, it is not here, the lofty image of my
yearning desire, of my fervent love! O Brambilla! Brambilla!
And I must miserably languish in this vile prison and nevermore
play the White Moor! Oh! Oh! Oh!"

"Who is carrying on so terribly up there anyway?" cried up a
voice from the street. Instantly Giglio recognized the voice of
the old *ciarlatano* and a ray of hope fell into his distressed
heart.

"Celionati," Giglio called down very plaintively, "dear Signor
Celionati, is it you I glimpse there in the moonlight? I am here
in a birdcage, in a sorry plight. They have locked me up here
like a bird. O Lord! Signor Celionati, you are a virtuous man
who will not abandon his neighbor, you have wonderful powers

at your disposal, help me, oh, help me out of my accursedly painful situation! O freedom, golden freedom, who values you more than he who sits in a cage though the bars of the cage be made of gold?"

Celionati burst out laughing, but then he said, "You see, Giglio, this comes of your accursed folly and your crazy fancies! Who asked you to enter the Pistoja Palace in preposterous disguise? How could you sneak into a gathering to which you were not invited?"

"What!" cried Giglio, "The handsomest of all costumes, the only one in which I could show myself before the adored princess, you call that a preposterous disguise?"

"It is," replied Celionati, "it is precisely your handsome get-up that is to blame for their treating you this way."

"But am I a bird then?" cried Giglio, full of irritation and anger.

"In any event," continued Celionati, "the ladies have taken you for a bird, and in particular for one they are absolutely bent on having, namely for a greenhorn!"

"O Lord!" said Giglio at his wit's end, "I, Giglio Fava, the famous tragic hero, the White Moor, I, a greenhorn!"

"Now Signor Giglio," cried Celionati, "just be patient, sleep if you can, very gently and quietly. Who knows what good things the coming day will bring you?"

"Have mercy!" shrieked Giglio. "Have mercy, Signor Celionati! Set me free from this accursed prison! Never again will I set foot in the damnable Pistoja Palace."

"Actually," replied the *ciarlatano,* "actually, you don't deserve having me stand up for you, because you disdained all my good instructions and tried to throw yourself into the arms of my mortal enemy, the Abbate Chiari, who, I want you to know, has plunged you into this misfortune by his vile sham poetry, which is full of falsehood and deceit. You're really a good boy, and I am an honest, softhearted fool, as I have often proven already; so I will save you. I hope that in return you will buy a pair of new spectacles tomorrow and a replica of the Assyrian tooth."

"I'll buy anything from you that you want me to! Only get me freedom! Freedom! I'm almost suffocated as it is!"

So said Giglio, and up by way of an invisible ladder the *ciarlatano* climbed to him and opened a large flap forming the siding of the cage. Through the opening, the unlucky greenhorn wedged himself out with effort.

But at that moment there arose a confused din in the palace and repugnant voices squeaked and whimpered in medley.

"All ye spirits!" cried Celionati. "Your flight has been noticed, Giglio! Hurry and make good your escape!"

With the strength of desperation Giglio pushed himself all the way through, dropped recklessly down onto the street, picked himself up, and, having sustained not the slightest injury, ran off in full fury.

"Yes," he cried, completely beside himself as he arrived in his little room and caught a glimpse of the silly outfit in which he had struggled with his Self, "yes, that mad monster lying bodiless there, that is my Self, and these princely garments the dark demon stole from the greenhorn and hoaxed onto me, so that those most beautiful ladies in their unfortunate deception would take me for the greenhorn. I'm talking nonsense, I know, but that is correct, for I have actually become crazy because the Self has no body. Ho, ho! Up and at 'em! Up and at 'em, my dear, sweet Self!"

With that he tore the fine garments off in fury, threw himself into the maddest of all masquerade costumes, and ran for the Corso.

All the joy of heaven pulsed through him as a charming angel of a girl, tambourine in hand, invited him to dance.

The copper engraving included with this chapter shows this dance of Giglio's with the unknown beauty. But what happened after that, the kind reader will learn in the following chapter.

SIXTH CHAPTER

How one dancing became a prince, fainted into a charlatan's arms, and then doubted his cook's talents at
supper. *Liquor anodynus* and much ado without a cause.
Knightly duel of friends sunk in love and melancholy
and the tragic outcome thereof. Disadvantage and im-
propriety of taking snuff. A girl's Free Masonry and
a newly invented flying machine. How old Beatrice put
on a pair of spectacles and then took them off her
nose again.

She

Turn! Faster turn! Restlessly whirl on,
mad and merry dance! Ha! How lightning swift all things fly
past! No rest! No halt! Myriads of colored figures go crackling
up like scattering sparks from fireworks and vanish into the
black night. Pleasure pursues pleasure and cannot catch her, and
therein precisely lies the pleasure anew. Nothing is more boring
than being rooted to the ground and having to account for every
glance and every word! That is why I should never want to be
a flower; much rather a golden beetle that whirs and buzzes
around your head till you can't hear yourself think for the noise!
But where is rationality anyway when the whirl of frantic pleasure sweeps it away? At one moment too heavy, it tears loose its
mooring threads and sinks into the abyss; at another moment
too light, it goes flying up into the misty round of the sky. In a
dance it is not possible to maintain a rational rationality, and
so we shall rather give it up entirely as long as our *tours* and our
pas continue. And for that reason I do not wish to account to
you in any way for my words, you gay and fleet companion!
See how I circle round you, eluding you at the moment when
you thought you would catch me and hold me fast! And now!
And now again!

He

And yet!—no! Missed again! But all that counts in a dance is knowing how to watch and keep the proper equilibrium. Hence the need that every dancer has of holding something in his hand as a balancing pole. That is why I shall draw my broadsword and wave it in the air. So! What do you think of this leap? Of this stance, where I entrust my entire Self to the center of gravity in the toe of my left foot? You call it antic frivolity. But it is precisely the rationality by which you set no store, although without it nothing is understood, and it is also the equilibrium necessary for many things. What? With colored ribbons aflutter around me as I hover balanced on my left tiptoe, with my tambourine raised high aloft, you want me to give up all rationality, all equilibrium? I'll throw my cape-end at you to blind you so you will stumble into my arms! No! No! As soon as I grasped you, you would no longer exist, you would vanish into nothingness! Who are you then, mysterious creature born of air and fire, who belongs to the earth and peers up enticingly from the water? You cannot escape me! You start to sink, I fancy I will hold you tight, and you float up into the air. Are you really the doughty elemental spirit who kindles life into life? Are you sadness, fervent desire, rapture, the heavenly joy of existing? Over and over again the same *pas*, the same *tours*! And yet, beautiful girl, your dance is forever new, and that is surely the wonderful thing about you.

The Tambourine

If, O Dancer, you keep hearing me clatter and click and clang, you either imagine I want to hoax you with all sorts of stupid and simple twaddle, or that I am a loutish thing that cannot grasp the tone and beat of your melodies, and yet it is I alone who keep you in tone and beat. Therefore listen, listen, listen to me!

The Sword

You fancy, O girl who dance, that wooden, dumb, and dull as I am, beatless and toneless, I can be of no use to you. But know that it is my brandishings alone whence float forth the tone and the beat of your dance. I am sword and zither, and I can wound the air with sound and song, with lunge and thrust. And I keep you in tone and beat. Therefore listen, listen, listen to me!

She

How the unison of our dance rises higher and ever higher! Oh, what steps! What leaps! Ever more daring, ever more daring, and yet they succeed because we understand dancing better and better!

He

Ha! A thousand glittering circles of fire ring us round! What rapture! Stately fireworks, never can you explode, for your material is as eternal as time. Yet—stop! Stop! I am burning, I am collapsing in fire!

The Tambourine and the Sword

Hold firm, hold firm to us, Dancer!

He and She

Alas for me! Dizziness—whirling—spinning seizes us! Down we go!

Thus, word for word, went the wonderful dance that Giglio Fava danced in the most delightsome way with the most beautiful lady, who could after all be none other than Princess Brambilla herself, until his senses were on the point of vanishing in the riot of exultant pleasure. But that did not happen. Rather, it seemed to Giglio as if he were sinking into the arms of the most beautiful lady just as Tambourine and Sword were once again exhorting them to hold firm. Nor did this happen either. The person in whose embrace he was lying was by no means the princess, but old Celionati.

"I do not know," Celionati began, "I do not know, my dearest Prince—for in spite of your bizarre disguise I recognized you at the first glance—how you came to let yourself be so crudely deceived, when you are usually a sensible and reasonable gentleman. It is a good thing that I just happened to be standing here and caught you in my arms when the loose wench was right on the point of taking advantage of your dizziness to kidnap you."

"I thank you," replied Giglio, "I thank you very much for your goodwill, dearest Signor Celionati. But what you were saying there about gross deception I do not understand at all, and I regret that my wretched dizziness prevented me from finishing the dance with the loveliest and most beautiful of princesses, because it would have made me totally happy."

"What," Celionati went on, "what are you saying? Do you really think that was Princess Brambilla who was dancing with you? No! There precisely lies the vile deception, in that the princess palmed off a person of low estate on you so she could pursue another love affair the more undisturbed."

"Could it be possible," cried Giglio, "that I have been taken in?"

"Consider," continued Celionati, "consider that if your dancing lady had really been Princess Brambilla, if you had successfully finished your dance, at that very moment the great mage Hermod would have had to appear and conduct you and your high bride into your kingdom."

"That is true," answered Giglio. "But tell me how it all came about and with whom I was actually dancing."

"You shall," said Celionati, "you shall learn everything. But if you have no objections, I shall accompany you to your palace in order to be able to talk more quietly with you there, O princely sir."

"Be so kind," said Giglio, "be so kind as to guide me there, because I must confess that the dance with the presumed princess has so affected me that I am walking as in a dream and in all truth do not know at the present moment where in Rome my palace is situated."

"Just come with me, most gracious lord," cried Celionati as he took Giglio by the arm and walked away with him.

Straight as a string their route led to the Pistoja Palace. While they were standing on the marble steps leading up to the portal, Giglio scrutinized the palace from top to bottom and then said to Celionati, "If this really is my palace, which I do not mean to doubt, then some odd hosts fell upon me who are carrying on some mad business up there in those very beautiful rooms and who act as if the house belonged to them and not to me. Saucy ladies decked out in alien finery take sensible, genteel people— and may the saints preserve me, but I think this befell me myself, the master of the house—for the rare bird which they are supposed to catch in nets woven by gentle hands and fairy's contriving, and that gives rise to great disorder and disturbance. It seems to me as though I was locked up here in a vile cage, and that is why I would prefer not to enter again. If it were possible, dearest Celionati, that for today my palace could be situated somewhere else, I would be very grateful."

"Your palace, most gracious lord," replied Celionati, "can hardly be situated elsewhere than right here, and it would run counter to all propriety for you to turn away to an alien house. You have but to reflect, O my Prince, on the fact that everything we are doing and everything that was done here is not real but is rather a *capriccio* fabricated from beginning to end, and you will not suffer the slightest inconvenience at the hands of those mad folk plying their affairs upstairs there. Let us enter with total assurance."

"But tell me," cried Giglio, detaining Celionati as the latter was about to open the door, "but tell me: did Princess Brambilla not ride in here with the magician Ruffiamonte and a numerous retinue of ladies, pages, ostriches, and asses?"

"Quite so," replied Celionati, "but that cannot prevent you, who are at least as much entitled to the palace as the princess is, from coming in likewise, even if that is done right now in all silence. You will presently feel entirely at home inside."

With that Celionati opened the door of the palace and shoved Giglio in ahead of him. In the vestibule everything was dark and still as the grave. But as Celionati knocked softly at a door, there presently appeared a little and very pleasing Pulcinella with lighted candles in his hands.

"If I am not mistaken," said Giglio to the little fellow, "if I am not mistaken, I have already had the honor of seeing you, my dearest Signor, on the roof of Princess Brambilla's coach."

"That is so," answered the little fellow. "I was then in the service of the princess. In a manner of speaking, I still am, but primarily the unfailing chamberlain of your most gracious Self, dearest Prince."

Pulcinella lighted both arrivals into a magnificent room and then discreetly retired, observing that he would pop up anywhere, wherever and whenever the prince bade, at the touch of a spring; for, though he was the sole jester in livery here on the downstairs floor, he was replacing a whole corps of servants by dint of his dash and mobility.

"Ha!" cried Giglio, gazing about the richly and splendidly appointed room. "Ha! Now I recognize that I really am in my palace, in my princely room. My impresario had it painted, could not pay for the job, and gave the painter a box on the ear for dunning him, whereupon the stage carpenter thrashed the impresario with a Fury's torch. Yes! I am in my princely home! But you were going to wrest me from a frightful deception on the score of the dance, best Signor Celionati. Speak, I pray you, speak. But let us sit down."

After both Giglio and Celionati had seated themselves on soft cushions, the latter began, "Know, my Sovereign, that the person foisted upon you in the princess's stead was none other than a pretty milliner named Giacinta Soardi."

"Is it possible?" cried Giglio. "But I believe this girl has as her lover a miserable beggarly player named Giglio Fava?"

"Quite so," answered Celionati, "but would you believe that Princess Brambilla is chasing after precisely that miserable beggarly player, that stage prince, in highway and byway, and only for that reason confronted you with the milliner in the hope that you might perhaps, by a mad and insane misunderstanding, fall in love with the latter and thus divert her from the stage hero?"

"What a thought!" said Giglio. "What a mischievous thought! But believe me, Celionati, it is only an evil demonic spell that is confusing everything and knocking everything topsy-turvy, and that spell I shall destroy with this sword, which I shall wield with valiant hand, and I shall annihilate that wretch who presumes to permit my princess to love him."

"Do that," replied Celionati with a roguish laugh, "do that, dearest Prince! It means a great deal to me to have that ridiculous person removed from my path, the sooner the better."

Now Giglio thought of Pulcinella and the services for which he had offered himself. He pressed some hidden spring or other and Pulcinella popped up at once, and, since he was able to replace a whole roster of the most various servants, just as he had promised, thus cook, cellar master, table waiter, and cupbearer were all present now, and a tasty meal was prepared in a few seconds.

After making a good showing, Giglio found that, as far as food and wine were concerned, it was too obvious that one and only one person had prepared, brought, and served everything, because everything tasted the same. Celionati opined that perhaps Princess Brambilla might for that very reason have dismissed Pulcinella from her service for the time being because, in his overeager conceit, he wanted to be in charge of everything by himself alone—a point over which he had often quarreled with Arlecchino, who presumed to the very same thing in the very same way.

In the extremely remarkable original *capriccio* which the narrator is closely following, there is a lacuna at this point. Musically speaking, the transition from one key to the next is missing, so that the new chord comes in without any of the proper preparation. Indeed, it might be said that the *capriccio* broke off with an unresolved dissonance. It says, namely, that the prince—none other can be meant than Giglio Fava who was threatening death to Giglio Fava—was suddenly stricken with ghastly stomach gripes, which he laid to Pulcinella's cooking, but that then, after Celionati had administered *liquor anodynus*,[1] he went to sleep; whereupon a great noise arose. We do not discover either what this noise signified or how the prince—or Giglio Fava—together with Celionati, got out of the Pistoja Palace.

The continuation goes approximately as follows:

As the day was beginning to decline, there appeared on the Corso a masker who caught the attention of everyone by his

[1] Latin for "pain medicine."

oddity and bizarre appearance. On his head he wore a curious cap adorned with two long rooster feathers and to go with it a mask with a nose like an elephant's trunk, on which was perched a huge pair of spectacles, then a jerkin with thick buttons and to go with it a pretty pair of sky-blue silk breeches with dark red bows, pink stockings, white shoes with dark red laces, and a handsome pointed sword at his side.

The kind reader already knows this costume from the First Chapter and realizes therefore that beneath it can be concealed none other than Giglio Fava. But hardly had this masker strolled up and down the Corso a couple of times than there sprang forth a mad Captain Pantalone Brighella, the like of whom has already several times appeared in this *capriccio*, and accosted the masker with eyes flashing in anger, crying, "So I finally meet you, infamous stage hero! vile White Moor! You won't get away from me this time! Draw your sword, oaf, and defend yourself, or I'll run you through with my wooden sword!"

With that the fantastic Captain Pantalone flourished his wooden broadsword in the air. Giglio, however, did not in the least lose his composure at this unexpected attack but rather said very calmly and quietly, "What kind of a coarse boor is this that wants to duel with me here without understanding the first thing about what true chivalric manners are? Listen to me, my friend! If you actually do recognize me as the White Moor, why, then you must know that I am a hero and a cavalier like any other and that only true courtesy bids me go about in sky-blue breeches, pink stockings, and white shoes. That is ballroom costume in King Arthur's manner. And along with it, my trusty sword flashes at my side, and I shall meet you in knightly combat if you attack me in knightly fashion, and if you are anybody that amounts to anything and not a boor translated into the Roman manner!"

"Forgive me," said the masker, "forgive me, O White Moor, if I make light for a moment of what I owe the hero and the knight. But as surely as princely blood flows in my veins, I will show you that I have read excellent chivalric books with as much profit as you have."

Whereupon the princely Captain Pantalone stepped a few paces back, held out his sword toward Giglio in fencing position

and with the tone of the utmost benevolence asked, "Is it agreeable?"

Daintily saluting his opponent, Giglio snatched his sword from its sheath, and the combat started. It was soon apparent that both the Captain and Giglio knew considerable about such knightly business. Firmly rooted in the ground remained their left feet, while their right ones now lunged forward with a thud for bold attack, now drew back to defensive position. Flashing, their blades crisscrossed, like lightning thrust followed thrust. After a hot and menacing pass the two swordsmen were obliged to rest. They looked at each other, and amid the fury of the duel such a love surged up within them that they fell into each other's arms and wept abundantly. Then the battle began anew with redoubled strength and adroitness. But now just as Giglio was about to fend aside a well calculated thrust of his opponent's, that thrust caught fast in the ribbon bow of his left pantleg so that the bow dropped off with a groan. "Halt!" cried Captain Pantalone. The wound was scrutinized and found insignificant. A couple of pins sufficed to fasten the bow back on again.

"I," said Captain Pantalone now, "I shall take my sword into my left hand because the weight of the wood is tiring my right arm. You may retain your light rapier in your right hand."

"Heaven forbid," answered Giglio, "I should do you such an injustice! I too shall take my sword into my left hand. That way it is right and proper, so I can hit you all the better."

"Come to my arms, good and noble comrade," cried Captain Pantalone.

The swordsmen embraced each other again and howled and sobbed extraordinarily over the magnificence of their conduct, and fell furiously on one another again.

"Halt!" cried Giglio this time, as he noticed that his thrust had caught in his opponent's hat brim.

At first the latter would not hear of any injury, but since the brim was falling down over his nose, he was obliged to accept Giglio's magnanimous offer. The wound was insignificant. The hat, once Giglio set it aright, still remained a noble felt. With intensified love the swordsmen gazed at one another; each had tried and found the other honorable and valiant. They embraced, wept, and high flamed the ardor of renewed battle.

Giglio left himself open, against his breast rebounded his opponent's sword, and he fell lifeless to the ground.

Despite the tragic outcome, the people broke into loud laughter as Giglio's corpse was carried off, until the whole Corso vibrated, while Captain Pantalone cold-bloodedly thrust his wooden broadsword back into its sheath and strolled off down the Corso with proud tread.

"Yes," said old Beatrice, "yes, I am determined to show that ugly old charlatan, that Signor Celionati, the door, if he shows himself here again and tries to turn my sweet and lovely child's head for her. And when you come right down to it, Master Bescapi is in cahoots with his nonsense."

In a way, old Beatrice might well be right, for since the time when Celionati had taken an interest in visiting the pretty milliner, Giacinta Soardi, her whole inner being seemed as if turned upside down. She was lost in a continual and everlasting dream and at times talked such fantastic and confused nonsense that the old woman was concerned for her sanity. As the kind reader can already gather from the Fourth Chapter, Giacinta's main idea, around which everything revolved, was to the effect that the rich and splendid Prince Cornelio Chiapperi was in love with her and would pay her suit. Beatrice opined on the contrary that Celionati, Heaven only knew why, was out to play a hoax on Giacinta; if everything was honest and aboveboard with this love of the prince's, then it was simply incomprehensible why he had not long since sought out his beloved at her home, since princes were not usually so obtuse about things like that. What was more, the couple of ducats slipped them by Celionati were not at all worthy of a prince's largess. When you came right down to it, there wasn't any Prince Cornelio Chiapperi; and if there really was one, why, old Celionati himself, as she well knew, up there on his platform in front of San Carlo had told the people that the Assyrian Prince Cornelio Chiapperi had vanished after having his molar tooth extracted and was being searched for by his fiancée, Princess Brambilla.

"Don't you see," cried Giacinta as her eyes flashed, "don't you see? There you have the key to the whole mystery, there you have the reason why the good and noble prince is concealing himself so carefully. Since he is all on fire with love for me, he is afraid of Princess Brambilla and her claims, and yet he cannot make up his mind to leave Rome. Only in the oddest disguise does he dare to show himself on the Corso, and it is precisely on the Corso where he has given me the most unambiguous proofs of his tenderest love. But soon the golden star of fortune will rise in all its clarity for him, that dear prince, and for me. Do you remember a certain foppish actor that used to pay court to me, one Giglio Fava?"

The old woman felt that it took no special memory for that, inasmuch as poor Giglio, who was still preferable to her over the stuck-up prince, had been at her house only day before yesterday and thoroughly enjoyed the tasty meal she had prepared for him.

"Would you," continued Giacinta, "would you believe it, old woman, that Princess Brambilla is chasing after that starveling wretch? So Celionati assured me. But just as the prince still shies at appearing in public as mine, so the princess still has all sorts of qualms about giving up her former lover and elevating the actor Giglio Fava to her throne. But at the moment when the princess gives Giglio her hand, the prince in full happiness shall receive mine."

"Giacinta!" cried the old woman. "What nonsense! What fantasies!"

"And," Giacinta went on to say, "and what you say about the prince's having so far disdained to search out his beloved in her own little room, that is downright false. You have no idea of the stratagems the prince uses in order to see me unobserved. For you must know that, along with other laudable qualities and accomplishments that he possesses, my prince is also a great magician. I will forbear recalling the fact that he visited me once at night in a form so small, so dainty, so charming, that I could have eaten him up. But he often appears here in the midst of our little room, right while you are present, and it is your fault that you do not see either the prince or all the splendors that are revealed. I enjoy less having our narrow quarters open out into a great and splendid ceremonial hall with marble walls and gold-worked tapestries, damask couches, and tables and chairs of ebony and ivory, than I enjoy having the walls vanish altogether, so that I can walk hand in hand with my beloved in the most beautiful garden that anyone can possibly imagine. I am not at all surprised that you, old woman, are not able to breathe the heavenly fragrances wafted in that Paradise, because you have the nasty habit of stuffing your nose with snuff and even in the presence of the prince you cannot do without fetching forth your snuffbox. But you should at least remove those swathes from around your ears so you can hear the singing of that garden, which captivates the senses wholly and completely and before which all earthly sorrow vanishes, even toothache. You simply cannot find it improper for me to permit the prince to kiss me on both shoulders, for you can see how wings of butterflies instantaneously grow there, the most beautiful, shining wings of many colors, and how I rise high, high into the air. Ha! That is the real joy of all, when I go sailing that way with the prince through the azure of the sky. Then everything that earth and heaven contain, all wealth and treasures that were only dreamed of hidden in the deepest mine of creation, unclose before my enraptured gaze, and everything, everything belongs to me! And you, old woman, say the prince is stingy and leaves me in poverty in spite of his love? But perhaps you mean I am rich only when the prince is present, but not even that is true. Look, old woman, see how at this moment when I am only talking about the prince and his magnificence, our room has become so beautifully adorned. See these silken draperies, these hangings, these mirrors, but above all that delightful wardrobe whose exterior is worthy of its rich contents. All you have to do is open it and the rolls of gold will fall into your lap. And what do you say to these trim ladies-in-waiting and maids and pages whom the prince has assigned to my service in the interim until the whole glorious court assembles about my throne?"

With these words Giacinta stepped up to that wardrobe which the kind reader saw in the First Chapter and in which hung very rich but also very odd and fantastic costumes which Giacinta had trimmed at Master Bescapi's behest and with which she now began a soft conversation.

The old woman watched Giacinta's carryings-on and shook her head, then began: "God comfort you, Giacinta! but you are ensnared in a wicked illusion, and I shall send for your confessor to drive out the devil that is haunting this place! But I still say it's all the fault of that crazy mountebank that put the prince into your head, and of that ridiculous costumer who had you work on the masquerade costumes. But I shall not scold. Reflect, my lovely child, my dear Giacintinetta, come to your senses, be nice the way you used to be!"

Silently Giacinta sat down on her workbench, propped her little head in her hand, and gazed pensively down at the floor.

"And if," the old woman went on, "and if our good Giglio gives up his capers—but wait—Giglio! Hey! Looking at you now that way, Giacintinetta, it comes back to me what he once read us out of that little book. Wait—wait—wait—it fits you to a T."

Out of a basket and from under ribbons, pieces of lace, and scraps of silk and other trimming materials the old woman produced a little neatly bound book, put her spectacles on her nose, crouched down in front of Giacinta, and read:

"Was it on the solitary mossy bank of a forest brook, was it in a scented jasmine arbor? No, I remember now, it was in a friendly little room lighted by the rays of the setting sun, that I glimpsed her. She was sitting in a low armchair, her head propped on her right hand, so that her dark curls willfully straggled and peeped out from between her white fingers. Her left hand lay in her lap and playfully tugged at the silk ribbon that had come untied from the slim body it had girdled. Involuntarily the movement of that hand seemed to be followed by her little foot whose tip just protruded from beneath the profuse folds of her garment and which was tapping softly, softly up and down. I tell you there was so much grace, so much heavenly charm upon her whole figure that my heart quivered with a nameless rapture. I wished for the ring of Gyges: she should not see me, for I feared she would vanish into air like a dream image if she were touched by my glance. A sweet and blessed smile played about her mouth and cheek, gentle sighs forced their way through her ruby-red lips and struck me like burning shafts of love. I was startled, because I thought I had called her name aloud in the abrupt pain of fervent bliss. But she did not notice me, she did not see me. Then I ventured to look into her eyes which seemed to be fixed upon me, and in the reflection of that blessed mirror there arose the wonderful magic garden into which that angelic creature had withdrawn. Shining castles in air opened their gates and forth from them streamed a merry and motley folk who joyously exulted in proffering the richest and most splendid gifts to the most beautiful girl. But all those gifts were merely hopes, yearning desires that emerged from the depths of her inner being to agitate her bosom. Higher and more vehemently, like waves of lilies, rose and fell the lace at her dazzling breast and a shimmering blush gleamed on her cheeks. For now the mystery of music awoke and spoke supreme things in celestial tones. You may believe that now I too was actually standing within the reflex of that wonderful mirror in the midst of the magic garden."

"That," said the old woman as she clapped the book shut and took her spectacles off her nose, "that is all very prettily and nicely said, but Lord in Heaven! what roundabout talk to express nothing more, really, than that there is nothing more charming, and for men of sense and reason nothing more seductive, than a pretty girl sitting lost in thought and building castles in the air.

"And, as said, that fits you to a T, my Giacinta, and all that stuff you have been chattering away about the prince and his stunts is nothing more than the dream in which you are lost, expressed in words."

"And," replied Giacinta as she rose from the workbench and clapped her hands like a delighted child, "and if it really were true, wouldn't I look just like the charming magic picture you were just reading about? And so you may know it, those were words of the prince that involuntarily crossed your lips when you were starting to read to me out of Giglio's book."

SEVENTH CHAPTER

How atrocious things were imputed to a nice young man
in the Caffè Greco, how an impresario felt remorse, and
how an actor's dummy died of tragedies by the Abbate
Chiari. Chronic dualism and the double prince who
thought crosswise. How someone saw things upside
down because of eye trouble, lost his country, and did
not go walking. Quarrel, strife, and separation.

The kind reader cannot possibly complain
that the author is tiring him out in this story with too long
journeys back and forth. Everthing lies nicely together in a little
circle that can be traversed with a few hundred steps: the Corso,
the Pistoja Palace, the Caffè Greco, etc., and, apart from the
little jump over to the land of Urdargarten, everything stays
within that little, easily traversable circle. Thus, it requires only
a few paces for the kind reader again to find himself in the Caffè
Greco where, four chapters ago, the mountebank Celionati told
German youths the strange and wonderful story of King Ophioch
and Queen Liris.

So, then! In the Caffè Greco a handsome young man, nicely
dressed, was sitting all by himself and seemed lost in profound
thought. Thus not until after two men, who had meanwhile
stepped in and come toward him, had already cried twice and
three times: "Signor! Signor! My best Signor!" did he wake from
his reverie and with courteously aristocratic dignity inquire
how he might be of service to the gentlemen.

The Abbate Chiari—it must be stated that the two men were
none other than the Abbate Chiari himself, the famous author
of the even more famous *White Moor*, and the impresario who

had supplanted tragedy with farce—the Abbate Chiari began immediately: "My best Signor Giglio, how does it happen that you are no longer to be seen, that you have to be looked for with difficulty through all of Rome? Behold here a repentant sinner whom the power and the might of my word have converted, who wants to make good all the wrong he has done you and abundantly compensate for all your damages."

"Yes," spoke up the impresario, "yes, Signor Giglio, I freely confess my incomprehension, my blindness. How was it possible for me to mistake your genius, to doubt even for a moment that in you alone was all my support! Come back to me, on my stage receive anew the admiration and the loud, tempestuous applause of the world!"

"I do not know," replied the nice young man as he gazed in complete astonishment at both the abbate and the impresario, "I do not know, gentlemen, exactly what it is you wish of me. You address me with a strange name, you speak to me of completely unfamiliar things, you act as if I were known to you, although I scarcely recall ever having seen you in my life."

"You're right," said the impresario, bright tears coming into his eyes, "you're right, Giglio, in treating me so disdainfully, in acting as if you didn't know me at all. I was an ass to drive you off the boards. But, Giglio! Don't be implacable, my boy! Give me your hand!"

"Think," the abbate interrupted the impresario, "think of me, good Signor Giglio, and of The White Moor, and of the fact that, after all, you could not garner more fame and honor in any other way than on the stage of this worthy man, who has sent Arlecchino to the Devil together with his whole sweet retinue and once more has achieved the good fortune of receiving and producing tragedies by me."

"Signor Giglio," the impresario went on, "you may set your own salary. In fact, you may select your costume for the White Moor yourself as your choice dictates, and it won't make any difference to me about a couple more false curls or a couple more packages of spangles."

"But I tell you," cried the young man, "that everything you are stating is still an insoluble riddle to me."

"Ha!" shrieked the impresario in full fury now. "Ha! I understand you, Signor Giglio Fava, I understand you very well, I understand you very well, I know everything now. That accursed Satan of a—I shall not speak his name lest poison cross my lips—*he* has caught you in his nets, *he* has you fast in his talons. You are signed up, you are signed up! But ha, ha, ha! Too late you will come to regret it when from that scoundrel, from that pitiful master costumer who is driven by the insane illusion of a ridiculous vanity, you come to—!"

"I beg you," the young man interrupted the angry impresario, "I beg you, dearest Signor, do not get into such a heat, just stay nice and calm. I now divine the entire misunderstanding. You take me, do you not, for an actor named Giglio Fava, who, as I have heard, is supposed to have shone formerly in Rome as an excellent actor, although in actuality he never amounted to much?"

Both the abbate and the impresario stared at the young man as if they were seeing a ghost.

"Apparently," the young man continued, "apparently you gentlemen have been absent from Rome and have only returned at this moment. Otherwise I should be very much surprised if you had not heard what all Rome is talking about. It would grieve me if I were the first from whom you heard that that actor Giglio Fava, whom you are looking for and who appears to be so valuable to you, was struck down yesterday on the Corso in a duel. I myself am only too convinced of his death."

"Oh, fine!" cried the abbate. "Oh, fine, oh, beyond all measure find and splendid! So it was the celebrated actor Giglio Fava who was struck down by a senseless, preposterous fellow yesterday so that he kicked both legs up in the air? Indeed, my best Signor, you must be a stranger in Rome and little acquainted with our carnival pranks; otherwise you would realize that when the people picked up the alleged corpse and started to carry it away, they had in their hands nothing but a pretty dummy made out of pasteboard, over which the populace then broke forth in immoderate laughter."

"To me," the young man went on to say, "to me it is unknown to what degree the tragic actor Giglio Fava did not actually consist of flesh and blood and was composed only of pasteboard. It is certain, however, that at the autopsy his entire insides were discovered to be stuffed with acting parts from the tragedies of a certain Abbate Chiari and that the surgeons attributed the death-dealing quality of the wound which Giglio Fava sustained from his opponent solely to the horrendous glut and total breakdown of all digestive organs by indulgence in viands devoid of strength and sap."

At these words of the young man, the whole circle of bystanders burst out in resounding laughter.

Unnoticed during this remarkable conversation the Caffè Greco had filled up with its usual clients, and it was primarily the German artists who had formed a circle around the speakers. If the impresario had previously gotten angry, the abbate's inner fury now burst forth still more vehemently. "Ha!" he shrieked. "Ha! Giglio Fava, that was what you were driving at! It's you I have to thank for the whole scandal on the Corso! Wait—my vengeance shall strike you—pulverize you—!"

But as the outraged poet burst out in vulgar abuse and, with the support of the impresario, even made as if to attack the nice young man, the German artists seized both of them and threw them rather ungently out the door so that they flew like streaks of lightning past old Celionati who was on his way in, and who shouted "Bon voyage!" after them.

As soon as the nice young man caught sight of the mountebank he went up to him swiftly, took him by the hand, led him to a remote corner of the room, and began: "If only you had come sooner, dearest Signor Celionati, in order to deliver me from two tiresome people who insisted on taking me for the actor Giglio Fava, whom I—ah, but you know that!—struck down on the Corso yesterday in my unhappy paroxysm. These persons imputed all sorts of atrocious things to me. Tell me, am I really so like that Fava that people can take me for him?"

"Have no doubt," replied the *ciarlatano* courteously, even almost reverently, "have no doubt, most gracious lord, but that, insofar as your pleasant facial features are concerned, you do indeed look rather like that actor. Hence, it was very wise to remove your double from your path, which you most skillfully went about doing. As far as the preposterous Abbate Chiari is concerned, together with his impresario, you may rely on me, my Prince! I shall extricate you from all attacks that might delay your total recovery. Nothing is easier than setting a director at odds with a stage poet to the point that they fall upon one another furiously and in raging combat devour each other, like those two lions of which nothing remained but the two tails that were found on the battlefield as a memento of perpetrated murder. But do not take too much to heart your resemblance to the pasteboard tragedian. For I just heard that the young people there who delivered you from your persecutors also think you are none other than that same Giglio Fava."

"Oh!" said the nice young man softly. "Oh, my dearest Signor Celionati, do not for Heaven's sake betray who I am! You, of course, know why I have had to remain so long concealed until I was entirely well again."

"Have," replied the mountebank, "have no fear, my Prince. I shall, without betraying you, tell them as much about you as is needful to win the respect and friendship of those young men without its so much as occurring to them to inquire your name and rank. For the time being, pretend as if you were paying us no attention at all, look out the window or read newspapers; then you can join in our conversation later. But so that what I say will not embarrass you, I shall speak in the language which alone really befits the things pertaining to you and your illness, and which for the time being you do not understand."

Signor Celionati took a seat as usual among the young Germans, who were still talking amid much laughter about how they had with utmost speed expedited the departure of the abbate and the impresario when the latter had gone after the nice young man. Then several of them asked the old man whether that wasn't really the well-known actor Giglio Fava leaning out the window there, and when the old man denied this and declared rather that it was a young foreigner of high lineage, the painter Franz Reinhold—the kind reader has already seen him and heard him talk in the Third Chapter—said he simply could not understand how people could claim to see a resemblance between this foreigner and the actor, Giglio Fava. He had to agree that the mouth, nose, forehead, eyes, and build of both might be similar in external form; but the spiritual expression of the face, which was the thing that really produced resemblance and which most portrait artists, or rather face copiers, could never grasp and therefore could never turn out true likenesses, precisely that expression was so worlds apart in the case of these two that he, for his part, would never have taken the foreigner for Giglio Fava. Fava really had a meaningless face, whereas in this foreigner's face there was something odd, the significance of which he himself did not understand.

The young people invited the old mountebank to tell them something again that would be like the wonderful story of King Ophioch and Queen Liris, which had especially pleased them, or rather to relate the second part of that tale itself, which he must have heard from his friend in the Pistoja Palace, the magician Ruffiamonte, otherwise known as Hermod.

"What," exclaimed the charlatan, "what second part? What second part? Did I suddenly stop that time, clear my throat, and then as I made a bow, say: 'To be continued'? And what is more, my friend, the magician Ruffiamonte, has already given a reading of the further developments of that story in the Pistoja Palace. It is your fault and not mine that you missed the class, which was attended, as is now the fashion, by ladies eager for learning. And if I were to go through all that again, it would cause horrible boredom for a certain person who never leaves us and who was present at that class, and who knows everything anyway. I mean the reader of the *capriccio* entitled *Princess Brambilla*, a story in which we ourselves appear and play our parts. So, nothing about King Ophioch and Queen Liris and Princess Mystilis and the many-colored bird! But about myself, about myself I will talk, if that meets with your approval, you frivolous fellows!"

"Why frivolous?" asked Reinhold.

"Because," continued Master Celionati in German, "because you look upon me as someone who exists merely to tell you fairy tales sometimes which only sound comical on account of their comicality and pass the time that you spend listening to them. But I tell you the author had something quite different in mind when he invented me, and if he should be looking on when you often treat me so casually, he could very well think I had slipped out of character. Enough! None of you shows me the reverence and respect that I deserve on the basis of my profound knowledge. Thus, for example, as far as knowledge of medicine is concerned, you are of the base opinion that I sell home remedies as arcana without any study of the fundamentals and that I claim to cure all illnesses with the same prescriptions. But the time has come to teach you better.

"From far, far away, from a land so distant that Peter Schlemihl for all his seven-league boots would have to keep running for a whole year in order to reach it, a young and very distinguished man has journeyed here to have recourse to my helpful art, inasmuch as he is suffering from an illness which can be termed the oddest and at the same time the most dangerous that there is and whose cure actually does rest with an arcanum the possession of which presupposes magic consecration. Namely, the young man is suffering from 'chronic dualism.' "

"What?" they all cried as they broke out laughing. "What? What are you saying, Master Celionati? 'Chronic dualism?' Is there such a thing?"

"I can plainly see," said Reinhold, "that you are about to regale us once again with something mad and fantastic, and afterwards you will dodge the issue."

"Ah," replied the mountebank, "ah, my son Reinhold, you shouldn't be the one to cast such a reproach at me. With you I have never dodged the issue, and since you, I believe, understood the story about King Ophioch aright and have even gazed into the clear mirror waters of the Urdar Spring yourself—but before I say anything further about the illness, gentlemen, be informed that the patient whose cure I have undertaken is precisely that young man looking out the window over there, the one you took to be the actor, Giglio Fava."

All looked over curiously at the stranger and agreed that in the otherwise spiritual features of his face there was nevertheless something indefinite and muddled which led one to infer a dangerous illness which in the last analysis consisted of a hidden madness.

"I think," said Reinhold, "I think that by your 'chronic dualism' you meant nothing more, Master Celionati, than that curious folly whereby the true Self is sundered from itself, a condition in which the genuine personality can no longer hold its ground."

"Not bad," replied the mountebank, "not bad, my son! And yet misfired. But if I am to account to you for the odd illness of my patient, I am almost afraid I won't succeed in making it clear and plain to you, primarily because you are not physicians and because I must therefore refrain from all technical terminology. Well! I will take a chance as chances go, and will first direct your attention to the fact that the author who invented us and to whom we must remain serviceable if we really want to exist at all, prescribed absolutely no time limit on our existence and actions. Hence, it is very pleasant for me to assume, without committing an anachronism, that you have heard the report about the double Crown Prince in the writings of a certain German author of great wit.[1] A princess found herself—to cite still another German writer of like wit[2]—in circumstances different from those of the country, namely, pregnant. The people were hoping and waiting for a prince; the princess, however, outdid this hope exactly twice over when she gave birth to two extremely charming princelets who were twins and yet to be termed a singleton, because they were born with their posteriors grown together. Despite the fact that the court poet maintained that Nature had not been able to find room in a single human body for all the virtues which the future heir to the throne should bear within him, and despite the fact that the ministers consoled the sovereign, who was somewhat dismayed by this dual blessing, by saying that four hands could wield the scepter more potently than two and that the whole gubernatorial sonata would sound more resonant and grand à quatre mains, yes!—in spite of all these things, enough circumstances nevertheless arose to cause many a justified doubt. First off, the great difficulty in inventing a practicable and yet attractive model for a certain little stool gave rise to the well-founded concern over how things would go with an appropriate form for the throne in the future; similarly, a commission composed of philosophers and tailors was able only after three hundred and sixty-five sittings to come up with the most comfortable and at the same time most attractive form for the dual trousers. But what appeared to

[1] Georg Christoph Lichtenberg (1742–1799) author of *Dass du auf dem Blocksberg wärst* (1799).

[2] Jean Paul Richter (1763–1825), in his *Komischer Anhang zum "Titan."*

be the worst problem of all was the total disparity of mind which revealed itself ever more and more in the two. If one prince was sad, the other was merry; if one wanted to sit, the other wanted to run. Suffice it to say that their inclinations never agreed. And yet it simply could not be claimed that one was of this and the other of that definite temperament, for in the opposition of constant alternation, one nature seemed to shade off into the other. This had to be explained on the basis of the fact that a spiritual conjunction manifested itself along with the physical one, and the greatest dissension resulted. They thought crosswise, so that neither one ever rightly knew whether he himself had really thought what he thought or whether his twin had thought it. And if that isn't confusion, then there never was any. Now if you will assume that just such a crosswise-thinking double prince is inside a man's body as *materia peccans*,[3] then you have sorted out the illness I am talking about, the manifestation of which is primarily to be seen in the fact that the patient does not of himself catch on."

Meanwhile the young man had approached the company unnoticed, and now when everyone was gazing silently at the mountebank as if waiting for him to continue, he began, after making a courteous bow: "I do not know, gentlemen, whether you mind my joining your company. People seem to like me everywhere else when I am quite healthy and cheerful, but of course Master Celionati has told you so many fantastic things about my illness that you will not want to be burdened with me myself."

In the name of all the rest, Reinhold assured the new guest he was welcome, and the young man took a seat in the circle.

The mountebank withdrew, after once again cautioning the young man to keep to his prescribed diet.

Then there happened what always happens—they immediately began to talk about the party who had just left the room and more than anything else questioned the young man about his fantastic physician. The young man assured them that Master Celionati, having taken courses to advantage both in Halle and in Jena, had acquired a very fine schooling, so that

[3] Latin, meaning literally, "sinning matter," i.e., body components causing disease.

full confidence could be placed in him. Otherwise, too, in his opinion, he was a very pretty and agreeable man who had the sole, though to be sure very grave, shortcoming of often running too much to allegory, a thing which really was prejudicial to him. Surely Master Celionati had spoken very fantastically about the illness he had undertaken to cure. Reinhold explained how, according to the mountebank's statement, the young man had a double Crown Prince inside him.

"You see," said the young man with a pleasant smile, "you see, don't you, gentlemen? Once again that is pure allegory, and yet Master Celionati knows my malady very exactly, and he knows that I am suffering only from an eye disorder which I brought on myself by wearing glasses too early. Something must have become disarranged in my retina, because unfortunately I see everything upside down most of the time, and thus it comes about that the most serious things often seem uncommonly funny to me, and contrariwise, the funniest things often seem uncommonly serious to me. This often causes me horrible suffering and such vertigo that I can hardly stand upright. Mainly, Master Celionati thinks, my recovery depends on my taking frequent and vigorous exercise. But, good Heavens! How am I to manage that?"

"Now," exclaimed one of the company, "since you, best Signor, are perfectly healthy and on your feet as far as I can see, I know—"

At that moment, in stepped a person already known to the kind reader, the celebrated Master Costumer Bescapi.

Bescapi walked up to the young man, bowed very low, and began: "My most gracious Prince!"

"Most gracious Prince!" cried everyone together and looked at the young man with astonishment.

But he said with calm mien, "Chance has betrayed my secret contrary to my will. Yes, gentlemen, I really am a prince, and an unhappy one at that, because I strive in vain for the splendid and mighty realm that is my heritage. If I said previously that it is not possible for me to take the proper exercise, that comes from my total lack of land and space besides. Precisely because I am confined within such strait limits, the numerous figures become confused and dart and tumble higgledy-piggledy until I can arrive at no clarity. Which is a very bad thing, inasmuch as, according to my innermost and truly essential nature, I can exist only in clarity. Through the efforts of my physician, however, as well as through those of this worthiest of all worthy ministers, I think I can regain my health by a joyous union with the most beautiful of all princesses and become great and powerful once more as I actually should be. Most solemnly I invite you, gentlemen, to visit me in my states and in my capital. You will find yourselves really very much at home there and will not want to leave me again, because only with me will you be able to live a genuine artist's life. Do not think, dear gentlemen, that I am biting off more than I can chew or that I am a vain boaster! Just let me be a healthy prince once again, who knows his people even when they stand on their heads, and you will discover how well I wish you all. I shall keep my word, as surely as I am the Assyrian Prince Cornelio Chiapperi! My name and country I shall withhold from you for the present. You will learn both in good time. Now I must take counsel with this excellent minister concerning some important affairs of state; after that I must pay a call on Folly and see, as I stroll through the court, whether any good jokes have sprouted in the manure beds."

With that the young man took the master costumer by the arm and both walked away.

"What do you say," said Reinhold, "what do you say, people, to all that? I get the impression that the motley throng of maskers from a mad fairy tale comedy is chasing figures of all kinds about in faster and faster circles until they can no longer be recognized or distinguished from one another. But let us get masks and go to the Corso. I surmise that the mad Captain Pantalone who fought the frantic duel yesterday will show up once again today and that he will do all sorts of fantastic things."

Reinhold was right. Captain Pantalone was very gravely walking up and down the Corso as though still in the resplendent glory of his yesterday's triumph but without doing anything mad as usual, although his infinite gravity gave him an appearance almost more comical than he usually maintained. The kind reader has already guessed before, but now knows for a certainty, who is hidden beneath that mask. None other, namely, than Prince Cornelio Chiapperi, the happy betrothed of Princess Brambilla.

And Princess Brambilla, why, she must herself be the beautiful lady who majestically walked down the Corso in rich and sumptuous garments with a waxen mask on her face. The lady seemed to have been on the lookout for Captain Pantalone, for she was adroit about circling around him until it looked as if he could not escape her, and yet he wormed his way out and continued his grave strolling. Finally, however, just as he was about to set off at a rapid pace, the lady took him by the arm and with a sweet and lovely voice said, "Yes, it is you, my Prince! Your gait and this attire worthy of your rank—you never donned a finer!—have given you away. Oh, tell me, why do you flee from me? Do you not recognize in me your life, your hope?"

"I really," said Captain Pantalone, "I really do not know who you are, beautiful lady. Or rather, I do not dare to guess, inasmuch as I have so often been the victim of vile deception. Before my eyes princesses have been transformed into milliners, actors into figures of pasteboard, until I have made up my mind to put up with no illusions and fantasies any more but to annihilate them both mercilessly wherever I come across them."

"Then start," cried the lady angrily, "then start with yourself! For you yourself, my worthy Signor, are nothing more than an illusion. But no," the lady went on softly and tenderly, "but no, beloved Cornelio, you know what princess is in love with you, how she came here from lands afar to seek you out, to be yours! And then, did you not swear to remain my knight? Speak, beloved!"

The lady had taken Pantalone's arm anew, but he held out his pointed hat to her, drew his broad sword, and said, "See! Gone is the token of my chivalry, gone are the rooster feathers from my open helmet. I have renounced my service to ladies, because they all reward me with ingratitude and faithlessness."

"What are you saying!" cried the lady angrily. "Are you insane?"

"Light," Captain Pantalone went on to say, "light me but on my way with the glittering diamond on your forehead! Fan me but with the plumes you plucked from the many-colored bird! I am proof against all magic. I know and I shall stick to it that the old man in the sable cap is right: my minister is an ass and Princess Brambilla is chasing after a wretched actor."

"Ho, ho!" cried the lady, still more angrily than before. "Ho, ho! If you dare address me in that tone, I shall only tell you that, if you claim to be a melancholy prince, that actor whom you term wretched and whom I can sew together again even if he has temporarily come apart, still seems to me far more worthy than you. Go right along to your milliner, to little Giacinta Soardi, whom you were chasing after anyway, I hear, and elevate her to your throne—for which you lack so much as a piece of land to erect it anywhere. God be with you for now!"

With that the lady walked away with a rapid step as Captain Pantalone called after her in a shrill voice: "Haughty! Faithless! This is how you reward my fervent love? But I know how to find consolation!"

EIGHTH CHAPTER

How Prince Cornelio Chiapperi could not find consolation, how he kissed Princess Brambilla's velvet slipper, and how both were then entangled in a net. New marvels of the Pistoja Palace. How two magicians rode on ostriches through the Urdar Spring and took up position in the lotus flower. Queen Mystilis. How familiar persons again appear and the *capriccio* entitled *Princess Brambilla* comes to a happy End.

Meanwhile it seemed as if our friend Captain Pantalone, or rather the Assyrian Prince Cornelio Chiapperi—for the kind reader knows that none other than that esteemed princely person was concealed beneath the mad caricature of a mask—yes, indeed, it seemed as if he simply had not been able to find consolation. For on the Corso the following day he was loudly lamenting that he had lost the most beautiful of all princesses and that, if he did not find her again, he was going to run himself through with his wooden sword for sheer despair. But since his gestures amid this woe were the most comical that anybody could possibly see, it was not long before he saw himself ringed around with maskers of all sorts who had their fun with him.

"Where is she?" he cried in a woebegone voice. "Where has she gone, my lovely betrothed, my sweet life? Was it for this that I had my finest molar tooth extracted by Master Celionati? Was it for this that I went chasing after my Self from one nook to another in order to find myself? Yes, was it for this that I really found myself, to pine a miserable life away without possession of love and joy and appropriate landed property? People! If one of you knows where the princess is, open your yap and tell me and don't let me go on lamenting here for nothing, or run to that most beautiful creature and inform her that the most faithful of all knights, the most dapper of bridegrooms is raging enough here from sheer longing and fervent desire, and that all Rome could go up like a second Troy in the flames of his love-fury if she doesn't come at once and put out the fire with the moist moonbeams of her blessed eyes!"

The crowd broke out in uncontrollable laughter, but a shrill voice cried: "Insane Prince, do you imagine Princess Brambilla will come to you? Have you forgotten the Pistoja Palace?"

"Ho, ho!" answered the prince. "Quiet, impertinent green-horn! Be glad you got out of the cage! People! Look at me and tell me if I am the real many-colored bird that is to be caught in nets?"

Again the crowd broke forth in uncontrollable laughter, but at the same moment Captain Pantalone fell to his knees as though beside himself. For before him, she herself was standing, that most beautiful one, in full splendor of all blessedness and grace and in the very garments in which she had first appeared on the Corso, except that instead of the little hat, a magnificently glittering diadem rested upon her brow, and from it rose plumes of many colors.

"I am yours," cried the prince in supreme ecstasy. "I am yours now, wholly and completely. See these feathers on my storm helmet! They are the white flag which I have run up, the signal that I surrender to you, you heavenly creature, utterly and unconditionally!"

"This had to be," replied the princess, "you had to surrender to me, the rich monarch, otherwise you would have been without your true homeland, and you would be a miserable prince. But swear eternal faith to me now by this symbol of my infinite regency!"

With that, the princess drew forth a dainty velvet slipper and extended it to the prince, who kissed it thrice after solemnly swearing eternal and changeless faith to the princess as surely as he hoped to exist. As soon as this had happened there rang forth a loud, piercing: "Brambure bil bal—Alamonsa kikiburva son-ton—!" The couple was surrounded by those ladies veiled in rich robes who, as the kind reader will recall, rode into the

Pistoja Palace in the First Chapter; behind them stood the
twelve richly clad Moors who now, instead of their long pikes,
were holding in their hands tall and wondrously gleaming peacock feathers which they flourished in the air. The ladies cast
veils of netting over the couple, hiding them densely and ever
more densely and finally in total night.

But now as the mist of netting fell away amid the sound of
horns, cymbals, and little drums, the couple found themselves
in the Pistoja Palace, in fact in the very room into which the
impertinent actor Giglio Fava had forced his way a few days
before. But more splendid, more splendid by far did the room look
now than before. Instead of the single suspended lamp that had
then lighted the room, some hundred now hung there so that
everything seemed to be all ablaze. The marble columns that
supported the lofty dome were entwined with luxuriant flower
garlands. The odd foliage of the roof seemed to be astir with
life, though one could not be sure whether with gay-plumaged
birds, or with charming children, or with wonderful animal
forms, and from the folds of the golden drapery of the throne-
canopy there shone forth, now here, now there, the friendly and
laughing faces of lovely maidens. As before, the ladies were
standing about in a circle, but far more sumptuously dressed,
and they were not making nets but rather were strewing splendid flowers about the room from golden vases, or swinging
censers from which a delicious odor rose as smoke. In tender
embrace upon the dais stood the magician Ruffiamonte and
Prince Bastianello di Pistoja. That the latter was none other
than the mountebank Celionati need hardly be said. In back of
the princely couple, that is to say, in back of Prince Cornelio
Chiapperi and Princess Brambilla, stood a little man in a very
brightly colored robe, holding in his hands a neat little ivory
casket, the cover of which was open and in which was contained nothing but a little glittering sewing needle, at which he
was gazing fixedly with a very bright smile.

The magician Ruffiamonte and Prince Bastianello di Pistoja
at last relinquished their embrace and only pressed each other's
hands a bit more. But then with a loud voice the prince called
to the ostriches: "Hey, there, good folk! Bring us the great book

so that my friend here, the honorable Ruffiamonte, can read off
what still is left to be read!'' The ostriches, clapping their wings,
hopped off and fetched the great book, which they laid upon
the back of a kneeling Moor and opened.
The mage, who looked uncommonly handsome and youthful
in spite of his long white beard, stepped up, cleared his throat,
and read the following lines:

Italy!—Land of brighter sunny skies
That kindle earth's delight to glorious bloom!
O Rome of beauty, your hilarious cries

At masking time deliver gloom from gloom!
Here frisk the merry forms of fantasy
Upon a stage shrunk to an egg's small room;

Here is the world of light hobgoblinery.
Genius it is, who from the Self gives birth
To Non-Self, rends its heart, and magically

Transmutes the pain of life to lofty mirth.
Land, city, world, and Self are found; themselves
The couple see in heavenly clarity

And in true union recognize themselves,
While on them shines life's deepest verity.
No more will super-clever folly deal

Numbness to mind by dull asperity.
The master's wondrous needle did reveal
The realm; mad pranks of magic did redeem

Genius and thereon set the noble seal,
And to life may now wake him from his dream.
Hark! Now begins a sweet upsurge of tone

And all things fall to silence, listening;
Shimmering azure lights the heavens' dome,
Far fountains, forests, whisper rustling.

O magic land of wondrous things, arise!
Rise to give yearning in exchange for yearning
When they themselves in Love's spring recognize.

The water surges. Plunge into its flow!
Strive on with might! Not far the shore's edge lies,
And lofty rapture gleams in fiery glow!

The mage clapped the book shut. At that moment a fiery mist rose from the silver funnel he was wearing on his head and filled the room more and ever more. And amid harmonious sounds of bells and harps and trumpets everything began to stir and move about. The dome rose aloft and became the bright arch of heaven, the columns became tall palm trees, the gold cloth fell away and turned into a bright and gleaming carpet of flowers, and the great crystal mirror melted into a clear and resplendent lake. The fiery mist that had arisen out of the mage's funnel had now been wholly dispersed, and cool and aromatic breezes wafted through the magic garden that stretched as far as the eye could see, with its superb and lovely bushes and trees and flowers. Louder rang the music, a happy jubilation arose, and a thousand voices sang:

Hail! Hail! to fair and far-off Urdar Land!
Its Spring shines clear and mirror-bright,
Sprung are the fetters that the Demon spanned!

Suddenly everything fell silent: music, jubilation, singing. Amid profound silence the mage Ruffiamonte and Prince Bastianello di Pistoja swung themselves up astride the two ostriches and swam out toward the lotus flower which rose like a gleaming island from the middle of the lake. They climbed into the chalice of the lotus, and those with good eyesight who were gathered around the lake plainly observed how the two magicians took a very small but also very pretty porcelain doll out of a little box and thrust it into the chalice of the blossom.

It befell that the pair of lovers, namely Prince Cornelio Chiapperi and Princess Brambilla, started up from the daze into which they had sunk and involuntarily looked into the clear and mirror-bright lake at whose margin they were standing. But as they caught sight of themselves in the lake, they *recognized* themselves for the first time; they looked at each other, burst out laughing in laughter comparable in its wonderful kind only to that of King Ophioch and Queen Liris, and then in supreme rapture fell into each other's arms.

And as soon as the couple laughed, then, oh! the splendid miracle! Up from the chalice of the lotus flower rose a woman of divine form, growing taller and taller until her head towered into the blue sky, while at the same time it was observed that her feet were planted in the uttermost depths of the lake. In the glittering crown upon her head sat the mage and the prince gazing down upon the populace, who broke forth in extravagant jubilation, drunk as they were with delight, and cried: "Long live our great Queen Mystilis!" while the music of the magic garden resounded with full chords.

And again a thousand voices sang:

> Yes, from the depths rise raptures into light
> And fly up where the dome of heaven gleams.
> Behold the queen who has won us outright!

> Around her goddess' head float sweetest dreams,
> Her footfall opens every glorious shaft.—
> True life is understood in its full streams
> By those who recognized themselves and—laughed!

It was past midnight and the crowds were pouring out of the theaters. Then old Beatrice closed the window from which she had been looking out and said, "The time has come for me to be getting everything ready, for soon my master and my mistress will be coming and surely they will be bringing good Signor Bescapi along with them." The old woman had bought up all the things for a tasty meal today, just like the time when Giglio had had to carry up her basket filled with dainties. But unlike that occasion, she did not have to fuss about in the narrow hole that passed for a kitchen and in the sorry little room rented from Signor Pasquale. Rather, she held sway over a spacious hearth and over a bright chamber, just as the gentlefolk were actually able to move comfortably about in three-to-four not too large rooms, in which there were numerous tables and chairs and other very tolerable furnishings.

As the old woman now spread a fine linen tablecloth over the table she had moved out into the middle of the room, she said with a smirk: "Hm! It's really awfully nice of Signor Bescapi not only to have moved us into these pretty quarters but also to have supplied us so generously with all the necessaries. Poverty must now have left us for good!"

The door opened and in walked Giglio Fava with his Giacinta.

"Let me," said Giglio "let me put my arms around you, my sweet, lovely wife! Let me tell you from the bottom of my soul that only since the moment I married you has the purest and most glorious joy of life been mine. Every time I see you play Smeraldina or other roles born of the true jest, or stand at your side as Brighella or Truffaldino or some other fanciful humorist, a whole world of the quickest, wittiest irony arises within me and kindles my acting. But tell me, my life, what wholly special spirit came over you today? Never have you flung such lightning-flashes of the most charming feminine humor from your inner heart, never were you so beyond measure lovely in the pertest and most fanciful vein."

"I might," answered Giacinta as she pressed a light kiss on Giglio's lips, "I might say the same thing about you, my beloved Giglio! You too were more magnificent than ever today, and maybe you yourself did not notice how we went on improvising our big scene for more than half an hour amid the continuous and genial laughter of the audience. But don't you remember what today is? Had you no intimation of the fateful hours in which this special inspiration seized upon us? Don't you recall that it is exactly a year today since we looked into the splendidly clear Urdar Lake and recognized ourselves?"

"Giacinta," cried Giglio in joyous astonishment, "Giacinta, what are you saying? It lies behind me like a beautiful dream, the land of Urdar, the Spirit of Urdar—but no! It was no dream, we did recognize ourselves. O my dearest Princess!"

"O!" answered Giacinta, "my dearest Prince!"

And now they embraced anew and loudly laughed and exclaimed alternately: "There lies Persia!—and there is India!—

but over here is Bergamo—and here is Frascati—our kingdoms adjoin!—no! No! They are one and the same kingdom,
and in it we rule as a mighty princely couple, it is the beautiful
and splendid land of Urdar itself! Ha! What joy!"
And now they went about the room exulting and again fell
into each other's arms and kissed each other and laughed.
"Aren't you," grumbled old Beatrice as they did so, "aren't
you just like wanton children! Already married for a whole
year and still making love and billing and cooing and jumping
about and—O my Savior! You almost knocked the glasses off
the table! Ho, ho! Signor Giglio, don't sling your cloak-ends into
my stew here! Signora Giacinta, take pity on the chinaware
and let it survive!"
But the two of them paid no attention to the old woman and
went carrying on as before. Finally Giacinta caught Giglio by
the arms, looked into his eyes, and said, "But tell me, dear
Giglio, you recognized him, didn't you, the little man behind us,
the one in the colored robe and holding the ivory casket?"
"Why," replied Giglio, "why shouldn't I, my dear Giacinta?
It was good Signor Bescapi, after all, with his creative needle,
our faithful impresario now and the man who first put us on
the stage in the form suited to our essential selves. And who
would have thought that that crazy old charlatan—"
"Yes," Giacinta interrupted Giglio, "yes, that old Celionati in
his tattered mantle and with his hat riddled with holes—"
"—that that was really supposed to be the fabulous old
Prince Bastianello di Pistoja?" These words were spoken by
the stately and elegantly dressed man who had just stepped
into the room.
"Oh!" cried Giacinta as her eyes lit up with delight. "Oh! most
gracious sir, is it really you? How happy we are, my Giglio and
I, to have you look us up in our little quarters. Do not refuse to
have a little bite to eat with us, and then you can go ahead and
explain what there really is to those matters with Queen
Mystilis, the Land of Urdar, and your friend, the magician Hermod, alias Ruffiamonte. I am not quite clear about all that yet."
"It needs," said the Prince of Pistoja with a gentle smile, "it
needs no further explanation, my sweet and lovely child. Suffice it to say that you saw through it yourself and that you also

got this smart fellow here, who well suits you as a husband, to
see through it too. You see, with my mountebank's career in
mind, I could throw around all sorts of mysterious and at the
same time boastful sounding words; I could say that you are
Fantasy, whose wings first require Humor in order to soar
aloft, while without the body of Humor you would be nothing
but wings and would float away, a plaything of the breezes,
upon the air. But I shall not do so, though not for the reason that
I might go too far over into allegory and thus commit an error
for which Prince Cornelio Chiapperi has already reprimanded
old Celionati in the Caffè Greco. I shall merely say that there
really does exist an evil demon who wears sable caps and black
dressing gowns who pretends to be the great mage Hermod,
and who is able to bewitch not only people of the ordinary sort,
but even queens like Mystilis. It was very malicious of the
demon to make the disenchantment of the princess dependent
upon a miracle that he considered to be impossible. In that little
world called the theater, namely, there was supposed to be found
a couple who were not only themselves animated by true
fantasy and humor in their inner beings, but who would also be
able to recognize that mood of the spirit objectively, as in a
mirror, and thereby project it into external life so that it might
have the effect of mighty magic upon the great world within
which the little world is enclosed. Thus, if you will, the theater
was supposed to represent, at least in a certain way, the Urdar
Spring into which people could look. In you, dear children, I
felt sure I could produce that disenchantment and so wrote to
my friend, the mage Hermod. As soon as he arrived and got out
at my palace, what pains he did take with you! But you know
about that, and if Master Callot had not intervened and taunted
you, Giglio, out of your hero's jacket—"

"Yes," Signor Bescapi interrupted the prince, whom he had
followed in, "yes, most gracious lord, a hero's jacket of many
colors! In connection with this dear couple, please remember
me a little, the way I helped along with this great task!"

"To be sure!" replied the prince. "And because you were a
wonderful man in your own right, namely, a costumer who
knew how to wish fanciful people into the fanciful outfits he
made up, I used your help and finally made you the impresario

of the odd theater where irony and genuine humor hold sway."

"I have," said Signor Bescapi, smiling very cheerfully, "I have always seemed to myself like someone who sees to it that not everything is spoiled in the cutting, as, for instance, in form and style."

"Well said," cried the Prince of Pistoja, "well said, Master Bescapi!"

While the Prince of Pistoja, Giglio, and Bescapi now went on talking of this and of that, Giacinta with pretty industry was decorating the room and the table with flowers that old Beatrice had had to fetch in haste, and lighting many candles, and, when everything looked bright and festive, she seated the prince in the armchair that she had fixed up with covers and hangings until it was well nigh comparable to a throne.

"A certain party," said the prince before sitting down, "a certain party of whom we all need to stand very much in fear, because he will surely pass very severe judgment on us and perhaps even contest our very existence, might perhaps say that I came here in the middle of the night without having any occasion to do so, just on his account, so I could tell him what you had to do with the disenchantment of Queen Mystilis, who in the last analysis is really Princess Brambilla. That certain party is wrong. For I tell you I have come here and that I shall always come here in the fateful hour of your recognition, to console myself with the thought that we and all others are to be deemed rich and happy who have succeeded in seeing and recognizing life and themselves and their total existence in the wonderful sun-clear mirror of the Lake of Urdar."

Here abruptly breaks off the source work from which, O kind reader, the Editor of these pages has worked. There is only an obscure tradition to the effect that the Prince of Pistoja, as well as impresario Bescapi, both enjoyed the macaroni and the Syracusan wine at the home of the young people. It is also to be surmised that on that same evening, as well as subsequently, many wonderful things befell that happy actor-actress pair, inasmuch as they had come in close contact with Queen Mystilis and with powerful magic.

Master Callot would be the only person who could supply further information on that score.

 MASTER FLEA

A Fairy Tale
in Seven Adventures of Two Friends

by E. T. A. HOFFMANN

FIRST ADVENTURE
Introduction

In which the kind reader learns as much as he needs
to know about the life of Mr. Peregrinus Tyss. The distribution of Christmas gifts at Bookbinder Lämmerhirt's
house in Kalbächer Lane and the beginning of the first
adventure. The two Alines.

O nce upon a time—
What author would dare nowadays to begin his tale this way?
"Out-of-date! Boring!" cries the kind, or rather the unkind,
reader who, in accordance with the ancient Roman poet's wise
advice, wants to be taken directly in medias res. He feels as if
some long-winded babbler of a guest, just arriving, were settling
himself down and clearing his throat to start on his endless
sermon, and he impatiently claps shut the book he has barely
begun. The present Editor of the amazing Tale of Master Flea,
however, is of the opinion that the above beginning is very good,
in fact the best a story can have, and that is the reason why the
foremost storytellers, such as nursemaids, old wives, etc., have
in all times made use of it. But since every author writes pref-
erably to be read, he (the aforementioned Editor, that is) absolutely does not wish to deprive the kind reader of the pleasure
of actually being his reader. Hence, he will inform him straight
off without any further to-do that the heart of this same Peregrinus Tyss, of whose odd destiny this story will treat, had
never thumped with such anxious joy of expectation on any
Christmas Eve as precisely on this one with which the narrative
of his adventures begins.

253

Peregrinus was to be found in a dark room adjoining the main hall where his Christmas gifts were customarily presented to him. There he was stealing softly back and forth, listening a bit at the door, and then again he would quietly sit down in the corner and with closed eyes inhale the mystic fragrances of marzipan and *pfefferkuchen* that wafted from that room. Then sweet mysterious shudders would course through him whenever he quickly opened his eyes, again to be dazzled by the bright streaks of light which penetrated the cracks of the door and danced hither and thither across the hall.

At last the little silver bell sounded, the doors of the room were thrown open, and in rushed Peregrinus into a whole fiery sea of flickering Christmas lights. Peregrinus halted, frozen before the table on which the most beautiful gifts were arranged in pretty and dainty order, and only a loud "Oh!" escaped from his bosom. Never had the Christmas tree borne such rich fruit, for from the branches that bent beneath their sweet burden hung all the candies that ever had a name, and in between them many a golden nut and many a golden apple from the garden of the Hesperides. The amount of choicest toys, fine lead soldiery, hunting sets of the same material, open picture books, etc, simply cannot be described. He did not venture yet to touch any of these riches bestowed upon him, but he could only strive to master his amazement and to grasp the happy notion that all this was now actually his.

"O my dear parents! O my good Aline!" Peregrinus kept exclaiming in his sensation of supreme delight.

"Well," replied Aline, "have I done it right, Peregrinus? Are you pleased right from the heart, my child? Don't you want to look at all these lovely things closer by? Don't you want to try out the new rocking horse, this fine bay here?"

"A splendid horse," said Peregrinus, gazing upon the bridled rocking horse with tears of joy in his eyes, "a splendid horse, of real Arabian stock." And he immediately mounted the proud and noble steed. But however excellent a horseman Peregrinus may have been, he must this time have done something or other amiss, for the wild Pontifex (that was the horse's name) reared with a snort and threw him so that he cast his legs pitiably into the air. But before the deathly frightened Aline could rush to his aid Peregrinus had already scrambled up and seized the horse's rein just as it was lashing out rearward and starting to run away. Once again Peregrinus swung himself astride and, summoning all his equestrian arts and applying strength and skill, brought the wild stallion under control until it trembled, panted, groaned, and in Peregrinus recognized its mighty master. When Peregrinus dismounted, Aline led the humbled creature away to its stall.

This somewhat stormy cavalcading which had set up an excessive din in the room and perhaps in the entire house, was now over, and Peregrinus sat down at the table to inspect the other gleaming presents quietly and more closely. With gratification Peregrinus consumed a bit of marzipan, while he put this or that jointed doll through its evolutions, cast a glance into this or that picture book, and then held a review of his army, which he found suitably uniformed and which he properly judged to be invincible because not a single soldier had a stomach inside of him, and finally walked over to his hunting set. With annoyance he perceived that there was only a fox-and-hare set, while the stag hunt as well as the wild boar hunt were missing altogether. Those sets had to be there. No one knew that better than Peregrinus, who had bought everything himself with more pains and care than can be told.

Oh, yes! It would seem quite necessary to protect the kind reader from the most arrant misunderstandings he might be involved in, if the author were to go on heedlessly with the narration without considering that he very well knows what sort of Christmas exposition is in question here, whereas this is unknown to the kind reader, who wants to find out what he does not know.

Anyone would be very much mistaken who thought that Peregrinus Tyss was a child whose kindly mother or some other female creature devoted to him and, after romantic fashion named Aline, were presenting him with Christmas gifts. Nothing of the sort!

Mr. Peregrinus Tyss had achieved thirty-six years, hence approximately the best ones. Six years earlier it was said of him that he was a very handsome man. Now he was correctly called a man of fine appearance. Always, however, both then and now, the fault condemned by all was that Peregrinus was too retiring, that he did not know life, and that he was obviously suffering from an unwholesome melancholy. Fathers with marriageable daughters opined that the good Tyss could not do better, in order to be cured of his melancholy, than to marry: he had free choice and no reason to be afraid of being "given the mitten." These fathers' opinions were correct at least in respect to this last point, inasmuch as Mr. Peregrinus Tyss, besides being, as was said, a man of fine appearance, possessed a very considerable fortune which his father, Mr. Balthasar Tyss, a very respectable merchant, had left him. Any girl who has, insofar as love is concerned, got beyond extravagance—that is to say, has turned at least twenty-three or twenty-four—will rarely reply to such highly gifted men's innocent question: "Will you make me happy, my dear, with your hand?" in any other way than by saying with blushing cheeks and lowered eyes: "Speak to my dear parents. I obey their command alone. I have no will of my own." And the parents fold their hands and say: "If such is God's will, we have nothing against it, son."

But to nothing did Mr. Peregrinus Tyss seem less disposed than to marriage. For besides being shy of human beings in general, he displayed an odd idiosyncrasy toward the female sex in particular. The proximity of a lady brought out beads of sweat on his brow, and if he was directly addressed by a young girl pretty enough, he got into a state of alarm that tied his tongue and precipitated a convulsive shudder through all his limbs. Possibly this was the reason why his aged stewardess was of such extraordinary ugliness that in the district where Mr. Peregrinus Tyss resided she passed in the eyes of many for a curiosity out of natural history. Her black bristles of half-grey hair suited her red, rheumy eyes well enough, and her thick copper nose suited her pale blue lips well enough to complete the portrait of a Blocksberg candidate, so that a couple of centuries earlier she would hardly have escaped the stake instead of being deemed now a very good-natured person by Mr. Peregrinus Tyss and even by other people. And such she was in fact, and therefore it was to be overlooked in her that into the day's succession of hours she interwove so many little nips of brandy for the needs and nourishment of her body and perhaps overly often pulled a huge black lacquered box out of her bodice and fed her conspicuous nose generously with real Offenbach snuff.[1] The kind reader has already observed that this remarkable person was that same Aline that arranged the display of Christmas gifts. Heaven knows how she had come by the illustrious name of "the Queen of Golconda."[2]

But if fathers wished that the rich, eligible Mr. Peregrinus Tyss would renounce his shyness of women and get married without further delay, old bachelors on the other hand said that Mr. Peregrinus was doing quite right not to marry, since his temperament was not suited to it.

Distressing, however, was the fact that at the word "temperament" many persons made a very mysterious face and, upon being questioned more closely, let it be understood not unclearly that Mr. Peregrinus Tyss unfortunately was sometimes a trifle touched in the head, a fault which had marked him from early years. Many people who considered poor Peregrinus touched in the head belonged principally to those who are firmly convinced that the nose is the best leader and guide on the great highway of life, which one must follow in keeping with reason and prudence, and who put on blinders sooner than let themselves be enticed aside by many a fragrant thicket and many a flowery meadow lying along the way.

And it is actually true that Mr. Peregrinus had in him and about him much that was odd and of which people could not make head or tail.

It has already been said that the father of Mr. Peregrinus Tyss was a very rich and respectable merchant, and when it is further added that he owned a very handsome house on the cheerful Horse Market, and that in this house, indeed in the same room where Christmas gifts used to be presented to the little Peregrinus, the adult Peregrinus was receiving his Christmas gifts on this occasion as well, then there can be no doubt but that the place where the amazing adventures were going on which are

---

[1] A cheap grade of snuff made in the town of Offenbach.

[2] The French story, *Aline, Reine de Golconde* (1761), by Stanislas de Boufflers (1738–1815) had served as the basis for various operas and ballets, among them an opera of the same title by Henri Montan Berton (1767–1844), which Hoffmann had conducted in Bamberg, on October 21, 1808, at his debut as conductor there.

to be narrated in this story, is none other than the famous and beautiful city of Frankfurt-on-the-Main.

About the parents of Mr. Pereginus there is nothing particular to be said except that they were upright, quiet people of whom no one could report anything but good. The boundless esteem which Mr. Tyss enjoyed on the Exchange he owed to the fact that he always speculated correctly and safely, that he gained one large sum after the other, yet never became noisy about it, but remained modest as before, and never bragged of his wealth but merely gave proof of it by haggling neither over small things nor over great ones, and that he was forbearance itself to insolvent debtors who had chanced upon misfortune, even deservedly.

For a very long time Mr. Tyss's marriage had remained unfruitful, until finally, after almost twenty years, Mrs. Tyss had delighted her spouse with a pretty and lusty boy, who was precisely our Mr. Peregrinus Tyss.

You can imagine how boundless was the joy of the parents, and even now all the people in Frankfurt still speak about the magnificent baptismal celebration that old Tyss gave and at which the noblest and most antique Rhine wine was broached, as if it were a matter of a coronation banquet.[3] But what is posthumously praised even more in old Mr. Tyss is the fact that to that baptismal celebration he invited a couple of people who in their hostile attitude had rather often done him harm, and also other people whom he fancied *he* had harmed, so that the banquet turned into a regular festival of peace and reconciliation.

Ah, the good Mr. Tyss did not know, did not dream, that this same babe whose birth so delighted him would so soon cause him sorrow and care.

From the very first, the boy Peregrinus displayed a very peculiar temperament. For after he had screamed uninterruptedly, day and night, for several weeks, without anyone's discovering any physical malady, he suddenly became quiet and froze into a motionless insensitivity. He seemed impervious to the least impression, and the little countenance, which seemed to belong to a lifeless puppet, was contorted neither with smil-

[3] Frankfurt-on-the-Main was the coronation city of the Holy Roman Emperors.

ing nor with weeping. His mother maintained she had been frightened by the old bookkeeper who these twenty years had been sitting mute and numb with the same lifeless face over the ledger in the office, and she shed many scalding tears over the little automaton.

Finally a godmother hit upon the happy thought of bringing little Peregrinus a very gaily colored and, when you come right down to it, ugly harlequin. The child's eyes became animated in marvelous fashion, his mouth distended into a soft smile, he reached out for the doll and pressed it tenderly to him as they handed it over. Then the boy looked again at the motley manikin with such wise and eloquent glances that it seemed as if perception and comprehension had suddenly wakened within him, as a matter of fact with lively vivacity, as is usual in children of that age. "He is too wise," said the godmother, "you won't keep him down! Just look at his eyes. He is already thinking much more than he should!"

This dictum gave great comfort to old Mr. Tyss, who had more or less resigned himself to the idea that after many years of futile hopes he had begotten a Simple Simon. But he was soon overtaken by new worries.

The age was long past when children usually begin to talk, and still Peregrinus had not uttered a sound. He would have been taken for a deaf-mute, had he not often looked with such an attentive glance at the person speaking to him, indeed by joyous and by sad expressions giving testimony to his interest, so that there could be no doubt but that he not only heard, but also understood, everything. His mother meanwhile, experienced no slight astonishment when she found confirmation of what the nurse had told her. At night, when the boy was lying in bed and thought no one was listening, he spoke individual words to himself, in fact whole phrases, and with so little gibberish that long practice might be presupposed. Heaven has bestowed upon women a very special and sure tact in correctly grasping human nature as it unfolds in growth, now in this way, now in that way, and this is the reason why they are as a rule the best educators, at least for the child's first years. In keeping with this tact, Mrs. Tyss was far from letting the boy notice her observation and trying to force him to speak. Rather, she was able by other and skillfull means to bring it about that of his own accord he no longer kept his fine talent for speaking hidden but let it shine forth to the world, and to the wonder of all let himself be heard, slowly, to be sure, but distinctly. Yet he constantly showed a certain aversion toward speech and liked best to be left quietly to himself.

Hence Mr. Tyss was released from worry about the failure of speech, but only to encounter later a still greater worry. For when the infant Peregrinus had grown into a boy and was supposed to learn efficiently, it seemed as though things could be conveyed to him only with the greatest effort. With reading and writing, as with speaking, all went oddly. At first there just wasn't any success at all, and then all of a sudden he could do them excellently and beyond all expectation. Meanwhile one tutor after another quit the house, not because the boy displeased them, but because they simply could not make anything out of his nature. Peregrinus was quiet, well-mannered, industrious, and yet when it came to actual systematic learning the way the tutor wanted it, this was out of the question, since he had a head only for such things, gave his whole soul only to such things as appealed to his inmost feelings. Everything else he allowed to pass by him without a trace. What did appeal to his feelings was everything that was wondrous, everything that aroused his imagination, in which he then lived and had his being. For example, he once received as a gift a sketch of the city of Peking with all its streets, houses, and so forth, which occupied the entire wall of his room. At sight of the fairy-tale city and the wondrous folk that seemed to throng its streets, Peregrinus felt as if translated by the stroke of a magic wand into another world where he must become at home. With ardent avidity he seized upon everything about China, about the Chinese, about Peking, that he could get his hands on, was at pains to pronounce with a fine singsong voice, in accordance with their description, the Chinese sounds which he found drawn anywhere. In fact, he tried, with the aid of the shears, to give as Chinese a cut as possible to his dressing gown, which was of the finest calamanco, in order to be able to promenade with delight about the streets of Peking in keeping with the usage. Absolutely nothing else could excite his attention, to the great annoyance of the tutor, who was trying to impart to him the history of the Hanseatic League, as old Mr. Tyss had expressly wished, but who now had to learn to his sorrow that Peregrinus was not to be dislodged from Peking. For this reason he personally caused Peking to be dislodged from the boy's room.

Old Mr. Tyss had already taken it as an evil omen that, as a child, Peregrinus preferred counter chips to ducats and then displayed a decisive aversion to large moneybags and account books and notation pads. But what seemed strangest of all was the fact that he could not hear the word "exchange" without shuddering spasmodically and insisting he felt as if someone were running a knife-point back and forth over a pane of glass. Peregrinus was ruined as a merchant, Mr. Tyss could not fail to see, right from the start, and gladly as he would have seen his son walk in his footsteps, he gave way in this desire on the assumption that Peregrinus would devote himself to some definite profession. It was a principle with Mr. Tyss that even the richest man must have an occupation and by virtue of it a definite position in life. He had a horror of unoccupied people, and to precisely such inoccupation Peregrinus wholly inclined for all the learning which he had acquired in his own way and which was chaotically jumbled within him. This was old Tyss's greatest and most oppressive worry. Peregrinus wanted to know nothing about the actual world, whereas the older man lived exclusively in it, and it could scarcely have turned out otherwise but that, the older Peregrinus got, the worse became the dissension between father and son, to the no small sorrow of the mother, who was heartily willing to allow Peregrinus— otherwise good-natured, devoted, the best of sons—his concern with downright fancies and dreams—a concern frankly incomprehensible to her—and who could not comprehend why his father insisted on burdening him with a definite occupation.

Upon the advice of proven friends, old Tyss sent his son to the University of Jena. But when he returned after three years, the old man cried out in anger and chagrin: "Just as I thought! Jack the Dreamer he went down, and Jack the Dreamer he comes back!" Mr. Tyss was quite right insofar as Peregrinus was utterly unchanged in his whole being but had remained totally the same. Yet Mr. Tyss did not give up hope of bringing the degenerate Peregrinus to reason, thinking that if he were once thrust into business by force, he might perhaps wind up by liking it and might change his mind. He sent him to Hamburg with commissions that did not require special knowledge of business, and recommended him, what's more, to a friend there who was supposed to assist him faithfully in every way.

Peregrinus arrived in Hamburg and handed over to his father's business friend not only the letter of recommendation but all the papers which concerned his errands, and then disappeared, no one knew where.

Whereupon the business friend wrote to Mr. Tyss:

Yours of the — received by the hand of your son. The latter, however, has not been seen since, but quickly departed from Hamburg without leaving any message. There is not much doing here in pepper, cotton is slack, in coffee only the middling grade is moving; on the other hand, lump sugar is holding up nicely and indigo also shows steady signs of becoming fashionable in various quarters. I have the honor, etc.

This letter would have plunged Mr. Tyss and his spouse into no slight consternation, had it not been for the fact that a letter from their lost son himself arrived by the same post, in which he excused himself with the most sorrowful expressions for having found it absolutely impossible to carry out the assigned commissions according to his father's wish and said that he had felt irresistibly drawn to distant regions from which he hoped to return home happier and more cheerful after a year's time.

"It's a good thing," said the old gentleman, "for the youngster to look about in the world. They'll shake him out of his daydreams there." As for the mother's concern that her son might lack for money on his grand tour and that hence his thoughtlessness in not writing where he was going was much to be censured, the old gentleman laughingly replied: "If the youngster lacks money, he will make friends all the sooner with the real world, and if he didn't write us where he intends to travel, he knows where his letters can reach us."

It has remained unknown where Peregrinus actually went on

his journey. Many assert he had been in far-off India; others, however, claim that he more or less imagined that. This much is certain, that he must have been very far away, for not after a year's time, as he had promised his parents, but only after the lapse of three full years, did Peregrinus come back to Frankfurt, and then on foot and in rather pitiable shape.[4]

He found the parental house locked up tight and not a soul stirring inside, ring and knock as he would.

Then finally there came along a neighbor from the Exchange, whom Peregrinus asked if Mr. Tyss was perhaps away on a journey. The neighbor reeled back quite terrified and cried out: "Mr. Peregrinus Tyss! Is it you? Have you finally come?—then you don't know?"

Suffice it to say that Peregrinus learned that both his parents had died, one after the other, during his absence, that the courts had taken custody of the estate, and that they had publicly summoned him, whose residence was completely unknown, to return to Frankfurt and claim the inheritance from his father.

Peregrinus stood speechless in front of the neighbor. For the first time, the sorrow of life pierced his heart, and he saw in ruins the lovely shining world in which he had happily dwelt before.

The neighbor perceived how completely incapable Peregrinus was of performing the least thing that was needed. He took him therefore to his own house and with the greatest celerity looked after everything himself, so that Peregrinus found himself that very evening in the house of his parents.

Utterly exhausted, utterly crushed by a grief such as he had never known before, he sank into his father's big armchair, which still stood in the same place as it had formerly stood.

Then a voice said, "It is good that you are here again, dear Mr. Peregrinus. Oh, if you had only come sooner!"

Peregrinus looked up and saw directly in front of him the old woman whom his father had hired in his early childhood as a nurse, primarily because she could hardly find a place on ac-

[4] *Peregrinus* is the Latin adjective meaning "from foreign parts." From it derive the Italian word *pellegrino*, the French *pèlerin*, and the English "pilgrim."

count of her frightful ugliness, and who had never left the house again.

For a long time Peregrinus stared at the woman. At last, oddly smiling, he began: "Is it you, Aline?—my parents are still alive, aren't they?" With that, he rose, walked all through the rooms, looked at every chair, every table, every picture, and so on. Then he said quietly: "Yes, everything is just as I left it, and that is the way it shall stay, too!"

From that moment Peregrinus began the strange life that was indicated right at the outset. Withdrawn from all society, he lived with his old nurse in the large and spacious house, at first all alone in the utmost solitude, until finally he rented out a couple of rooms to an old man who had been a friend of his father's. This man seemed quite as shy of people as Peregrinus was. There was good reason why both of them, Peregrinus and the old man, got along very well, for they never saw each other.

There were only four family holidays that Peregrinus observed very solemnly, and these were the birthdays of his father and mother, the first day of the Easter season, and his own christening anniversary. On these days Aline had to set the table for as many persons as his father used to invite and prepare the same dishes as were customarily served, as well as put out the same wine as his father had offered. It goes without saying that, in the manner customary through so many years, the same silver had to be used now, and the same plates, the same glasses, just as they had been used then and just as they were, still undamaged in the inherited property. Peregrinus strictly insisted upon that. When the meal was ready, Peregrinus sat down to it alone, ate and drank only a bit, listened to the conversation of his parents and of the imagined guests, and only modestly answered this or that question which someone of the party addressed to him. When his mother had pushed back her chair, he got up with the others and took leave of each person in the most courteous manner. Then he withdrew to a remote room and left to Aline the distribution of the many still untouched dishes and the wine to homeless people, which command of her master that loyal soul was wont to carry out most conscientiously. Peregrinus began the celebration of his father's and mother's birthdays in the early morning by carrying a pretty bouquet, as he had done in his boyhood, into the room where his parents were accustomed to have breakfast, and by reciting verses which he had learned by heart. On his own christening anniversary he could not, of course, sit down at the table, for he had not been born long, and Aline therefore had to look to everything, such as urging the guests to drink, and generally, as they say, to do the honors of the table. Otherwise everything went as at the other festivals. Besides the latter, there was one other special day of joy in the year for Peregrinus, or rather evening of joy, and that was the distribution of Christmas gifts, which had stirred his young soul with sweet and innocent delight more than any other pleasure.

He himself carefully bought multicolored Christmas candles, toys, and dainties with the same intention as his parents had given him gifts in his boyhood years, and then the distribution proceeded as the kind reader has already learned.

"I'm still very sorry," said Peregrinus, after he had played for some time yet, "I'm still very sorry that the stag hunt and the wild boar hunt have been mislaid. Where can they have gone!— Oh! Look there!" At that instant he caught sight of a still unopened box, for which he reached out quickly, expecting to find the missing hunting sets in it. But when he opened it he found it empty and drew back as if stricken by an abrupt fright. "Odd," he then said softly to himself, "that's odd. What is there about this box? It seemed to me as if something menacing jumped out toward me which my eye's glance was too dull to catch!"

Aline, when he asked her, assured him that she had found the package among the toys but that she had exerted all her strength in vain to get it open. She had thought that something special was contained in it and that the cover would yield only to the skillful hand of the master. "Odd!" repeated Peregrinus. "Very odd! And I had been looking forward especially to that hunting set. I hope this doesn't forbode some evil! But who is going to fuss about such fancies on Christmas Eve, when they really have no foundation! Aline! Bring the basket!" Aline directly fetched a big white basket with handles, into which Peregrinus very carefully packed the toys, the confections, and the candles, and then hung the basket on his arm, took the big Christmas tree on his shoulder, and started out on his way.

Mr. Peregrinus Tyss had the admirable and cheerful habit of taking his entire fund of gifts, just as he had prepared them in order to dream himself back for a couple of hours into his lovely, contented boyhood, and of appearing unexpectedly like Father Christmas himself with shining, many-colored presents amid some needy family where he was aware that merry children were on hand. And then, when the children were in their loudest, liveliest delight, he would slip softly away and often would walk the streets half the night through, because he was unable to control himself because of the profound emotion that choked his heart and because his own house seemed to him like a gloomy tomb where he and all his joys were buried. This time the gifts were destined for the children of a poor bookbinder named Lämmerhirt, an able, industrious man who for some time had worked for Mr. Peregrinus and with whose three lively boys, ranging from five years to nine, Mr. Peregrinus was acquainted.

Bookbinder Lämmerhirt lived in the highest story of a narrow house in Kalbächer Lane and, considering that the winter's storm was now whistling and raging and that it was wildly raining and snowing all together, you can imagine that Mr. Peregrinus did not arrive at his destination without great exertion. From Lämmerhirt's windows a couple of sorry candles gleamed down, and laboriously Peregrinus climbed the steep stairs. "Open up!" he cried, as he knocked at the door of the room. "Open up! Open up! Father Christmas is bringing gifts to good children!"

The bookbinder, quite terrified, opened the door but did not recognize the snow-covered Peregrinus until after he had peered at him for some time.

"Most respected Mr. Tyss!" cried Lämmerhirt in astonishment. "Most respected Mr. Tyss, how in Heaven's name do I come to have this special honor on this blessed Christmas Eve?"

Mr. Peregrinus did not let him finish the speech, but crying loudly, "Children, children! Look sharp! Father Christmas is giving gifts!" he took possession of the big drop-leaf table that stood in the middle of the room and immediately began to produce the well-covered Christmas presents from his basket. The wet and dripping Christmas tree, to be sure, he had had to leave outside the door. Still the bookbinder could not grasp

what all this was supposed to be about. His wife understood
better, for she was laughing toward Peregrinus with tears in her
eyes, but the boys kept standing far off, silently devouring with
their eyes each present as it emerged from its covering and
often unable to repress a loud exclamation of joy and wonder-
ment. And now when Peregrinus finally had neatly sorted out
and arranged the gifts according to the age of each child, and
lighted all the candles, crying: "Come on, come on, children!
These are the presents that Father Christmas has given you!"
then, still not quite grasping the idea that all this was to belong
to them, they broke into a gleeful shout, leaped and whooped,
while the parents set about the task of thanking the benefactor.

The thanks of the parents, and even of the children, that was
precisely what Mr. Peregrinus sought to avoid every time, and
hence he wanted to get quietly away as usual. He was already at
the door, when it suddenly opened and there in the bright
shimmer of the Christmas candles a young and magnificently
dressed lady was standing before him.

It is seldom of any avail when an author undertakes to
describe for the kind reader exactly how this or that very handsome person who appears in his story looked, as regards shape,
height, posture, color of eyes and hair, and it seems much better,
in contrast, to give him the entire person in the bargain without
this traffic in details. It would suffice perfectly here, too, to
give assurance that the lady that stepped up to the deathly
frightened Peregrinus was uncommonly pretty and lovely, were
it not absolutely necessary to mention certain singularities
which this little person had about her.

Namely, the lady was indeed small, somewhat smaller than
was quite fitting, but, for all of that, built very finely and
daintily. Her face, otherwise beautifully formed and full of expression, took on something strange and odd by virtue of the
fact that the pupils of her eyes were more vivid and her finely
drawn eyebrows somewhat higher than ordinary. The ladykin
was dressed, or rather adorned, as if she were coming from a
ball. A splendid diadem glittered in her black hair, rich lace only
half covered her full bosom, her lavender and yellow checked
dress of heavy silk clung to her slender body and fell in folds
down just far enough to allow the daintiest white-shoed feet to

be seen, just as the lace sleeves were short enough and her white glacé gloves went just far enough up to allow the loveliest part of her dazzling arm to be seen. A rich necklace and jeweled earrings completed her costume. It was inevitable that the bookbinder was quite as confounded as was Mr. Peregrinus and that the children should leave their toys to stare open-mouthed at the strange lady. But since women customarily are the least astonished at something odd and unusual and generally get control of themselves the fastest, the bookbinder's wife found words first and asked what could be done for the lovely unknown lady.

The lady now stepped all the way into the room, and this was the moment the alarmed Peregrinus tried to use to beat a hasty retreat. But the lady seized him by both hands as she murmured with a sweet little voice: "So Fortune is favorable to me after all! So I have overtaken you after all! O Peregrin, my dear Peregrin, what a beautiful, blessed encounter once again!"

With that she raised her right hand in such a way that it touched Peregrin's lips and he was obliged to kiss it, despite the fact that cold drops of sweat were standing out on his brow. The lady did now let go of his hands and he could have fled, but he felt held by a spell that would not let him leave the spot, like some poor little beastie fascinated by the gaze of the rattlesnake.

"Allow me," the lady was saying now, "allow me, my dearest Peregrin, to take part in the lovely celebration which you, with a noble hand, with tender heartfelt spirit, have prepared for good children. Allow me to contribute something toward it also."

From a dainty little basket which was hanging from her arm and which was only now noticed for the first time, she drew forth all sorts of pretty toys, arranged them with lovely eagerness on the table, led the boys up, pointed out to each one whatever she had intended for him, and in all of this was able to be so nice with the children that you could never hope to see anything more gracious. The bookbinder thought he was in a dream, but his wife was smiling slyly, because she was convinced that there was undoubtedly something special between Mr. Peregrin and the strange lady.

While the parents were being amazed and the children delighted, the strange lady seated herself on an old rickety sofa and down beside her pulled Mr. Peregrinus Tyss, who, as a matter of fact, was himself scarcely sure any longer whether he actually was that person.

"My dear," she then began murmuring softly in his ear, "my dear, cherished friend, how happy, how blissful I feel at your side."

"But," stammered Peregrinus, "but most respected lady—"

But suddenly, Heaven knows how, the strange lady's lips came so close to his, that before he could think about kissing them, he had already kissed them. And that he should thereupon have completely lost his speech anew, can be imagined.

"My sweet friend," the strange lady now continued as she moved so close to Peregrinus that she was all but sitting on his lap, "my sweet friend, I know what is troubling you, I know what has painfully touched your gentle, childlike spirit this evening. Oh, yes!—but be of good cheer! I shall bring you what you have lost and whatever you hardly dared hope to find again."

With that, from the same little basket in which the toys had been, the strange lady drew forth a wooden box and put it into Peregrinus's hands. It was the stag and wild boar hunting sets which he had missed on the Christmas table. It would be difficult to describe the odd feelings that crisscrossed within Peregrinus's being.

If the whole apparition of the strange lady, in spite of all her grace and charm, had about it something ghostly which even the others, who did not fear the proximity of a woman as much as Peregrinus did, could not help sensing with a shiver through all their limbs, poor Peregrinus, already distressed enough, could not fail to be struck by a profound horror as he perceived that the lady was most minutely aware of everything that had taken place in the utmost privacy. And in the midst of this horror, whenever he raised his eyes and the triumphant glance of those very beautiful black eyes shone forth from beneath their long silky lashes, and when he felt the lovely creature's sweet breath and the electric warmth of her body, then the nameless woe of an ineffable longing such as he had never known sought to bestir itself in wondrous shudders. Then for the first time his whole way of life and the playing with the distribution of Christmas gifts seemed childish and insipid to him, and he felt ashamed that the lady should know of it. And now it seemed to him again as though the lady's gift were living proof that she understood him as no one else on earth and that the most intimate, most profound sense of tenderness had guided her when she sought to please him in this way. He decided to preserve the dear gift eternally, never to let it out of his hands, and, carried away by an emotion that completely overwhelmed him, he pressed to his heart with vehemence the box in which the stag and wild boar hunting sets was contained.

"Oh!" murmured the ladykin. "Oh, what delight! You are pleased with my gift! Oh, my sweet Peregrin, then my dreams, my premonitions have not misled me."

Mr. Peregrinus Tyss recovered a bit, so that he was capable of saying very distinctly and audibly: "But my best and most respected young lady, if only I knew who on earth I had the honor of—"

"Roguish man," the lady interrupted him as she lightly tapped his cheek, "roguish man, you pretend not to know your own true Aline! But it is time for us to give these good people elbowroom here. See me out, Mr. Tyss!"

As Peregrinus heard the name Aline, he naturally could not help thinking of his old nurse, and now he really felt as though a windmill were whirling in his head.

And now, as the strange lady took leave of the bookbinder, his wife, and his children in the most cheerful and gracious way, and as the bookbinder, for sheer astonishment and awe, could only stammer incomprehensible things, the children acted as if they had long been acquainted with the stranger. The wife said, "Such a nice, kind gentleman as you, Mr. Tyss, deserves to have such a beautiful, kindhearted fiancée, who even into the night helps perform works of charity. I congratulate you with all my heart!" The strange lady expressed her thanks with emotion, assured them that her wedding day would be a festival for them as well, earnestly forbade anyone to accompany her, and took a small candle from the Christmas table herself to light her way down the steps.

You can imagine how Mr. Tyss felt about all this as the strange lady laid her arm in his. " 'See me out, Mr. Tyss,' " he thought to himself. "That means down the stairs as far as the carriage that is waiting at the door, and where the servant or perhaps a whole retinue of servants is waiting. For, when all is said and done, this is some mad princess who—Heaven deliver me quickly from this strange torment and preserve the little mind that I have!"

Little did Mr. Tyss dream that everything that had happened up to now had been only the prelude to his wondrous adventure, and for that reason he did well, quite unintentionally, to implore Heaven beforehand for the preservation of his mind.

As the pair came down the steps, the door of the house was opened by unseen hands, and when Peregrinus and the lady had emerged, it was closed again in the same way. Peregrinus was totally unaware of this, for he was much too astonished by the fact that there was not the slightest trace of a carriage in front of the house, or of a servant waiting.

"In Heaven's name!" cried Peregrinus. "Where is your carriage, my lady?"

"Carriage?" replied the lady. "Carriage? What carriage? Did you think, dear Peregrinus, that my impatience, my anxiety to find you would have permitted me to have myself brought here quite calmly by vehicle? Through storm and tempest, driven by hope and yearning, I have raced about until I found you. Thank Heaven that I have succeeded. And now take me home, dear Peregrinus. My residence is not very far off."

With all the power at his command Mr. Peregrinus dismissed the thought that it was quite impossible for the lady, dressed as she was in white silk shoes, to have walked even a few steps without spoiling her entire costume in the storm and rain and snow, whereas now not the slightest trace of any disarray of her very careful toilette was to be seen. He resigned himself to accompanying the lady still further and was happy that the weather had changed. The wild storm was past, not a cloudlet was in the sky, the full moon shone down in friendly wise, and the winter night was felt only in the sharp and cutting wind.

But scarcely had Peregrinus gone a few steps when the lady

began to whimper softly, and then broke out in loud lamentations that she was going to freeze in the cold. Peregrinus, whose blood was streaming at white heat through his veins and who therefore had not felt any of the cold, who had not even thought about the fact that the lady was so lightly clad and had not even thrown a shawl or kerchief over her, suddenly realized his boorishness and started to wrap the lady in his coat. But the lady rejected this, lamenting, "No, dear Peregrin, that won't help me! My feet! Oh, my feet! I will perish of this terrible pain."

Half fainting, the lady was on the point of collapsing as she cried with dying voice: "Carry me, carry me, sweet friend!"

Then, without further ado, Peregrinus lifted the feather-light ladykin in his arms like a child and carefully wrapped her with his coat. But hardly had he walked on a short distance with the sweet burden when strongly and ever more strongly the wild frenzy of ardent passion possessed him. He covered the back of the lovely creature's neck and her bosom with burning kisses as she nestled close to his heart while he continued to run through the streets half bereft of his senses. Suddenly he felt as though he were waking with a start from his dream. He found himself right in front of a house door, and looking up, he recognized his own house on the Horse Market.

Now it occurred to him for the first time that he had not inquired of the lady for her residence. He pulled himself together by force and asked: "My lady! Heavenly, divine creature, where do you live?"

"Why," replied the lady as she raised her head, "why, dear Peregrin, here, here in this house. I am your poor Aline, you know, and I live with you! Just hurry and have them open the door."

"No, never!" shouted Peregrinus in horror as he let the lady sink to the ground.

"What?" cried the latter. "What! Peregrin, you mean to reject me, and yet you know my terrible fate, you know that, child of misfortune that I am, I have no shelter, that I must perish here miserably if you don't take me in as you used to do? But perhaps you want me to die—so be it then! Carry me at least as far as the fountain so they won't find my corpse in front of

your house—ah! Yonder stone dolphins will perhaps have
more pity than you. Alas for me! Alas for me! The cold!"
The lady collapsed in a faint.

Then anguish of heart and despair seized Peregrin's bosom
as if by icy tongs and crushed it tight. Wildly he cried, "Then
come what may, there is nothing else I can do!" And he picked
up the lifeless woman, clasped her in his arms, and gave a
strong tug at the bell. Swiftly Peregrin ran past the lackey who
had opened the door, and while still on the stairs, without
waiting as he usually did until he got to the top to knock very
softly, shouted, "Aline, Aline! Light, light!" and this so loudly
that the whole entrance hall re-echoed.

"What? What? What's this? What does this mean?" Thus
cried the old Aline, opening her eyes wide as Peregrinus un-
wrapped the fainting lady from his coat and with tender cau-
tion laid her down on the sofa.

"Quick!" he cried. "Quick, Aline, fire in the fireplace! Fetch
smelling salts—tea—punch—feather beds!"

But Aline did not stir from the spot, and staring at the lady,
she kept right on with her "What? What? What is this? What
does this mean?"

Then Peregrinus spoke about a countess, perhaps even a
princess, whom he had encountered at bookbinder Lämmerhirt's house, who had been seized with fainting on the street,
whom he had had to carry home, and then, since Aline still
remained motionless, he shouted, stamping his foot as he did so,
"In the Devil's name, fire, I say—tea—smelling salts!"

Then there was a glitter of pure mica in the old woman's eyes,
and it seemed as though her nose flared higher with a phos-
phorescent gleam. She took out her big black snuffbox, struck
the cover until it rang, and took a mighty quantity of the contents. Then she set both arms akimbo and with a mocking tone
said, "Well, just look! A countess! A princess! And they find
her at the poor bookbinder's house in Kalbächer Lane, and she
is seized with fainting on the street! Ho, ho! I know perfectly
well where such finely dressed little ladies are to be found at
night! Fine pranks, I must say, a pretty scene you're making
me! Bringing a loose wench into an honorable house, and to
brim the measure of sinfulness, calling on the Devil on the holy

Christmas Eve. And I, in my old days, am supposed to lend my hand to it yet? No, my fine Mr. Tyss, you'll look for someone else to do that. I'll have no part of it. And tomorrow I'm leaving your service."

And with that the old Aline walked out and slammed the door so vehemently behind her that everything rattled and rang. Peregrinus wrung his hands in anguish and despair. No sign of life was to be seen in the lady. But just at the moment when in his horrible distress Peregrinus had found a bottle of eau de cologne and was just about to rub the lady's temples dexterously with it, she jumped up from the sofa quite gaily and friskily and cried, "At last, at last we are alone! At last, my Peregrinus, I can tell you why I followed you to bookbinder Lämmerhirt's residence and why I could not leave you tonight. Peregrinus! Let me have the captive that you have locked up in your room. I realize that you are in no way obliged to do so, that it depends entirely on your goodness of heart, but it is just such a good, true heart that I know you have, and for that reason, my good, dearest Peregrin, let me have him, that captive!"

"What," asked Peregrinus in the profoundest astonishment, "what captive? Who is supposed to be a captive in my house?"

"Yes," continued the lady as she grasped Peregrin's hand and tenderly pressed it to her heart, "yes, I must confess that only a great and noble spirit will cede advantages which a favorable fortune has conferred upon him, and true it is that you will renounce many a thing that would have been easy for you to achieve if you hadn't delivered up the captive. But—consider, Peregrin, that Aline's entire fate, entire life, depends upon the possession of that captive, that—"

"If you don't want," Peregrinus interrupted the lady, "if you don't want me, angelic young lady, to take everything for a feverish delusion and perhaps go insane myself on the spot, then just tell me who it is you are talking about, about what captive?"

"What?" replied the lady. "Peregrin, I don't understand you. Do you mean to deny perhaps that he actually has fallen into your hands? Wasn't I myself there when he, at the time you bought the hunting set—"

"Who?" screamed Peregrin quite beside himself. "Who is

this *he*? This is the first time in my life that I have seen you, my dear young lady. Who are you, and who is this *he*?"

Then the lady, completely dissolved in grief, fell at Peregrin's feet and cried as the tears streamed profusely from her eyes, "Peregrin, be human, be merciful! Give him back to me! Give him back to me!"

And all this while, Mr. Peregrinus kept shouting, "I'm going mad! I'm going crazy!"

Suddenly the lady collected herself. She seemed much taller than before, her eyes flashed fire, her lips quivered, and she shouted with a wild gesture, "Ha, barbarian! There is no human heart in you. You are implacable—you want me to die, to be destroyed—you won't give him back to me! No, never—never. Ah! luckless creature that I am, I am lost—lost!" And therewith the lady rushed out of the room and Peregrin heard her running down the stairs and heard her screams of lamentation filling the whole house, until downstairs a door was violently slammed shut.

Then everything was death-still, as in a grave.

SECOND ADVENTURE

The Flea Tamer. The sad fate of Princess Gamaheh in Famagusta. The ineptitude of the Spirit Thetel and noteworthy microscopic experiments and amusements. The pretty Dutch girl and the strange adventure of young Mr. George Pepusch, a former Jena student.

There was at this time a man in Frankfurt who practiced a most odd art. He was called the Flea Tamer by virtue of the fact that he had succeeded, to be sure not without the greatest effort and exertion, in putting culture into these tiny animals and in training them to do all sorts of clever tricks.

On a table top of the finest white marble polished to a gleam, you saw with the greatest astonishment fleas that pulled little cannon, caissons, and munitions wagons, while others ran alongside with muskets on their shoulders, cartridge pouches on their backs, and sabers at their sides. At the command of the virtuoso, they executed the most difficult evolutions, and everything seemed merrier and more sprightly than with real, full-sized soldiers because the marching consisted of the daintiest entrechats and aerial leaps and the left-flanks and right-flanks of pretty pirouettes. The entire complement had an astounding aplomb, while at the same time the commander seemed to be an able ballet master. Almost prettier and more wonderful still were the little gold coaches drawn by four, six, or eight fleas. The coachmen and lackeys were rose bugs of the smallest kind, barely visible to the naked eye, but who it was that sat inside could not rightly be discerned.

Involuntarily one was reminded of the equipage of Queen Mab which the doughty Mercutio describes so beautifully in Shakespeare's Romeo and Juliet that one quite understands how often it has passed over his very nose.

Not until the whole table had been viewed with a magnifying glass, however, was the skill of the Flea Tamer revealed in full measure. Only then was the splendor to be seen, and the delicacy of the harnesses, the close work on the weapons, the luster and daintiness of the uniforms, all of which aroused the profoundest admiration. It seemed to surpass comprehension what instruments the Flea Tamer must have used in order to fashion neatly and in proportion certain small accessories—spurs, for example, coat buttons, and the like—and that labor, which otherwise passed for the tailor's masterpiece and which consisted of nothing less than turning out a pair of perfectly fitting riding breeches for a flea—where it must be admitted the taking of the measurements was the hardest part—seemed by comparison a perfectly easy and slight thing.

The Flea Tamer had an infinite run of customers. All day long the hall was never empty of curious people who did not shrink from the high admission charge. Visitors were numerous in the evenings, too, almost more numerous in fact, since then came such persons as set no great store by such waggish tricks but who came to admire a thing which gained the Flea Tamer a quite different esteem and the genuine respect of a natural scientist. This thing was a night microscope, which, like the solar microscope by day, and in a way similar to a magic lantern, cast the brightly illuminated object against a white wall with a sharpness and a distinctness that left nothing to be desired. Along with this, the Flea Tamer also did a business in the finest microscopes that you could ever wish to find and for which people willingly paid very dear prices.

It chanced that a young man named George Pepusch[1]—the

---

[1] A Johann Christoph Pepusch (1667–1752) arranged the music for John Gay's The Beggar's Opera (1728), that perennially popular work which assumed new guise in 1928 as Die Dreigroschenoper (The Threepenny Opera) with text by Bert Brecht and music by Kurt Weill. Doubtless Hoffmann came upon the name in Ernst Ludwig Gerber's "Dictionary of Musicians" (Historisch-Biographisches Lexicon der Tonkünstler), 1792; reissued 1813.

kind reader will presently come to know him better—had the desire to visit the Flea Tamer, though it was late in the evening. While yet on the steps he heard quarreling that was getting more and more vehement and which finally passed into wild screaming and raging. Just as Pepusch was about to enter, the door of the hall flew open violently and in frantic throng the people plunged toward him, death-pale horror on their faces. "The damned wizard! The Devil's henchman! I'll denounce him to the High Council! He'll be thrown out of town, the conjuring fraud!" Thus shrieked the people pell-mell and, driven by fear and terror, they kept trying to get out of the building as fast as possible.

A glance into the hall revealed at once to young Pepusch the reason for this frightful horror which had driven the people out. Inside, everything was alive. A revolting confusion of the most loathsome creatures filled the entire room. The races of the plant lice, of the beetles, of the spiders, of the slime worms, magnified to excessive size, were extending their proboscises, walking about on tall, hairy legs, and hideous ant lions were seizing and squashing with their jagged claws the gnats which were defending themselves and flailing about with their long wings, while in among them writhed vinegar eels, paste eels, and hundred-tentacled polyps, and from all the intermediate spaces peered Infusoria with distorted human faces. Never had Pepusch beheld anything more revolting. He was just on the point of feeling a profound horror, when something coarse flew into his face and he saw himself enveloped in a cloud of dense flour-dust. But therewith his horror was dispelled, for he knew at once that the coarse thing could be nothing else than the round powdered wig of the Flea Tamer, and such indeed it was.

When Pepusch had wiped the powder out of his eyes, the crazy, revolting population of insects had vanished. The Flea Tamer was sitting completely exhausted in his armchair.

"Leeuwenhoek,"[2] Pepusch cried to him, "Leeuwenhoek, do you see now what comes of your carryings-on? Here you have

[2] Anton van Leeuwenhoek (1632–1723) was the famous Dutch merchant and scientist who improved the microscope and first observed blood corpuscles, bacteria, and Infusoria.

had to seek refuge again among your vassals in order to keep people from pitching onto you! Isn't that so?"

"Is it you?" said the Flea Tamer in a weak voice. "Is it you, good Pepusch? Oh, the jig is up for me, absolutely up. I'm a goner! Pepusch, I begin to think you really meant well by me, and that I didn't do well not to pay attention to your warnings."

Now, as Pepusch calmly asked what had happened, the Flea Tamer turned in his armchair toward the wall, covered his face with both hands, and tearfully called to Pepusch just to take a magnifying glass and inspect the marble top of the table. Already with his naked eye Pepusch discerned that the little coaches, the soldiers, etc., were standing and lying dead and that nothing stirred or budged any more. The trained fleas also seemed to have taken on a wholly different form. With the aid of the magnifying glass, Pepusch very soon discovered that there was not one single flea left, but that what he had taken for them were black peppercorns and fruit pits stuck in the harnesses and uniforms.

"I just don't know," the Flea Tamer now began very mournfully and overcome with grief, "I just don't know what evil spirit struck me blind so that I didn't notice the desertion of my troops before all the people had stepped up to the table and prepared to look. You can imagine, Pepusch, how the people, when they saw themselves deceived, first complained and then burst out in flaming anger. They accused me of the foulest deception, and as they kept getting more and more heated and wouldn't listen to any excuse, they were going to pitch onto me to get revenge. What better could I do, in order to escape a thorough drubbing, than immediately to set the big microscope into operation and surround the people entirely with creatures from which they recoil, as is the habit of the mob?"

"But," asked Pepusch, "but tell me now, Leeuwenhoek, how could it happen that your well-trained troops, who have displayed so much loyalty, should suddenly be off and away without your becoming immediately aware of it?"

"Oh," wailed the Flea Tamer, "oh, Pepusch, he has left me, he by whose virtue alone I was master, and he it is to whose base treason I ascribe my blindness and all my misfortune!"

"Didn't I," replied Pepusch, "didn't I warn you long ago not to base your business on tricks which, as I well know, you couldn't perform without the possession of the master? And now you have found out how that possession, in spite of all your efforts, is in jeopardy." Pepusch now gave the Flea Tamer further to understand that he absolutely couldn't comprehend how, even if he had to give up these tricks, this could so upset his life, since the invention of the night microscope as well as his skill in the construction of microscopic lenses in general had long since firmly established him.

The Flea Tamer assured him, however, that quite different matters were involved in these tricks, and that he could not surrender them without renouncing himself and his entire existence.

"But where is Dörtje Elverdink?" Such was Pepusch's inquiry as he interrupted the Flea Tamer.

"Where is she!" shrieked the Flea Tamer, wringing his hands. "Where is Dörtje Elverdink? Gone! That's what she is! Gone— disappeared. Strike me dead at once, Pepusch, for I see the anger and the fury gaining on you more and more. Make short work of it with me!"

"Now you see," said Pepusch with a lowering glance, "now you see what comes of your folly and your silly carryings-on. Who gave you the right to lock poor Dörtje in like a slave, and then, just to attract customers, to deck her out in splendor like a marvel of natural history? Why did you do violence to her affection and not allow her to give me her hand, when you must have noticed how deeply we loved each other? So she has fled? Very well. At least she is no longer in your power, and even if I don't know at this moment where to look for her, I am convinced that I will find her. Here, Leeuwenhoek, put on your wig and resign yourself to your fate. That is the best and most sensible thing you can do now."

The Flea Tamer clapped his wig onto his bald head with his left hand, while with the right he grasped Pepusch by the arm.

"Pepusch," he said, "Pepusch, you are my true friend; for you are the only person in the whole city of Frankfurt who knows that I have been lying in my grave in the old church in Delft since the year 1725,[3] and yet you didn't betray that fact

[3] Hoffmann's error for 1723.

to anyone even when you were angry with me on account of Dörtje Elverdink. Although I sometimes can't quite get it into my head that I actually am that Anton van Leeuwenhoek whom they buried in Delft, nevertheless, when I consider my works and reflect upon my life, I have to believe it over again, and it is for that reason very pleasant for me that people really don't talk about it any more. I realize, my dearest Pepusch, that, as far as Dörtje Elverdink is concerned, I have not acted properly, although in quite a different sense from what you may think. I did quite right in declaring your suit a silly and purposeless effort, but wrong insofar as I was not completely frank with you and did not tell you what the case with Dörtje Elverdink actually is. Then you would have seen how laudable it was to talk wishes out of your head which, in realization, could not have been other than disastrous. —Pepusch! Sit down with me and let me tell you a marvelous history!"

"I may as well," replied Pepusch, with a poisonous glance as he sat down on an upholstered armchair opposite the Flea Tamer.

"Since you," the Flea Tamer began, "since you, my dear friend Pepusch, are quite conversant with history, you doubtless know that King Sekakis lived for many centuries in intimate liaison with the Queen of the Flowers, and that the beautiful and lovely Princess Gamaheh was the fruit of that love. It may be less well-known, and I cannot tell you, by what means the Princess Gamaheh came to Famagusta. Many claim, and not without cause, that the princess was supposed to hide in Famagusta from the repulsive Leech Prince, sworn enemy of the Queen of the Flowers.

"Suffice it to say that in Famagusta it chanced that the princess was strolling once in the refreshing cool of the evening and entered a dark and lovely cypress grove. Enticed by the lovely rustling of the evening breeze, the murmur of the brook, and the melodious twittering of the birds, the princess lay down on the soft fragrant moss and fell presently into deep sleep. But precisely the enemy whom she had sought to escape, the ugly Leech Prince, stuck his head up out of the slime of the water, caught sight of the princess, and fell in love with the beautiful sleeper to the point that he could not resist the desire to kiss her. Softly he crept up and kissed her behind the left ear. Now you realize, friend Pepusch, that the lady whom the Leech Prince ventures to kiss is lost, because he is the meanest bloodsucker in the world. And so it came about that the Leech Prince kept on kissing the poor princess until all life had departed from her. Then he fell, quite glutted and drunken, upon the moss and had to be taken home by his servants, who quickly came squirming up from the slime. In vain did the Root Mandragora work itself out of the ground and lay itself upon the wound which the crafty Leech Prince had kissed upon the princess; in vain did all the flowers rise at the lament of the Root and join in the disconsolate lamentation! Then it chanced that the Spirit Thetel was just coming along that way, and he too was deeply touched by Gamaheh's beauty and by her unhappy death. He took the princess into his arms, pressed her to his bosom, strove to breathe life into her with his breath, but she did not waken from her deathly sleep. Then the Spirit Thetel caught sight of the repulsive Leech Prince, whom—he was that sluggish and besotted—his servants had not been able to get down into his palace, flamed up in anger, and threw a whole fistful of salt crystals upon the body of the ugly enemy, so that the latter directly poured forth all the purple ichor that he had sucked from the Princess Gamaheh and then, amid many twitchings and grimaces, gave up the ghost in revolting fashion. But all the flowers that stood round about dipped their garments in this ichor and in eternal memorial of the murdered princess, dyed them such a magnificent red as no painter on earth can produce. You realize, Pepusch, that the finest dark red gillyflowers, amaryllis, and cheiranthus come from precisely that cypress grove where the Leech Prince kissed the beautiful Gamaheh to death. The Spirit Thetel was about to hurry away, for he still had much to do before nightfall in Samarcand; he cast, however, one more glance at the princess, stopped as though held by a spell, and observed her with the most profound sadness. Suddenly a thought occurred to him. Instead of going on his way, he picked the princess up in his arms and with her soared aloft high into the air.

"At that very time two wise men, one of whom, let it not be concealed, was I myself, were observing the courses of the stars from the gallery of a lofty tower. High above them they perceived the Spirit Thetel with the Princess Gamaheh, and at the same instant it occurred to one of them—ah! but that has nothing to do with the case for the time being! Both mages had recognized the Spirit Thetel but not the princess, and they racked their brains with all sorts of surmises as to what the apparition might signify, without being able to come up with anything certain, or even plausible. Soon afterwards, however, the sad fate of the Princess Gamaheh became generally known in Famagusta, and then the mages were able to explain the appearance of the Spirit Thetel with the girl in his arms.

"Both suspected that the Spirit Thetel must surely have found a means of bringing the princess back to life, and they made up their minds to inquire in Samarcand, where, according to their observation, he had patently directed his flight. But in Samarcand all was silence on the score of the princess. No one knew a thing.

"Many years had passed. The two mages had quarreled, as is wont to happen among learned men, the more often the more erudite they are, and they shared only the most important discoveries with each other from old and iron habit. You have not forgotten, Pepusch, that I was myself one of those mages. Hence, I was not a little astonished at a communication from my colleague which contained the most fantastic and at the same time the most glorious news concerning the Princess Gamaheh that anyone would ever have dreamed. This is how it was. Through a scientific friend, my colleague had received from Samarcand the most beautiful and rarest tulips, as completely fresh as if they had just been cut from their stems. He was primarily concerned with the microscopic examination of the inner parts and particularly of the pollen. So he dissected a lovely lavender and yellow tulip, and in the midst of the flower-cup he discovered a curious little seed-pellet which struck his curiosity in a very special way. But what was his amazement when, by means of the application of the finder lens, he clearly perceived that the seed-pellet was none other than the Princess Gamaheh, who seemed to be slumbering quietly and sweetly, couched upon the pollen of the tulip-cup.

"Far as the distance was that separated me from my colleague, I nevertheless set out instantly and hastened to him. He, meanwhile, had put aside all operations in order to grant me the satisfaction of the first view, probably in the fear that, acting by his own lights, he might spoil something. I was soon convinced of the total correctness of my colleague's observation, and, like him, I was also of the firm conviction that it must be possible to rescue the princess from her slumber and restore her to her previous form. The sublime intellect inherent in us caused us presently to discover the proper means. Since you, friend Pepusch, understand very little, nothing at all, in fact, about our art, it would be entirely supererogatory to describe to you the various operations which we then undertook in order to achieve our purpose. It will suffice if I tell you that by means of the skillful use of various lenses, which for the most part I prepared myself, we succeeded not only in educing the princess unharmed from the pollen, but also in advancing her growth in such a fashion that she soon had attained her natural stature. Granted, life was still lacking, and whether it were possible to produce this for her depended upon the last and most difficult operation. With the aid of a fine Kuff solar microscope we projected her image and neatly detached the reflection from the white wall, smoothly and without any damage. As soon as the reflection floated free, it shot like a lightning flash into the lens, which was shattered in a thousand pieces. Before us stood the princess, fresh and full of life. We set up a shout of joy, but all the greater was our horror as we noticed that the circulation of her blood was blocked at just the point where the Leech Prince had kissed her. She was just on the point of collapsing lifeless, when we saw a little black dot appear at the point behind her left ear and then disappear again just as quickly. The stoppage of the blood ceased immediately, the princess recovered once more, and our work was a success.

"Each of us, I and my colleague, knew perfectly well what priceless value the possession of the princess could have for him, and each strove for it, thinking he had a better right than the other. My colleague alleged that the tulip, in the flower-cup of which he had found the princess, had been his property, and that he had made the initial discovery, which he had communicated to me, so that I could be considered only as an assistant who could not expect as the reward of my labors the work itself, with which I had only helped. I, on the other hand, cited the fact that I had discovered the last and most difficult operation by which the princess had been brought to life, and that my colleague had only assisted in the execution thereof, by which token, if he had had claims of ownership to the embryo in the pollen, the living person nevertheless belonged to me. We argued for several hours until finally, when we had shouted ourselves hoarse, a compromise was worked out. My colleague surrendered the princess to me, in exchange for whom I delivered to him a very important and secret lens. But precisely this lens is the cause of our present total enmity. My colleague asserts that I have fraudulently made off with this lens. But that is a gross and shameless lie, and even though I actually know that he has lost the lens in the course of delivery, I can still declare on my honor and conscience that I am not to blame for that, and I simply don't understand how that could have happened. The lens, you see, is not so small but that a grain of powder must be, at most, eight times larger.

"Look, friend Pepusch, I have now given you my entire confidence. Now you know that Dörtje Elverdink is none other than the Princess Gamaheh restored to life. Now you realize that a simple young man such as you can have no hope of such a lofty, mystic alliance—"

"Stop!" George Pepusch interrupted the Flea Tamer and smiled a trifle satanically toward him. "Stop! One confidence is worth another, and so for my part I will confide to you that I knew sooner and better than you everything that you have been telling me here. I can't marvel enough at your stupidity and at your absurd presumption. Understand what you could not have helped knowing long ago, were it not that your science, except insofar as lens-grinding is concerned, is so miserable; understand that I am myself the Thistle Zeherit, which stood where the Princess Gamaheh had laid her head and about which you have found it prudent not to speak at all."

"Pepusch," cried the Flea Tamer, "are you in your right mind? The Thistle Zeherit blooms in far-off India, specifically in that lovely mountain-girt vale where sometimes the wisest mages of the earth are wont to assemble. Archivarius Lindhorst can best instruct you on that score.[4] And you, whom I have seen running to the schoolmaster here in your laced-up jacket, whom I have known as a Jena student emaciated and yellowed with studying and hunger, you claim to be the Thistle Zeherit? Tell that to somebody else, but don't bother me with it."

"What a wise man," said Pepusch, laughing, "what a wise man you are, Leeuwenhoek. Well, think of my person as you will, but don't be silly enough to deny that the Thistle Zeherit bloomed forth in glowing love and longing at the moment when Gamaheh's sweet breath fell upon it, and that when it touched the lovely princess's temple, she too, sweetly dreaming, fell in love. Too late the Thistle spied the Leech Prince, whom it would otherwise have instantly killed with its spines. But it would have been possible to bring the princess back to life with the help of the Root Mandragora, if the oafish Spirit Thetel had not interfered, with his clumsy attempts at rescue. It *is* true that Thetel reached in anger into the salt-box, which on journeys he usually wore at his belt, the way Pantagruel carried his medicinal bark,[5] and threw a hefty handful of rock salt at the Leech Prince, but the claim that he killed him by doing so is quite false. All the salt landed in the mud and not a single grain of it hit the Leech Prince, whom the Thistle Zeherit killed with his spines and thus avenged the death of the princess, and then dedicated himself to death. No one but the Spirit Thetel, who interfered in things that didn't concern him, is to blame for the fact that the princess had to lie so long in flower-sleep. The Thistle Zeherit awoke much sooner. For the death of both was but the insensibility of flower-sleep, out of which they could return to life, albeit in different form. You would certainly brim the measure of your vulgar error if you were to imagine that the Princess Gamaheh bore precisely the form that Dörtje Elverdink now bears, and that you were the one who restored her to life. With you, my good Leeuwenhoek, things went as

---

[4] Archivarius Lindhorst is the great and benevolent mage in Hoffmann's earlier tale, *The Golden Pot (Der goldene Topf)*.

[5] See Rabelais, *Gargantua and Pantagruel*, Book II, chapter 28.

they did, in the truly remarkable tale of the Three Oranges,[6] with that hapless servant who set two maidens free from the oranges without first making sure of the means of keeping them alive, so that they then perished wretchedly before his eyes. Not you, no, but the one who has escaped from you and whose loss you feel and bewail so much, he was the one who completed the work which you began ineptly enough."

"Ha!" shrieked the Flea Tamer, completely beside himself. "Ha! My premonition! But you, Pepusch, you, to whom I have shown so much goodness, instead of standing by me in my misfortune, you dish me out all sorts of unseemly clownish jokes."

"The clownish jokes be upon your head!" cried Pepusch, thoroughly provoked. "You will rue your folly too late, you conceited charlatan!—I am going to look for Dörtje Elverdink. But just so that you won't bother honorable people any further—"

Pepusch reached out for the screw which turned on the whole microscopic machine.

"Kill me outright!" screamed the Flea Tamer.

But at that instant everything came crashing down and the Flea Tamer collapsed on the floor in a faint.

"How can it be," said George Pepusch to himself when he got out on the street, "how can it be that a man who has a nice warm room at his disposition, and a well-fluffed-up bed, goes chasing about the streets at night in the nastiest storm and rain? —If he has forgotten his key, and if besides, love and foolish desire impel him." In this way he was obliged to answer himself. For his entire action now seemed foolish to him. He recalled the moment when he had first seen Dörtje Elverdink—

Several years previously the Flea Tamer had been displaying his feats in Berlin and had been having no slight success as long as the business had novelty. But it was not long before people had seen their fill of trained and drilled fleas, and then they didn't consider worthy of admiration even the tailoring, the harness work and saddle work, or the weapons' design for

---

[6] Gozzi's eighteenth-century fairly-tale comedy, *L'amore delle tre melarance*, the basis for Prokofiev's twentieth-century opera, *The Love of Three Oranges*.

the use of the tiny creatures, although at first the talk had been of incomprehensibility and magical life, and the Flea Tamer seemed to have passed wholly into oblivion. Presently, the talk was that a niece of the Flea Tamer's, who had not put in an appearance before, was now in attendance at the performances. This niece was reported to be such a pretty, lovely girl, and so delightfully costumed besides, that it was simply not to be described. The easily stirred world of the modern young gentlemen who, as proficient concert masters, are accustomed to set the tone and tempo in society, flocked in, and since in this world only extremes avail, the Flea Tamer's niece aroused wonder such as never had been known. Soon it was *ton* to visit the Flea Tamer. Anyone who had not seen his niece was not permitted to speak, and thus the man's venture was promoted. But no one could manage the given name "Dörtje," and since just at that time the magnificent Bethmann was bringing out all the lofty graciousness, all the ravishing charm, all the womanly tenderness ever embodied in the sex, in the role of the Queen of Golconda,[7] and this role seemed to be an ideal of the ineffable magic with which a feminine creature is able to delight everyone, people conferred upon the Dutch girl the name of "Aline."

At the time when George Pepusch came to Berlin, Leeuwenhoek's lovely niece was the talk of the day, and even at the table d'hôte of the hotel where Pepusch had taken lodgings, the talk was of almost nothing else but the charming little marvel who delighted all the men, young and old, and indeed even the women themselves. Pepusch was urged to betake himself directly to the supreme summit of all current activity in Berlin and to see the beautiful Dutch girl. Pepusch had a sensitive, melancholy temperament. In any pleasure he perceived too soon the bitter aftertaste which comes from the black Stygian rivulet that runs through our whole life, and this made him gloomy, withdrawn, indeed often unjust to everyone around him. One can imagine that in this way Pepusch was little disposed to go running after pretty girls. For all of that, however, he did go to the Flea Tamer's, more to see confirmed his predetermined

---

[7] Friederike Bethmann-Unzelmann (1760–1815) sang the title role of the opera in Berlin beginning in April, 1804.

opinion that here, as so often in life, lurked only a bizarre illusion, than for the sake of the dangerous marvel. He found the Dutch girl quite pretty, charming, pleasing, but as he watched her he was forced to smile complacently at his own sagacity, by means of which he had already guessed that the heads which the girl had completely turned must have been somewhat wobbly from the very start.

The beauty had completely in her control that light, unconstrained tone that testifies to the finest social breeding. With that gracious coquetry that extends the fingertips familiarly to a man and simultaneously numbs his courage to grasp them, this lovely little thing knew how to attract those who were storming her from all sides as well as how to hold them within the limits of the most delicate propriety.

No one bothered about the stranger Pepusch, who found sufficient leisure to observe the beauty in all her action and being. But as he peered longer and longer into her lovely little face, there stirred in the deepest depths of his inner being a dull recollection, as though he had somewhere seen the Dutch girl before, though in quite different circumstances and dressed quite differently, just as it seemed to him as if he himself had been of an entirely different form at that time. In vain he struggled to bring this recollection to some clarity, although the notion that he actually had seen the little lady gained constantly in certitude. The blood rushed to his face as finally someone lightly tapped him and whispered into his ear: "The lightning bolt has struck you, too, has it not, Master Philosopher?" It was his neighbor from the table d'hôte to whom he had declared that he considered the ecstasy into which everyone was plunged a curious madness that would vanish as quickly as it arose. Pepusch noticed that during the time he had been staring at the little lady with unaverted gaze, the hall had become empty, so that the last persons were now walking away. Only now did the Dutch girl seem to notice him. She bowed to him with gracious friendliness.

Pepusch could not get the Dutch girl out of his head. During the sleepless night he kept tormenting himself to get somehow on the track of that recollection, but in vain. Only the sight of the beauty could put him on that track, he decided quite rightly, and the very next day, and all the days ensuing thereafter, he did not fail to make his way to the Flea Tamer's and stare for two or three hours at the pretty Dörtje Elverdink.

When a man cannot get rid of the thought of a charming lady who has caught his attention in one way or another, then this is for him the first step toward love, and thus it came about that at the moment when he thought he was merely pondering over that dim recollection, Pepusch was already completely in love with the beautiful Dutch girl.

Who cared any longer now about the fleas, over whom the Dutch girl, attracting everyone to herself, had won the most resplendent victory? The Flea Tamer himself felt that he was playing a somewhat silly role with his fleas, and hence locked up his troops until some other time, and with considerable skill gave a different form to his spectacle and gave the leading role to his beautiful niece.

Specifically, the Flea Tamer had had the happy thought of organizing evening *causeries*, to which people subscribed at a fairly high fee, and at which, after he had displayed several pretty optical tricks, the further entertainment of the company devolved upon his niece. The beauty allowed her social talent to shine to the full, then she used the slightest lag to give the company new impetus by her singing, accompanying herself upon the guitar. Her voice was not strong, her technique was not tremendous—often, in fact, it was contrary to the rules—but the sweet tone, the clarity and deftness of her singing were wholly in keeping with her lovely person, and finally, when she allowed the languishing gaze from beneath her black, silken eyelashes to gleam like moist moonglow down over the spectators, every heart was choked and the censure of the stubbornest pedant could not but fall silent.

At these evening *causeries* Pepusch zealously pursued his study, that is to say he stared at the Dutch girl for two hours and then left the hall with the others.

Once he was standing closer than usual to the Dutch girl and clearly heard her say to a young man: "Tell me, who is that lifeless ghost who stares at me every evening for hours at a time and then goes away without a sound?"

Pepusch felt himself deeply offended. He raged and stormed

about his room and acted so frantically that no friend would have recognized him in that wild creature. He swore up and down never to see the malicious Dutch girl again. But on the very next evening he did not fail to make his way to Leeuwenhoek's at the customary hour and wherever possible to stare with fixed gaze at the beautiful Dörtje. Going up the steps he was really very shocked to be going up the steps, and with the utmost swiftness he had made the resolution at least to keep a good distance away from the seductive creature. And he actually carried out this resolution by creeping off into a corner of the hall. But the attempt to lower his eyes failed utterly, and, as was said, he gazed into the Dutch girl's eyes more fixedly than ever.

He himself did not know how it came about that Dörtje Elverdink was suddenly standing in the corner right beside him.

With a small voice that was a sweet murmuring melody, the lovely creature was saying: "Sir, I don't recall having seen you elsewhere than here in Berlin, and yet I find so much that is familiar in the features of your face, in your entire person. Indeed, I feel as though we had been quite close friends a very long time ago, in a very distant land, and under very different, curious circumstances. I beg you, sir, resolve my uncertainty, and unless a resemblance is perhaps deceiving me, let us renew the friendly relationship that rests in obscure memory like a beautiful dream."

At these gracious words of the beautiful Dutch girl, Mr. George Pepusch had a very odd feeling. His heart was choked, and, while his forehead was burning, a chill was running through all his limbs as if he lay ill with the most violent fever. Though this may have meant nothing other than that Mr. Pepusch was over his ears in love with the Dutch girl, there was nevertheless another reason for the utterly confused state which robbed him of all speech, in fact almost of all recollection. For as Dörtje Elverdink was telling of how she thought she had known him long ago, it seemed to him as if within him, as in a magic lantern, a new picture were suddenly being thrust forward, and he glimpsed a far-off Yore that lay a long way behind the time when he had first tasted mother's milk, and in which he himself, as well as Dörtje Elverdink, moved and had their being. Enough! The thought which was just then becoming clear through much reflection and which was assuming firm outlines, flashed forth at this moment; and this thought was nothing less than that Dörtje Elverdink was the Princess Gamaheh, daughter of King Sekakis, and whom he had loved at that green time when he had still been the Thistle Zeherit. It was well that he did not expressly communicate this notion to other people; otherwise he might perhaps have been taken for mad and locked up—although the *idée fixe* of a partially insane person may often be nothing else but the irony of an existence which preceded the present one.

"But, good heavens! You seem to be mute, sir!" Thus spoke the little lady as she touched George's bosom with the daintiest little fingers. But from the tips of those fingers an electric ray darted into George's heart, and he woke from his insensibility. In total ecstasy he seized the little lady's hand, covered it with ardent kisses, and cried: "Heavenly, divine creature!" and so on. The kind reader can probably imagine what all else George Pepusch cried at that moment.

Suffice it to say that the little lady accepted George's protestations of love in a way that was all he could wish for, and that the fateful minute in the corner of Leeuwenhoek's hall produced a love affair which translated the good Mr. George Pepusch first into heaven, and then again, by virtue of its alternation, transferred him to hell. For, since Pepusch was of a melancholy temperament and morose and suspicious besides, it could not fail but that Dörtje's conduct should give him occasion for many a petty jealousy. Precisely that petty jealousy, however, stimulated Dörtje's somewhat roguish humor, and it was her joy to torment poor Mr. George Pepusch in the subtlest way. But since any given thing may be pressed only up to a certain point, it came finally to an outburst with Pepusch of his long-contained wrath.

He happened to be speaking once about that wonderful time when, as the Thistle Zeherit, he had so tenderly loved the beautiful Dutch girl, who was then the daughter of King Sekakis, and was recalling with all the enthusiasm of the most fervent love that precisely that relationship and the fight with the Leech Prince had already given him the most incontestable right to

Dörtje's hand. Dörtje Elverdink assured him that she remembered that time and that relationship very well, and that the first glimmer of recollection had entered her soul when Pepusch had gazed at her with his Thistle-look. The little lady was able to talk so charmingly of these wondrous things, she acted so enthusiastic about her love for the Thistle Zeherit, who had been predestined to study at Jena and then to rediscover the Princess Gamaheh in Berlin, that Mr. George Pepusch fancied himself in the Eldorado of all delight. The pair of lovers were standing by the window and the little lady was allowing the lovesick George to put his arm around her. In this intimate position they were exchanging fond talk, for the dreamy conversation about the marvels of Famagusta was turning into fond talk. Just then a very handsome officer of the Hussar Guards happened to walk by in a brand-new uniform and in a very friendly way waved to the little lady, whom he knew from evening parties. Dörtje had her eyes half closed and her little head turned away from the street. Anyone would have thought it would have been impossible for her to see the officer. But mighty is the magic of a gleaming new uniform! The little lady, roused perhaps by the significant clatter of the sword on the pavement, opened her little eyes bright and clear, slipped out of George's arms, threw the window up, kissed her hand to the officer, and gazed after him until he had disappeared around the corner.

"Gamaheh!" cried the Thistle Zeherit, beside himself. "Gamaheh! What does this mean? Are you making fun of me? Is this the fidelity you swore to your Thistle?"

The little lady turned on her heel, broke into a shrill laugh, and cried, "Come, come, George! If I am the daughter of worthy old King Sekakis, and if you are the Thistle Zeherit, then that darling officer is the Spirit Thetel, who really pleases me much better than the gloomy, prickly Thistle."

With that the Dutch girl ran out the doorway, but, as can be imagined, George Pepusch fell directly into rage and despair and ran wildly down the steps and out of the house as if a thousand devils were after him. As fate would have it, George encountered a friend, who was seated in a post carriage and on the point of departure. "Wait! I'm going with you!" Thus shouted the Thistle Zeherit, and he swiftly flew home, put on an overcoat, thrust money into his pocket, gave the landlady the key to his room, climbed into the post carriage, and rode off with his friend.

Despite this inimical separation, however, the love for the beautiful Dutch girl had not been extinguished in George's heart at all, and no more could he make up his mind to renounce the just claims which he, as the Thistle Zeherit, felt he had to Gamaheh's hand and heart. Accordingly, he renewed those claims when he met Leeuwenhoek again in The Hague some years later, and how zealously he prosecuted them in Frankfurt as well, the kind reader has already learned.

In total desperation Mr. George Pepusch was rushing about in the night through the streets, when his attention was caught by the flickering and uncommonly bright gleam of a light that fell upon the street through a crack in a window shutter on the ground floor of a respectable house. He thought the room must be on fire, and hence he clambered up on the grille fence to look into the room. But his astonishment was boundless at what he beheld.

A cheery, bright fire was blazing on the hearth, which was directly opposite the window. Before this hearth was sitting, or rather lying in a wide, old-fashioned armchair, the little Dutch girl, adorned in the finery of an angel. She seemed to be sleeping, while a very old and withered man was kneeling in front of the fire and, with spectacles on his nose, was peering into a pot in which apparently some drink was being heated. Pepusch was in the act of clambering up still higher to get a better look at the group, when he felt himself seized by the legs and pulled violently downward. A harsh voice cried: "Just look at the rascal! Isn't that the limit! Off, you scamp, to the dog-kennel!" It was the night watch who had noticed George climbing up to the window and who could imagine nothing else but that he was trying to break into the house. All protestations notwithstanding, Mr. George Pepusch was hauled away by the watchman, to whose aid the passing patrol had hurried up, and in this wise his nocturnal wanderings were happily concluded in the guardhouse.

THIRD ADVENTURE

Appearance of a small monster. Further clarification of
the fate of the Princess Gamaheh. Remarkable bond of
friendship entered into by Mr. Peregrinus Tyss and
revelation of who the old gentleman is who rents lodgings in his house. Very marvelous effect of a fairly small
microscopic lens. Unexpected arrest of the hero of the
story.

Anyone who has gone through such
things in a single evening as had Mr. Peregrinus Tyss, in fact
anyone who finds himself in a mood like his, may find it quite
impossible to sleep well. Restlessly Mr. Peregrinus kept twisting
about on his bed, and whenever he fell into those fantasies
which customarily precede sleep, he was once again holding the
sweet little creature in his arms and sensing hot and ardent
kisses on his lips. Then he would start up and fancy he was
hearing Aline's lovely voice, still awake. With passionate yearning he hoped she might not have fled, and yet he feared once
again that she might enter forthwith and enmesh him in an in-
extricable net. This struggle between contrary emotions con-
stricted his heart and at the same time filled it with a sweet
anguish never known before.

"Do not go to sleep, Peregrinus, do not go to sleep, noble
man! I must speak with you this very instant!" Thus came a
whisper close in front of Peregrinus, and it kept on: "Do not go
to sleep! Do not go to sleep!" until he finally opened his eyes,
which he had been holding tightly shut, in order to see the
lovely Aline more clearly.

By the shimmer of the night lamp he distinguished a little

295

monster hardly a span in length sitting on his white coverlet. For the first moment he was horrified by it, but then he courageously reached toward it with his hand to make sure if his imagination were not deceiving him. Directly the little monster had vanished without a trace.

Although the exact portrayal of the beautiful Aline, Dörtje Elverdink, or the Princess Gamaheh—for the kind reader has long since known that one and the same person is only apparently divided into three persons—could probably be omitted, it is, on the other hand, absolutely necessary to describe with full exactness the little monster that sat on the coverlet and caused Mr. Peregrinus some degree of horror. As has been mentioned, the creature was hardly a span in length. In its birdlike head was stuck a pair of round, gleaming eyes, and out of the sparrowlike beak protruded a long pointed thing like a thin rapier, and just above the beak two horns thrust forth from the forehead. The neck, birdlike as well, began just back of the head, but then became thicker so that, without interruption of the form, he grew down into a formless body that had almost the shape of a hazelnut and was covered with dark brown scales like an armadillo. Weirdest and oddest of all, however, was the formation of the arms and legs. The former had two joints and were rooted in the two cheeks of the creature, right by the beak. Directly beneath these arms was a pair of feet, and then further on another pair, all two-jointed like the arms. These rear feet seemed to be the ones on whose efficiency the creature really seemed to rely, for, besides the fact that these feet were perceptibly longer and stronger than the others, the creature was wearing very fine golden boots on them, with diamond spurs.[1]

Now if, as was said before, the little monster had vanished without a trace as soon as Peregrinus had reached for it, he would certainly have taken everything for an illusion of his excited senses, had it not been that right underneath, in the corner of the bed, a faint voice was audible, which was to be

---

[1] Except for the golden boots and diamond spurs, the description follows the large and detailed drawings of the flea made by seventeenth- and eighteenth-century microscopists. An example, appearing in several places in this volume, is reproduced most prominently facing the title page.

heard saying: "Good heavens, Peregrinus Tyss, can I have been so mistaken in you? Yesterday you treated me so nobly, and now that I am about to prove my gratitude to you, you reach out a murderous hand toward me? But perhaps my shape has displeased you and I did the wrong thing to show myself to you microscopically, just so you would surely notice me—something that is not so easy as you might think. I am sitting now precisely as before on your white bedspread, and yet you don't see me at all. Don't take it amiss, Peregrinus, but your optic nerves are really a bit too coarse for my slim figure. Just promise me that I will be safe with you and that you won't do anything hostile to me, and I will come closer to you and tell you many a thing which you won't go wrong in finding out."

"Tell me," replied Peregrinus Tyss to the voice, "just tell me first who you are, dear unknown friend, and we shall go on from there. Meanwhile I can assure you in advance that anything hostile is contrary to my nature and that I shall continue to treat you nobly, although at the moment I can't understand in what way I can have previously proven my nobility toward you. But do go on preserving your incognito, because the sight of you is not especially pleasing."

"You are," the voice went on to say, after clearing its throat a bit, "you are, I repeat with pleasure, a noble man, Mr. Peregrinus, but not particularly deeply initiate in learning, and in general a bit inexperienced, otherwise you would have recognized me at the first glance. I could speak somewhat boastfully; I could say that I am one of the mightiest kings, and that I am master over many, many millions. Out of native modesty, and because in the last analysis the term "king" is not quite appropriate, I will pass over that. Among the people at whose head I have the honor to stand, a republican constitution happens to prevail. A senate, which may consist of at the most forty-five thousand nine hundred and ninety-nine members, occupies, for the sake of easier supervision of voting, the position of the ruler; but whoever stands at the head of this senate actually bears the name of "Master," because he must have attained mastership in all things in life! Without further ado then, I shall now reveal to you that I, who am here speaking with you without your being able to see me, am none other than Master

Flea. That you know my people I do not doubt in the least, for, worthy sir, you have surely refreshed and strengthened many a one of my people before this with your own blood. You must therefore be aware at least that my people are animated by an almost indomitable sense of freedom and actually are made up of nothing but harebrained madcaps who are inclined to elude solid formation by incessant hopping about. You realize what a talent is involved in being Master of such a people, Mr. Peregrinus, and by that token you will have the proper respect for me. Assure me of that, Mr. Peregrinus, before I speak any more."

For a few minutes Mr. Peregrinus Tyss felt as though a large windmill, driven by stormy waves, were turning inside his head. But then he became calmer, and it just seemed to him as though the apparition of the strange lady at bookbinder Lämmerhirt's was just as fantastic as what was going on now, and that perhaps this was nothing but the proper continuation of the odd story in which he had become involved.

Mr. Peregrinus declared to Master Flea that he now respected him quite uncommonly for the sake of his rare gifts, and that he was all the more eager to learn more from him, inasmuch as his voice had a very nice sound, and a certain gentleness of speech gave evidence of his fine and dainty physical structure.

"Thank you," Master Flea went on to say, "thank you very much, dear Mr. Tyss, for your good opinion, and I hope to convince you presently that you have not been mistaken in me. In order for you to discover, my good man, what service you performed for me, it is necessary to communicate my entire biography to you. Hear me, then! My father was the famous—

"Oh! But it just occurs to me that readers and listeners have noticeably lost the fair gift of patience, and that extensive life histories, formerly loved best of all, are now abominated. Hence, rather than being thorough, I shall only fleetingly and episodically touch on what directly relates to my stay with you.

"By virtue of the fact that I actually am Master Flea, you must, dear Mr. Peregrinus, recognize in me a man of the most widely encompassing erudition, of the deepest experience in all the branches of learning. And yet, you cannot measure the degree of my knowledge by your standards, since the marvelous world in which I live with my people is unknown to you. What would be your astonishment if your mind were to be opened for that world, which would seem to you the strangest and most incomprehensible magic realm? Precisely for this reason you should not find it at all surprising if everything that originates in that world appears to you as a confused fairy tale thought up by an idle brain. But do not be led astray by that. Trust my words.

"You see, my people are far superior to you human beings in many things, for example, in the matter of seeing through the secrets of Nature, in strength and skill, spiritual and physical skill. However, we too have our passions, and these, as with you, are often the source of many a discomfort, in fact of total calamity. Thus, I too was loved by my people, indeed worshiped. My masterdom could have brought me to the highest level of happiness, had I not been blinded by an unhappy passion for a person who dominated me utterly without ever being able to become my spouse. Our sex is in general reproached with a very particular preference, a preference that exceeds the limits of propriety, for the fair sex. However well-grounded this reproach may be, nevertheless everyone knows, on the other hand—oh, but no more digressions!

"I saw the daughter of King Sekakis, the beautiful Gamaheh, and instantaneously fell so horribly in love with her that I forgot my people, forgot myself, and lived only in the bliss of hopping about on her loveliest neck, on her most beautiful bosom, and tickling the exquisite creature with sweet kisses. She often stretched out her rosy fingers toward me, but without being able to catch me. I took this for pleasant fondling, for the lovely dalliance of felicitous love!—how foolish is the mind of a lover, even though he be Master Flea himself. Suffice it to say that poor Gamaheh was attacked by the loathsome Leech Prince who kissed her to death. But I could have succeeded in saving the beloved girl, if a silly loudmouth and a bungling lout had not got mixed up in the affair without being asked, and spoiled everything. The loudmouth was the Thistle Zeherit, and the bungler was the Spirit Thetel. As the Spirit Thetel soared into the air with the sleeping princess, I gripped tight the Brussels lace that she happened to be wearing about her neck, and in that way was Gamaheh's loyal traveling companion without being noticed by the Spirit. It happened that we flew over two mages that were on a high tower observing the course of the stars. One of those mages focused his glass so sharply upon me that I was downright blinded by the shine of the magic instrument. A powerful dizziness came over me, I tried in vain to hold on tightly, I plunged past help down from the terrible height, fell right onto the nose of the observing mage. Nothing but my lightness and my extraordinary agility kept me alive.

"I was still too dazed to jump down off the mage's nose and get to complete safety, when the monster, that treacherous Leeuwenhoek—that was the mage's name—neatly caught me with his fingers and put me directly under a Russwurm universal microscope. Despite the fact that it was nighttime and hence he had to light the lamp, he was far too practiced an observer and far too experienced in science not to recognize me at once as Master Flea. Highly delighted that a happy chance had played this distinguished captive into his hands, and determined to take all possible advantage of the fact, he threw poor me into chains, and thus began an anguished captivity, from which I was not released until yesterday forenoon by you, Mr. Peregrinus Tyss.

"Possession of me gave the accursed Leeuwenhoek total power over my vassals, whom he soon gathered around him in droves and upon whom he superimposed with barbaric cruelty a so-called culture, which soon robbed us of all freedom and all enjoyment of life. As for academic subjects and the sciences and arts in general, Leeuwenhoek very quickly discovered to his astonishment and annoyance that we were almost more erudite than he himself. The higher culture which he forced upon us consisted primarily in our becoming something, or at least in our having to represent something. Precisely that becoming something, that representing something, gave rise to a number of requirements that we had not previously known and which we now had to fulfill by the sweat of our brows. The cruel Leeuwenhoek turned us into statesmen, military men, professors, and I don't know what all. And these had to parade about in the costumes of the various professions, had to bear weapons, etc. Thus there arose among us tailors, cobblers, hairdressers, embroiderers, button makers, weaponsmiths, belt makers, sword cutlers, wheelwrights, and a host of other artisans that worked only to benefit an unnecessary and harmful luxury. Worst of all was the fact that Leeuwenhoek had his eye on nothing but his own advantage, that he displayed us cultivated people to the public and got money for it. What was more, he got all the credit for our culture and he received the praise which was due to us alone. Leeuwenhoek knew perfectly well that, once I was lost, there would be an end to his mastery over my people. That was all the more reason for him to entwine constantly the magic that held me in thrall to him, and the more tormented was my unhappy captivity.

"With ardent yearning I kept thinking of the lovely Gamaheh and pondered means of getting news of her fate. But what the shrewdest intelligence could not think up, the favor of chance produced of itself. My mage's friend and confederate old Swammerdam,[2] had discovered the Princess Gamaheh in the pollen of a tulip and had confided this discovery to his friend. By means which I shall omit to expatiate upon, good Mr. Peregrinus Tyss, since you would not understand especially much of them, the gentleman succeeded in restoring the princess to her natural form and in summoning her back to life. In the long run, however, the two highly learned gentlemen were just as much bungling louts as the Spirit Thetel and the Thistle Zeherit. In their eagerness they had forgotten the main thing, and thus it came about that at the very moment when the princess had awakened to life, she started to sink down anew into death. I alone knew what was the matter. My love for the beautiful Gamaheh, which flamed up more strongly than ever in my bosom, gave me a giant's strength; I wrenched my chains asunder; with one mighty leap I sprang upon the lovely girl's shoulder—only one little sting sufficed to start the arrested blood pulsing. She lived again!

"But now I must tell you, Mr. Peregrinus Tyss, that that sting has to be repeated if the princess is to go on blooming in beauty

---

[2] Jan Swammerdam (1637–1680), a Dutch entomologist whose researches were published, under the title of *Biblia naturae*, in 1737–38 at the centenary of his birth. He had discovered the corpuscular structure of the blood even before Leeuwenhoek but did not make the discovery public. Hoffmann incorrectly doubles the final "m" in his name, which we here spell in its proper Dutch form, and often abbreviates it to "Swammer."

and youth, otherwise she would in a few months' time shrivel up into an old withered crone. Thus, as you will realize, I am absolutely indispensable to her, and only out of fear of losing me can there be explained the black ingratitude with which Gamaheh rewarded my love. Namely, she delivered me without further ado to that abominable tormentor, Leeuwenhoek, who threw me into fetters stronger than those I had borne before— but to his own destruction.

"In spite of all the precautions of old Leeuwenhoek and of the beautiful Gamaheh, I finally succeeded after all in escaping from my prison in an unguarded hour. Although I was much hampered in my escape by the heavy riding boots that I had not had time to kick off of my feet, I still managed to get as far as the shop of the toy dealer where you were making purchases. It was not long before Gamaheh too, to my no small terror, entered the store. I thought I was lost. Only you could help me, noble Mr. Peregrinus. Softly I lamented my distress to you, and you were kind enough to open for me a box, into which I made haste to jump and which you then just as quickly carried away with you. Gamaheh looked for me in vain, and only much later discovered how and where I had fled. Now that I had my freedom, Leeuwenhoek had also lost his power over my people. They all set themselves free, slipped away, and to the mockery of the tyrant left peppercorns, fruit pits, and the like stuck in their garments.

"Once again my cordial thanks, good, noble Mr. Peregrinus, for the great deed of kindness that you did for me and which I can appreciate as no one else can. Allow me to spend a bit of time with you as a free man. In many a very important affair of your life I can be so useful to you that you would hardly believe it. It might well be deemed dangerous that you have flamed forth in ardent love for that lovely creature—"

"What are you saying," Peregrinus interrupted the invisible little fellow, "what are you saying, Master? I—I have flamed forth in love?"

"Precisely so," Master Flea went on. "Just imagine my horror, my terror, when you stepped in yesterday with the princess in your arms, all aflame with wild passion, when she applied all the seductive wiles that are unfortunately only too much at her disposal, to move you to deliver me up! But not until then did I grasp your magnanimity in its full scope, when you stood firm, when you pretended so skillfully that you knew nothing at all about my staying with you, that you simply did not understand what the princess was actually asking of you."

"But," Peregrinus interrupted Master Flea again, "but that was in fact the case. You attribute to me as merits, dear Master Flea, things that I have never dreamed of. In the shop where I was buying the toys I noticed neither you nor the pretty lady who sought me out at bookbinder Lämmerhirt's, and whom you are so oddly pleased to call Princess Gamaheh. I was totally unaware of the fact that, among the boxes that I took with me and in which I fancied there were lead soldiers and hunting sets of the same material, there was an empty one in which you were contained. And how in the world could I have guessed that you were the captive that the lovely girl kept asking for so urgently? Don't be eccentric, Master Flea, and don't let yourself dream things of which there is not the slightest intimation in my soul."

"You are trying," replied Master Flea, "neatly to elude my expressions of gratitude, good Mr. Peregrinus, and to my great comfort that gives me new and vivid proof of your unselfish way of thinking. Know, noble man, that Leeuwenhoek's and Gamaheh's efforts to seize me again shall remain wholly vain as long as you grant me your protection. You would have to turn me over voluntarily to my tormentors, all other means are fruitless. Mr. Peregrinus Tyss, you are in love!"

"Oh, do not," Peregrinus broke into the Master's speech, "oh, do not speak that way! Do not call love a momentary and foolish transport that is now already over!"

Mr. Peregrinus felt fiery blushes rising in his face and making a liar of him. He crept under the covers.

"It is," continued Master Flea, "it is no wonder at all that you too could not withstand the wondrous charm of the Princess Gamaheh, especially when she used many a dangerous wile to catch you. The storm is not over yet. Many a magic spell that is in the repertory of many charming women who are not exactly the Princess Gamaheh, will yet be invoked by that malicious little creature in order to involve you in the toils of her love.

She will try to get such complete control over you that you shall live only for her and for her wishes, and then—alas for me! It will depend on whether your nobility is strong enough to prevail over your passion, whether you will prefer to yield to Gamaheh's wishes and plunge anew into misery not only your protégé but also that poor people which you wrested from its base servitude, or whether you will resist the wicked and false enticements of a seductive creature and thus establish my and my people's welfare. Oh, if you would! If you could! Promise me the latter!"

"Master," answered Mr. Peregrinus, drawing the covers away from his face, "dear Master, you are right. Nothing is more dangerous than the enticements of women. They are all false, malicious; they play with us as the cat plays with the mouse, and for our tenderest efforts we gain nothing but scorn and mockery. That was why the cold sweat of death always used to stand out on my forehead whenever a female creature came near, and I do think that there must be something very peculiar about the beautiful Aline, or, if you wish, about the Princess Gamaheh, despite the fact that I simply cannot understand with my homely, sound human reason all this that you have told me, and although I seem rather to feel as if I were in a confused dream or as if I were reading the *Arabian Nights*. However, be that as it may, you have entrusted yourself to my protection, dear Master, and nothing shall prevail upon me to deliver you to your enemies. I don't want to see that seductive wench again. I solemnly promise that, and I would give you my hand on it, if you had one that could take mine and return my honorable pressure." With that, Mr. Peregrinus extended his arm far out across the coverlet.

"Now," said the invisible little fellow, "now I am completely reassured, completely put at ease. Even though I don't have any hand to extend to you, permit me at least to sting you in your right thumb, partly to prove to you my intense joy, partly to seal the more firmly the bond of our friendship."

Mr. Peregrinus at that moment felt a sting in the thumb of his right hand, a sting that hurt so painfully that it could have come only from the first master of all fleas.

"You sting," cried Peregrinus, "you sting like a little demon."

"Take that," replied Master Flea, "as a vital sign of my good and true intention. But it is fitting that as a pledge of my gratitude I should present you with a gift which belongs among the most extraordinary that art has ever produced. It is none other than a microscope, which a very skillful and expert optician among my people produced while he was still in Leeuwenhoek's service. To you the instrument will seem a bit subtle, for in fact it is about a hundred and twenty times smaller than a grain of sand; but its use admits of no special size. I put this lens, namely, in the pupil of your left eye, and thereupon that eye will become microscopic. The effect will surprise you, and so I shall maintain silence on that score for the present and merely request you to permit me to undertake the operation at a time when I am convinced that the microscopic eye cannot fail to perform great service for you. And now, sleep well, Mr. Peregrinus. You do need some rest yet."

And now Peregrinus actually went to sleep and did not wake until it was bright morning.

His ear caught the familiar scratching of old Aline's broom sweeping out the adjoining room. A small child aware of some misbehavior or other could not be so afraid of his mother's switch as Peregrinus was of the old woman's reproaches. At last the old woman softly entered with his coffee. Mr. Peregrinus squinted through the bed curtains, which he had pulled together, and was not a little surprised at the clear sunshine that was spread across the old woman's face.

"Are you still asleep, dear Mr. Tyss?" asked Aline in the sweetest tone that lay in her throat.

Much heartened, Peregrinus replied just as amiably, "No, dear Aline. Just set my breakfast on the table and I will get up immediately."

But when Peregrinus finally did get up, it seemed to him as if there wafted through the room the sweet breath of that lovely creature who had lain in his arms. He felt so cozy, and yet at the same time so uneasy. He would have given anything in the world to know what had happened to the secret of his love, for that most charming of creatures had appeared and disappeared again just like that secret itself.

While Mr. Peregrinus was trying vainly to drink his coffee

and enjoy his white bread, each bite of which grew larger in his mouth, old Aline came in and busied herself with one thing and another, murmuring to herself all the time: "Amazing! —incredible!—what all doesn't happen to a body!—who would have thought it!"

Unable, for the sheer beating of his heart, to endure it any longer, Peregrinus asked: "What is so amazing, dear Aline?"

"All sorts of things, all sorts of things!" replied Aline, smiling roguishly as she continued about her task of straightening up the room.

Poor Peregrinus's heart was on the point of bursting, and involuntarily he cried out in a tone of the most painful yearning: "Ah, Aline!"

"Yes, Mr. Tyss, here I am. What would you like?" So spoke the old woman and came and stood squarely in front of Peregrinus as though awaiting his command.

Peregrinus stared into the coppery and frightfully distorted face of the old woman, and all his reticence broke forth from the profound vexation that suddenly filled him.

"What has become," he asked in a rather gruff tone, "what has become of the strange lady who was here last evening? Did you open the house door for her? Did you get her a carriage as I ordered? Did the lady get back to her residence?"

"Open the door?" said Aline with a damnable grin that was supposed to look like a sly smile. "Get a carriage? Take to her residence? No need of all that! The beautiful lady, the dear little thing, stayed in this house. She is still here and probably won't be leaving the house right away."

Peregrinus started up in joyous terror. The old woman now related how the lady had run down the stairs in such a way that her sight and hearing had failed her, and how old Mr. Swammer had been standing below in the doorway of his room with a huge branched candlestick in his hand. With numerous bowings and scrapings, quite contrary to his customary manner, the old gentleman had invited the lady into his room, and she had slipped in, too, immediately and without objection, and Mr. Swammer had then securely locked and bolted the door.

All the same, the misanthropic Mr. Swammer's conduct had seemed much too odd to her, not to do a bit of listening at the

door and peep through the keyhole. There Mr. Swammer had
stood in the middle of the room and had talked so stirringly
and so dolefully to the lady that tears had come into her, the
old woman's, eyes, although she had not understood one single
word because Mr. Swammer's language was foreign. She hadn't
been able to believe anything but that Mr. Swammer was making an effort to bring the lady back to virtue and the fear of
God, for he had become more and more excited, until the lady
had fallen to her knees and kissed his hand very submissively,
and wept a little as she did so. But Mr. Swammer had raised
the lady up very kindly, kissed her on the brow—he had had
to bend way over to do so—and then led her to a chair. Very
zealously Mr. Swammer had made a fire in the fireplace, fetched
some spices, and, as far as she could discern, had begun to
brew some mulled wine. Unfortunately, she, the old woman, had
at that point taken some snuff and sneezed hard. Then a shock
had gone through all her limbs and she had been annihilated, as
it were, when Mr. Swammer had stretched out his arm toward
the door and shouted with a fearful voice that pierced the very
marrow: "Get thee gone, eavesdropping Satan!" She just didn't
know how she had got upstairs and into bed. When she had
opened her eyes in the morning she thought she was seeing a
ghost. For she had beheld Mr. Swammer in front of her bed in a
handsome sable mantle with tie-bands and tassels of gold, his
hat on his head, and his cane in his hand.

"Good Dame Aline," Mr. Swammer had said to her, "I must
go out on important errands and will perhaps not return for several hours. See to it that no noise is raised in the entrance hall
in front of my door, and that absolutely no one ventures to enter
my room. An aristocratic lady, as you may well know, a foreign,
wealthy, wondrously beautiful princess has taken refuge with
me. In former times I was her private tutor at her royal father's
court, and therefore she has confidence in me, and I shall and
must protect her against all wicked attacks. I am telling you this,
Dame Aline, so that you will show the lady the respect which
befits her rank. She will, if Mr. Tyss so permits, claim your
services, and you shall, good Dame Aline, be royally rewarded
for them, insofar as you can maintain silence and betray the
princess's presence to no one."

With that, Mr. Swammer had walked quickly away.

Mr. Peregrinus Tyss asked the old woman whether it did not seem strange to her that the lady whom he, as he could assure her again, had met at bookbinder Lämmerhirt's in Kalbächer Lane, should be a princess and should have taken refuge with old Mr. Swammer.

It was the opinion of the old woman, however, that she would trust Mr. Swammer's words more than her own eyes, and that she therefore thought that everything that had occurred at bookbinder Lammerhirt's and in the room here had been either a magical illusion, or else that terror and confusion in her flight had brought the princess to such fantastic behavior. Besides, she was going to find out everything herself from the princess very soon.

"But," Mr. Peregrinus went on, actually only for the sake of prolonging the conversation about the lady, "but what has happened to your suspicion, your bad opinion that you entertained of the strange lady yesterday?"

"Oh," replied the old woman with a smirk, "oh, that is all past and done. All one has to do is look at the dear lady in the right way to know that she is a grand princess, and so angelically beautiful besides, as only a princess can be. After Mr. Swammer had gone out, I had to have a peek at what the good lady was doing, and I looked through the keyhole. There lay the lady stretched out on the sofa with her angel's head propped on her hand, so that her black locks poured through her little lily-white fingers—a very pretty sight. And the lady was dressed in real silver taffeta that allowed her dainty bosom and round little arms to shimmer through it. On her little feet she was wearing golden slippers. One of them had fallen off so that it could be seen that she had no stockings on. The little bare foot peeped out from beneath her dress, and she was playing with her toes, so that it was a cunning sight to behold. But surely the lady is still lying downstairs in the same position as before on the sofa, and if you are inclined, dear Mr. Tyss, to apply yourself to the keyhole, you—"

"What are you saying!" Peregrinus interrupted the old woman vehemently. "What are you saying! Am I to surrender to that seductive sight, which might perhaps sweep me away to all kinds of follies?"

"Courage, Peregrinus! Resist the temptation!" was heard in a whisper close by Peregrinus, who recognized the voice of Master Flea.

The old woman smiled mysteriously and said, after she had been silent for a few minutes, "I will come right out and tell you, dear Mr. Tyss, just how the matter looks to me. The strange lady may or may not be a princess, but this much is certain: she is very grand and rich, and Mr. Swammer is taking a very active interest in her, and besides, must have known her for a long time. And why did the lady run after you, dear Mr. Tyss? I say, because she has fallen mortally in love with you, and love makes one completely blind and mad and leads even princesses to the oddest and most unpredictable tricks. A gypsy woman once prophesied to your late lady mother that you would some day become happy as the result of a marriage just when you were least thinking of such a thing. And now this is to come true!"

And with that the old woman began anew to describe how perfectly lovely the lady looked.

It can be imagined how Peregrinus felt himself besieged. "Stop!" he finally burst forth, "Do stop talking about such things, Dame Aline. The lady is supposed to be in love with *me*? How ridiculous! How absurd!"

"Hm," said the old woman, "if that weren't the case, then the lady would not have sighed so piteously, then she would not have cried out so sorrowfully: 'No, my dear Peregrinus, my sweet friend, you will not, you cannot be so cruel to me! I will see you again and taste all the bliss of heaven!' And our old Mr. Swammer, the strange lady has turned him quite upside down. Have I ever received a single *Kreuzer* from him, apart from the *Kronentaler* at Christmas time? And this morning he gave me this fine, shiny *Karolin*, and with such a friendly look as he never before had on his face, as a tip in advance for the services that I will perform for the lady. There is something behind this. What do you want to bet, Mr. Swammer winds up playing the matchmaker in your house, Mr. Tyss!"

Again Aline spoke of the sweetness and charm of the lady

with enthusiastic words that sounded odd enough in the mouth
of a withered old woman, until Peregrinus, all fire and flame,
jumped up and shouted as though mad: "Come of it what may—
down, down to that keyhole!"

In vain warned Master Flea, who had leaped into the scarf
of the amorous Peregrinus and hidden there in a recess of a
fold. Peregrinus did not hear his voice, and Master Flea learned
what he ought long since to have known, namely, that something may be done with the most headstrong people, but not
with a lover.

The lady was, in fact, still lying on the sofa just the way the
old woman had described, and Peregrinus discovered that no
human language was adequate to express in words the divine
magic that lay upon all her lovely form. Her gown, of actual
silver taffeta with strange, many colored embroidery, was quite
fantastical and could quite appropriately pass for the negligee
of the Princess Gamaheh, the one that perhaps she was wearing
in Famagusta at the moment when the malicious Leech Prince
kissed her to death. At least the garment was so bewitching
and at the same time so uncommonly strange, that the conception of it seemed neither to have sprung from the head of the
most brilliant theatrical seamstress nor to have been planted in
the mind of the most sublime milliner.

"Yes, it is she, it is Princess Gamaheh!" So murmured Peregrinus, as he trembled for sweet bliss and thirsting desire. But
now, when the lovely girl sighed: "Peregrinus, my Peregrinus!"
then Mr. Peregrinus Tyss was seized by the total madness of
passion, and only a nameless anguish that robbed him of all
power of decision restrained him from breaking down the door
by force and throwing himself at the feet of the angel.

The kind reader already knows how matters stand with the
magic charmε and the supernatural beauty of little Dörtje Elverdink. The Editor can give his assurance that, after he too had
peeped through the keyhole and caught sight of the girl in her
fantastical dress of silver taffeta, he could say nothing but that
Dörtje Elverdink was a very pretty and charming doll. But since
no young man has ever fallen in love for the first time with any
creature except a supernatural one, an angel whom nothing
on earth resembles, let Mr. Peregrinus also be permitted to con-

sider Dörtje Elverdink a similarly magical and supernatural being. "Pull yourself together, think of your promise, worthy Mr. Peregrinus Tyss. You intended never to see the seductive Gamaheh again, and now—! I could thrust the microscope into your eye, but you will have to preceive for yourself without it that the malicious girl has long had her eye on you, and that everything she does is a deceitful wile to lead you on. Just believe me. I mean it for your good!" So whispered Master Flea from within the fold of the cravat. But for all the anxious doubts that rose from within Peregrinus, he still could not tear himself away from the enchanting sight of the girl, who knew very well how to use the advantage of being allowed to think herself unobserved, and also, by altering her seductive postures, how to drive poor Peregrinus quite beside himself.

Mr. Peregrinus might perhaps be standing yet at the door of the fateful room, had not the bell rung loudly and had not the old woman called to him that old Mr. Swammer was coming back. Peregrinus flew up the stairs and into his own room. There he gave himself over totally to his thoughts of love. But with those thoughts, there returned those doubts which Master Flea's exhortations had roused in him. A flea had quite literally been put in his ear, and he fell into all sorts of disquieting reflections.

"Do I," he thought, "do I not have to believe actually that the lovely creature is the Princess Gamaheh and the daughter of a powerful king? But if such is the case, then I must consider it folly, madness, to aspire to the possession of so exalted a personage. Then, too, she herself asked for the delivery of a captive upon whom her life depended, and if that coincides exactly with what Master Flea told me, then I can hardly doubt but that everything that I might interpret as love for me, is perhaps only a device to subject me entirely to her will. And yet—to give her up—to lose her—that is hell, that is death!"

Mr. Peregrinus Tyss was disturbed in these painful reflections by a gentle, shy knocking at the door. The person who entered was none other than Mr. Peregrinus's lodger.

Old Mr. Swammer, otherwise a shriveled, misanthropic, sullen man, seemed suddenly to have become twenty years younger.

His brow was smooth, his eye animated, his mouth friendly. Instead of his ugly black wig, he was wearing his own white hair, and instead of his dark grey overcoat, a handsome coat of sable fur, just as Aline had described him. With a cheerful, indeed joyous countenance, formerly not characteristic of him at all, Mr. Swammer advanced toward Peregrinus. He did not wish, Mr. Swammer said, to disturb his dear landlord in any task; his duty as a lodger, however, required that he notify the landlord the first thing in the morning that, during the preceding night, he had been obliged to give shelter to a helpless woman who wished to escape the tyranny of a wicked uncle, and hence would be spending some time in the house, for which the permission of the kind landlord would meanwhile be needed, for which he was herewith applying.

Involuntarily Peregrinus asked who the helpless woman might be, without thinking that that was, in fact, the most purposeful question he could ask in order to get on the track of the strange mystery.

"It is," replied Mr. Swammer, "it is right and proper for the landlord to know whom he is harboring in his house. Know then, honored Mr. Tyss, that the girl who has taken refuge with me is none other than the pretty Dutch girl, Dörtje Elverdink, niece of the famous Leeuwenhoek, who, as you know, displays here the wonderful microscopic arts. Leeuwenhoek is otherwise my intimate friend. But I must confess that he is a hard man and that he has shamefully mistreated poor Dörtje, who is, moreover, my godchild. A stormy scene which took place last evening forced the girl to flee, and it seems natural that she should seek help and comfort from me."

"Dörtje Elverdink," said Peregrinus, half in a dream. "Leeuwenhoek! Perhaps a descendant of the naturalist Anton van Leeuwenhoek who constructed the famous microscope?"

"It cannot be said precisely," replied Mr. Swammer smiling, "that our Leeuwenhoek is a descendant of that famous man, since he is the famous man himself, and since it is only a fable that he was buried in Delft almost a hundred years ago. Do believe that, my dearest Mr. Tyss, otherwise you might even be in doubt that I, although I am for brevity's sake and in order not to have to answer questions about subjects of my science for every curious fool now called Swammer, am actually the famous Swammerdam. Everyone maintains that I died in the year 1680, but you will observe, worthy Mr. Tyss, that I stand alive and well before you; and that *I* am really *I*, I can demonstrate to anyone, even the simplest, out of my *Biblia naturae*.[3] You do believe me, worthy Mr. Tyss?"

"So many odd things," said Peregrinus in a tone that testified to his inner confusion, "so many odd things have happened to me very recently, that, if everything were not the clear perception of my senses, I should have to doubt it eternally. But now I believe in everything, however mad and senseless it may be! It is possible that you are the late Mr. Jan Swammerdam and hence, as a ghost, know more than other ordinary people. But as far as the flight of Dörtje Elverdink is concerned, or of the Princess Gamaheh, or whatever the lady's name may be, you are in profound error. Hear, then, how that happened."

Very calmly now, Peregrinus related the adventure that he had experienced with the lady, from her entrance into Lämmerhirt's room, up to her reception in Mr. Swammer's chamber.

"It seems to me," said Mr. Swammer, when Peregrinus had concluded, "it seems to me as though all that you have been pleased to relate is nothing but a remarkable, although very pleasant, dream. I shall, however, venture no opinion on that score and shall ask you for your friendship, of which I shall perhaps have grave need. Forget my morose behavior, and let us approach each other more closely. Your father was a man of discernment and my closest friend, but as concerns knowledge, profound reason, mature judgment, and practiced and true insight into life, the son outdoes the father. You don't know how I esteem you, my best and worthiest Mr. Tyss."

"Now is the time!" whispered Master Flea, and at that instant Peregrinus felt a tiny fleeting pain in the pupil of his left eye. He knew that Master Flea had put the microscopic lens into his eye, but indeed he could not have imagined the effect of that lens. Behind the cornea of Swammer's eyes he perceived curious nerves and filaments, whose wondrously tangled course he was able to follow far into the brain and to discern as Swam-

[3] An actual work on insects written by Jan Swammerdam of Amsterdam. (See note 2 above.)

mer's thoughts. They went approximately as follows:

"I would never have believed that I would get off so cheaply here, that I would not be better questioned. But if papa was a dull character by whom I never set any store, the son is still more confused in mind, to whom a large portion of childish silliness was allotted. Here this Simple Simon tells me the whole situation with the princess and never supposes that she has already told me all that herself, for my conduct with her would necessarily presuppose an earlier intimate relationship. But what's the use? I have to act nice with him because I need his help. He is naïve enough to believe everything I say, in fact to make many a sacrifice for my advantage out of sheer simplicity of goodness, for which he will gain no other reward but that, when all has gone well and Gamaheh is mine again, I will bluntly laugh at him behind his back."

"It just seemed to me," said Mr. Swammer as he stepped up close to Mr. Peregrinus, "it just seemed to me as though there were a flea on your neck-cloth, worthy Mr. Tyss!" His thoughts ran: "Confound it! Why, that was really Master Flea! That would be a damnable mischance if Gamaheh had not been mistaken."

Peregrinus stepped back quickly, assuring him that he didn't mind fleas at all.

"Then," continued Mr. Swammer bowing deeply, "then I take my leave of you most submissively, my dear and most worthy Mr. Tyss." His thoughts ran: "I wish black-feathered Satan would consume you, you damned rascal!"

Master Flea removed the microscopic lens from the pupil of Peregrinus, who was wholly sunk in astonishment, and then said, "Dear Mr. Peregrinus, you have now witnessed the wonderful effect of the instrument which has not its equal in the whole world, and you will see what superior advantage it gives you over people when their innermost thoughts lie revealed before your eyes. If you were to wear this lens constantly in your eye, however, the constant realization of thoughts would burden you down to the ground. For only too often would there be repeated the bitter offense that you have just experienced. I shall be with you constantly, whenever you leave your house, either in your neck-cloth, in your jabot, or in some comfortable and appropriate place. If you wish to know the thoughts of the person with whom you are speaking, you have only to snap your fingers, and immediately you shall have the lens in your eye."

Mr. Peregrinus Tyss, comprehending the incalculable advantage of this gift, was about to pour forth the most impassioned thanks, when two deputies of the High Council entered and announced to him that he was accused of a serious crime, and that this accusation must have as its consequence his present arrest and the seizure of his papers.

Mr. Peregrinus swore by all that was high and holy that he was not aware of the slightest crime. One of the deputies opined with a smile that perhaps within a few hours his total innocence would be made clear. Until then, however, he would have to submit to the orders of the authorities.

What else was there for Mr. Peregrinus Tyss to do but to get into the carriage and let himself be transported to the prison?

One may imagine with what sensations he passed by Mr. Swammer's room.

Master Flea was sitting in the captive's neck-cloth.

FOURTH ADVENTURE

Unexpected encounter of two friends. Counselor Knarrpanti and his painful principles. The Thistle Zeherit's
desperation of love. Optical duel of two mages. Somnambulistic condition of the Princess Gamaheh. The thoughts
of her dream. How Dörtje Elverdink almost speaks the
truth and how the Thistle Zeherit runs off with the
Princess Gamaheh.

News spread very fast of the watchman's
blunder in arresting Mr. Pepusch as a nocturnal prowler who
was trying to burglarize. Certain irregularities were meanwhile
claimed to have been observed in his papers, and that was the
reason for his being requested to produce some resident citizen
or other of Frankfurt as surety, and meanwhile having to make
the best of his stay in the burgomaster's quarters.

There in a very nice room sat George Pepusch, thinking this
way and that way of whom he could ever produce in Frankfurt
as his surety. He had been so long away that he was forced to
fear he had been forgotten even by those who had formerly
known him very well, and as for other addresses, he was at a
complete loss.

In a thoroughly bad humor he looked out the window and
began to curse his fate aloud. Just then another window was
opened right next to him, and a voice cried, "What? Am I seeing
right? Is it you, George?" Mr. Pepusch was not a little astonished to catch sight of the friend with whom he had had the
most intimate association during his sojourn in Madras.

"Deuce take it! How can anybody be so forgetful, in fact, so
stunned out of his wits! I did know that you had come in safely

to your home port. I heard marvels in Hamburg about your strange way of life, and now that I get here, I don't even think of looking you up. But anybody that has such things on his mind as I have—well, it's good that chance has brought you to me. You see that I am under arrest, but you can get me out instantly if you will furnish surety that I really am the George Pepusch that you have known for these long years, and not a rascal, not a robber!"

"I," cried Mr. Peregrinus Tyss, "am indeed a splendid, irreproachable surety now, when I am under arrest myself for a serious crime that I am not aware of, in fact, of which I haven't the faintest notion."

But it might be advisable to interrupt the conversation of the two friends who had found each other again in a way they had not expected, and to tell the kind reader what was behind the arrest of Mr. Peregrinus Tyss. It is hard, impossible in fact, to demonstrate how rumors get started. They are like the wind: no one knows where it comes from or where it goes to. Thus, the rumor had spread in the city that on Christmas Eve a very aristocratic lady had been abducted in an incomprehensible way from a large party that had gathered at the home of a rich banker. Everyone was talking about it, named the banker by name, and complained loudly that the police must not be very vigilant if such a deed of violence could be carried out without timidity. The council could not get around initiating investigations. All the guests who had been at the banker's house on Christmas Eve were interrogated. Each one said that in any case, as far as he had heard, an aristocratic lady had been abducted from the party, and the banker felt it a great pity that such a trick should have been perpetrated in his house. Meanwhile no one could give the name of the abducted lady, and when the banker submitted the list of his guests it was learned that not a single one of the ladies who had been present was missing. If the same could be said of all the native and foreign ladies and maidens in the entire city, of whom none had sustained any harm on Christmas Eve, then the council recognized, as it could hardly fail to do, the rumor as wholly unfounded and the entire matter as settled.

But then there appeared before the council a person, odd both

as to his dress and as to his whole manner, who said he was a
Privy Counselor and had the name of Knarrpanti.[1] Thereupon
he drew from his pocket a paper with a big seal on it and
handed it over with a courteous bow and with an expression
which clearly indicated how surprised the council would be at
the high dignity which he, Privy Counselor Knarrpanti, represented and at the important commission he had received,
and what respect would now be shown him. Knarrpanti was a
very important man, a so-called factotum at the court of a petty
prince, whose name the Editor cannot recall, and about whom
there is to be said only that he was constantly short of money,
and that, of all the state organizations he knew from history,
none pleased him more than the secret State Inquisition as it
formerly existed in Venice. Some time previously, this prince had
actually lost one of his princesses, no one knew quite how. And
now when the rumor of the abducted aristocratic lady reached
Knarrpanti, who happened to be in Frankfurt borrowing money
wherever possible for his master, he immediately wrote to the
prince that his efforts had been successful in getting on the
track of the lost princess. Whereupon he received commission
at once to pursue the abductor and to use every means to discover the princess and to take possession of her, cost what it
might. This commission was accompanied by a courteous letter
to the council, begging the same to assist Privy Counselor
Knarrpanti to the utmost in his investigations and, upon his
motion, to arrest the abductor and bring him to trial. This letter
was the paper which Knarrpanti handed over to the council in
his audience, and from which he promised himself such a great
effect.

The council replied, saying that the rumor of an aristocratic
lady's having been abducted had been refuted as groundless,
that it had been fully ascertained, on the contrary, that no one
had been abducted, that hence there could be no question of
handing over an abductor, and that Privy Counselor Knarrpanti,

[1] Privy Counselor Knarrpanti and his case against the hero parody the
real-life Police Director Heinrich von Kamptz and his prosecution of the
real-life student, Gustav Asverus, for "demagogic activity" in 1819. See
the Introduction, pp. xxiii–xiv.

disburdened of all further investigations, would have no need of assistance.

Knarrpanti listened to all this with a self-satisfied smile and gave assurance that his uncommon sagacity had already succeeded in capturing the perpetrator. With the reminder that, if there were a perpetrator, then there must have been a per-petrated act, Knarrpanti opined that, if once the perpetrator were handed over, then the act perpetrated would be dis-covered automatically. Even if the chief accusation could not be determined on account of the obduracy of the accused, all the same, only a shallow, irresponsible judge would not be able to inquire a little here and inquire a little there, a thing which would not put the slightest little stain upon the accused and which would justify the arrest. He must, he said, now urgently move for the swift arrest of the abductor of his princess, and that abductor was none other than Mr. Peregrinus Tyss, who had long been known to him as highly suspicious, and whose papers he requested be immediately impounded.

The council was amazed at this saucy accusation against a quiet, irreproachable citizen and rejected Knarrpanti's proposal with considerable animation.

Knarrpanti did not in the least lose his composure, but with a certain offensive arrogance that was peculiar to him, assured them that if it was authentication of his accusation that was wanted beforehand, he could very easily produce it. He was willing to prove by two witnesses that Mr. Peregrinus Tyss had, on Christmas Eve, dragged a beautifully dressed girl by force into his house.

More to show up fully the absurdity of this assertion than really to probe into the case, the council decided to give both proposed witnesses a hearing. Both of them, a neighbor of Mr. Peregrinus Tyss, who just happened on that fateful Christmas Eve to be entering his own house, as well as the watchman, had observed the whole scene only from a distance as Peregrinus had carried the mysterious beauty past, but they agreed in testifying that in any event Mr. Tyss had taken a finely dressed lady into his house. They both claimed to have noticed further that the lady had struggled a good deal and lamented piteously.

To the question of why they had not hurried to the assistance of the lady in distress, they answered that such a thing had not even occurred to them. The deposition of these witnesses put the council in no slight embarrassment, since Mr. Peregrinus seemed really to have incurred the guilt of the crime of which he was being accused. Knarrpanti spoke like a Cicero and demonstrated how the circumstance of no lady's now being missing decided nothing at all, inasmuch as the lady might well have fled again out of Peregrinus's house and from pure shame have concealed the entire event. Who the lady was, as well as what Mr. Tyss might be up to in other dangerous love adventures, all that would surely be shown from the criminal's papers, and he invoked the council's love of justice, according to which surely no execrable action should go unsuspected. The council decided in the first place to accede to the application of the worthy Privy Counselor, and thus it came about that poor Peregrinus Tyss's sudden arrest, as well as the seizure of his papers, ensued.

Let us return to the two friends, who have their heads stuck out of the windows of their cells.

Peregrinus had told his friend in detail how, upon his return to Frankfurt, he had found himself orphaned and how he had since then been living a solitary, friendless life in complete isolation and solely amid the memories of former days in the midst of the noisy city.

"Oh, yes," replied Pepusch morosely, "I have heard about that. People have told me the tomfooleries that you carry on in order to spend your life in childish reveries. You are trying to be a hero of the tender emotions and the childlike state, and therefore you flout the just claims which life and human society make upon you. You give pretentious family feasts, and dispense among the poor the delicious foods and expensive wines that you had served to the dead. You give yourself Christmas gifts and pretend you are still a child, and then you present to poor children the gifts which are the kind that are customarily lavished on spoiled children in the homes of wealthy parents. But you don't stop to consider that it is a sorry kindness to the poor things when you titillate their palates once and they doubly feel their misery afterwards, when from gnawing hunger they have to eat barely edible food that many a dainty lap dog would reject. Ha! How I despise these feedings of the poor, when I consider how what is squandered on them in one day would nourish them in a moderate fashion for months on end! You shower the children of poor people with shiny toys and don't stop to think that a brightly painted wooden sword, a rag doll, a cuckoo, or some trivial candy given them by their father and mother would please them just as much, and perhaps much more. Besides, they will stuff themselves and eat themselves sick on your accursed marzipan, and with the awareness of more resplendent presents that will continue to be denied them in the future, the seed of dissatisfaction and discontent is planted in their souls. You are rich, you are full of vigor, and yet you withdraw from all communication and frustrate every friendly approach of spirits that are well-disposed toward you. I am prepared to believe that the death of your parents was a great shock to you. But if everyone who suffered a painful loss were to creep into his shell, by the Devil! the world would be a charnel house and I wouldn't want to live in it. But man! don't you realize that you are being ruled by the stubbornest kind of selfishness, which is concealed behind a silly misanthropy? Go on, go on, Peregrinus! I cannot respect you any more, can no longer be your friend, if you don't change your life and don't give up this damnable management of your household."

Peregrinus snapped his fingers, and immediately Master Flea thrust the microscopic lens into his eye.

The thoughts of the angry Pepusch ran: "Isn't it a pity that such a likable, sensible fellow should have gone off into such ominous bypaths, which could lead him finally to the total debilitation of all his better powers? But it is sure that his gentle, melancholically disposed temperament could not bear the blow dealt him by his parents' death, and that he sought comfort in a behavior that borders on insanity. He will be lost if I don't rescue him. So I will go after him all the harder, paint him the picture of his folly in all the harsher colors, the more I esteem him, the more truly I am and remain his friend."

By these thoughts Peregrinus recognized that in the morose

Pepusch he had found his old true friend again, unchanged.

"George," said Peregrinus after Master Flea had again removed the microscopic lens from his eye, "George, I shan't argue with you over what you say about the blameworthy aspects of my way of life, because I know that you mean it very well. But I must tell you that it makes my heart swell whenever I am able to make a day of joy for the poor, and if that is detestable selfishness, even if in doing so I think of no one so much as myself, then I am at least sinning unconsciously. These are the flowers in my life, which otherwise seems to me like a dreary, barren field full of thistles."

"What," George Pepusch broke forth vehemently, "what are you saying about thistles? Why do you despise thistles and oppose them to flowers? Do you have so little experience of Nature as not to know that the most wondrously magnificent of flowers that can possibly be, is none other than the blossom of a thistle? I mean the *Cactus grandiflorus.*[2] And is the Thistle Zeherit not precisely the most beautiful cactus under the sun? Peregrinus, I have kept it a secret from you for so long, or rather, had to keep it a secret because I myself did not have a clear realization of it, but now you must know that I am myself the Thistle Zeherit, and for that reason I do not want to and absolutely shall not give up my claims to the hand of worthy King Sekakis's daughter, the lovely, heavenly Princes Gamaheh. I found her, but at that very moment demonic watchmen and city militiamen seized me and dragged me off to prison."

"What!" cried Peregrinus, half-frozen with astonishment, "You, too, George, are involved in this oddest of all stories?"

"What story?" asked Pepusch.

Peregrinus did not hesitate to tell his friend everything, as he had told Mr. Swammer, of what had happened at bookbinder Lämmerhirt's and subsequently at his house. He did not even conceal the appearance of Master Flea, though, as one may imagine, he did conceal the possession of the mysterious lens.

---

[2] "Torch thistle" (*Fackeldistel*) and "opuntia" are terms for varieties of flowering cactus or prickly pear. An exceptionally beautiful species is the American *Cactus grandiflorus* or *Cereus grandiflorus,* sometimes called "Queen of the Night."

George's eyes burned, he bit his lips, he clasped his brow in his hand, he cried in full fury as Peregrinus concluded: "The wretch! The hussy! The traitress!" In the self-torment of desperate love he had every little detail of Dörtje's conduct repeated in order to drain greedily every last drop of the poison cup that Peregrinus had handed him without realizing it. Intermittently he kept muttering: "In his arms—to his bosom—ardent kisses—" Then he leaped back from the window and ran about the room gesturing like a madman.

In vain Peregrinus called to him to listen further, that he had many comforting things yet to say to him. Pepusch did not abate his raving.

The room was thrown open and a delegate from the council announced to Mr. Peregrinus Tyss that no legal ground had been found for his continued detention and that he might return to his residence.

The first use Peregrinus made of his recovered freedom was to present himself as surety for the arrested George Pepusch, on whose behalf he testified that he really was the George Pepusch with whom he had lived in intimate friendship in Madras[3] and that he was known to him as a man of means and of unspotted reputation. Of the Thistle Zeherit, the most beautiful of all torch thistles, Peregrinus prudently made no mention, for he realized that under the prevailing circumstances this might have been more detrimental than helpful to his friend.

Master Flea poured himself out in very philosophical and instructive observations to the effect that the Thistle Zeherit, despite a harsh and peevish exterior, was very human and understanding, although he constantly showed himself a little too arrogant. When you came right down to it, the Thistle had quite rightly disparaged Mr. Peregrinus's way of life, even though this had been done in terms somewhat too harsh. For his part, he would really like to advise Mr. Peregrinus to go out into the world from now on.

"Believe me," said Master Flea, "believe me, Mr. Peregrinus, it will afford you many an advantage if you leave your solitude. In the first place, you would no longer have to be afraid of ap-

[3] The city on the west coast of India.

pearing shy and embarrassed, since, with the mysterious lens in your eye, you will be master of the thoughts of people, and since it will therefore be quite impossible for you not to maintain proper tact everywhere. How firmly, how calmly you can now step before the most exalted heads, when their innermost thoughts lie clear before your eyes. If you move freely in the world, your blood will flow more easily, all gloomy brooding will cease, and, what is best of all, brightly colored ideas and thoughts will rise in your brain, the image of the beautiful Gamaheh will lose some of its splendor, and soon you will be in better condition to keep your word to me."

Mr. Peregrinus felt that both George Pepusch and Master Flea meant him well, and he made up his mind to follow their sage advice. But as soon as he heard the sweet voice of the dear beloved, which spoke and sang rather often, he could not think how it would be possible to leave the house that had become a Paradise for him.

At last, however, he prevailed upon himself to take a walk in public. Master Flea had put the lens in his eye and had taken up a station in his jabot, where he was sure of being rocked gently back and forth.

"Do I finally have the rare pleasure of seeing my dear, good Mr. Tyss again? You make yourself scarce, dear friend, and everyone thirsts for you. Let us step in somewhere or other and drink a bottle of wine, friend of my heart! How delighted I am to see you!" Thus called out to him a young man whom he had scarcely seen two or three times. His thoughts ran: "So the silly misanthrope is putting in an appearance once again? But I have to flatter him because I will soon be wanting to borrow money from him. Surely he won't be devil-bound and accept my invitation? I don't have a groschen on me and no innkeeper will give me credit any more."

Two very daintily dressed young girls chanced to cross Peregrinus's way. They were sisters, distantly related to him.

"Oh!" cried one laughing. "Oh, Cousin, so we meet you for once? It is not nice of you at all to barricade yourself the way you do, so that no one sees you. You have no idea how fond Mamma is of you, because you are such a sensible person. Promise me to come and see us soon. There! Kiss my hand." Her thoughts ran: "Well! What is this? What has happened to Cousin? I meant to throw him straight into terror and fright. He used to run away from me, from every woman, and now stops and looks me strangely in the eye and kisses my hand without any shyness? Could he be in love with me? That is all I would need! Mother says he is a little foolish. What difference does that make? I'll take him. A foolish man is precisely the best one when he is as rich as Cousin is."

Her sister had merely whispered with downcast eyes and deep red cheeks: "Yes, come and visit us soon, dear Cousin!" Her thoughts ran: "Cousin is a very handsome man, and I don't understand why Mother calls him ridiculous and insipid, and can't abide him. If he comes to our house he will fall in love with me, because I am the prettiest girl in all Frankfurt. I will take him, because I want to marry a rich man so I can sleep until eleven o'clock and wear more expensive shawls than Mrs. von Lersner."

A passing surgeon had them stop his carriage as he caught sight of Peregrinus, and called out the door: "Good morning, my good Tyss! You look like life itself! Heaven keep you in good health! But if anything should happen to you, think of me, the old friend of your late father. I help powerful physiques like that onto their feet in quick time! Farewell!" His thoughts ran: "I think the man is constantly healthy out of pure stinginess. But he is looking so pale, so distraught, he seems finally to have something bothering him. Well, if he gets into my hands he won't get up from his bed so soon. He will pay roundly for his stubborn good health."

"Most cordial greetings, noble sir!" called out to him an old merchant directly afterward. "You see how I run and chase and how I have to torment myself for the sake of business. How wise you were to withdraw from business, although with your insight you could not have failed to double the wealth of your excellent father." His thoughts ran: "If only the fellow would get into business, the addled simpleton would lose all his wealth in speculations in a short time, and that would be a delight. His old papa, that used to take pleasure in pitilessly ruining other honest people when they were trying to help themselves up by means of a little bankruptcy, would turn over in his grave."

Many more such decisive contradictions between words and thoughts came Peregrinus's way. He constantly directed his answers more to what the people thought than to what they said, and thus it was inevitable that, since Peregrinus had penetrated into people's thoughts, they just could not make out what to think of Peregrinus. At last Mr. Peregrinus felt weary and bewildered. He snapped his fingers, and directly the lens disappeared out of his left eye.

As Peregrinus stepped into his house he was surprised by a strange spectacle. A man was standing in the middle of the entrance hall and looking with unaverted gaze through an oddly shaped lens at Mr. Swammer's door. On the door sun-bright circles were wavering in rainbow hues. These became concentrated in a fiery dot which seemed to penetrate right through the door. When this happened, a dull groan was heard, punctuated by sounds of pain, which seemed to be coming from within the room. To his horror Peregrinus thought he recognized Gamaheh's voice.

"What do you want? What are you doing here?" exclaimed Peregrinus as he made for the man, who actually seemed to be practicing infernal arts. Meanwhile, faster and faster, more and more fiery, the rainbow circles flickered, ever more burning became the dot, and ever more painful tones of anguish resounded from inside the room.

"Ah!" said the man as he gathered up his lenses and quickly put them in his pocket. "Ah, see who is here, the master of the house! Forgive me, good Mr. Tyss, for operating here without your kind permission. But I had come to you to request that very permission. Then the good and friendly Aline told me that you had gone out, and the business here would allow of no postponement."

"What business?" asked Peregrinus, rather gruffly. "What business is there here that won't allow of any postponement?"

"Could you," continued the man with a repulsive smile, "could you not know that my unnatural niece, Dörtje Elverdink, has run away? Why, you were arrested, although quite unjustly,

as her abductor. Hence, if it comes to that, I shall testify with
much pleasure to your complete innocence. Not to you did my
faithless niece run away, but to Mr. Swammerdam, who used
to be my friend, but who has now turned into my enemy. She
is here in this room, I know, and alone, too, because Mr. Swammerdam has gone out. I can't get in because the door is tightly
locked and bolted, and I am much too good-humored to use
force. On that account, however, I am taking the liberty of
tormenting the little lady a bit with my optical torture instrument, so that she will acknowledge, in spite of her affected
status as a princess, that I am her lord and master!"

"You are the Devil, sir!" shouted Peregrinus at the height of
fury. "You are the Devil, sir! but not the lord and master of the
lovely, heavenly Gamaheh. Out of my house, and practice your
Satan's arts wherever you like, but here they shall come to
naught, I shall see to that!"

"Don't" said Leeuwenhoek, "just don't get overexcited, dear
Mr. Tyss. I am an innocent man who intends nothing but what is
good. You don't know who it is you are taking such an interest
in. It is a little monster, a little basilisk, who is sitting in that
room in the form of the loveliest of little ladies. Granted that
she might run away if her stay with insignificant me thoroughly
displeased her; but was the faithless traitress free to rob me of
my most beautiful jewel, my soul's best friend, without whom I
cannot live, cannot endure? Was she free to abduct Master Flea
from me? You don't understand, most respected sir, what I
mean, but—"

At this point Master Flea, who had jumped up from Mr. Peregrinus's jabot and taken a safer and more comfortable position in
his neck-cloth, could not restrain himself from breaking forth
in a fine mocking laughter.

"Ha!" cried Leeuwenhoek as though stricken with sudden
terror. "Ha! What was that? Could it be possible? Yes, here, in
this place!—allow me, most worthy Mr. Peregrinus!" Thereupon Leeuwenhoek stretched out his arm, stepped up close to
Mr. Peregrinus, and was on the point of grabbing his neck-cloth.

But Peregrinus dodged him adroitly, seized him with a strong
hand, and dragged him toward the door of the house, intending
to throw him out with no more ado. Just as Peregrinus found

himself right by the door with Leeuwenhoek, who was wearing himself out in futile protestations, the door was opened from the outside and in rushed George Pepusch with Mr. Swammerdam behind him.

As soon as Leeuwenhoek caught sight of his enemy Swammerdam, he wrenched himself loose with a supreme effort of his final strength and planted himself with his back to the door of the fateful room where the beautiful lady was held captive.

Perceiving this, Swammerdam drew a little telescope out of his pocket, pulled it out to its full length, and went after his enemy, crying loudly, "Draw, damn you, if you have the courage to!"

Swiftly Leeuwenhoek had a similar instrument in his hand, pulled it likewise out to its full length, and screamed, "Come on, I'll meet you! You will soon feel my power!"

Both now put the telescopes to their eyes and fell furiously upon one another with sharp, murderous strokes, now lengthening, now shortening their weapons by folding or extension. Now there were feints, parries, volts, in short all possible fencing tricks, and the tempers seemed to be getting ever more excited. Whenever one of them was hit, he would scream loudly, jump into the air, and do the most amazing capers, the handsomest entrechats and pirouettes, like the best solo dancers on the Parisian stage, until the other one fixed his folded telescope firmly on him. And when the same thing happened to the latter, he did precisely the same thing. Thus they alternated in the most frantic leaps, in the wildest gestures, in the most furious shouts. The sweat dripped from their brows, their bloodshot eyes bulged from their heads, and since nothing but their mutual looking through the telescopes was visible, and no other cause for their St. Vitus's dance, one was compelled to take them for lunatics escaped from a madhouse. The whole business was very amusing to behold.

Mr. Swammerdam finally succeeded in dislodging the wicked Leeuwenhoek from his stance by the door, which he was maintaining with stubborn bravery, and in shifting the battle to the remote end of the entrance hall.

George Pepusch perceived the moment, pushed open the now free door, which was neither locked nor bolted, and slipped into the room. Immediately he rushed out again, shouting: "She is gone—gone!" and rushed out of the house with the swiftness of lightning.

Both Leeuwenhoek and Swammerdam had hurt each other badly, for both of them were hopping and dancing about in mad fashion, and their howling and screaming were making music that seemed to be like the wailing of the damned in hell. Peregrinus did not rightly know what he should do to separate the raging pair and thus put an end to a scene which was as ridiculous as it was horrible. Finally the two of them became aware of the fact that the door of the room was standing wide open, forgot both battle and pain, put up their destructive weapons, and rushed into the room.

It struck heavily upon Mr. Peregrinus Tyss's heart that the most beautiful of girls had fled from his house. He cursed the detestable Leeuwenhoek to hell. Then from the stairs the voice of Aline was heard. She burst into loud laughter and kept crying intermittently, "What all a body doesn't live to see! Amazing! Incredible! Who would ever have dreamed of such a thing!"

"What," asked Peregrinus meekly, "what incredible thing has happened now?"

"O dear Mr. Tyss," the old woman cried to him, "just come up here quickly, just walk into your room."

With a roguish giggle the old woman opened the door of his room for him. As he stepped in, there, O marvel! O rapture! the lovely Dörtje Elverdink came skipping to meet him, dressed in that seductive gown of silver taffeta, just as he had glimpsed her in Mr. Swammer's room.

"At last, at last I get to see you again, my sweet friend," breathed the little lady, and snuggled up so close to Peregrinus that he could not do anything else but put his arms around her in the tenderest fashion, in spite of all his good resolutions. His senses were on the point of failing him for sheer rapture and transport of love.

It has, however, often occurred that, right in the midst of the supreme ecstasy of the most abounding bliss, a person has bumped his nose right sharply, and, awakened suddenly by the terrestrial pain, has fallen from the blissful Beyond into the vulgar Here. Just so did it befall Peregrinus. Namely, just as he was bending down to kiss Dörtje's sweet mouth, he bumped his not inconsiderable nose horribly against the diadem of glittering diamonds that the little lady was wearing in her black locks. The sharp pain of the encounter with the angularly cut stones brought him sufficiently to his senses so that he noticed the diadem. But the diadem reminded him of the Princess Gamaheh, and therewith he could not fail to recall everything that Master Flea had said to him about that seductive creature. He considered how a princess, the daughter of a mighty king, could not possibly set any store by his love, and how her entire love-exuding conduct must likely be nothing but hypocritical trickery through which the traitress intended to regain possession of the magical flea. With these considerations there glided through his inmost being an icy stream, which, if it did not completely extinguish the flames of love, did at least dampen them.

Peregrinus gently unwound himself from the little lady's arms as she held him in loving embrace, and with downcast eyes softly said, "Oh, good heavens! Why, you are the daughter of the mighty King Sekakis, the beautiful, lofty, splendid Princess Gamaheh! Forgive me, Princess, if an emotion which I was unable to resist, swept me off to folly, to madness. But you yourself, Your Highness . . ."

"What," Dörtje Elverdink interrupted Peregrinus, "what are you saying, my dear friend? I, the daughter of a mighty king? I a princess? Why, I am your Aline, who will love you to the point of madness if you—but, what has come over me? Aline, the Queen of Golconda? But she is with you in your house. I have talked with her. A good, kind woman, but she has gotten old, and long since no longer pretty as at the time of her marriage to a French General![4] Alas for me! I must not be the right one. I never reigned in Golconda, did I? Alas for me!"

The little lady had closed her eyes and was beginning to sway and collapse. Peregrinus took her over to the sofa.

"Gamaheh," she went on saying as though speaking in a somnambulistic trance, "Gamaheh, you say? Gamaheh, the daughter of King Sekakis? Yes! I remember, in Famagusta! I

---

[4] In Berton's opera, the Queen of Golconda recognizes the French General Saint-Phar as her former fiancé and marries him.

was actually a beautiful tulip—no, no, I already felt love and longing in my bosom. No more of that, no more of that!" The little lady was silent. She seemed about to pass wholly into slumber. Peregrinus undertook the dangerous enterprise of putting her into a more comfortable position. But no sooner had he put his arms gently around the lovely girl, than he felt a concealed needle prick him sharply in his finger. From habit he snapped his fingers. Master Flea, however, took that for the prearranged signal and immediately put the microscopic lens into the pupil of his eye.

As usual, Peregrinus saw beyond the cornea the strange network of nerves and veins which penetrate into the depths of the brain. But through that network were intertwined brightly shining silver threads a hundred times more delicate than the most delicate of spider webs, and precisely these strands, which seemed to be endless, as they branched forth out of the brain into a something inaccessible even to the microscopic eye, possibly entangled thoughts of a more sublime kind with others of a variety more readily comprehensible. Peregrinus perceived, intermingled at random, flowers that were being transformed into human beings, and then again human beings that flowed away into the earth to emerge glittering as jewels and minerals. And in among these moved all sorts of strange animals, which were transformed countless times and which spoke wondrous languages. No phenomenon was congruous with any other, and in the woeful lamentation of heartrending melancholy that resounded through the air the dissonance of the phenomena seemed to be expressed. Yet precisely this dissonance ennobled the fundamental harmony the more, which triumphantly broke forth and conjoined everything that had seemed sundered into everlasting and nameless delight.[5]

[5] The author's contemporaries would have recognized this scene, retained in the girl's subconscious memory from a previous existence, as the condition of the primeval universe. Nature, in exuberance of creative activity, was experimenting at random with forms but had not yet fixed on any definite pattern. Hence, elements easily assembled in all forms—animal, vegetable, mineral, human, and cosmic—and just as easily dissolved and reassembled in new configurations. Grotesque incongruities occasioned the "dissonances," but all dissonances blended with the "cosmic" harmony.

"Do not be confused," whispered Master Flea, "do not be confused, good Mr. Peregrinus, those are the thoughts of her dream that you are seeing there. If perhaps something further lies beyond them, this is not the time to probe the matter any further. Just call the seductive little creature by her right name and then question her any way you please."

Since the little lady bore various names, it might, as one could imagine, have proven difficult for Peregrinus to hit upon the right one. But Peregrinus cried, without thinking in the least about the matter: "Dörtje Elverdink! Dear, sweet girl! Can it be no illusion? Is it possible that you really could love me?"

Immediately the little lady woke from her trancelike state, opened her eyes, and said with flashing glance, "What doubt of that, my Peregrinus? Can a girl very well do what I have done if the most ardent love does not fill her heart? Peregrinus, I love you as no one else, and if you will be mine, then I am yours with all my soul, and I shall remain with you because I cannot give you up, and not merely in order to escape my uncle's tyranny."

The silver threads had vanished, and the properly ordered thoughts ran: "How has this come about? First I pretended love for him merely to get Master Flea back for me and for Leeuwenhoek, and now I have become fond of him in earnest. I have caught myself in my own snare. I scarcely think of Master Flea any more. I should like to belong eternally to the man who seems to me more lovable than all that I have ever seen until now."

One can imagine how these thoughts fired all the blessed rapture in Peregrinus's heart. He fell to his knees before the lovely girl, covered her hands with a thousand glowing kisses, called her his delight, his heaven, his total happiness.

"Now," whispered the little lady as she drew him softly to her side, "now, my dear one, you will surely not refuse me a wish upon whose fulfillment depends the peace, in fact the entire existence of your beloved."

"Ask," replied Peregrinus as he tenderly embraced the little lady, "ask anything, my sweet life, anything you desire. Your slightest wish is my command. Nothing in the world is so dear to me that I would not sacrifice it for you, for your love, with joy."

"Woe is me!" whispered Master Flea. "Who would have thought that the faithless creature would triumph? I am lost!"

"Then listen," the little lady went on, after she had ardently returned the fiery kisses which Peregrinus had pressed upon her lips, "then listen. I know in what way the—"

The door burst open and in stepped Mr. George Pepusch.

"Zeherit!" shrieked the little lady in desperation and sank back lifeless into the sofa.

The Thistle Zeherit, however, flew to the Princess Gamaheh, took her into his arms, and ran off with her at lightning speed.

Master Flea was saved this time.

FIFTH ADVENTURE

Remarkable trial and further wise and understanding behavior of Privy Counselor Knarrpanti. Thoughts of young poetic enthusiasts and lady authors. Peregrinus's observations concerning his life and Master Flea's erudition and rationality. Rare virtue and steadfastness of Mr. Tyss. Unexpected outcome of a scene which threatened to have tragic consequences.

The kind reader will recall that the papers of Mr. Peregrinus Tyss had been impounded in order to get closer on the track of an action that had not taken place. Both the delegate of the council and Privy Counselor Knarrpanti had read minutely through every piece of writing, every letter, and every scrap of paper that had been found—not excluding laundry lists and grocery lists—and now as a result of their investigations were of wholly opposite opinions.

The delegate maintained that the papers contained not one single word which could have relation to a crime of the kind that Peregrinus, according to the accusation, was supposed to have committed. Privy Counselor Knarrpanti's spying falcon-like eye had, on the other hand, discovered a great deal in Mr. Peregrinus Tyss's papers to show him as an extremely dangerous man. In earlier youthful years Peregrinus had kept a diary. In this diary there were a host of insidious passages which not only cast a very disadvantageous light on his notions relative to the abduction of a young woman, but clearly demonstrated that he had already committed that crime several times.

Thus it read: "There is really something lofty and magnificent about this abduction!" And again: "And yet I have carried

off the loveliest one of all!" And again: "From him I have taken
these Mariannes, these Philines, these Mignons!" And again: "I
love these abductions!" And again: "It was proper, it was necessary for Julia to be abducted, and that was what happened when
I had her surprised on a solitary walk in the woods and carried
off by masked men."

Besides these wholly decisive passages in the diary there was
also found a letter from a friend, in which it said insidiously:
"I should like to ask you to have Friederike abducted from
him in any place and by any means you can."

All these mentioned quotations, together with a hundred
other sentences, wherever the words "abduction," "abduct,"
and "abducted" occurred, the wise Knarrpanti had not only
underscored heavily with red pencil, but he had listed them on
a separate sheet, which looked very pretty and with which work
he was particularly pleased.

"You see," said Knarrpanti to the council delegate, "you see,
most worthy colleague, didn't I tell you so? This Peregrinus
Tyss is an infamous, horrible person, a regular Don Juan. Who
knows what has become of the unhappy sacrificial victims of
his lust, these Mariannes, these Philines, and who all? It was
high time that a check was put on this monster, otherwise this
dangerous man might have turned the good city of Frankfurt
into a thousand sorrows by his abduction plots. What crimes the
man has already committed according to his own confession!
Look at this passage, dear colleague, and judge for yourself
what monstrous designs this Peregrinus had in mind."

The diary entry which the wise Privy Counselor Knarrpanti
pointed out to the council delegate read: "I was unfortunately
murderously lazy today." The word "murderously" was underlined three times,[1] and Knarrpanti wanted to know whether
anyone could very well display more criminal intentions than
by regretting not having committed a murder on a certain day!

The delegate repeated his opinion that there was not the
slightest trace of a crime to be detected in Mr. Peregrinus Tyss's
papers. Knarrpanti incredulously shook his head, and the dele-

[1] Police Director von Kamptz had so underlined in red pencil the word
"*mordfaul*" ("murderously lazy") in the impounded diary of Gustav
Asverus, the student arrested in 1819 for "demagogic activity."

gate asked him to listen once more to those passages he had himself excerpted as suspicious, but in better context. The kind reader will presently be completely convinced of Knarrpanti's sublime slyness.

The delegate opened the insidious diary and read: "Today I saw in the theater for the twentieth time and with the same delight Mozart's *Abduction from the Seraglio. There is really something lofty and magnificent about this abduction.*" And again: "*All the flowers might please me, and yet I have carried off the loveliest one of all.*" And again: "*From him I have taken these Mariannes, these Philines, these Mignons;* for he was too deeply involved in these characters, indulging in reveries with the old Harper and quarreling with Jarno. *Wilhelm Meister is no book for such as are recovering from serious nervous disorders.*"[2] And again: "*Jünger's Abduction is a charming comedy.*[3] *I love these abductions* because they breathe a particular vitality into the plot." And again: "*The too little thought out plan got me into terrible straits. It was proper, it was necessary for Julia to be abducted, and that was what happened when I had her surprised on a solitary walk in the woods and carried off by masked men.* I was uncommonly pleased with this new idea, which I carried through on a broad enough scale. Altogether, this tragedy was a very funny piece of bungling on the part of the inspired youth, and I am sorry I threw it into the fire."

The letter read: "You see Friederike so often in company, you lucky fellow! Apparently Moritz will let no one get near her and monopolizes her entire attention. If you were not so foolish, so shy of women, *I should like to ask you to have Friederike abducted from him in any place and by any means you can.*"

Knarrpanti still insisted that even the context did not make matters any better, for it was precisely the crafty slyness of criminals to veil such expressions in such a way that they might pass at first glance for wholly indifferent, wholly innocent. As special proof of such slyness the profound Knarrpanti pointed

[2] Marianne, Philine, Mignon, the Harper, and Jarno are characters in Goethe's novel, *Wilhelm Meister.*
[3] Johann Friedrich Jünger's comedy, *Die Entführung (The Abduction),* 1792.

out to the delegate a verse which appeared in Peregrinus's papers and in which there was mention of an *endless conducting* by Fate. Knarrpanti prided himself not a little on his sagacity in discovering immediately that the word "abduction" had been truncated in that verse in order to remove it from attention and suspicion.

Still the council did not wish to enter into any further proceedings against the accused Peregrinus Tyss. The jurists employed an expression which may be allowed to stand here on account of the fact that it looks strange in the Tale of Master Flea, and, although the "marvelous" may be termed the real adornment of a fairy tale, the "strange" is not to be disallowed as a pleasing ornamental addition. They said (the jurists, that is) that there was a total lack of a *corpus delicti*. But the wise Counselor Knarrpanti stuck to it that he didn't give a damn about the *delictum* if he could just get his hands on a *corpus*, and the *corpus* was the dangerous abductor and murderer, Mr. Peregrinus Tyss. The Editor begs the kind reader who is not familiar with legal jargon, and in particular all lovely lady readers, to get a young jurist to explain this passage. The jurist in question will immediately strike his breast and begin: "In the language of the law it says—and so on."

Only the occurrence during the night, about which the witnesses had spoken, was considered by the delegate to be a subject on which Mr. Peregrinus Tyss should have to submit to an interrogation.

Peregrinus became no little embarrassed when he was questioned by the delegate about how the matter had gone. He felt that if he departed from the truth in any detail the whole story would inevitably bear the mark of falsehood, or at least of the highest unlikelihood. Hence he found it expedient to keep still altogether, and to defend himself by saying that, as long as no definite and actual crime was ascertained of which he could be accused, he did not consider it necessary to answer questions about individual events in his life. Knarrpanti gloated at this statement by the accused and found his entire suspicion thereby confirmed.

He told the delegate rather frankly that he did not know how to go about this thing rightly, and the delegate was clearheaded and understanding enough to realize that a hearing conducted by Knarrpanti himself would occasion Peregrinus no disadvantage and might rather give the matter a turn to his advantage.

The ingenious Knarrpanti had more than a hundred questions ready, with which he now went after Peregrinus and which, as a matter of fact, were often not so easy to answer. Primarily they were addressed to the purpose of finding out what Peregrinus had been *thinking*, both in general throughout his life and also on this and that particular occasion, as, for example, upon the writing of these suspicious words in his papers.

Thinking, Knarrpanti held, was already a dangerous operation in and of itself, and with dangerous people became just that much more dangerous. Further, there were such artful questions as, for example, who had the elderly man been, in the blue overcoat and with hair cut short, with whom he had reached an agreement on the twenty-fourth of March of the preceding year at noon at the table d'hôte, concerning the best way to prepare Rhine salmon? Or again: did he himself not see that all the mysterious passages in his papers rightly aroused suspicion, and might not what he had omitted to write down contain much more suspicious matter, in fact a full confession of the deed?

This method of investigation, in fact Privy Counselor Knarrpanti himself, seemed so odd to Peregrinus that he was curious to ascertain the thoughts of the crafty fox.

He snapped his fingers, and swiftly the obedient Master Flea had the microscopic lens in his eye.

Knarrpanti's thoughts ran approximately thus: "I don't myself think the young man has abducted our princess, who ran off several years ago with a strolling player, or that he even could have done so. But I couldn't let the opportunity pass to make a big fuss in my best interest. My little master was beginning to be indifferent toward me, and at court they were calling me a tiresome dreamer. In fact, they rather often found me ridiculous and insipid, although no one was superior to me in intelligence and taste, and not one of them understood so well as I do, the little services by which one gets into the good graces of the master. Did I not even help the prince's valet polish the shoes? And then came that abduction story like a boon from heaven. With the news that I had got on the track of the runaway princess, I suddenly raised myself again to the position of respect that I had almost lost. Once again they find me intelligent, wise, clever, and, above all, so loyally subservient to the master that I am called a pillar of the state, upon which all well-being depends.

"Nothing will or can come of this affair, because the actual abduction can not be proved in this man's case. Just for that reason I mean to torment the young man with questions and cross-questions as much as I can. For, the more I do this, the higher my interest in the case and my lively zeal on behalf of my master will be praised. All I need to do is make the young man impatient and squeeze a few snippy answers out of him. These I will then mark with good strong red pencil, add a few remarks to them maybe, and before you know it, there the man will be in an ambiguous light, and out of the whole business there will develop a hateful atmosphere that will do him harm and prejudice him even in the eyes of such quiet, naïve people as this delegate here. Blessed be the art of lending a tinge of hateful significance to the most indifferent matter. It is a gift that Nature gave me and by virtue of which I get my enemies off my neck and remain myself in the best of well-being. I have to laugh that the council is so impressed at how set I am on actually ascertaining the truth, because I really have only myself in mind, and I look upon the whole case as a means of increasing my importance with my master, and thus of acquiring as much approbation and money as I possibly can. Even if nothing comes of it, no one can say that my efforts have been useless. It will be said rather that I was right after all, and that by the steps I took I at least hindered the rascally Peregrinus Tyss from abducting the already abducted princess after the fact."

When Peregrinus saw through the sublime counselor's thoughts this way, it was natural for him to maintain proper composure and, instead of becoming restive as Knarrpanti wanted him to, to bring Knarrpanti's cleverness to naught by very skillful answers. The council delegate seemed to be getting his own pleasure out of this. After Knarrpanti had closed his endless interrogation, chiefly for lack of breath, Peregrinus, unasked and in a few words, told the delegate that the young lady whom he had carried into his house on Christmas Eve at her own express request, was none other than the niece of the optical artificer Leeuwenhoek, Dörtje Elverdink by name, and that she was now staying with her godfather, Mr. Swammer, who rented rooms in his house.

This account was found acceptable, and the extraordinary abduction trial was ended.

Knarrpanti, to be sure, pressed for still further interrogation and read his astute trial transcript in the council, but his masterpiece aroused only universal, resounding laughter. It was then found to be very advisable for Privy Counselor Knarrpanti to leave Frankfurt and to carry the amazing official record with his own hands to his master as a result of his efforts, as proof of his sagacity and of his lively zeal of office. The bizarre abduction trial became the talk of the city, and to his no small annoyance the worthy Knarrpanti was forced to observe that, whenever he passed by, the people held their noses with all the marks of disgust and revulsion, and got up from their seats whenever he was about to sit down at the table d'hôte. He soon got out of the city. And thus Knarrpanti had to leave with shame and dishonor the field on which he had hoped to gather laurels.[4]

All this which has been related here in sequence had actually occupied a period of several days, for no one should imagine that Knarrpanti was able to compose a considerable folio volume in a short time. But his remarkable trial transcript resembled such a volume. Knarrpanti's daily harassment, his preposterous and arrogant behavior roused profound depression in Peregrinus, and this was further intensified perceptibly by the uncertainty in which he hung in the matter of the beautiful lady's fate.

As the kind reader learned at the close of the Fourth Adventure, George Pepusch had, with the speed of lightning, swept the little lady out of the arms of the amorous Peregrinus and left the latter stunned with amazement and fright.

When finally Peregrinus had come to his senses, jumped up, and pursued his robberlike friend, everything in the house was empty and still. In answer to his repeated shouts old Aline had padded forth in bedslippers from the most distant room and

[4] This scene was suggested by Tobias Smollett's *Peregrine Pickle*, Vol. III, *Pipes holds his nose*, etc.

assured him she had not noticed the entire occurrence in the slightest way.

Peregrinus was almost beside himself over the loss of Dörtje. But Master Flea was heard with comforting words: "You don't know," he said in a tone that could not fail to inspire confidence in the most hopeless man, "you don't know yet, dear Mr. Peregrinus Tyss, whether the beautiful Dörtje Elverdink has actually left your house. As far as I understand such things, she is not far away. I feel as though I sense her presence. But if you are willing to trust my friendly advice and follow it, leave the beautiful Dörtje to her fate. Believe me, the little lady is a thing that changes like the weather. Assuming that she is now genuinely fond of you, as you told me she is, how long will it be before she plunges you into such sorrow and misery that you will lose your mind over it, like the Thistle Zeherit? Again I say to you, give up your solitary life. You will be the better for it. What girls have you already known, that you should esteem Dörtje as the most beautiful one? What woman have you approached with friendly words of love, that you should believe that only Dörtje can love you? Go on, go on, Peregrinus! Experience will convince you of something better. You are a very handsome, stately man, and I would not have to be so intelligent and perspicacious as Master Flea really is, if I did not foresee that the happiness of love will still laugh for you in quite a different way from what you now imagine."

By the fact that he went to public places, Peregrinus had already broken the ice, and it was less difficult for him now to visit companies from which he had formerly held aloof. Master Flea did him excellent service the while with his microscopic lens, and Peregrinus is said to have kept a diary during this time and to have set down the most fantastic and most amusing contrasts between words and thoughts as they daily befell him. Perhaps the Editor of the odd tale called *Master Flea* will some time in the future find opportunity to bring to light many a further item worthy of mention from that diary. Here it would only hold up the story, and for that reason not be welcome to the kind reader.

This much can be said, that many a locution became stereotyped with the thoughts that accompanied it; as for example,

"I solicit your kind advice," goes in thought: "It is absurd enough to think that, in a matter long since decided, I should actually seek his advice; but that flatters him!"; "I trust you completely," goes: "I have known for a long time that you are a rascal!" And so on. Finally, it may be mentioned also that many people did put Peregrinus into great embarrassment with his microscopic observations. These included the young men who got extremely enthusiastic about everything and could pour themselves forth in a gushing stream of the most magnificent style of speaking. Among these, young poets seemed to speak most profoundly and most superbly, as they paraded their downright fantasy and genius and were obliged to endure much adoration, primarily from ladies. Paired with them were the writing ladies, who had right at their fingertips' all the profundities of existence here below, as well as all the genuinely philosophical insights that penetrated to the very core of the social life, as people call it, and could rehearse it all in splendid words like a holiday sermon.

If Peregrinus was amazed to see the silver threads put forth tendrils out of Gamaheh's brain into an undiscoverable Something, he was no less astonished at what he perceived in the brains of the aforementioned people. He saw, to be sure, the strange weft of veins and nerves, but at the same time he noticed that, when these people spoke especially magnificently about art and knowledge, about the tendencies of the higher life, these threads did not proceed at all into the depths of the brain, but grew back forward again, so that one could not speak at all of clear perception of thoughts. He communicated his observation to Master Flea, who was sitting as usual in the fold of his neck-cloth. It was Master Flea's opinion that what Peregrinus took for thoughts, were none at all, but only words striving in vain to become thoughts. If Mr. Peregrinus Tyss now became jolly in many ways in society, his faithful companion, Master Flea, also remitted much of his seriousness and proved a roguish little voluptuary, an amiable roué. Not a single beautiful throat, not a single nape of a woman's white neck could he see, but that he leaped out of his hiding place at the first opportunity and onto that inviting spot, where he knew how to dodge skillfully every ambush of pointed fingers. This maneuver included a double interest. For one thing, he found his own pleasure in it, and then he also wanted to draw Peregrinus's glances toward beauties that would overshadow Dörtje's image. And yet it all seemed to be effort wasted, for not a single lady whom Peregrinus approached with full assurance and without any timidity seemed to him so pretty or so charming as his little princess. But what in the last analysis held his love firmly to his little lady was the fact that with none of them did he find words and thoughts so in agreement with his tastes, as with her. He thought he was never going to be able to give her up, and he declared this unreservedly. Master Flea was not a little perturbed.

One day Peregrinus noticed that old Aline was smiling roguishly to herself, taking snuff more frequently than usual, clearing her throat, murmuring unintelligible things, in short, was acting with her entire being like someone who has something on his mind and would like to get rid of it. What was more, she kept answering everything with "Yes! There's no way of telling. We shall have to wait and see!" whether these remarks fitted the situation or not.

"Just speak," cried Peregrinus at last, full of impatience, "just speak right out, Aline, and say what is the matter again, without stealing around me this way with mysterious looks."

"Oh!" cried the old woman, clutching her withered fists together. "Oh! the dear, darling little sugar-doll, the dear sweet thing!"

"Whom do you mean?" Peregrinus interrupted the old woman with annoyance.

"Why," said the latter, smirking as before, "why, whom else should I mean but our dear princess downstairs in Mr. Swammer's rooms, your lovely fiancée, Mr. Tyss."

"Woman," Peregrinus flared up, "wretched woman, she is here, here in this house, and you don't tell me this until now?"

"Where," replied the old woman without losing her composure in the least, "where else could the princess very well be except here, where she has found her mother?"

"What!" cried Peregrinus, "what are you saying, Aline?"

"Yes," said the old woman raising her head, "yes, Aline, that is my right name, and who knows what all will not come to light yet in a short time, before your marriage?"

Without paying the slightest attention to the impatience of Peregrinus, who kept conjuring her by all the angels and devils just to talk, to relate, the old woman disposed herself comfortably in an armchair, fetched forth her snuffbox, took a big pinch of the stuff, and then demonstrated to Peregrinus circumstantially and with many words that there was no greater or more harmful shortcoming than impatience.

"Calm," she said, "calm, my boy, is what you need above all things. Otherwise you run the risk of losing everything at the very minute when you think you have won it. Before you hear one little word from me, you will have to sit down quietly over there and not for anything interrupt me in my story."

What was there left for Peregrinus to do but obey the old woman? As soon as he had sat down, she proceeded to narrate things which were odd and strange enough to hear.

As the old woman told the story, the two gentlemen, Swammerdam and Leeuwenhoek, had had a prime tussle around the room for some further time and had raved and ranted horribly while doing so. Then everything had become quiet. A dull groaning had meanwhile caused the old woman to fear that one of the two was wounded mortally. But when the old woman had peeped curiously through the keyhole, she beheld something quite different from what she had thought. Swammerdam and Leeuwenhoek had seized George Pepusch and were punching and kneading him with their fists so that he was getting thinner and thinner, and in the process he was groaning in the way the old woman had heard. Finally, when Pepusch had gotten as thin as a thistle stalk, they attempted to poke him through the keyhole. Poor Pepusch was already hanging with half of his body out into the entrance hall when the old woman fled in terror. Soon afterwards the old woman had heard ringing laughter and saw Pepusch in his natural form being led home quite peaceably by the two mages. In the doorway the beautiful Dörtje was standing and beckoning the old woman to come in. She wanted to get dressed in her finery and had need of the old woman's help in the process.

The old woman simply could not talk enough about the

great quantity of dresses that the little lady had produced from all sorts of old closets and shown to her, each one of which was richer and more magnificent than the other. Then the old woman asserted that surely only an Indian princess could own such jewels as the little lady: her eyes still hurt from the dazzling glitter. The old woman went on to tell how she had talked about one thing and another with the darling child in the course of the dressing, how she had thought of the late Mr. Tyss and of the lovely life that used to be led in this house, and how finally she had come round to the topic of her deceased relatives.

"You know," the old woman said, "you know, dear Mr. Tyss, that nothing is more precious to me than my late auntie, the calico printing lady. She had been in Mainz, and I think in India too, and she could pray and sing in French. If I have that auntie to thank for my unchristian name of Aline, I am willing to forgive her for that in her grave, because I gained from her alone my genteel manner of living, my politeness, and my understanding of how to use words prettily. And then, as I was relating a great deal about my auntie, the little princess inquired about my parents, grandparents, and so on and so on back in the family. I poured out my heart, I spoke without reserve about how my mother had been almost as beautiful as I am, although I excel in consideration of my nose, which I get from my father and which has been customary in that form in the family since human memory can recall. And then I came to speak also about the church consecration, when I danced the allemande with Sergeant Häberpiep and wore the sky-blue stockings with the red clocks in them. Well, dear God, we are all weak and sinful creatures. But, Mr. Tyss, you should have seen for yourself how the little princess, who at first had kept giggling and laughing so it was a joy to hear, had become more and more silent and kept looking at me with such strange glances that I actually felt downright uncanny. And just imagine, Mr. Tyss, suddenly, before I knew it, there was the little princess down on her knees in front of me trying to kiss my hand and crying, 'Yes! it is you, now I recognize you! Yes! It is you yourself!' And when I asked in all astonishment what this was supposed to mean—"

The old woman stopped, and when Peregrinus urged her just

to go on talking, she very solemnly and thoughtfully took a big pinch of snuff and said, "You will find out soon enough, my lad, what else took place. There is a time and an hour for everything!"

Peregrinus was just about to press the old woman still more sharply to tell him more, when she burst forth in shrill laughter. With a somber face Peregrinus reminded her that his room was not precisely the place to carry on her foolish antics with him. But, setting her arms akimbo, the old woman seemed to be on the point of choking. The fiery red color of her countenance passed over into a pretty cherry-brown, and Peregrinus was standing ready to throw a glass of water into the old woman's face when she got her breath and resumed speaking.

"Can you," she said, "can you help laughing at the silly little thing? No, there is no love like that any more on earth! Just imagine, Mr. Tyss—" and the old woman burst out laughing anew.

Peregrinus felt his patience running out. Finally he made out with difficulty that the little princess was under the illusion that he, Mr. Peregrinus Tyss, was absolutely bent on marrying the old woman, and that she, the old woman, had had to give her her solemn promise to refuse his hand.

To Peregrinus it seemed as though he were involved in some evil witchcraft, and he began to feel so uncanny that the honorable old woman herself started to look to him like a spectral creature from whom he could not flee fast enough.

The old woman would not let him leave, because she had to confide to him very quickly something that concerned the little princess.

"It is certain," said the old woman confidentially, "it is certain that now your fine and gleaming star of fortune, dear Mr. Peregrinus, has risen, but it will now be up to you to keep that star favorable. When I assured the little lady that you were astonishingly in love with her and that you were far from wanting to marry me, she said that she would not be convinced of that and would not be able to give you her beautiful hand until you had granted her a wish which she had long cherished in the depths of her heart. The little lady maintains that you have taken a darling little Negro boy into your house, who has escaped from her service.[5] Of course I denied that, but she insists that the boy is so tiny that he could live in a nutshell. Now, this boy—"

"Nothing will come of that," cried Peregrinus vehemently, who had long since known what the old woman was driving at, and with violence he left the room and the house.

It is an old and traditional custom for the hero of the story, when he is seized by vehement emotions, to rush out into the forest, or at least into the shrubbery situated in a solitary place. The custom is good because it actually obtains in life. Directly afterwards it could not happen otherwise with Mr. Peregrinus Tyss but that he should keep running so long in one spurt from his house on the Horse Market until he had put the city behind him and reached a nearby place overgrown with bushes. Since, further, in a romantic story no place overgrown with bushes must lack for rustling leaves, sighing and whispering evening breezes, murmuring fountains, babbling brooks, and the like, just so, we may believe that Peregrinus found all these things in his place of refuge. Upon a mossy stone that lay half in the mirror-bright brook, whose curling waves splashed about it, Peregrinus sat down with the firm intention, as he reflected upon the odd adventures of the moment, of seeking and finding the Ariadne clew that would show him the way back out of the labyrinth of most extraordinary riddles.

It may well be that the rustling of the bushes recurring in measured pauses, the monotonous sound of the water, and the even clatter of a distant windmill presently assumed the quality of a basic tone, in time with which the thoughts are reined in and given form so that they no longer go rushing about without

[5] At the beginning of Act II of *A Midsummer Night's Dream*, Puck explains:

> ... Oberon is passing fell and wrath,
> Because that she, as her attendant, hath
> A lovely boy stolne from an Indian King,
> She never had so sweet a changeling,
> And jealous Oberon would have the childe ...
> . . . .
>   all their Elves for feare
> Creepe into Acorne cups and hide them there.

rhythm and beat, but turn into recognizable melody. Then, after he had been in this pleasant spot for some time, Peregrinus arrived at quiet contemplation.

"Actually," said Peregrinus to himself, "no fantastical fairy-tale writer could think up crazier and more confused events than I have been living through in reality in the short span of a few days. Charm, delight, and love itself come to meet the misogynic hermit, and one glance, one word, suffices to kindle flames in his bosom, whose martyrdom he shunned without knowing it! But the place, the time, the whole appearance of the strange and seductive creature are so mysterious that an odd magic seems to be visibly involved, and not long after that, a little, tiny, generally despised beast displays knowledge, understanding, and even a marvelous magic power. And this beast talks about things that are incomprehensible to all ordinary comprehension, and in a way as if all this were but the thousand-times-repeated Yesterday and Today of common life behind the meat platter and the wine bottle.

"Have I come too close to the flywheel turned by the dark, unknown powers, and has it caught me up in its oscillations? Can one help thinking one's mind must inevitably be lost over things like this, if they cut through our lives? And yet I find myself well off, for all of that. In fact, it no longer strikes me as particularly odd that a king of the fleas has entrusted himself to my protection and in exchange has confided a secret to me which reveals the secret of inner thoughts and thereby elevates me above all the deceptions of life.

"But where will all this lead? Where can it lead? What if behind this strange mask of a flea there were an evil demon who was trying to lure me to destruction, who was bent on robbing me in vile fashion of all the blessedness of love that might flower for me in the possession of Dörtje? Would it not be better to get rid of the little monster straightaway?"

"That," Master Flea interrupted Peregrinus's monologue, "that was a very unmannerly thought, Mr. Peregrinus Tyss! Do you fancy that the secret I have confided to you is a slight one? Can that gift not pass for the most decisive mark of my genuine friendship? Shame on you for being so distrustful! You feel amazement at the comprehension and the mental powers of a tiny, otherwise despised little beast, and that testifies—don't take this amiss—at least to the limitations of your scientific education. As far as the thinking and self-determining soul of beasts is concerned, I wish you had read the Greek Philo,[6] or at least the treatise of Hieronymus Rorarius, *Quod animalia bruta ratione utantur melius homine,* or his *Oratio pro muribus.*[7] Or that you knew what Lipsius[8] and the great Leibnitz[9] thought about the mental capacity of beasts, or that you were familiar with what the erudite and profound Rabbi Maimonides[10] said concerning the souls of animals. Then you would hardly take me for an evil demon on account of my comprehension or try to measure the mass of intellectual rationality according to its physical extension. I think that in the last analysis you are inclined to the astute opinion of the Spanish physician Gomez Pereira,[11] who finds nothing more in animals than artful mechanisms without capacity to think, without freedom of the will, who move involuntarily and automatically. But no, I will not consider you so tasteless as all that, good Mr. Peregrinus Tyss. Rather, I shall firmly believe that you have long since learned better through my slight person.

"Moreover, I don't quite know what surprises you so, estim-

---

[6] In the first century Philo Judaeus composed a treatise on the existence of reason in animals. Hoffmann surely knew no more about that treatise than he could find written about it in the *Dictionnaire historique et critique* of Pierre Bayle (1647–1706), which he might have read either in the French original or in German translation.

[7] Hieronymus Rorarius (1485–1556), an Italian scholar, published these two works in 1547: *That Irrational Animals Use Reason Better Than (Does) Man* and *Oration on Behalf of Mice.* Again, Hoffmann's knowledge of them came from Bayle's *Dictionnaire.*

[8] Justus Lipsius (1547–1606), a Dutch scholar, credited animals with the capacity for cognition in the course of his book on the physiology of the Stoics, *Justi Lipsii physiologiae stoicorum libri tres,* Antwerp, 1637.

[9] The well-known Gottfried Wilhelm von Liebnitz (1646–1716), German mathematician and philosopher, rejected the claims made by Hieronymus Rorarius for the cognitive abilities of animals, yet attributed to animals a capacity analogous to the human reason, an "*analogon rationis.*"

[10] The Jewish philosopher Moses Maimonides (1135–1204) denied that animals had powers of cognition but claimed that they did have the ability to express their will, for thus the Godhead operated through them.

[11] Gomez Pereira (born *circa* 1500) published in 1554 the treatise *Antonina Margarite de immortalitate animae* (Antonina Margarite on the Immortality of the Soul), which dealt with matters in the areas of medicine and theology. Pereira is considered a precursor of Descartes.

able Mr. Peregrinus, or in what way you are able to separate
into wonderful and non-wonderful the manifestations of our beings, which are really only ourselves over again, since they mu-
tually determine us and we them. If you are amazed at something because it has never happened to you, or because you
fancy you do not see the connection between cause and effect,
that only testifies to the natural or diseased dullness of your
perception, which impairs your powers of cognition. But—
don't take this amiss, Mr. Tyss—the funniest part of the matter
is the fact that you want to divide yourself into two parts, one
of which recognizes and willingly believes the so-called marvels, while the other is greatly astonished at this credulity.
Has it ever struck you that you believe in the images of dreams?"

"I beg you," Peregrinus interrupted the little speaker, "I beg
you, good man, how can you talk about dreams, which are only
the result of some disorder in our bodily or mental organism?"

At these words of Mr. Peregrinus Tyss, Master Flea struck up
a laugh that was as delicate as it was mocking. "Poor Mr.
Tyss," he said to the somewhat chagrined Peregrinus, "poor
Mr. Tyss, is your intelligence so little enlightened that you do
not see the ridiculousness of such opinions? Since the time
when Chaos condensed to formative matter—the World-Spirit
has been forming all forms out of that available material, and
from it dreams proceed with their images. These configurations are sketches of what has been or perhaps of what will be,
sketches which the Mind quickly draws at its pleasure, when
the tyrant named Body releases him from his slave's service.
But here is neither the time nor the place to refute you and
convince you of something better. Possibly that would be of
no use either. There is just one further thing that I want to
reveal to you."

"Speak," cried Peregrinus, "speak or be silent, dear Master.
Do whichever you think is more fitting, for I realize sufficiently that, small as you are, you have infinitely more comprehension and profound knowledge. You force me to unconditional trust, even though I don't wholly understand your fancy
ways of talking."

"Listen, then," Master Flea resumed, "listen, then, and know
that you are involved in the history of the Princess Gamaheh in

a very special way. Swammerdam and Leeuwenhoek, the Thistle
Zeherit and the Leech Prince, and the Spirit Thetel besides, are
all seeking possession of the beautiful princess, and I must confess myself that my old love has unfortunately been aroused
and that I was foolish enough to share my mastery with that
lovely faithless creature. But you, you, Mr. Peregrinus, are the
chief personage. Without your consent the beautiful Gamaheh
can belong to no one. If you want to find out the actual, profound substance of the matter, which I do not know myself,
then you must discuss it with Leeuwenhoek, who has found
out everything and who will surely drop many a word, if you
will take the trouble and know how to sound him out properly."

Master Flea was about to continue his speech when, in full
fury, a person rushed out of the bushes and made for
Peregrinus.

"Ha!" shrieked George Pepusch—for it was he—with wild
gestures. "Ha!" Faithless, treacherous friend! Do I find you
here? Do I find you in this fateful hour? Up, then, pierce this
bosom, or fall by my hand!"

With that Pepusch pulled a pair of pistols out of his pockets,
put one pistol into Peregrinus's hand and, with the other in his
own, struck a stance, crying, "Shoot, cowardly poltroon!"

Peregrinus took up a position but assured him that nothing
would bring him to the unholy madness of entering into a duel
with his only friend without so much as guessing the cause for
it. At the very least he would not in any case murderously attack his friend first.

Then Pepusch broke into a wild laugh, and at the same instant the bullet from the pistol which Pepusch had fired went
through Peregrinus's hat. Without picking up the hat, which had
fallen to the ground, the latter stared at his friend in deep
silence. Pepusch approached to within a few steps of Peregrinus
and muttered dully: "Shoot!"

Then Peregrinus fired the pistol quickly into the air.

Howling like a madman, George Pepusch now fell upon his
friend's bosom and with heartrending tone cried, "She is dying! She is dying from love of you, unhappy man! Hurry—save
her—you can do it! Save her for yourself and let me perish in
wild despair!"

Pepusch ran away so fast that Peregrinus had immediately lost sight of him.

But now it fell heavily upon Peregrinus's heart to think that his friend's wild behavior must be caused by something horrible that had happened to the lovely little lady. He hurried quickly back to the city.

As he entered his house the old woman came to meet him, wailing aloud that the poor, beautiful princess had suddenly been taken ill in the most violent way and would probably die; old Mr. Swammer himself had just gone to fetch the most famous physician that there was in Frankfurt.

With death in his heart, Peregrinus slipped into Mr. Swammer's room, which the old woman opened for him. There lay the little lady, pale and rigid as a corpse on the sofa, and not until he had knelt down and bent over her did Peregrinus perceive her faint breathing. As soon as Peregrinus took hold of the ice-cold hand, a painful smile played about her lips and she whispered, "Is it you, sweet friend? Have you come to see her once again who loves you so unutterably? Alas! She is dying because she is unable to breathe without you!"

Dissolved in bitterest grief, Peregrinus poured forth asseverations of his tenderest love and kept repeating that nothing in the world was so dear to him but that he would sacrifice it for the lovely girl. His words turned to kisses, but in these kisses, like the breath of love, words became audible again.

"You know," these words may have gone, "you know, my Peregrinus, how much I love you. I can be yours and you mine, I can get well on the spot, you will behold me blooming in fresh and youthful splendor like a flower which the morning dew revives and which raises its sunken head in joy—but—give me the captive, my dear, beloved Peregrinus, or else you will see me pass away before your eyes amid nameless anguish of death!—Peregrinus—I can endure no more—it is over—"

With that the little lady, who had halfway sat up, sank back into the pillows, her bosom was vehemently rising and falling in a death struggle, her lips were turning blue, her eyes seemed to set.

In wild anguish, Peregrinus grabbed at his neck-cloth. But of his own free will Master Flea leaped upon the white throat of the little lady, crying in the tone of profoundest sorrow as he did so: "I am lost!"

Peregrinus stretched out his hand to seize the Master. But suddenly it seemed as if an unseen power were restraining his arm, and thoughts quite different from those which had filled him up to now, went through his head.

"What!" he thought. "Because you are a weak man who surrenders to mad passion, who in the frenzy of aroused desire accepts as truth what may after all be nothing but deceptive illusion, are you willing to betray faithlessly one who has yielded himself to your protection? Because of those things you are willing to put a free and harmless little people in chains of everlasting slavery? Because of those things you are willing to destroy hopelessly the friend whom you have found to be the only one whose words accord with his thoughts? No—no— Get control of yourself, Peregrinus! Rather endure death than break faith!"

"Give—me—the—captive—I am dying!" stammered the little lady with failing voice.

"No!" cried Peregrinus, as in fierce despair he swept the little lady into his arms. "No! Never!—but let me die with you!"

At that instant a high, melodious sound was heard, as though little silver bells were being struck. Suddenly, with the shimmer of fresh roses on her lips and cheeks, Dörtje leaped up from the sofa, and breaking forth into convulsive laughter, went hopping about the room. She seemed as though stung by the tarantula.

In horror Peregrinus beheld the uncanny spectacle, and so did the physician who stood in the doorway, blocking the entrance of Mr. Swammer who was trying to follow him in.

SIXTH ADVENTURE

Strange behavior of traveling charlatans in a tavern, together with adequate drubbing. Tragic history of a little tailor in Sachsenhausen. How George Pepusch astonished honorable people. The horoscope. Amusing battle of familiar people in Leeuwenhoek's room.

All passers-by stopped, stretched out their necks, and peered through the windows into the tavern. Denser and denser gathered the crowd, more and more angrily everyone kept elbowing up and pushing, madder and madder became the confusion, the laughter, the frenzy, the jubilation.

The uproar was being caused by two strangers who happened to be in the tavern. Besides the fact that their figures, their dress, and their whole appearance had something foreign about them which was offensive and at the same time ridiculous, they were carrying on such odd tricks as had never been seen before. One of them, an old man of repulsively dirty aspect, was dressed in a long and very tight overcoat of shiny material, a faded black in color. At one moment he could make himself tall and thin, then again he shrank up into a short, fat character, and the odd thing was that as he did so he squirmed like a slippery worm. The other one, hair powdered and curled, in gaily colored silk coat, nether garments of the same material, big silver buckles, looking like a *petit maître* from the latter half of the past century, by contrast, kept flying up to the ceiling again and again and letting himself come down gently, while he kept warbling out-of-tune songs in a hoarse voice and in a

354

completely unknown language. According to the tavern keeper's statement, both of them had come into the bar, one shortly after the other, like perfectly sensible, proper people, and called for wine. Then they had looked more and more sharply into each other's faces and had begun to discourse. Although their language was incomprehensible to all the guests, their tone and ·gestures indicated that they were involved in a quarrel which was getting ever more violent.

Suddenly they had stood there, transformed into their present forms, and had begun to carry on in the maddest fashion, attracting more and ever more spectators.

One of the spectators cried out, "The one that flies up and down so prettily, he must be Degen, mustn't he, the watchmaker from Vienna, who invented the flying machine and with it came tumbling down out of the air and onto his nose?"[1]

"Oh, no," replied another, "that isn't Degen the bird. I'd sooner think it was the little tailor from Sachsenhausen, if I didn't know the poor thing had been burned."

I do not know whether the kind reader knows the history of the little tailor from Sachsenhausen. Here it is:

History of the Little Tailor from Sachsenhausen

It befell that a gentle, pious, little tailor in Sachsenhausen came out of church of a Sunday all dressed up and with his dear wife. The air was raw, and the little tailor had eaten nothing the night before except half of a soft-boiled egg and a pickle, and that morning one little bowl of coffee. Hence he felt a little faint and pitiful, because, what's more, he had sung pretty hard in church, and he yearned for a dram in his stomach. All week long he had been busy, and also nice to his dear wife, for whom he had made up a nice petticoat out of a piece of material that had fallen under the bench while he was cutting it. So his dear wife kindly allowed the little tailor to step into the apothecary's and have a dram to warm himself up. And step into the apothecary's he did, and ordered same. The clumsy apprentice, who had stayed behind alone in the shop because the black-

[1] Degen was a real person (1756–1815) who made attempts at flight in Vienna and in Paris in the early years of the nineteenth century.

guard of a pharmacist—and in fact all the other cleverer people —had left, got hold of the wrong thing and brought down from the cabinet a sealed bottle in which there was no stomach elixir, but inflammable air that balloons are filled with. The apprentice poured out a glassful, and this the little tailor put right into his mouth and eagerly drained the air like a pleasing cordial. Right off he felt queer. He felt as though he had a pair of wings on his shoulders, or as though someone were playing catch with him. For ell-high and higher yet he just had to rise up in the apothecary's shop and sink down again. "Oh, jiminy, jiminy!" he kept shouting. "What a spry dancer I have turned into!" But the apprentice's mouth was hanging open for sheer amazement. Then it happened that someone opened the door, causing the window opposite to fly open. In streamed a strong draft through the shop, caught the little tailor, and quick as the wind he was out the open window to the ends of air. He was never seen again. It befell after some time that the people of Sachsenhausen glimpsed a ball of fire in the air one evening. It lighted up the whole area with dazzling brilliance and then went out and fell to earth. They all wanted to know what had fallen, and they ran to the spot, but they didn't find anything but a little lump of ashes. But with it there was the tongue of a shoe buckle, a scrap of egg-yellow satin with colored flowers in it, and a black thing that looked almost like the black horned knob of a cane. They all pondered how things like that could fall out of the sky in a fire-ball. But when the dear wife of the escaped tailor came along, and when she saw the things that had been found, she wrung her hands, carried on most miserably, and cried, "Oh, misery, that is my darling's shoe buckle. Oh, misery, that is my darling's Sunday vest. Oh, misery, that is my darling's cane knob!" But a great savant explained that the cane knob was not a cane knob but a meteor or a terrestrial object that didn't turn out right. In this way the people of Sachsenhausen and of the whole world learned that the poor little tailor who had been given inflammable air by the apothecary's apprentice instead of a dram for his stomach, had been burned up in the upper air and had fallen to earth as a meteor or as some terrestrial object that had not turned out right.

End of the History of the Little Tailor from Sachsenhausen

The waiter finally became impatient when the curious stranger did not stop making himself now big, now little, without paying any attention to him, and held the bottle of Burgundy that he had ordered, right under his nose. Directly the stranger sucked fast to the bottle and did not let go until the last drop had been drained. Then he fell unconscious into the armchair and was able to stir only weakly.

The customers had observed with astonishment that he had gone on swelling up as he drank, and now appeared very fat and shapeless. The flying antics of the other one now seemed to cease. Panting and quite out of breath, he kept trying to come down, but when he saw that his opponent was lying there half dead, he quickly fell upon him and began to beat him hard with his clenched fists. The host hauled him off and declared he would throw him out of the house immediately if he wouldn't be quiet. If they wanted to display their juggling tricks, they might do so, but without brawling and pounding each other like low rowdies.

The aerialist seemed a bit miffed to think that the tavern keeper took him for a juggler. He asserted that he was anything but a cheap performer that practiced trivial arts. Besides, he had held the position of ballet master in the theater of a famous king; right now he was free-lancing as a bel-esprit, and his name was Legénie, as his trade required. If in righteous anger he had jumped a little higher than was proper over that accursed fellow there, that was his affair and did not concern anybody.

The host said that all that still didn't justify pommeling. To which the bel-esprit retorted that the host didn't know that malicious, crafty fellow, otherwise he would cordially grant him a black-and-blue back. The fellow had formerly been a French customs officer, but was now living by bloodletting, cupping, and barbering, and his name was Monsieur Leech. Clumsy, loutish, gluttonous, he was a burden to all. It wasn't enough that the good-for-nothing swilled away the wine from his mouth everywhere they met, just as he had done here, but the villain was up to nothing less right now than snitching from him his beautiful fiancée, that he was planning to carry home from Frankfurt.

The customs officer had heard everything the *bel-esprit* had stated. He blazed at him with his little eyes that darted poisonous fire and then said to the host: "Tavern keeper, don't believe a word of what he's babbling there, that gallows-bird, that useless buffoon. A fine ballet master indeed! He squashes the dainty ballerinas' toes with his elephant's feet, and when he pirouettes he knocks a tooth out of the *maître du spectacle*'s jaw in the wings and his opera glasses away from his eyes! And his poetry, it has feet as clumsy as he is, and they sway back and forth like drunken men and stomp your thoughts to a pulp. And then the conceited driveler thinks that because he sometimes flutters clumsily through the air like a peevish gander, the most beautiful lady can't fail to be his fiancée."

Shrieked the *bel-esprit*: "You spiteful worm of Satan, you're going to feel the gander's beak!" and started after the customs officer again in full fury.

But the host grabbed him from behind with strong arms, and amid the most inexpressible jubilation of the assembled crowd, threw him out the window.

Now that the *bel-esprit* was gone, Monsieur Leech had immediately resumed the solid, straightforward shape with which he had entered the place. The people outside took him for someone quite different from the person who had been able to extend himself so, and dispersed. The customs officer thanked the tavern keeper most obligingly for the help he had lent him against the *bel-esprit*, and, to bring this grateful mindedness right out into the open, offered to shave the tavern keeper, without any sort of emolument, and in such a light and pleasing way as he had never in his life experienced before. The tavern keeper felt his beard, and since at the moment it seemed to him as though the hair was growing long and bristly, he consented to Monsieur Leech's proposal. The customs official began to prepare for the business with light and practiced hand. But presently he cut the tavern keeper's nose so severely that bright drops of blood welled forth. Taking this for sly malice, the tavern keeper jumped up furiously and grabbed the customs officer, who went flying out the door as fast and as nimbly as the *bel-esprit* had gone through the window. Not long afterwards there arose an unseemly racket in the entrance hall. The tavern keeper hardly took time to swab his injured nose sufficiently with German tinder and ran out to see what the devil was causing the new uproar.

There, to his no small astonishment, he saw a young man who had grabbed the *bel-esprit* with one hand and the customs officer by the shirt front with the other hand, and as his fiery eyes rolled wildly, was screaming furiously, "Ha! you brood of Satan! you shan't get in my way, you shan't rob me of my Gamaheh!" Simultaneously the *bel-esprit* and the customs officer were screeching, "A madman! Save us, tavern keeper! He wants to murder us! He mistakes us for someone else!"

"Hey, there!" cried the tavern keeper. "Hey, there! dear Mr. Pepusch in a dull voice. He seemed as though awakening from a queer fellows? Aren't you perhaps mistaken about them? This is the ballet master, Mr. Legénie, and this is the customs officer, Monsieur Leech."

"Ballet master Legénie? Customs officer Leech?" repeated Pepusch in a dull voice. He seemed as though awaking from a dream and having to collect his thoughts. Meanwhile two honorable citizens had also stepped out of the bar, who also knew Mr. George Pepusch and who urged him to remain calm and to let the silly strangers go. Once again Pepusch repeated, "Ballet master Legénie? Customs officer Leech?" and let his arms drop lifelessly down.

Quick as the wind, the released men were off, and to many a person on the street it appeared as though the *bel-esprit* flew away over the roof of the opposite house, while the beard-trimmer disappeared in the slime that had gathered between the stones just in front of the door.

The citizens pressed the completely disconcerted Pepusch to step into the bar and drink a bottle of genuine Niersteiner with them. Pepusch accepted their offer and seemed to swallow down the noble wine with pleasure and appetite, although he sat there quite stiffly and silently and replied not a word to anything said to him. At last his features brightened, and he said quite affably, "You did well, you good people and friendly companions, to prevent me from killing those wretches on the spot when they were in my power. But you don't know what dire creatures had disguised themselves beneath those odd masks."

Pepusch stopped, and one can imagine with what taut curiosity the citizens listened for what Pepusch would now reveal. The tavern keeper had come over, too, and all three, the citizens and the tavern keeper, leaned over the table with folded arms, put their heads close together, and held their breath so as not to miss a syllable that came from Pepusch's mouth.

"You see," Mr. George Pepusch continued very softly and solemnly, "you see, you good men, the one that you call ballet master Legénie is none other than the evil, clumsy Spirit Thetel; the one that you take for the customs officer Leech is the abominable bloodsucker, the loathsome Leech Prince. Both are in love with the Princess Gamaheh, who, as you surely know, is the beautiful, glorious daughter of the mighty King Sekakis, and they are here to alienate her from the Thistle Zeherit. Now that is the silliest nonsense that ever dwelt in a stupid brain, because, apart from the Thistle Zeherit, there is just one single creature in the whole world to whom the beautiful Gamaheh can belong, and perhaps that creature will also enter in vain into combat with the Thistle Zeherit. For soon the Thistle shall bloom at midnight in full splendor and force, and in his love-death[2] will gleam the dawn of the higher life. Now I am myself the Thistle Zeherit, and there you have the reason, good people, why you cannot blame me for being furious with those traitors and for taking the whole story very much to heart."

The people opened their eyes very wide and, speechless and open-mouthed, stared at Pepusch. They were, as the saying goes, thunderstruck, and the thunder was still rolling in their ears.

Pepusch tossed off a large glass of Roman wine and then, turning to the tavern keeper, said, "Oh yes, tavern keeper, soon you will live to see it. Soon I shall bloom as the *Cactus grandiflorus*, and all around there will be the tremendous fragrance of the loveliest vanilla. You can take my word for that."

All the tavern keeper could say was a stupid: "Well, if that doesn't beat the dickens!" The other two men, however, exchanged knowing glances, and one of them, taking George's hand, said with an ambiguous smile, "You seem to be just a

---

[2] The German word here is *Liebestod*, and this is the first occurrence of that fateful word in literature.

trifle excited, dear Mr. Pepusch. How would it be if you had a little glass of water—?"

"Not a drop!" Pepusch cut short the well-meant advice. "Not a drop! Was water ever poured into boiling oil without stirring up the fury of the flames? You claim I am excited? As a matter of fact that may be the case, but maybe the Devil could stay calm if he had gone around shooting at a friend, as I have been doing, and then put a bullet through his own brains! Here! I put the murder weapon in your hands, and now everything is over."

Pepusch pulled a pair of pistols out of his pocket. The tavern keeper staggered back, but the two citizens reached for them and, as soon as they had the murder weapons in their hands, burst out in intemperate laughter. The pistols were made of wood, a set of children's toys from the Christmas trade.

Pepusch seemed not to take any notice of what was going on around him. He sat lost in thought and kept repeating over and over: "If I could only find him! If I could only find him!"

The tavern keeper took courage and discreetly asked, "Whom do you mean, actually, good Mr. Pepusch? Who is it that you can't find?"

"If you know," said Pepusch solemnly, looking the tavern keeper sharply in the eye, "if you know anyone comparable in might and in wondrous power to King Sekakis, name me his name and I will kiss your feet! Besides, I was meaning to ask you whether you knew of anyone acquainted with Mr. Peregrinus Tyss, who could tell me where I might find him at this moment."

"There," replied the tavern keeper with a friendly smirk, "there I can help you, excellent Mr. Pepusch, and I can inform you that the good Mr. Tyss was here not more than an hour ago and had a small glass of Würzburger. He was much absorbed in thought, and all of a sudden, when I merely mentioned what news there was from the stock exchange, he exclaimed: 'Yes, sweet Gamaheh! I have given you up! Be happy in my George's arms!' Then a curious, delicate voice said, 'Let us go now to Leeuwenhoek and have a look at the horoscope!' Right away Mr. Tyss emptied his glass in a great hurry, and, together with the voice without a body, was off. Apparently both of them, the

voice and Mr. Tyss, have gone to Leeuwenhoek, who is *in
lamento* because all his trained fleas have died."

Then up sprang George in full fury, seized the tavern keeper
by the throat, and shrieked, "What are you saying, you oaf of a
leech-messenger? Given her up? Given her up? Gamaheh—
Peregrinus—Sekakis...?"

The tavern keeper's account was precisely in line with the
truth. He had heard Master Flea summoning Mr. Peregrinus
with his silver voice to go to the microscopist Leeuwenhoek
—the kind reader knows for what purpose. And Peregrinus had
actually started out on his way there.

Leeuwenhoek received Peregrinus with a saccharinely repulsive cordiality and with that humble way of making compli-
ments in which arduously forced recognition of superiority
expresses itself. But since Peregrinus had the microscopic lens
in his eye, all of Mr. Anton van Leeuwenhoek's cordiality, all
his humility, availed him naught. Rather, Peregrinus immediately recognized the ill-humor, indeed the hatred, that filled the
microscopist's soul.

While he was asserting how much Mr. Tyss's visit honored
and delighted him, his thoughts were: "I wish black-feathered
Satan would hurl you ten thousand fathoms down into the
abyss, but I have to be friendly and submissive with you, because the accursed constellation has put me under your control
and my whole existence is in a certain way dependent upon
you. But maybe I can outwit you, because you are a simple
ninny for all your genteel ancestry. You think the beautiful
Dörtje Elverdink loves you and may even be going to marry
you? Just apply to me on that score, and then, in spite of the
power that resides within you without your knowing it, you
will fall into my hands, and I shall do everything in my power
to ruin you and to get possession of Dörtje as well as of
Master Flea."

Naturally, Peregrinus regulated his behavior by these thoughts
and took good care not to mention the beautiful Dörtje Elverdink by so much as a single word. He pretended to have come
in order to view Leeuwenhoek's collection of curiosities from
natural history.

And now, while Leeuwenhoek was opening the big cabinets,

Master Flea said very softly in Peregrinus's ear that his (Pere-grinus's) horoscope was lying on the table by the window. Cau-tiously Peregrinus approached and cast a sharp glance at it. There he saw all sorts of lines that crisscrossed mystically, and other wondrous signs. But since he was totally lacking in astrological knowledge, he might look at it as sharply as he would: everything remained unclear and confused to him. Only, it did seem strange to him that he could not help recognizing very clearly as himself that red, gleaming dot in the middle of the chart on which the horoscope had been drawn up. The longer he looked at the dot, the more it took on the shape of a heart, and the more burningly red it became. And yet it glit-tered only as if through cobwebs, with which it was overgrown.

Peregrinus observed how Leeuwenhoek kept trying to draw him away from the horoscope, and very sensibly decided to ask his friendly enemy straight out and with no further ado, about the meaning of the mysterious chart, as long as he was running no risk of being put off with lies.

Maliciously smiling, Leeuwenhoek assured him that nothing could give him greater pleasure than explaining to his very esteemed guest those signs upon the chart, which he had him-self drawn up from his slight knowledge of such things.

His thoughts ran: "Ho, ho! So that's what you're up to, my shrewd fellow! Master Flea has not advised you badly at all, indeed! Explaining the mysterious chart, I should maybe set you right as to the magic potential of your worthy person? I could fib a bit for you, but what good would that do, when you wouldn't understand one iota about anything even if I told you the truth, but would stay as stupid as before? Out of pure con-venience, and so as not to put myself to the expense of direct inventions, I am going to tell you as much as I think proper about the symbols of the chart."

Peregrinus now knew that he was not going to find out every-thing, but that, at least, he would not be told falsehoods.

Leeuwenhoek put the chart on an easellike stand, which he had moved up from a corner to the middle of the room. Both of them, Leeuwenhoek and Peregrinus, sat down before the chart and contemplated it in silence.

"Perhaps," Leeuwenhoek began at last with a certain solemnity, "perhaps you do not even dream, Peregrinus Tyss, that those lines, those symbols on the chart which you are so attentively contemplating, are your own horoscope, which I have drawn up with mystic astrological skill, under favorable influence of the stars. You might ask me, Peregrinus, how I came by such arrogance, how I might penetrate into the intricacies of your life, how I should come to want to unveil your destiny, and you would have a perfect right to do so, were I not able to prove to you my inner vocation to that end. I don't know whether you are perhaps acquainted with the famous Rabbi Isaac ben Harravad, or at least have heard of him. Among other profound knowledge, Rabbi Harravad had the rare talent of being able to tell by looking at a person's face whether that person's soul had previously inhabited another body or whether that soul was to be considered as entirely fresh and new. I was still very young when the old rabbi died—of indigestion he had incurred from a tasty garlic dish. The Jews carried off his corpse so fast that the deceased did not have time to collect and take with him all his learning and talents, which illness had scattered about. Laughing heirs parceled them out among themselves, but I had fished up for myself that wondrous gift of vision at the very moment when it was poised on the tip of the sword which the Angel of Death was putting to the old rabbi's bosom. And in that way that wondrous gift passed to me, and I also can tell, as Rabbi Isaac ben Harravad could, from a man's face, whether his soul has ever inhabited another body or not.[3] Your countenance, Peregrinus Tyss, aroused in me, from the very first time I saw it, the oddest doubts and misgivings. The long pre-existence of your soul became *certain* to me, and yet every form antecedent to your present life remained wholly obscure. I had to have recourse to the stars and draw your horoscope in order to solve the mystery."

"And," Peregrinus interrupted the Flea Tamer, "and did you discover anything from it, Mr. Leeuwenhoek?"

"Of course I did!" replied Leeuwenhoek, assuming a still

[3] The author borrowed this episode from the famous *Dictionnaire historique et critique* of Pierre Bayle (1647–1706). Rabbi Isaac ben Harravad wrote circa 1200, but his works are known only from report. Hoffmann's details about his death are fanciful, but the further remarks of Leeuwenhoek are derived from a book about vampires, 1734, by Michael Ranfft.

more solemn tone. "Of course I did! I learned that the psychic principle which now animates the attractive body of my worthy friend, Mr. Peregrinus Tyss, had long since pre-existed, although only as an idea, without awareness of form. Look here, Mr. Peregrinus, observe attentively the red dot in the middle of the chart. That is not only you yourself, but that dot is also the form of which your psychic principle could not formerly become aware. As a gleaming garnet you lay at that time in a deep stratum of the earth, but, stretched out above you on the green lawn of the ground, slumbered the lovely Gamaheh, and only in that state of unconsciousness did her form also melt away. Strange lines and strange constellations intersect your life from that point on, when the idea assumed form and became Mr. Peregrinus Tyss. You are in possession of a talisman without knowing it. That talisman is that very same red garnet. It may be that King Sekakis wore it in his crown as a jewel, or that he was in some sense himself the garnet. Suffice it to say, however, that you now possess it. But a certain event must take place if its slumbering potential is to be awakened, and with the awakening of that potential of your talisman there will be decided the fate of an unhappy creature, who, until now, has led a wretched life of irreality between fear and unsteady hope. Alas! That sweet Gamaheh could achieve only a life of irreality through that profound magical potential, because the operative talisman had been stolen from us! You alone killed her, you alone can breathe life into her when the garnet will have leaped up in flame within your bosom!"

"And," Peregrinus interrupted the Flea Tamer anew, "and that event by which the potential of the talisman is to be awakened, can you explain that to me, Mr. Leeuwenhoek?"

The Flea Tamer stared goggle-eyed at Peregrinus, and looked just like someone who has suddenly been overtaken by great embarrassment and does not know what he is going to say. His thoughts ran: "Damnation! How has it happened that I said much more than I really meant to say? Couldn't I have at least kept my mouth shut about the talisman that this blessed clown bears within his body, and which gives him so much power over us that we shall all have to dance to his piping? And now I am supposed to tell him the event on which depends the awakening of the potential of his talisman! Dare I confess to him that I don't know myself, that all my skill is wrecked in trying to untie the knot into which all the lines become entangled —in fact, that when I contemplate this sidereal main symbol of the horoscope, I feel downright miserable and my honorable head seems to me myself like a prettily painted wig-maker's block formed out of vile pasteboard? Far from me be such a confession, which would humiliate me and put weapons in his hands against me. I'll palm off something on this ninny, who thinks he's so clever, something that will go through him like a shock and take away all his desire to probe any further into me."

"My very dear Mr. Tyss," said the Flea Tamer, pulling a very serious face, "my very dear Mr. Tyss, do not request me to talk about that event. You know that horoscopes instruct us clearly and completely about the entrance of definite circumstances, but, such is the wisdom of the Eternal Power, that the outcome of dangers threatened always remains obscure, and on that score only dubious interpretations are possible and permissible. I am much too fond of you as a good and excellent man of the heart, my good Mr. Tyss, to put you before the time into disquiet and anxiety. Besides, I would tell you at least so much that the event, which should give you awareness of your power, might also at the same moment destroy the present form of your existence amid the excruciating torments of hell! No, that *too* I shall keep from you. And now: not another word about the horoscope. Just do not be alarmed, my good Mr. Tyss, although the matter looks very bad, and I, for all my knowledge, can hardly predict a happy outcome for the adventure. Perhaps you will be rescued from the evil peril by a wholly unexpected constellation which is now still outside the scope of observation."

Peregrinus was astonished at Leeuwenhoek's crafty dissimulation. Meanwhile, the whole state of the matter, the situation in which Leeuwenhoek, without knowing it, without guessing it, stood in relation to him, struck him as so uncommonly delicious that he could not refrain from bursting out in ringing laughter.

"What," asked the Flea Tamer somewhat abashed, "what are you laughing about so hard, my most worthy Mr. Tyss?"

"You do very cleverly," replied Peregrinus still laughing, "you do very cleverly, Mr. Leeuwenhoek, to conceal the menacing event from me out of pure consideration. For besides being too much of a friend of mine to put me into anxiety and fright, you have another cogent reason, which consists of nothing other than that you yourself do not know the least thing about that event. All your efforts to untie that tangled knot were futile. Your entire astrology does not amount to much, and if Master Flea had not fallen unconscious on your nose, all your arts would be in a heartily bad way."

Fury enflamed Leeuwenhoek's face, he clenched his fists, he gnashed his teeth, he trembled and tottered so badly that he would have fallen out of his chair, had not Peregrinus grabbed him as firmly by the arm as George Pepusch had grabbed the tavern keeper by the throat. The tavern keeper had managed to save himself by an agile leap to one side. Immediately Pepusch had flown out of the door and he stepped into Leeuwenhoek's room at precisely the instant when Peregrinus was holding him down in the chair and he was muttering grimly between his teeth: "Accursed Swammerdam! Could you have done this to me?"

As soon as Peregrinus caught sight of his friend Pepusch, he let go of the Flea Tamer, stepped over to his friend, and anxiously inquired whether the horrible mood had passed, which had come over him with such destructive violence.

Pepusch seemed moved almost to tears. He maintained that in all his life he had never committed so many ill-mannered follies as he had this very day. Among them he reckoned primarily the fact that, after putting a bullet through his head in the forest, he had talked about extravagant things with good-natured people in a tavern—he himself no longer knew where it was, whether at Protzler's, at the Swan, at the Willow Inn, or some other place—and tried murderously to strangle the tavern keeper, just because he thought he had gathered from his broken utterances that there had happened the happiest possible thing that could befall him (Pepusch). All his mishaps would soon reach their climax now, for it was only too sure that the people had taken his talk and his whole behavior for the most vehement outbreak of madness, and, instead of enjoying the fruits of the joyous event, he would have to be afraid of being locked up in a madhouse.

At this point Pepusch brought up what the tavern keeper had mentioned concerning Peregrinus's conduct and remarks, and asked, blushing deeply and with downcast eyes, whether such a sacrifice, such a renunciation in favor of an ill-fortuned friend, as he inferred, was still possible or even thinkable at the present time, when heroism had vanished from the world.

At his friend's remarks, Peregrinus's heart was cheered within him. With ardor he assured him that he, for his part, was far from offending a proven friend in the least, that he solemnly disavowed all claims to the heart and hand of the beautiful Dörtje Elverdink, and that he gladly gave up a Paradise which, frankly, had welcomed him with its resplendent and alluring shimmer.

"And I," cried Pepusch, throwing himself upon his friend's bosom, "and I wanted to murder you! And because I did not believe in you, I shot myself! Oh, the madness, oh, the dreary actions of a troubled spirit!"

"I beg you," Peregrinus interrupted his friend, "I beg you, George, come to your senses! You talk about shooting yourself, and here you stand fresh and healthy before me! Now does that make sense?"

"You are right," replied Pepusch. "It seems as though I just couldn't tell you rationally how it really happened when I actually did put a bullet through my brain. Those people also claimed that my pistols were not especially genuine weapons of murder, that they weren't even made of steel, but only of wood, as a matter of fact, children's toys, and thus perhaps the duel could not have happened any more than the suicide could, except as an amusing bit of whimsy. Is it possible that we have changed roles, and that I am beginning self-mystification and fooling around with silly childish things just at the moment when you are emerging from your childish fable-world into real and vivid life? But, be that as it may, it is necessary for me to be certain about your nobleness and my good fortune, and then all the mists will soon be dispelled that darkened my sight, or that were perhaps deceiving me with illusions of Morgan le Fay. Come, my Peregrinus, walk down with me to see the lovely

Dörtje Elverdink. I will take my sweet fiancée from your hand."
Pepusch took his friend's arm and started to hurry away
with him. But the walk they proposed to take was to be spared
them. For the door opened and in stepped Dörtje Elverdink,
beautiful and gracious as an angel. But back of her was old Mr.
Swammer. Leeuwenhoek, who had sat there so long stiff and
mute, casting glances crackling with anger now at Pepusch, now
at Peregrinus, seemed as though struck by an electric shock
when he caught sight of old Swammerdam. He shook his
clenched fist at him and, with a voice shrill with fury, screamed,
"Ha! So you have come to make fun of me, you old treacherous monster? But you won't get away with it! Defend yourself.
Your last hour has struck!"

Swammerdam reeled back several steps, and when Leeuwenhoek was already proceeding to attack him with his telescope,
he pulled out a similar weapon in his defense. The duel that
had flared up in Mr. Peregrinus Tyss's house seemed about to
begin anew.

George Pepusch threw himself between the duelists, and as
with his left fist he skillfully knocked aside a murderous aim of
Leeuwenhoek's that would have stretched his opponent on the
floor, he struck down with his right fist the weapon that Swammerdam had opened up quick as a wink, so that it could do no
harm to Leeuwenhoek.

Then Pepusch loudly declared that he would not permit any
duel or any kind of a dangerous fight between Leeuwenhoek
and Swammerdam until he had learned in detail the cause of
their dissension. Peregrinus found his friend's conduct so rational that he did not scruple to step betwen the duelists and
make the same declaration as Pepusch.

Both Leeuwenhoek and Swammerdam were obliged to yield
to the friends. Moreover, Swammerdam maintained that he had
not come with any hostile intentions at all, but only to make a
peaceable settlement with Leeuwenhoek in the matter of Dörtje
Elverdink, and thus put an end to the feud that had gone on
only too long and that set at odds two complementary principles whose common research could exhaust the deepest well
of science. As he said this, he glanced with a smile at Mr.
Peregrinus, and thought that Peregrinus would, as he ventured

to hope, act as intermediary, considering that Dörtje had now actually fled to his arms.

Leeuwenhoek, on the contrary, maintained that the possession of Dörtje was the real apple of discord. Meanwhile, he said, he had discovered a new piece of spite in his unworthy colleague. Not only did he deny possessing a certain microscope which, on a certain occasion, he had kept by way of a compromise, in order to renew his usurpatory claims to possessing Dörtje; he had, what was more, given that microscope to someone else in order to torment and distress him, Leeuwenhoek, still more. Swammerdam meanwhile swore by all that was holy that he had never received the microscope and that he had good reason to believe that it had been maliciously smuggled away by Leeuwenhoek.

"The fools!" whispered Master Flea softly to Peregrinus. "The fools! They are talking about the microscope which is in your eye. You know that I was present at the peace treaty concluded by Swammerdam and Leeuwenhoek concerning possession of the Princess Gamaheh. When Swammerdam was just about to put into his left eye that microscopic lens, which he really did get from Leeuwenhoek, I snatched it away, because it was not Leeuwenhoek's rightful property, but *mine*. Say right out, Mr. Peregrinus, that you have the precious thing."

And Peregrinus made no bones of announcing straight off that *he* had the microscopic lens that Swammerdam was supposed to have gotten from Leeuwenhoek but did not get. Moreover, the treaty had never yet been put into effect, and neither one of them, neither Swammerdam nor Leeuwenhoek, had the unqualified right at the present time to look upon Dörtje Elverdink as his foster daughter.

After much talking back and forth, both parties to the quarrel agreed that Mr. Peregrinus Tyss should choose Dörtje Elverdink, who loved him most tenderly, for his spouse, and that then, after seven months, he should decide which of the two microscopists he would regard as foster father and father-in-law.

But charming and lovely as Dörtje Elverdink looked in her dainty costume, which seemed to have been tailored by amoretti, and for all the sweet, languishing glances of love that she kept casting at Mr. Peregrinus, the latter was keeping both his ward and his friend in mind. He remained true to his given word and declared once again that he was renouncing Dörtje's hand.

The microscopists were not a little taken aback when Peregrinus indicated George Pepusch as the one who had the greatest and the most justified claim to Dörtje's hand, and they were of the opinion that, at least at the present time, he simply did not have the power to determine their wills.

With a flood of tears pouring from her eyes, Dörtje Elverdink tottered over to Peregrinus, who caught her up in his arms just as she was about to collapse, half-fainting, to the floor. "Ungrateful man," she sighed, "you are breaking my heart by turning me away from you! But that is the way you want it. Take at least this farewell kiss and let me die!"

Peregrinus bent down, but as his lips touched the lips of the little lady, she bit him so ferociously on those same lips that the blood spurted forth. "Rudeness," she cried merrily as she did so, "thus must thou be punished! Come to reason, be nice, and take me, and let the other one scream as much as he will."

Meanwhile, the two microscopists had started up a new quarrel, Heaven knows over what. But George Pepusch threw himself inconsolably at the beautiful Dörtje's feet and cried out in a voice that sounded miserable enough to be coming from the throat of the most unhappy of lovers, "Gamaheh! Has the flame in your bosom completely died? Do you not recall the magnificent former time in Famagusta, nor even the lovely days in Berlin any more?"

"George," the little lady interrupted him, laughing, "you are an idiot, with your Gamaheh, and your Thistle Zeherit, and all the other crazy stuff that you saw in your dreams. I was fond of you, my lad, and still am, and I will take you, although the Great One yonder pleases me better, provided you will give me your sacred promise, in fact take a solemn oath, that you will apply all your powers—"

The little lady whispered something very softly into Pepusch's ear. But Peregrinus thought he heard Master Flea mentioned.

The quarrel between the two microscopists had meanwhile become more and more vehement. Once again they had laid hold of their weapons, and Peregrinus was trying to soothe their heated spirits, when once more the company was increased.

Amid revolting screeches and repulsive shrieks the door was thrown open and in rushed the *bel-esprit*, Monsieur Legénie, and the beard-trimmer, Leech. With a wild and horrible gesture they pounced on the little lady, and the beard-trimmer had already grabbed her by the shoulder, when Pepusch with irresistible force thrust the abhorrent enemy away, simultaneously seizing him around the whole of his elastic body and squeezing him in such a way that he shot up long and pointed and roared with pain as he did so.

While this was happening to the beard-trimmer, the two microscopists had instantly become reconciled upon the appearance of their enemies and were jointly beating the *bel-esprit* with much pleasure. And it did no good for the *bel-esprit* to rise up to the ceiling while he was being given a sound drubbing lower down. For both Leeuwenhoek and Swammerdam had snatched up short, thick cudgels, and as soon as the *bel-esprit* tried to come down, they beat him aloft again with blows skillfully applied to that part of the body which can best endure them. It was a dainty game of shuttlecock, in which the *bel-esprit* under duress had assumed the most wearying and at the same time the most thankless role, that of the bird.

The battle with the demonic intruders seemed to inspire great horror in the little lady. She clung tightly to Peregrinus and kept begging him to take her away from this menacing ruckus. Peregrinus was all the less in a position to refuse, for he could not help being convinced that his help was not needed on the battlefield. And so he took the little lady to her residence, that is to say into his lodger's rooms.

Suffice it to say that the little lady, as soon as she found herself alone with Mr. Peregrinus, tried all the arts of her coquetry anew in order to lure him into her net. Try as he would to keep firmly in mind that this was all falseness and had for its goal only to get his protégé into slavery, nevertheless he was seized by such confusion that he did not even think of the microscopic lens, which would have served him as a most effective antidote.

Once again Master Flea was in danger. But this time he was

rescued by Mr. Swammer, who entered with George Pepusch. Mr. Swammer looked uncommonly pleased. Pepusch, on the other hand, had fury and jealousy in his burning eyes. Peregrinus left the room.

With the bitterest and most profound gloom in his wounded heart, somber and absorbed in himself, he roamed the streets of Frankfurt. He walked out the gate, and on further, until he finally came to that lovely spot where the bizarre adventure with his friend Pepusch had occurred.

Once again he contemplated his marvelous fate. Lovelier, more gracious, in higher allurement of love than ever, the image of the little lady arose within him. His blood surged more forcefully in his veins, more violent became his pulse, his heart was on the point of bursting from ardent longing. He felt only too painfully the magnitude of the sacrifice he had made and by virtue of which he thought he had lost all of his life's happiness.

Night had come on by the time he returned to the city. Without noticing it, perhaps from unconscious shyness about going back to his house, he had passed through many side streets and come finally to Kalbächer Lane. A man wearing a knapsack on his back asked him whether bookbinder Lämmerhirt didn't live there. Peregrinus glanced up and noticed that he was really standing in front of the high, narrow house in which bookbinder Lämmerhirt lived. High up in the air he glimpsed the brightly lighted windows of the hard-working man, who was working right through the night. The door opened for the man with the knapsack and he went into the house.

Peregrinus felt deeply saddened to think that, in the confusion of the recent times, he had forgotten to pay bookbinder Lämmerhirt for various pieces of work that he had done for him. He decided to go down there the first thing on the following morning and settle his debt.

SEVENTH ADVENTURE

Hostile plottings of the microscopist confederates, together with their continued stupidity. New trials of Mr. Peregrinus Tyss and new perils of Master Flea. Röschen Lämmerhirt. The decisive dream and conclusion of the tale.

Although there is a total lack of definite information about the actual outcome of the battle in Leeuwenhoek's room, it is hardly to be presumed otherwise than that the two microscopists, with the help of young Mr. George Pepusch, must have won a complete victory over their evil enemies. Otherwise old Swammer would not have been so amicable and so pleased on his return, as he actually was. With the same glad and joyous mien, Swammer, or rather Mr. Jan Swammerdam, came in the next morning to see Mr. Peregrinus, who was lying in bed engaged in profound conversation with his protégé, Master Flea.

As soon as he caught sight of Mr. Swammerdam, Peregrinus did not fail to have the microscopic lens put into his eye immediately.

After many long and equally wearisome excuses for his early visit, Swammerdam finally sat down close by Peregrinus's bed. The old man absolutely would not hear of Peregrinus's getting up and throwing on a dressing gown.

In the oddest turns of phrase the old man thanked Peregrinus for the great acts of courtesy he had shown him, and which, he claimed, consisted of his not only having taken him into his house as a lodger, but also in his having allowed the household to be increased by a young, and sometimes too lively and too noisy, lady. Further, however, he was compelled to find the greatest courtesy of all in the fact that Peregrinus, not without making some sacrifice himself, had effected his (the old man's) reconciliation with his old friend and colleague, Anton van Leeuwenhoek. As Swammerdam told the story, their two hearts had inclined toward each other in the moment when they were attacked by the *bel-esprit* and the beard-trimmer and had to rescue the beautiful Dörtje Elverdink from the wicked monsters. The formal and solemn reconciliation of the estranged parties had then immediately ensued.

Leeuwenhoek quite as much as Swammerdam had recognized the favorable influence that Peregrinus had had on both of them. The first use they had made of their re-established alliance as friends consisted in their joint examination of the strangely and wondrously complex horoscope of Mr. Peregrinus Tyss and their attempt to interpret it as far as possible.

"What," said Mr. Jan Swammerdam, "what my friend Anton van Leeuwenhoek did not succeed in doing by himself, was brought to realization by our common powers, and thus this experiment was the second that we have undertaken with the most glorious success in spite of all the hindrances that rose to oppose us."

"The silly, shortsighted fool!" whispered Master Flea, who was sitting on the pillow right next to Peregrinus's ear. "He still thinks the Princess Gamaheh was brought to life by him. That's a fine life indeed, to which the clumsiness of the dullwitted microscopists had forced that poor girl!"

"My good man," continued Swammerdam, who had all the less been able to hear Master Flea inasmuch as he had been compelled to sneeze very hard just then, "most estimable Mr. Peregrinus Tyss, you are one of the World Spirit's very special elect, one of Nature's darlings. For you possess the most wondrous, most potent talisman, or, to speak more correctly and more scientifically, the most magnificent Tsilmenaja or Tilsemoht,[1] that ever sprang from the womb of earth watered by the

[1] Tsilmenaja and Tilsemoht were Chaldean words designating talismans, according to Friedrich Arpe's treatise on talismans and amulets, published in 1717 in Latin and in 1792 in German translation. This is the same work from which Hoffmann extracted the names: Gamaheh, Zeherit, Thetel, Sekakis, and Nacrao.

dew of heaven. It does honor to my art that it was I, and not Leeuwenhoek, who established that this lucky Tsilmenaja derives from King Nacrao, who reigned in Egypt long before the deluge. However, the potential of the talisman is, at the present time, dormant, until the rising of a certain constellation which has its focus in your worthy person. Something must and will come to pass with you yourself, my dear Mr. Tyss, which, at the same instant when the power of the talisman wakens, will give you knowledge of that awakening. Let Leeuwenhoek have said whatever he said about that very problematic dot in the horoscope, it was all a lie, because he knew less than nothing about that dot until I opened his eyes for him. Possibly, my dear Mr. Tyss, my dear friend even wanted to frighten you with some impending catastrophe. I know he is fond of frightening people needlessly. But trust your respectful lodger, who, with his hand on his heart, swears to you that you have absolutely nothing to be afraid of. I should, however, like to know whether at the moment you do not detect the possession of the talisman at all. And what are you pleased to think about the whole matter anyway?"

With these last words, Swammerdam, with a poisonous smile, peered as sharply into Peregrinus's eyes as if he meant to penetrate his profoundest thoughts. But there he could hardly succeed as well as Peregrinus could with his microscopic lens. By means of that lens Peregrinus discovered that it was not so much the common conquest of the *bel-esprit* and the beard-trimmer that had brought about the reconciliation of the two microscopists, as it was the mysterious horoscope. Possession of the potent talisman, that was what both were after now. As far as that certain mysteriously tangled knot in Mr. Peregrinus's horoscope was concerned, Swammerdam had remained in just as irksome ignorance as Leeuwenhoek, but he felt that within Peregrinus's self must lie the clue that would lead to discovery of that secret. That clue he now intended to elicit skillfully from Peregrinus unawares, and then, with Leeuwenhoek's aid, to cheat him of possession of the inestimable jewel before he knew its value. Swammerdam was convinced that the talisman of Mr. Peregrinus Tyss was to be considered of equal value to the wise Solomon's ring, since, like the latter, it conferred upon the owner the total mastery of the spirit realm.

Peregrinus repaid like with like as he himself mystified Mr. Swammerdam, who was trying to mystify him. He was able to reply skillfully in such covert language that Swammerdam could not help being afraid the charm was already beginning to work and that the secret would presently be disclosed to him, which neither he nor Leeuwenhoek had been able to discover.

Swammerdam lowered his eyes, cleared his throat, and stammered out some incomprehensible words. The man actually was in a bad position. His thoughts kept grumbling confusedly, "Devil take it! What is this? Is this that fellow Peregrinus talking to me? Am I the wise and learned Swammerdam or an ass!"

Finally he pulled himself desperately together and began, "But let us change the subject, most estimable Mr. Tyss, let us change the subject, and, as I see it, let us change to something fine and pleasant!"

As Swammerdam now went on to say, he, as well as Leeuwenhoek, had been overjoyed to discover the tender inclination of the beautiful Dörtje Elverdink for Mr. Peregrinus Tyss. Although each had been of a different opinion so long as each had thought that Dörtje must stay with *him,* and that love and marriage were out of the question, they had now been persuaded of a better idea. In Peregrinus's horoscope they thought they read that he must inevitably choose the beautiful and gracious Dörtje Elverdink as his spouse, if he was to do what was most salutary for all the conjunctures of his entire life. Neither doubted for an instant but that Peregrinus was engrossed by equally ardent love for the lovely little lady, and thus they regarded the matter as definitely settled. Swammerdam was further of the opinion that Mr. Peregrinus Tyss was also the only man who could drive his rival from the field with no effort at all, and that even the most menacing opponents, for example the *bel-esprit* and the beard-trimmer, would be helpless to do anything against him.

From Swammerdam's thoughts Peregrinus perceived that the

microscopists really thought they had found in his horoscope the unalterable necessity of his marriage to the little Dörtje Elverdink. It was only to this necessity that they were yielding, and from even the apparent loss of Dörtje they meant to gain the greatest advantage, namely to snag Mr. Peregrinus Tyss himself together with his talisman.

One can imagine how much confidence Peregrinus must have had in the wisdom and erudition of the two microscopists, when neither one had been able to solve the main point of the horoscope. Hence he set no store at all by that alleged conjuncture which was supposed to determine the necessity of his marriage to the beautiful Dörtje. Nor was it difficult for him in the least to state very definitely and firmly that he had renounced Dörtje's hand in order not to offend his best and closest friend, young George Pepusch, who had prior and better claims than he to the possession of that lovely creature, and that under no condition in the world would he break his pledged word.

Mr. Swammerdam raised his grey-green cat's eyes, which he had kept lowered so long, stared mightily at Peregrinus, and smiled like vulpine cunning itself.

If the bond of friendship with George Pepusch, he said, were the only scruple that was keeping Peregrinus from giving free play to his emotions, then that bond was broken at this very minute. For Pepusch, although he was suffering a bit from madness, realized that the pattern of the stars was opposed to his marriage to Dörtje Elverdink and that nothing could come of it but misfortune and ruin. Therefore Pepusch had renounced all claims to Dörtje's hand and had declared that, as far as that beautiful girl was concerned, who was going to belong to no one but to his dear friend Tyss, he intended to defend her against that clumsy lout of a *bel-esprit* and against the bloodsucking beard-scraper.

Icy shivers ran through Peregrinus as he perceived from Swammerdam's thoughts that everything he had said was true. Overwhelmed by the oddest and most contradictory emotions, he sank back into the pillows and closed his eyes.

Mr. Swammerdam invited Peregrinus most urgently to come

down and hear for himself the present state of affairs from Dörtje's and from George's lips. Then he took his departure in just as garrulous and ceremonious a manner as he had entered.

Master Flea, who was all this time sitting quietly on the pillow, suddenly leaped up on the peak of Mr. Peregrinus's nightcap. There he rose aloft on his long hind legs, wrung his hands, raised them imploringly to heaven, and in a voice half-choked with bitter tears cried, "Woe to poor me! I thought I was safe, and only now comes the most perilous trial! What is the use of all the courage, all the steadfastness of my noble protector, if everything, everything is opposed to me! I surrender! It is all over!"

"Why," said Peregrinus in a dull voice, "why are you carrying on so up there on my nightcap, dear Master? Do you think you are the only one who has something to lament about? Am I not myself in the most miserable condition in the world, since I am destroyed and ruined in my entire being and don't know what to do or which way to turn my thoughts? But don't think, dear Master Flea, that I will be foolish enough to venture near the rocks on which I and all my fine resolutions and decisions can founder. I shall take good care not to accept Swammerdam's invitation and see that seductive Dörtje Elverdink again."

"I really don't know," replied Master Flea after he had resumed his old place on the pillow next to Mr. Peregrinus Tyss's ear, "I really don't know whether I shouldn't advise you after all, however disastrous it may seem to be, to go right down to Swammerdam. It seems as though the lines of your horoscope are converging faster and faster now and as though you were yourself about to enter into the red dot. Let obscure Fate have resolved what it will, I realize that not even a Master Flea can evade such a resolution, and that it would be as silly as it would be useless to ask you to rescue me. Go down, then. See her. Take her hand, and deliver me into slavery. And so that everything may come to pass as the stars will it, without intrusion of any foreign element, do not make any use of the microscopic lens."

"But," said Peregrinus, "but, Master Flea, your heart once seemed so strong, your mind so firm, and yet you are now so despondent and dejected! You may be as wise as you will, yes,

Clement VII's touted Nuncio Rorar[2] may reckon your intelligence far beyond his, but all the same you have no very distinct concept of the firm will of man and you think too slightly of it. Once again! I shall not break my pledged word. And, so that you may see how firm is my decision not to see the little lady again, I'm going to get up and, as I proposed yesterday, go over and see bookbinder Lämmerhirt."

"O Peregrinus," cried Master Flea, "the will of man is a fragile thing. A passing zephyr will often snap it off. What a chasm lies between what one intends and what does happen! Many a life is nothing but a constant intending, and from sheer intending, many a person does not know what he wants himself. You intend not to see Dörtje Elverdink again, and who will be your guarantee that it won't happen in the next minute after you have pronounced this decision?"

And curious enough it was, that precisely what Master Flea with prophetic soul predicted, happened. Namely, Peregrinus got up, dressed, and, true to his purpose, started to go over to see bookbinder Lämmerhirt. But, as he was going past Swammerdam's rooms, the door opened wide, and Peregrinus himself did not know how it happened, but all of a sudden he was standing at Swammerdam's arm in the middle of the room right in front of Dörtje Elverdink, who gaily and unconcernedly was throwing him a hundred kisses and joyously calling to him in her little silver bell of a voice, "Good morning, my darling Peregrinus!"

But someone else was standing there in the room, and that was Mr. George Pepusch, who was peering out the open window and whistling a little song. Now he shut the window with a bang and turned around. "Ah, just look!" he cried, as though only now catching sight of his friend Peregrinus. "Ah, just look! You've come to visit your fiancée. That is right and proper, and a third party is a nuisance. So I shall get myself out of here right away. But let me tell you first, my good friend Peregrinus, that George Pepusch disdains any gift tossed his way as alms to a poor sinner by his merciful friend! Your sacrifice be damned! I'm not going to be beholden to you for anything.

---

[2] Rorar, Nuncio of Pope Clement VII, is the same person as Hieronymus Rorarius, referred to in note 7 to p. 349.

Take her, this lovely Gamaheh who loves you so warmly, but watch out that the Thistle Zeherit doesn't strike root and burst the walls of your house asunder."

George's tone and his whole manner bordered on the brutality of braggadocio. and Peregrinus was filled with the most profound annoyance as he perceived how completely Pepusch had misunderstood him in all his actions.

"It never," he said without concealing that annoyance, "it never entered my mind to get in your way. The madness of jealous infatuation speaks in you, otherwise you would consider how innocent I am of everything you are brooding over in your heart. Don't expect me to kill the serpent which you are nourishing in your bosom to your own self-torment! And I want you to know that I gave you no gift and that I made no sacrifice for you, when I renounced the beautiful girl, perhaps the highest happiness of my life. I was forced to do so by other, loftier obligations, by an irrevocable promise!"

In wild anger Pepusch clenched his fist and raised it in his friend's direction. Then the little lady jumped in between the two friends and took Peregrinus's hand as she cried out laughingly, "Oh, do let the oafish Thistle go! He has nothing but crazy nonsense in his head, and, in good thistle fashion, he is stubborn and peevish, without knowing what he wants himself. You are mine and you shall stay mine, my sweet, darling Peregrinus!"

And with that the little lady pulled Peregrinus down on the sofa and without further ado sat on his lap. After a good chewing of his nails, Pepusch ran wildly out the door.

Dressed once more in her fabulously alluring gown of silver taffeta, the little lady was just as charming as before, and just as full of amorous attraction. Peregrinus felt the electric warmth of her body streaming through him, and yet icy, uncanny chills blew intermittently like the breath of death. For the first time he thought he noticed something oddly lifeless and rigid in the little lady's eyes, and the tone of her voice and even the rustling of the strange silver taffeta seemed to betray an alien creature never to be trusted. His heart was heavy, recalling that Dörtje had also been dressed in taffeta that other time when she had spoken just as she thought. Just why he found the taffeta menacing, he didn't himself know, but the idea of taffeta and uncanny business were connected with each other, just as a dream will connect the most heterogeneous things, and just as one will declare that everything is insane when he cannot see its profounder significance.

Far from offending the sweet little thing with possibly false suspicions, Peregrinus suppressed his feelings by force and merely waited for a favorable moment to wriggle loose and flee from the serpent of Paradise.

"But," said Dörtje finally, "but, you seem so cool to me today, my sweet friend, so unfeeling! What is on your mind, my life?"

"A headache," replied Peregrinus as noncommittally as possible. "A headache—whims—foolish notions—nothing more than that is disturbing me somewhat, my lovely child. Let me go out in the open air and it will all be gone in a few minutes. Besides, I still have an errand to do."

"That is all a lie!" cried the little lady, jumping up suddenly. "That is all a lie! And you are a nasty ape that needs to be tamed!"

Peregrinus was glad when he found himself out on the street. But Master Flea was joy unconfined, as he kept snickering and laughing there in Peregrinus's neck-cloth, and clapping his front paws together till they smacked aloud.

Peregrinus found this gaiety of his little protégé somewhat annoying, because it disturbed his thinking. He begged Master Flea to be quiet, for serious people had already gazed at him with looks full of reproach, thinking he was the one that was snickering and laughing and carrying on so foolishly in the open street.

"Oh, fool that I was!" cried Master Flea nonetheless, desisting in his outbursts of immoderate joy, "Oh, dullwitted fool that I was, to think that I could doubt of the victory when no further struggle was necessary. Yes, Peregrinus, it just couldn't be any other way. You had triumphed at the moment when the very death of the beloved was unable to shatter your resolution. Let me rejoice, let me exult, for I should have to be very much deceived if the bright sun should not rise soon to shed light on all the mysteries."

As Peregrinus knocked at Lämmerhirt's door, a soft feminine voice called, "Come in!" He opened the door, and a girl who was alone in the room came to meet him and asked him pleasantly what she could do for him.

Let it suffice the kind reader to say that the girl may have been about eighteen years old, that she was more tall than short, and slender in the purest symmetry of her limbs, that she had light brown hair and dark blue eyes, and a skin that seemed to be the soft downy tissue of lilies and roses. But more than all that, the girl's face expressed that tender mystery of virginal purity and high heavenly loveliness that many an old German painter has caught in his pictures.

The minute Peregrinus looked into the lovely maiden's eyes, he felt as if he had been lying in heavy, burdensome fetters which a benevolent power had now loosened, and that an angel of light was standing in front of him, by whose hand he would enter into the kingdom of nameless rapture of love and yearning.

As the girl, blushing at Peregrinus's fixed stare, modestly lowered her eyes, she repeated her question: What did the gentleman desire?

With effort, Peregrinus stammered out the inquiry: Was this where bookbinder Lämmerhirt lived? And now, as the girl replied that Lämmerhirt did indeed live here, but that he had gone out on errands, Peregrinus spoke incoherently about some bookbinding that he had commissioned, about some books that Lämmerhirt was supposed to get for him. Finally he got on something of an even keel and recalled the de luxe edition of Ariosto which Lämmerhirt was supposed to bind in red morocco with rich gold trim.

And then it seemed as though an electric spark went through the girl, and she clapped her hands and cried with tears in her eyes, "O lord! You are Mr. Tyss!" She made a motion as though she were going to seize Peregrinus's hand, but stepped back quickly, and a deep sigh seemed to relieve her full heart. Then a charming smile shone on the maiden's face like a lovely dawn, and she poured forth a stream of thanks and blessings on Peregrinus for being her father's, her mother's benefactor, and not only that—no—his generosity, his kindness, the way he had given the children presents just this past Christmas and had spread joy and happiness. She quickly cleared off her father's armchair, which was laden with books, manuscripts, pamphlets, and unbound sheets of printed matter, moved it toward him, and with gracious hospitality invited Peregrinus to sit down. Then she brought forth the neatly bound Ariosto, passed a linen cloth gently over the morocco binding, and with beaming look handed Peregrinus this masterpiece of the bookbinder's art, well aware that Peregrinus would not withhold his praise of her father's fine workmanship.

Peregrinus took several gold pieces out of his pocket. Noticing this, the lovely girl quickly asserted that she did not know the price of the work and therefore could not accept any payment; Mr. Peregrinus might, however, be so kind as to wait a few minutes, for her father would be back immediately. It seemed to Peregrinus that the worthless metal was melting into a lump in his hand. He put the gold pieces back into his pocket quicker than he had taken them out. And now that Peregrinus had mechanically let himself down into Lämmerhirt's broad armchair, the girl fetched up her own chair. Out of instinctive politeness, Mr. Peregrinus jumped up and started to move the chair, but it came about that, instead of the chairback, he caught hold of the girl's hand. And as he ventured to press the precious thing softly, he thought he felt a barely perceptible counter pressure.

"Kitty, Kitty, what are you doing!" With these words the girl turned and picked up off the floor the ball of yarn which the cat, beginning a mystic web, was holding between its forepaws. Then with childlike unconcern she took hold of the arm of the rapture-engulfed Peregrinus, led him back to the armchair, and begged him to sit down once more, while she herself sat down opposite him and took some needlework in hand.

Peregrinus was rocking in a storm upon a rolling sea. "O Princess!" The word slipped out, how, he didn't himself know. The girl looked at him in fright. Then it seemed to him as if he had committed a crime against the lovely creature, and in the softest, most melancholy tone he exclaimed, "My dearest, dearest Mademoiselle!"

The girl blushed and with lovely virginal shame said, "My

parents call me Röschen. Call me that too, dear Mr. Tyss, for I
am one of the children for whom you have done so many kind
things and by whom you are so highly regarded."

"Röschen!" cried Pereginus, completely beside himself. He
would have liked to throw himself at the lovely maiden's feet,
and scarcely could he hold himself back from doing so.

Röschen proceeded to tell him, as she went on working
quietly, how, since the time when her parents had fallen into
the bitterest want on account of the war, she had been taken in
by a cousin in a small neighboring town, and how this cousin
had died a few weeks before, and how she had then come back
to her parents.

Peregrinus heard only Röschen's sweet voice, without understanding much of the words, and he was not convinced that he
was not dreaming blessedly until Lämmerhirt came into the
room and greeted him with the most cordial welcome. It was
not long before his wife and the children followed him, and,
as in the unfathomable mind of man, thoughts, impulses, and
feelings intersect in odd and variegated confusion, it happened
that Peregrinus, even amid the ecstasy which allowed him to
glimpse a never-dreamed-of heaven, suddenly recalled how the
surly Pepusch had found fault with his giving of gifts to the
Lämmerhirt children. He was pleased to learn in answer to his
inquiry, that none of the children had ruined his stomach on
the candy, and the friendly and earnest way, indeed the certain
pride, with which they looked up at the high glass cupboard
which contained the shining toys, showed that they considered
the last gifts as something extraordinary which would probably
never happen again.

So the ill-tempered Thistle was wrong.

"Oh, Pepusch," said Peregrinus to himself, "no pure ray of
true love descends into your gloomy and troubled spirit!" And
by that Peregrinus meant again more than gifts of candy and
toys.

Lämmerhirt, a gentle, quiet, pious man, looked with obvious
pleasure at Röschen, who had been busily going out and coming
back in, bringing bread and butter, and who was now preparing
elegant sandwiches for her brothers and sisters at a little table
in the further corner of the room. The happy youngsters were

crowded closely around their dear sister, and if they opened their mouths a little wider than necessary in pardonable childish eagerness, it did no particular harm to the domestic idyll. Peregrinus was delighted with the lovely girl's activity, without Werther's Lotte and her bread-and-butter slices coming into his mind as he did so.

Lämmerhirt came closer to Peregrinus and in a low voice began to speak about Röschen, saying what a dear, good, pious child she was, whom Heaven had lent the gift of external beauty also, and how he expected to meet with nothing but joy from the lovely child. But, he added as his face lit up with delight, but the thing that warmed the very cockles of his heart was, that Röschen also had an inclination toward the noble art of bookbinding, and in the few weeks since she had been with him had made uncommon progress in fine, delicate workmanship, so that she was already much more skillful than many a lout of an apprentice that squandered morocco and gold for years on end and put the letters on crooked and askew until they looked like drunken peasants reeling out of a tavern.

Very confidentially the delighted father whispered into Peregrinus's ear, "It just has to come out, Mr. Tyss, or else it will burst my heart, I can't help it—do you know that my *Röschen* did the gilt work on the edges of the Ariosto?"

As soon as Peregrinus heard this, he quickly reached for the neat morocco volumes as though he had to make himself master of the sacred objects before an adverse chance could rob him of them. Lämmerhirt took this for a sign that Peregrinus wanted to leave and so begged him to put up with a few more minutes with the family. Precisely this, however, reminded Peregrinus that he really must be tearing himself away. He quickly settled the bill, and Lämmerhirt shook his hand as usual at parting; his wife did likewise, and so did Röschen! The boys were standing in the open doorway, and, so that the folly of love might receive its due, Peregrinus snatched the remaining bit of bread-and-butter sandwich out of the hand of the youngest as he went by him, and on this he chewed away as he ran, as though pursued, down the steps.

"Well, well," said the little fellow, quite flabbergasted, "what was all that? He might have told me, that Mr. Tyss, if he was hungry. I would have been glad to give him my whole sandwich!"

Step by step Mr. Peregrinus Tyss made his way home, lugging the heavy quartos laboriously under his arm and with transfigured gaze receiving one bite after another of the fragmentary sandwich upon his lips, as though he were partaking of heavenly manna.

"There's another one gone overboard!" said a passing citizen. The man could not be blamed for thinking such a thing of Peregrinus.

When Mr. Peregrinus Tyss entered his house, old Aline came to meet him and with gestures that signified anxiety and worry, beckoned him toward Mr. Swammerdam's rooms. The door was open, and Peregrinus saw Dörtje Elverdink sitting stiffly in an armchair. Her shriveled face seemed to belong to a corpse that was already laid in its grave. Equally stiff, equally corpselike, were sitting in armchairs in front of her: Pepusch, Swammerdam, and Leeuwenhoek. "Is that," said the old woman, "is that ever a crazy, spooky business down here! Those three wretched men have been sitting there like that the whole blessed day. They don't eat anything, they don't drink anything, they don't say anything, and they hardly draw breath!"

As a matter of fact, Peregrinus felt something like horror come over him at this rather eerie sight. Meanwhile, as he went on up the stairs, the ghostly scene was drowned in the rolling sea of heavenly dreams in which the ecstatic Peregrinus had been floating since the moment he had seen Röschen. Desires, dreams, blissful hopes commonly overflow into the heart of a friend, but was there any other now for poor Peregrinus than the honorable heart of good Master Flea? To him he now wanted to pour forth his whole heart, he wanted to tell him all about Röschen—something which actually could not be properly told. But call as he would, coax as much as he would, no Master Flea was to be seen. He was off and away. Upon more careful investigation in the fold of his neck-cloth where Master Flea formerly took up lodging on trips out, Peregrinus found a tiny box, on which were written the following words:

Enclosed you will find the microscopic lens. If you look sharply into the box with your left eye, the lens will immediately be in the pupil. When you want to take it out again, all you have to do is to hold your eye up to the box, press the pupil gently, and the lens will fall to the bottom of the box.

I am working at business of yours and risking much in so doing, but for my dear protector I shall do everything as

Your most obedient

Master Flea.

For a sterling and able novelist, one who works together all human deeds and actions to his heart's desire with a sturdy, quill-equipped hand, here would be a capital opportunity of demonstrating practically, by Peregrinus's example—after such a novelist had discussed the matter sufficiently in theory—the enormous difference between being in love and loving. Much could be said in that case about sensual impulses, about the curse of Original Sin, and about the celestial spark of Prometheus which, in love, kindles the true affinity of spirit of the different sexes, which affinity then forms the actual and necessary dualism of Nature. And if the aforementioned spark of Prometheus should also kindle the torch of the marriage god along the way, like a sturdily and brightly burning household light by which one can well see to read and write and sew, and if a happy brood of offspring can occasionally get their little mouths as smeared up with cherry jam as any other brood, well —that is the way of things here below. Besides, a heavenly love like that goes very well as sublime poetry, and, as a matter of fact, the best that can be claimed for it is, that that kind of love is no empty phantom of the brain; there really is something to it, as many people can testify, for whom things have gone now well, now badly, with that kind of love.

The kind reader has long since guessed that Mr. Peregrinus Tyss had merely fallen considerably in love with the little Dörtje Elverdink, whereas, in the very first moment he glimpsed Lämmerhirt's Röschen, that lovely, angelic child, the true heavenly love had flamed up bright in his heart.

The present reporter of this wildest and strangest of all tales would reap but little gratitude, if, sticking stiffly and strictly to the goose step of the novelists that go strutting along, he could not refrain from rousing that extreme boredom necessary to every correct novel. Namely, by allowing himself leisurely rest and relaxation after each lap surmounted by the pair of lovers in the usual fashion. No! beloved reader, let us hasten to the goal like lusty and sturdy horsemen tearing along on stout runners and paying no heed to anything that lies to left or right. Here we are! Sighs, love plaints, sorrow, rapture, bliss, all converge in the focal point of that moment when the lovely Röschen, the charming carnation of lovely virginity upon her cheeks, confesses to the overjoyed Peregrinus Tyss that she loves him, indeed how she cannot tell him how much she loves him, how beyond all measure she loves him, how she lives in him alone, how he alone is her single thought and her single happiness.

The sly and sinister Demon has a habit of intruding into the brightest sunny aspects of life with his black claws, indeed, of darkening totally that sunlight by the somber shadow of his misfortune-bringing self. And thus it came about that evil doubts arose within Peregrinus, in fact, that a nasty suspicion stirred within his bosom.

"What!" a voice seemed to whisper to him. "What! That Dörtje Elverdink also professed love for you, and yet it was vile self-advantage that animated her and made her try to lure you to break your faith and turn traitor on your best friend, on poor Master Flea. I am rich. They say that a certain good-tempered behavior of mine, a certain frankness—termed naïveté by many—can win me the ambiguous favor of human beings, especially of women. And this one, that now professes love for you—"

Swiftly he reached for the fateful gift of Master Flea. He took out the little box, and started to open it to put the microscopic lens into the pupil of his right eye and in that way to penetrate Röschen's thoughts.

He glanced up, and the pure azure of those loveliest of eyes shone into his heart. Röschen, noticing his inner agitation, looked at him quite amazed and almost anxiously.

And then it seemed as if a sudden lightning flash shot through him, and the annihilating sense of the perversity of his mind overwhelmed his entire being.

"What is this?" he said to himself. "You want to penetrate with sinful sacrilege into the heavenly pure sanctuary of this angel? You want to spy on thoughts that can have nothing in common with the infamous conduct of common souls corrupted with things earthly? You want to profane the spirit of love itself, testing it with the vile arts of uncanny, menacing powers?"

He had hidden the little box with haste in his pocket. He felt as though he had committed a sin for which he would never, never be able to atone.

Quite overcome by grief and sorrow, he threw himself at the feet of the startled Röschen, cried out that he was a blasphemer, a sinful man who was not worthy of the love of an angelically pure creature like Röschen, and dissolved in tears.

Röschen, who could not imagine what dark spirit had come over Peregrinus, sank down beside him, put her arms around him, and whispered as she wept, "For Heaven's sake, my beloved Peregrinus, what is the matter? What has happened? What wicked enemy has come between us? Oh, come, come, sit down quietly beside me!"

Peregrinus, incapable of any voluntary movement, allowed himself to be silently and softly pulled up by Röschen.

It was a good thing that the old, rather rickety divan was loaded as usual with fascicules of books, finished bound volumes, and no small quantity of a variety of bookbinding tools. Thus Röschen had to clear away a lot of things in order to make room for herself and the contrite Mr. Peregrinus Tyss. That way, he gained time to recover, and his great sorrow and his heartrending melancholy passed over into the milder emotion of a wrong perpetrated but still allowing of atonement.

If, as far as his facial expression was concerned, he was comparable before to the disconsolate sinner over whom the sentence of damnation has been irrevocably pronounced, he now looked a trifle silly. That look, however, is a good prognostic every time in circumstances of this kind.

But now when both of them, Röschen and Mr. Peregrinus Tyss, were sitting together on the aforementioned rickety divan of the honorable master bookbinder Lämmerhirt, Röschen began with downcast eyes and half-ashamed smile: "I think I can guess, my darling, what has assailed your spirits so suddenly. I will confess that people have told me all sorts of strange things about the odd inhabitants of your house. The neighbor woman—well, you know how neighbor women are, they like to chatter and chatter and often they themselves don't even know about what. Well, these mean neighbor women have told me that a very wonderful lady was in your house on Christmas Eve. They said old Mr. Swammer had put her up in his quarters as his runaway niece, but that the person in question was setting her cap for you with strange enticements. But that is not the worst by a long shot. Just imagine, my darling Peregrinus, that old crone across the way—you know the one, the old woman with the pointed nose who always waves so friendly whenever she sees you, and about whom you once said when you saw her on her way to church on Sundays in her best gown of colored material—I can't help laughing whenever I think of it—that it made you think a bouquet of tiger lilies was walking across the street—that suspicious old crone has tried to put all kinds of nasty things into my head. However friendly her greeting may be to you, she is always warning me about you, and she claims that nothing less than satanic arts are practiced in your house, and that little Dörtje is nothing but a little imp in disguise, walking around in human form in order to trap you—and in very pretty and seductive disguise at that. Peregrinus, my dear, beloved Peregrinus, look into my eyes. You won't find the slightest trace of suspicion in them. I recognized your pure heart. Never have your words or your looks cast a shadowed breath on the bright, clear mirror of my soul. I trust you, I trust the thought of the happiness that will come to us when a firm bond unites us, and that has been proclaimed to me by sweet dreams full of love and yearning! Peregrinus! Let dark spirits have decided whatever they will over you, their power will be shattered and broken against your loyal self, which is firm and strong in love and unchanging faith. What would, what could destroy a love like ours? Put all doubts away. Our love is the talisman before which the spirits of the night flee away."

At that moment Röschen seemed to Peregrinus like a creature of a higher order, and her every word was comfort from heaven. An indescribable feeling of purest bliss flowed through his heart like the sweet soft breath of springtime. He was no longer the sinner, the presumptuous blasphemer that he had

considered himself to be; he felt with rapture that he realized
he was worthy of the love of this loveliest, most angelically
pure of virgins.

The master bookbinder Lämmerhirt returned with his family
from a stroll.

Peregrinus's and sweet Röschen's hearts were overflow-
ing, and at nightfall Peregrinus left the narrow dwelling of the
jubilantly delighted bookbinder and his good wife, both of
whom, out of sheer joy and bliss, sobbed a little more than was
really necessary—happily and blissfully engaged.

All the creditable and very authentic notes from which this
strange story has been taken, agree, and the centennial calendar
confirms it, that precisely on that night when Mr. Peregrinus
Tyss came home a happily engaged man, the full moon shone
very bright and friendly, so that the whole Horse Market was
adorned with its lovely silver radiance. Understandably, it appears that Mr. Peregrinus Tyss, instead of seeking his rest,
leaned out the open window, as is fitting and proper for lovers,
in order to linger a bit over the thought of his lovely fiancée as
he gazed at the moon.

And now, although it may redound to the obvious disadvantage of Mr. Peregrinus Tyss as far as the kind reader is concerned, but more particularly as far as the kind lady readers are
concerned, truth must be given its due, and it may not be passed
over in silence that, in spite of his bliss, Mr. Peregrinus twice
yawned so loudly and so immoderately that a somewhat tipsy
market laborer, who happened just then to be staggering across
the street, called up to him in a loud voice, "Hey! you up there
with the white nightcap! Don't swallow me!" And that was
the sufficient cause that made Mr. Peregrinus Tyss impatiently
slam the window down so that the panes rattled. Some even
maintain that during this scene he called out rather loudly,
"Uncouth clown!" But this cannot be absolutely attested, for
such a thing seems quite incompatible with his gentle temperament and his spiritual mood. Suffice it to say that Mr. Peregrinus Tyss threw down the window and betook himself to
his rest. Meanwhile, the need for sleep seemed to have been
obviated by that immoderate yawning. Thoughts upon thoughts
crisscrossed in his brain, and especially vividly appeared to him

that peril overcome when a sinister power had sought to lure him into an infamous application of the microscopic lens. And now it first dawned on him that Master Flea's fateful gift, however well he himself had intended it, was nevertheless in every respect a gift that belonged to Hell.

"What!" he said to himself. "A person who probes into the most secret thoughts of his brethren, does that fateful gift not bring upon him the ghastly fate that befell the Wandering Jew, who wanders through the most colorful throng in the world, without joy, without hope, without sorrow, in dull indifference that is like the *caput mortuum* of despair, as though he were wandering through an inhospitable and disconsolate desert? Ever hoping anew, ever trusting anew, and ever again bitterly disillusioned, how can it possibly be otherwise than that mistrust, evil suspicion, hatred, and greed for revenge will nest in his soul and consume every trace of the truly human principle, which is expressed in gentle trust and in heartfelt goodness? No! Your friendly face, your smooth words are not going to deceive me, you, in whose deep heart is perhaps hidden an unmerited hatred against me. I shall consider you my friend, I will show kindness to you as far as I am able, I will disclose my soul to you, because it makes me feel good to do so, and the bitter sensation of the moment when you disillusion me is to be reckoned as insignificant compared to the joys of a beautiful past dream. And even the loyal friends, who really do mean well —how unstable is the spirit of man! Can not an evil conjunction of adverse circumstances, a bad humor created by the iniquity of capricious chance, produce a fleeting thought of hostility in the souls of those friends? And precisely that thought is caught by the wretched lens; somber mistrust fills one's spirit, and in the most unjust anger, in insane delusion, I thrust the real friends out of my heart also, and deeper and deeper, down to the roots of life, the mortal poison of ill temper eats, dividing me from all existence here below and alienating me from my very self. No! It is blasphemy, infamous blasphemy to try, like that fallen Angel of Light who brought sin into the world, to make oneself equal to the Eternal Power who sees through the heart of man because He commands it. Away, away with the unholy gift!"

Mr. Peregrinus Tyss had seized the little box which contained the microscopic lens and was on the verge of hurling it with all his might against the ceiling.

Suddenly there, right in front of Mr. Peregrinus Tyss, on the bedspread, sat Master Flea in his microscopic form, very smart and handsome to behold in his shining scale-armor and the finest of polished golden boots.

"Halt!" he cried, "Halt! Most honored sir! Don't start any useless nonsense! You would annihilate a mote of the sun sooner than you throw that little indestructible lens so much as a foot away, as long as I am on hand. What is more, without your noticing it, I had hidden myself as usual in the fold of your neck-cloth while at the home of master bookbinder Lämmerhirt, and hence I was a witness to everything that went on. Similarly I have been listening in on your present edifying monologue and from it I have drawn many a lesson.

"First of all, you have only now allowed your spirit, purely animated by actual love, to flash forth in resplendent glory like a mighty beam of light from your inner being, so that, I fancy, the supremely decisive moment is approaching.

"Further, I too have come to realize that I was in gross error in the matter of the microscopic lens. Believe me, my most honored, proven friend, although I do not have the pleasure of being a human being, like you, but only a flea, albeit no ordinary one, but a graduate by virtue of my glorious status of Master, nevertheless I understand the human temperament very well and also the deeds and doings of human beings, among whom I permanently reside. Many a time those doings seem very funny to me, almost silly. Don't take that amiss, most honored sir! I say that only as Master Flea. You are right, my friend, it would be a nasty thing and could not possibly lead to good, if a human being could look into the brain of another without so much as a by-your-leave. For the dispassionate, cheerful flea, however, that gift of the microscopic lens is not harmful in the least.

"You well know, most honored—and presently, if Fate will have it so, most happy—Mr. Peregrinus, my nation is of a nimble, even volatile, spirited temper. It could be said that it consists of nothing but youthful, pert madcaps. At the same time, I, for my part, can boast of a special shrewdness about life that generally eludes you wise children of men. That is to say, I have never done anything at the improper moment. Now, biting people is the guiding concern of my existence. But I have always bitten at the right time and in the right place. Take that statement to heart, loyal and honorable friend!

"I now accept the return of that gift intended for you, which neither that chemical compound of a human being named Swammerdam, nor that Leeuwenhoek, self-consumed by petty envy as he is, can possess. I accept it from your hands and shall preserve it faithfully.

"And now, my most honored Mr. Tyss, give yourself over to slumber. Presently you will pass into a dream phantasmagoria, amid which the great moment will proclaim itself. At the proper time I shall again be with you."

Master Flea disappeared, and the radiance he emitted was quenched in the profound darkness of the room, the curtains of which were tightly drawn.

It came to pass as Master Flea had said.

Mr. Peregrinus Tyss fancied presently that he was lying on the bank of a murmuring forest brook, listening to the rustling of the wind, the whispering of the bushes, and the buzzing of the thousands of insects that whirred about him. Then it was as if strange voices were becoming audible, distinct and ever more distinct, so that finally Peregrinus thought he could understand words.

But only a confused chattering penetrated his ear, numbing his senses.

At last a voice, hollow and solemn but ringing clearly and ever more clearly, began with the following words:

"Unhappy King Sekakis, who disdained the understanding of Nature, you, who blinded by the evil spell of the cunning Demon, beheld the false teraphim instead of the true Spirit: on that fateful spot in Famagusta, buried in a deep stratum of the earth, lay the talisman. But since you destroyed yourself, there was no agency to kindle its frozen power. In vain you sacrificed your daughter, the beautiful Gamaheh. The despairing love of the Thistle Zeherit was in vain. Nevertheless, the bloodlust of the Leech Prince remained likewise powerless and inoperative. Even the loutish Spirit Thetel was compelled to relinquish his sweet prey. For so powerful was your half-extinguished idea still, O King Sekakis, that you were able to return the lost one to the primeval element from which she had sprung.

"Mad retail dealers in Nature, to think that the poor girl had to fall into your hands, that you should have discovered her amid the pollen of that fateful Haarlem tulip! To think that you had to torment her with your horrible experiments, imagining in your childish pride that you could effect by your vile arts what can be effected through the power of the slumbering talisman alone!

"Nor might it be vouchsafed to you either, Master Flea, to see through the mystery. Within your clear vision did not reside the power of penetrating into the depths of the earth to espy the frozen garnet.

"The stars moved on, their wondrous motions intersecting each other's orbits, and fearful constellations gave birth to that which is astounding, to that which is unfathomable to the foolish eye of man. And yet no sidereal conflict wakened the garnet. For that human spirit which was required in order to cherish and protect the garnet so that it might waken to joyous life in the recognition of what is highest in human nature—that spirit was not born: it is eternal!

"The miracle is accomplished. The moment has arrived."

A gleam flickered brightly past Peregrinus's eyes. He half awoke from his state of insensibility—and to his no small astonishment beheld Master Flea in his microscopic shape but enveloped in the most magnificent robe of many folds, holding a high-flaming torch in his forepaws, eagerly and assiduously prancing up and down the room and emitting high, piercing sounds as he did so.

Mr. Peregrinus sought to rouse himself wholly out of his sleep. But all of a sudden a thousand fiery lightnings flashed through the chamber, which seemed presently to be filled with a single glowing ball of fire.

And then a gentle, aromatic fragrance passed through the fierce fire, and the fire died quickly away to become the soft shimmer of moonlight.

Peregrinus found himself once more standing upon a magnificent throne, clad in the rich garments of an Indian king, with the glittering diadem upon his head, and in his hand instead of a scepter the meaningful lotus flower. The throne was erected in a hall that stretched as far as the eye could see, and its thousands of columns were slim cedars that reached the sky. From dark, clustering shrubs in between them the loveliest roses and all sorts of wondrous flowers, shedding fragrance, rose aloft as though in thirsting desire for the pure azure which with loving eyes gazed down and gleamed between the linked boughs of the cedar trees.

Peregrinus recognized himself. Within his own bosom he felt the garnet glow, kindled now with life.

In the furthest distance the Spirit Thetel was attempting to rise into the air, but he could not reach half the height of the cedars, and kept plopping down disgracefully upon the ground again.

And here the nasty Leech Prince was creeping back and forth in disgusting contortions, trying now to blow himself up fat in revolting fashion, and then again to draw himself out thin, and all the while he kept groaning, "Gamaheh! Mine in spite of all!"

In the middle of the hall sat Leeuwenhoek and Swammerdam upon colossal microscopes, pulling very woeful and piteous faces as they alternately cried reproachfully to each other, "You see, that was the dot in the horoscope, whose meaning you could not make out. The talisman is lost to us forever!"

Close by the steps of the throne, Dörtje Elverdink and George Pepusch seemed not so much to be asleep as sunk in profound oblivion.

Peregrinus—or King Sekakis, for we can now call him that—flung back the royal mantle whose folds covered his bosom, and from within him the garnet darted rays as dazzling as the fire of heaven through the broad hall.

With a dull moan the Spirit Thetel, just as he was about to fling himself once again into the air, crumbled away in countless flakes without color, and these, as if driven by a storm, vanished among the shrubbery.

With a ghastly sound of the most heartrending anguish the Leech Prince writhed and contracted and disappeared into the earth. A resentful roar was heard, as though the earth were unwilling to take the loathsome and unwelcome fugitive back into her womb. Leeuwenhoek and Swammerdam had fallen down off their microscopes, and by their anguished moaning and groaning and by their terrified death-rattles it was apparent that a cruel torment had seized them.

But Dörtje Elverdink and George Pepusch, or, as they are here more properly named, the Princess Gamaheh and the Thistle Zeherit, had awakened from their oblivion and knelt before the king, to whom they seemed to make supplication in yearning sighs. Yet they lowered their glances to the ground as though they were unable to endure the radiance of the gleaming garnet.

Very solemnly spoke Peregrinus now:

"Out of vile clay and out of feather-flock lost by a silly, clumsy ostrich, the evil Demon had kneaded you together, you, who, as the Spirit Thetel, were to deceive mankind. Therefore the ray of Love has annihilated you, you empty phantom of chaos, and you have been compelled to crumble away into insubstantial nothingness.

"And you too, bloodthirsty monster of night, loathsome Leech Prince, you have been forced to flee before the ray of the gleaming garnet into the womb of earth.

"But you, poor, deluded, wretched, hapless Swammerdam and deplorable Leeuwenhoek, your whole life was a constant and uninterrupted error. You aspired to fathom Nature without having any notion of the meaning of her inmost being. You presumed to force your way into her workshop and eavesdrop on her secret work, imagining you would succeed in beholding with impunity the fearful mysteries of those depths which are unfathomable to the human eye. Your hearts remained dead and frozen. Never did true love animate your spirits, never did the flowers speak to·you with sweet words, or the many-colored, light-winged insects. You imagined you were beholding the high and holy wonders of Nature in pious admiration and reverence, but even as in your insolent way you strove to probe the qualities of those marvels to their inmost core, you destroyed that reverence yourselves, and the knowledge for which you strove was only a phantom, by which you were deceived like curious and impertinent children. Fools! The garnet's ray will give you no comfort further, no hope."

"Ha, ha! There is still comfort, there is still hope. The old woman betakes herself to the old ones. There's love for you, there's fidelity for you, there's tenderness for you! And the old woman is now really a queen, and she takes her little Swammerdam and her little Leeuwenhoek into her kingdom, and there the pretty princes are, and they unravel silver threads and golden threads and silk patches and accomplish other sensible and very useful things."

Thus spoke old Aline, who stood there suddenly between the two microscopists, dressed in wondrous garments that almost equaled the raiment of the Queen of Golconda in the opera. As for the microscopists, they had shriveled up to the point where they seemed to be hardly a span high any more, The Queen of Golconda took the little fellows to her bosom, moaning and groaning as they obviously were, and caressed them and fondled them like little boys as she talked baby talk to them. And then the Queen of Golconda put her dainty little doll-babies into two little cribs neatly carved from the finest ivory, and rocked them as she sang:

> Sleep, my baby, go to sleep,
> In the garden walk two sheep,
> A black one and a white one,
> etc.

And while this was taking place, the Princess Gamaheh and the Thistle Zeherit went on kneeling on the steps to the throne.

Then spoke Peregrinus: "No! Dispelled is the error that troubled your lives, you beloved pair. Come to my bosom, my well-loved ones! The ray of the garnet will transpierce your hearts and you shall taste the blessedness of heaven."

With a sound of joyous hope they rose, both the Princess Gamaheh and the Thistle Zeherit, and Peregrinus pressed them tightly to his flaming heart. When he released them, they fell into each other's arms with high ecstasy. Gone was the deathly pallor from her face. Fresh, youthful life bloomed upon her cheeks and gleamed from her eyes.

Master Flea, who had stood so long beside the throne as a dainty gentleman-at-arms, suddenly took on his natural form, and with a shrill cry of "Old love rusts not!" sprang with a doughty leap upon the nape of Dörtje's neck.

But, O marvel! At the same moment Röschen lay like a cherub of Heaven at Peregrinus's bosom, glorious in the high, indescribable grace of lovely maidenhood, with the radiance of purest love shining upon her.

Then the boughs of the cedar trees rustled, and higher and more joyously the flowers raised their heads, and gliding birds of paradise sped through the hall, and sweet melodies streamed from the dark shrubbery, and, as though from the far distance, there resounded exultant jubilation, and a thousand-voiced hymn of the most rapturous delight filled the air, and in the sacred consecration of love the highest ecstasies of life were stirred and blazed up flashing, pure ether-fire of the sky!

Mr. Peregrinus Tyss had purchased a very pretty country house in the vicinity of the city, and here there was to be celebrated his own marriage and that of his friend George Pepusch and the little Dörtje Elverdink.

The kind reader will allow me to dispense with describing the wedding feast, as well as with telling how everything else went on that festive day. I shall gladly leave it to my beautiful lady readers to arrange the bridal attire of both brides precisely as the image of them hovers before their imaginations. One thing only needs to be mentioned: Peregrinus and his lovely Röschen were cheerful, childlike simplicity itself, while George and Dörtje, on the other hand, were profoundly withdrawn into themselves, and with their gazes lowered, seemed to see, to feel, and to think only of each other.

It was midnight when suddenly the aromatic fragrance of the large-blossomed torch thistle filled the whole broad garden, the whole villa.

Peregrinus woke from sleep. He thought he heard deeply sorrowful melodies of hopeless yearning, and a strange premonitory feeling seized him. He felt as though a friend were being torn by force out of his heart.

On the following morning the second bridal pair, namely George Pepusch and Dörtje Elverdink, were missing, and there was no little astonishment when it was learned that they had not so much as entered the nuptial chamber.

At that moment the gardener came in in great excitement and cried out that he didn't know what to make of it but that a rare miracle had opened in the garden. All night long he had dreamed of the *Cactus grandiflorus*, but only now had he discovered the reason for it. They should all come and look.

Peregrinus and Röschen went down into the garden. In the middle of a fine clump of shrubbery a tall torch thistle had shot up. Its blossom, withered now in the morning rays, was drooping, and around that blossom clung lovingly a lavender and yellow striped tulip, which had also died the death of the plants.

"Oh, my premonition!" cried Peregrinus, his voice quivering with deep sadness. "Oh, my premonition! It did not deceive me. The garnet's ray that kindled me to supreme life has caused your death, you pair bound together by the interlockings of a mysterious discord of dark powers. The mystery is revealed. The supreme moment of fulfilled yearning was also the moment of your death."

Röschen, too, seemed to sense the significance of the miracle. She bent down to the poor dead tulip and shed numerous tears.

"You are quite right," said Master Flea, who suddenly sat there in his charming microscopic form upon the torch thistle. "Yes, you are quite right, most worthy Mr. Peregrinus. Everything is just as you have just said, and I have lost my beloved forever."

Röschen had almost fled in horror at the sight of the little monster. But since Master Flea looked at her with such knowing and friendly eyes, and since Mr. Peregrinus acted so intimately with him, she took heart, looked him straight in his pretty little face, and she gained all the more confidence in the odd little creature when Peregrinus whispered to her: "This is my dear, good Master Flea."

"My good Peregrinus," Master Flea now said very tenderly, "my dear and lovely lady, I must leave you now and return to my people. But I shall remain ever true and amicably disposed toward you, and you shall perceive my presence in a manner that will delight you. Farewell, both of you, cordial farewell! All happiness to you both!"

During this time Master Flea had assumed his natural form and had vanished without a trace.

And as a matter of fact, it is said that Master Flea always proved a good house spirit in the family of Mr. Peregrinus Tyss, and that he was particularly active when, after the lapse of a year, a little Peregrinus brought joy to the happy couple. Then Master Flea sat by the lovely wife's bed and bit the nurse on the nose whenever she fell asleep; he also jumped into the improperly prepared broth of the patient and out again, etc.

But it was especially nice of Master Flea that he never failed on Christmas to provide the Tyss offspring with the daintiest toys constructed by the most skilled craftsmen among his people, and in this way he reminded Mr. Peregrinus Tyss very graciously of that fateful Christmas Eve distribution of gifts, which is also to be designated as the nest of the maddest and most wonderful occurrences.

At this point all further notes suddenly leave off, and the wondrous history of Master Flea reaches a happy and wished-for

End.

Composition and presswork by The TJM Corporation. Text and display set in Melior. Printed on Warren's University Text, an acid-free paper made expressly for the University of South Carolina Press and watermarked with the Press emblem. Bound in GSB S/535 by Nicholstone Book Bindery. Format by Robert L. Nance.